The Silver! Mine!

The Silver! Mine!

Christopher L. Haefner

Library of Congress Control Number: 2008906924
ISBN: Hardcover   978-1-4363-6082-1
                         Softcover   978-1-4363-6081-4

To order additional copies of this book, contact:
Xlibris Corporation
1-888-795-4274
www.Xlibris.com
Orders@Xlibris.com
49475

Summary

Bounded by fate, Mr. Faehner stands ready to fulfill a lifetime's ambition to find the silver! By his assertions, it lies somewhere in the extent of the vast "beyond"—beyond the reach of the long-ago played-out tunnels of the Pequea Silver Mine he has since come to own. He believes, as he has since he was twelve, that an unbelievable quantity and quality of the precious ore exists there, and he has spent his life in pursuit of it. Then, on the very day before the truth of its discovery can be made possible, he is prevailed upon by an inveigling young reporter who has crashed one of his momentous, "moments of my life" parties. Intrigued by the reporter's tenacity and integrity under duress, Mr. Faehner grants him an exclusive never-before-given interview—the chance of a lifetime. Amid the hours-long discussion, the reporter is taken on an extraordinary journey into the billionaire's private life. The storied past of intentional and unintentional achievement, of adversaries come-to-life once again, is told. All were part of the hope for the finding, for the silver!

The Inner View

The entrance to the Silver Hills Country Club was blocked, barricaded by two freestanding wooden trestles and guarded by two freestanding security officers who were employed there. Suddenly, a lone white car spilled in off the nearby highway and began a slow, tedious approach along the juncture road. The driver, a well-dressed young man, recognized the blockade and approached ever more slowly until he pulled up alongside one of the security attendants. Before he could begin, he was dutifully told that "orders were orders" and under no circumstances were any latecomers allowed onto the premises unless they were on the VIP list.

The young man pleaded his case in an exemplary manner, explaining that he was an out-of-town reporter and could an exception be made in his case since he too had been ordered to be here by his boss, the editor of the *Hazleton Review*. In order to appear to appease the persistent driver, the clever guard purposefully stepped away from the idling vehicle and only pretended to place the urgent call from the walkie-talkie he was carrying, supposedly to another station guard who was inside the facility and could question the powers-that-be. To make the plea seem authentic, he waited an unreasonable five full minutes before returning the unacceptable news. The offended young reporter drove off with a puff of dust and loose stone shooting up in an errant spray from his tires as he fled. The two officers looked up at each other and exchanged smiles.

Sometime later, the spacious auditorium was erupting with interludes of loud, raucous laughter, shouts, and lengthy periods of highly intense clapping as the keynote speaker paused often and on purpose during his well-rehearsed speech.

"In closing, let me remind you all of something I have spoken so often. Life is remarkable. But it can be made to be even more so by the thrust we put forth in our own determinations. Let no dream or desire go undone. Let no person stand in your way of it. Bring only those into it who willingly attest to your efficacious purposes." He glanced longingly at his beautiful wife for effect before continuing.

The effective pause rendered Mr. Faehner incapable of saying anything further. It felt conclusive. To signify this to his audience, he stepped away from the podium and received his wife who was ready to embrace him.

"I love you, Connie," he whispered softly to her.

The enthralled crowd of over 200 well-wishers began another round of applause for the man whose fortieth year of celebrated achievements was the centerpiece of the festivity. For the next half-hour, continued accolades spewed over him like silvery raindrops, soaking him with self-worth and dignity. Once he felt that his ego had been effectively boosted to the point of bursting, he made an abrupt departure from the crowded hall and fled into an adjoining alcove where he tried to recoup his composure. Alone, apart from the throng of well-wishers, he began to contemplate the events of his life—all that had led him to the moment of this day. Begun so long ago, he traced them back, memories all, to the point of their beginning. They were like the continuous spirals as seen on a crosscut section of an ancient tree, all leading back, all connected.

Just at that moment, his cell phone went off signaling that something of significance was occurring and required his immediate attention. He had previously let it be known to his subordinates that only matters of the highest priority should reach him.

"Yes, it's me," he answered in an annoyed voice.

"Sir, there's an intruder on the compound. What do you wish us to do?"

"A what? A who?" he spurted out.

"He's a young kid. He's identified himself as a newspaper reporter or something. He's from out of town."

"Bring him to me, to my office,"

The call was disconnected. Mr. Faehner felt slighted that his day, despite all his precaution, was being disrupted by an intruder.

"Why couldn't it had been something more standout," he proffered to himself as he made the long march through the interior of the complex, then up through to the second-level office, which overlooked the building front. Once he gained the office front, he stepped inside and went to go stand before one of the huge side windows, which overlooked an immense grassy field below. 200 yards distant, down slope, was the boundary extent of the country club, its property bounded by the wayward course of the Pequea Creek. Beyond the creek lay the Silver Mine property—1,000 acres of constituent wooded hills, surface streams and ponds, and lush green meadows. It was his Garden of Eden.

From his lookout point atop the high country club hill, he could survey a sizeable portion of the dreamscape he had made his life's pursuit. He gazed longingly at its variance and beauty and at the various perfunctory activities taking place there. There was mundane work being done at the park's amphitheater where the next day's country-music concert would undoubtedly draw in over five thousand listeners. Country Willie always sold the place out whenever he performed. Aside the peninsula-shaped ground where the amphitheater was located were the creek-side campgrounds, a half-mile segment of tree-lined campsites, which abutted the water's edge. They came complete with electrical hookups and fresh well water. From his commanding vantage point, he could see that all but one of the sites was occupied. The one lone spot was most likely due to a last-minute cancellation or an overdue guest. On the fringe of the campground was a small meandering stream, which received its flow from an overspill pipe situated up a small rise that bounded the lower pond. At the point of spillage, the pond water splashed over a man-made waterfall then across, alongside the campground, before emptying into the creek. On the other side of the stream was a vacant land. Here, on this forty-acre parcel, the land was left go. It had never, in all of its history, been tilled or toiled over. Here, a panoply of indigenous plant life continuously vied with each other for dominance of the specially regarded domain. In all the forty years since the Silver Mine's modern existence, not one species had been able to take over the land tract. They lived and thrived together in imperfect interspersed harmony, contending, yielding, but never completely relenting. A walk-through during a less prodigious time of year revealed just how diverse the biotic preserve was. Milkweed, pussy willow, thistle, rye grass, creeper, Queen Anne's lace, buttercups, and forget-me-nots all vied for space. Left in the luxurious state of nonintervention, this mass of lush area provided a well-placed habitat for the local wildlife.

Another area of well-intended space was the vast sloping meadow immediately uphill from the far-stretching campground. This acreage was the grazing pasture of the Sicilian donkeys, which had been at the Silver Mine since its inception. They were now, to Mr. Faehner's eyes, dots of dabbled black and gray amid a sea of green.

Tourists were meandering about, couples holding hands while keeping perfect stride on their joyous walks. Siblings young and old were engaged in rivalries and challenges involving games and sports. Farther up from the lowest portion of the property was the placid pond, which sat as the centerpiece between the huge bank barn and the prominent 1800 house. At the far edge of the pond, the property was dissected by Silver Mine Road, the only public thoroughfare that ran through the comprising one thousand acres of secluded land. Beyond the road was the property's upper portion, which consisted of an old 1890s kiln, an artifact museum, an upper pond, and the silver mine itself. All of these points of interest were bounded within acres and acres of wild-wooded hills, wild fields, and small cutting streams. Silver Mine Run ran straight through the property's center at the base of the hollow, which described the natural center of the opposing hills on either side of it.

The Silver Mine property was Mr. Faehner's eternal pride and joy. He never tired of looking out over it. Catching a peripheral view, he turned and directed his shining eyes toward an obscure extent of the western edge of the forty-acre preserve. There, he discerned the figures of two adolescent children playing amongst the weeds near a newly reconstructed stone bridge, which gapped the wide creek. The bridge had been rebuilt from an earlier era. In the early 1900s, it served an old trolley line, which ran out of Lancaster and down ten miles farther to the nestled little town of Pequea. The bridge had been reconstructed when the country club was being built because it allowed easy access from one property to the other. Without it, the distance to or from either piece of land was miles around.

Although the bridge was considered an access point, it was not. Since its inception, the heavy stone arch had all but stood silent. Steel gates blocked each side's entrance, and only Mr. Faehner had the keys to the locks. He had never once relinquished them to anybody and in the thirteen years since he had last used them had since forgotten where they were.

Watching the bridge brought back this realization, and it spurred in him the desire to find them once more. The intransigent keys were included on a list of other lost items and memorabilia whose whereabouts had long since eluded him. The list now consisted of an old long-lost Boy Scout knife and sharpening stone, a Cross pen given to him in a ceremony many years later for allowing that same old troop-of-his-youth to hold annual jamborees at the Silver Mine campground, and most prized of all was a set of slide film made from pictures taken back in 1974. That year, when he was only fourteen, he had hired a professional photographer to take pictures of the mine so he would always have something to remember the early years by, for posterity's sake. Almost as prized as the Silver Mine photos was a memorable collection of wallet-sized photos of grade-school and high-school sweethearts. Prior to his engagement to Connie, he tucked them away in a large white envelope, hid them, and never found them again.

Mr. Faehner was lured away from his contemplative lull by a decisive knocking on the door. Before pertaining to it, he tucked his white shirt into his white pants and adjusted his yellow tie to line up with the buttons on his shirt. Next, he reclipped the tie with his silver clip and looked at himself in a wall mirror.

"Come in," he said in a droned voice.

"Prisoner for you, sir," came the jovial response.

The familiar-looking security officer who was standing just to the left of and just in back of the detained individual shoved him gently forward beyond the threshold of the room. For the longest interval of time, Mr. Faehner remained perfectly still and silent. He regarded the insolent young buck like an old buck in the forest, looking him over, letting him look him over, all in the manner of creating an aura for the young buck to consider. Mr. Faehner knew nothing of the red-haired, skinny, twenty-year-old who now stood in awe of him other than that he was reputed to be a reporter from an out-of-town newspaper. The same could not be said of the reporter. In anticipation of this prestigious assignment, he had prepared for the intended event by enthusiastically delving into old files and reports and ascertaining many facts about his prospective person of interest.

Mr. Faehner was a man whose prestige went hand in hand with his prosperity. His property holdings in the county were extensive, so extensive in fact that he now owned almost 33 percent of the entire southern end. Tens of thousands of acres of some of the best green land ever formed were called his. Since 1990 when he first acquired the original Silver Mine tract, he had added to his ownership countless other parcels and properties so often, so voraciously, that many considered his relentless pursuit of land like that of a hungry pig in front of a slop trough.

Besides, the thousand-acre Silver Mine and the thousand-acre Silver Hills Country Club, Mr. Faehner owned a huge hotel and marina not far in the little town of Pequea. There also he was spending gobs of time and money reconstructing a roadway bridge and run-down houses. Most of the homes he built, he sold, but several he kept for the purpose of lending out to friends and family whenever somebody did something especially nice for him.

Mr. Faehner also owned a sprawling thousand-acre vineyard and winery located a few miles southerly distant from the Silver Mine. Though he was not a praised connoisseur of the vines, he did enjoy being in the business. To offset his lack of expertise in the field of grapes, he practiced a lackadaisical laissez-faire approach in dealing with the business. The only stipulation he had was that it made money. The Grapes of Rathe was run entirely by a former California wine master who tired of the strife he endured while practicing his craft under the thick-clouded corporate control of the conglomerated California Wine Makers Associations. He came on a promise to the lush, lucrative lands of Lancaster County that he would be free to pursue, as he saw fit, a way to promulgate his sometimes-antiestablishmentary methods for propitiating the latest, greatest, tastiest grapes in all the kingdom of the vine!

The advantage to Mr. Faehner for allowing this winemaker his fetish desire was that it afforded him yet another winning round in the real-life game of Monopoly he was playing in the county's southern end. Nobody, since William Penn himself, had ever owned such a vast amount of the fertile state—not by one's self.

In addition to these prosperous proprietaries, he also held deed to a hundred hundred-acre farms, all of which he leased out to local Pennsylvania Dutch farmers who he knew were the absolute best at getting things growing in the rich-soiled slopes. Often, they came to him and asked him to sell their particular land, but always he refused them, instead telling them to have patience in the Lord for if it was providence that they take private ownership of the land then they would and nothing he could ever do could prevent it.

Once though he did come through for a troubled Amish farmer who had had enough of the tactless development that was all the time encroaching upon his rural farm tract. Already, along the rural highway that abutted his land was a huge auto dealership, a monstrous retail store, and an out-of-the-way convenience store, which the Amish man considered anything but a convenience to anyone in the area who frequented it. Its prices were considerably higher than those of the nearest supermarket, and it was located miles out of the way of even the nearest home.

Knowing Mr. Faehner's affinity for acquiring land at any cost, the lone countryman approached the wealthy landowner and asked if he could find it in his heart to help him ward off the deep-pocket corporations who wanted only to get a foothold in the southern county so they could then slowly take over.

"I know just what in tarnation they're up to too," he gruffed. "They want to bring in their stores, claiming there's a need when really the need comes much, much after, once everything gets built up around them."

Mr. Faehner thought so too. And he was not one interested in the trade. He was intrigued by the farmer's concern for the future of the southern land, and so instead of just purchasing outright all of the available land along the tertiary road and keeping it for himself, he bought it and turned it over to the farmer at cost. The Amish man surprised him even further when, after the agreement, he came calling at the Faehner estate with a cashier's check for—, the total amount of cash he owed him!

Another time too, he extended his benevolence by buying a small 150-acre tract of wood and stream for a local hunting club. The small price of the acquisition was of no bother to him, but he did it more to secure the allegiance of its members not to advance their skills upon his burgeoning properties, all of which were off-limits to them and their like. It strengthened him too in that there were many advanced societal and political members in its ranks. And in life, he knew that you never knew when you might need someone of any associated background. He was no hunter as they were, but on several occasions, he had joined in their field frolics just to let them know that he was one of the boys and because he immensely enjoyed being in the great outdoors.

For his generous contribution, the Outdoor Odyssey Club had made him a lifetime honorary member, which allowed him to be in their good graces forever. This special inclusiveness, once stated, brought with it an entirely unexpected rippling effect. Once started, many, many, many, of the competing local municipalities all vied to have the up-and-coming southern-ender included in their realm too. Over time, it came to involve the consuetude constituency of every town, ville, crossroads, and community. He had been invited to appear on every supervisory board of every township, wherever and whenever his influence could be brought to the table. Because he never favored one over another, they aligned themselves together in one unity like a small confederacy, all happy just to be part of a new kingdom. They were a collection of like-minded, real-life puppets on a string: Frogtown, Hessville, Little Conestoga, Pequea, West Willow, Smithville, Mount Nebo, Rawlinsville, Drumore, Quarryville, Atglen, and Christiana. More and more, they relied on his input and opinions until they hardly made a move without him.

Meanwhile, the young reporter had been led into the office's inner sanctum. The security officer reported, mostly for the benefit of the bereft young man, that he would be standing guard just outside the main door for the duration of the interview.

Then, without the reporter's knowledge, Mr. Faehner operated his pocketed cell phone so it would ring his desk phone. He excused himself to answer it. Then, without explanation, he hurried over to one of the room's side doors, opened it, and began to walk through.

"Wait here for just one minute," he announced before disappearing into the awaiting void.

Unbeknownst to the reporter, Mr. Faehner had entered the offset room as it was referred to. Here, special surveillance equipment was used to monitor the disposition and moves of anyone in his office. From a little black chair, he listened and watched as the reporter waited, seemingly all alone. The idea was to ascertain. If the person on display exhibited any signs of discontent, it would be simultaneously viewed and taped so it could be used against them. Part of this well-planned ruse was to keep the charged in the dark, so to speak, about what fate lie ahead for them as had just happened to the young fellow. This way they would remain, for the time being, in a profound state of uncertainty and consternation. If there was any ulterior motive for their unintended appearance, it might come out while they thought they were alone. Often, the person would make remarks or even hurl hostile epithets into the room's empty spaces supposedly rehearsing for the big scene that was to follow once the "big" man showed his face once more. Often, it worked. On the occasions when this tactic was deployed, the "big" man would reenter the room armed with stipulated facts about the character and intent of the person being scrutinized.

This time, though, the charade was not working. The young man remained quiet and content. He had not uttered a syllable nor reached for the desk phone to call for help. He had not even walked about the room out of curiosity or derision to make a more evaluated assumption as to who this all-powerful person was.

There was another factor at work too, which availed the cause of the supplicated man. The day was being celebrated. Mr. Faehner was in just too good of a mood to turn it into a bad one. His head was spinning with joy, and he did not want anything to spoil it. He determined not to if he could help it. He made one last furtive glance at the visual monitor and ascertained that the depiction he had already surmised of the visitor was still accurate, then proceeded to turn off the surveillance system.

He reentered the main office and found his visitor sitting stiffly in one of the armchairs facing his personal desk. Face-to-face, he appeared to be a bit nervous as he was busy fidgeting with his fingers, tapping them together while his hands were joined at his lap. He seemed more like a young child waiting for a scolding for some misdeed.

"Sorry for the delay," Mr. Faehner elicited while taking up a position behind his immense silver-maple desk. "Now, let's get down to seriousness here. Who are you, and what exactly is your purpose for being here?"

"I'm from the *Hazleton Review*, sir, and I came here today to cover you. I expected to get here, get in, and find out something intriguing about you that I could later write about. It was an assignment."

The interview continued although not in the way the reporter originally intended. With roles reversed, the college-age intern went about explaining away in prosaic prose how he had been enjoined by his editor to get a real feel of what it actually meant to travel to a place and reap from it what he could in accordance with his ability. The dilemma, he countered, came when he encountered the seemingly insurmountable difficulty at the gate. He was late. But having come so far, he refused to give up. And all things considered, it seemed a rather ridiculous reason for prohibiting his entry. To counter this, the tenacious-minded twenty-year-old careened his automobile off into a patch of back-behind-the-building woods, then attempted to meander into the main building, pretending he had inadvertently wandered outside and was just making his way back.

Mr. Faehner listened attentively, appreciatively, to the young apprentice. He felt a lifting of his spirit the way he allowed the loquacious renderings and pleas to fill the room, which was quite a contrast from the way it might have gone many years earlier. At any earlier time in his storied career, he probably would not have given the guy a chance. His personality then was much more confrontational. He was snappy at insolent people no matter what, and conversations, if there were any, were much more one-sided. Now he sat with a great air of self-approval at the dignified way his contemporary could so freely speak his peace. Often in these midyears of his life, he found himself doing this, considering how life experience had changed him. Kinder qualities, which were always in him, now bubbled up into his everyday self-awareness and he responded to them, tendering them into each and every applicable situation.

He never forgot how he used to be. Before, even matters of the slightest indifference were treated as though they were matters of grave concern. People involved in those matters were treated accordingly. He pictured himself caught up in any one of those episodes; kicking things, screaming at people for incidents as unimportant as someone spilling a glass of water on a carpet or someone lighting up a cigarette in his car. Philosophically, he knew the reason for his lack of control. He had been conditioned into it. Having been through so, so many conflicts and controversies as he advanced through his career, he found it better to be on his guard. An enemy could be anyone. And because they were unforeseeable, it was always better to let them know that he was always ready for confrontation.

But he found his way out. His successive successes had given him confidence. Age had made him wiser. And his spirit, once so secreted away in the recesses of his being, was now free to float over him, its aura like a continuous mist about his body.

In this new day, this man's slight was but an annoyance, like a pesky fly that flew in then out of a can of soda. Mr. Faehner even felt affable about it.

Several times while the reporter rambled on, he had to put a hand to his face to stop himself from smiling. Leniency would have to be granted.

But then, suddenly, his own face turned serious. A reflection caught hold of him. Déjà vu. He envisioned something of himself in the opposite chair. Like the reporter, he too had spent so much time, energy, and effort pleading a cause like this to someone like him, someone supreme, who sat in power and judgment over him. He remembered how much he disliked it and the person who put him through it. He felt connected to the persistent young person and did not want to impress upon him anything similar to the feelings from the past that had been his experience. He became enlightened and ended the contest. He interrupted.

"So you've come to get a scoopful of me, haven't you? I'll tell you what. I'm going to give you three scoops or more. I'm going to give you the chance of a lifetime. But to tell my story, you'll have to listen to it all, and let me tell you, it is quite a lot."

He noticed instantly that the reporter was gleaming. He noticed too that he wasted no time in getting out his notepad and pen. He was glad to see too that the reporter had an admirable demeanor, that despite having just been in for it, he was more than willing to let bygones be bygones and move ahead to the more important detail of his work.

"Well, young man, if you are up to it, I'm going to give you the Pulitzer Prize-winning account of my life and career."

To Begin With . . .

"Wait, sir," the young man said in a halting voice. "If this is going to be enduring as you say, then please allow me to take a leak, so to speak. And I could use a sip of something too."

"That's fine, young man. The facility is over there. Drinks are in that compact cooler over there."

While the reporter busied himself at relinquishing his discomforts, Mr. Faehner suddenly snapped his fingers excitedly. He also exited the room and reentered the alcove to retrieve his cell phone, which he had inadvertently left there. He then placed a few well-intended calls to his wife and three subordinates informing them of his long-intended detainment. On his way back to his desk, he too obliged himself with a refrigerated beverage. After a brief stint of indecision, he plucked a Coke from the shelf, popped off the top tab, then began slugging some of the sugary syrup down into his parched throat.

Still waiting for the absent reporter, he, can-in-hand, sauntered over to the office side, which looked out upon his realm. He concentrated on the past, eyes fixed upon the bygone experiences. He counted them through in a backward momentum like leafing through a completed book, finish to start. To that first memorable day, he ventured, when the story first unfolded, back to that indelible "once upon a time."

That cradle event as it happened was as real to him now as it ever had been. Its impact had lost none of its verve. It was an eon ago so it seemed, but time, in its unending intervention, had done nothing to diminish its character or importance. Time, in fact, had served it to gain in its effect. Its intensification grew. From what had been a single day's dalliance came a contrivance, came a contingency, came another, came another, came another, and all of it a culmination from the first.

He filled the cup of his mouth with more of the thirst-quenching refreshment, swished it around to placate the bubbles, then proceeded to slowly swallow the savory liquid. It struck him funny that on this special day, that special day, that day of forty years ago, the day that had served as the crucible for everything else that had happened, the day whose events sparked every other and whose existence made it possible for this one so marked by jubilation had not even crossed his mind before this very moment!

Just at that moment, the facility door opened, and the young reporter returned. He too stopped off at the refrigerator and retrieved a beverage of his choosing for refreshment. Mr. Faehner was quite ready for him, to lull him into the depths of his private experiences, to bring him into it as though he were going to experience it for himself.

"Have you heard, my young friend, of the oft-stated expression about being in the right place at the right time?"

"Certainly, sir."

"Then you have heard it only two-thirds correct," Mr. Faehner returned aptly. "For the equation stated that way is grossly incomplete. To make it complete, one must add the third part of it."

"And what is that?" the reporter interjected.

"And that is that it has to be the right person in the right place at the right time. And in my case, that could not be more right."

"Shall I quote you on that, sir?"

"It means everything that you do."

The men of common cause faced each other, one knowing of the relevance of what was to come, the other awaiting to be nothing more than enlightened perhaps by a defined story of success, by a story that had had its ending known. But by a silence that stared at him, dared him to know more, the reporter started to sense more, that there was something more here than meets the eye.

Feeling somewhat more at ease, the reporter's inquisitive nature took over and without any consideration as to what he was saying, he made comment of the hangings on the paneled wall behind Mr. Faehner's chair. There, mounted to the walnut-stained grain were painted portraits of ten men. Underneath each was a caption disclosing who they were, in name only. From his seat, the reporter scrutinized them, half-expecting to recognize at least one or two, believing from their prominent position that they might be state-known or country-known personages.

Mr. Faehner, however, feigned indifference until, that is, an idea struck him. He immediately bounced out of his swivel chair and stood erect beside the frozen caricatures almost as though he were posing as one of the above. He was beset by them but at the same time bestowed upon by them by what they represented. He gave them, one and all, the all-powerful pointed finger and laughed in their faces. It was the highlight of his day, that moment.

"Why did you do that?" the befuddled reporter asked.

"You have hit upon it, my friend. The most perfect way of pursuing this epic tale. A chronology. A juxtaposition of these men, of who they were, and what they did to me. A telling. A *Who's Who* list of the men who came into my life and tried to stop me. A list of the men who failed."

With those words spoken, the reporter began to regard the mosaic of men more carefully, wondering what each of them had done so out of the ordinary that their eternal fate was to remain suspended on a reveling wall, evildoers forever.

"These men, who I poignantly remind myself of, were my combatants in life. They were competitors, rivals, and nemesises. They were conspirators, opponents, and antagonists—all. But though they defied me, though they stood in my way, they are the sole reason for my success. Through them, I learned to define myself, to defend myself. Through them, I became the man that I am."

"It sounds as if you were involved in quite a few little wars," the reporter speculated.

"They were wars," Mr. Faehner concluded. "And in each of them, my enemy met his Waterloo!"

The emphasis of the last characterizing word made the reporter lose control of his content-emptying composure. His own carbonated drink got caught down his windpipe, and he was instantly besieged by an expectorating cough, which, despite a valiant effort, he could not bring to cessation. Mr. Faehner reacted. He flew up out of his chair, which he had again rejoined and reached the gagging victim with not a moment to spare. In an act of desperation, he began slapping him repeatedly on the back until the fluid had been effectively vomited back into the mouth and reswallowed into the esophageal tube. When the unexpected incident was over, Mr. Faehner resumed his place behind his desk. Standing once again, he viewed the portraits one by one. Then, using one of his index fingers as a guide, he began indicating them, making a brief speech about who they were and whether or not they were yet among the living. As he did, he unintentionally began to soliloquize about having defeated them. He couldn't help it. They were like trophies; real-life heads mounted behind frame and glass, eyes which can no longer see, ears which can no longer hear, minds which can no longer think.

"I can no longer forget about them as I can to breathe," Mr. Faehner said in a colloquial voice.

"It sounds like they, even though they've met their end, have a considerable hold over you still," the reporter adduced.

"They do!" Mr. Faehner announced in a clarifying voice. "And it's right that they do. But it's in a better manner than you would expect. For despite their adversarial styles and tendencies, they discounted me who even as a young adolescent possessed a mind that was capable of outsmarting them. I enjoy reveling in that aspect of things. I'll bet they each rued the day when they first decided to do me in. But it was even worse than that. For unknowingly, unwittingly, each of them were, believe it or not, my mentors too. Each of them had an exact influence over me—an act for me to follow. As I struggled to defeat them, I endeavored to understand them—their philosophies, their intricacies, their depths. And I learned. They didn't realize that it is not the size of your opponent that matters but the size of his heart, and for me, this was a matter of the heart. That's another lesson for you, one that I give freely. Take it seriously."

Mr. Faehner afforded them a considerable pause before continuing. He wanted to collect his thoughts, for he had hit upon another perspective of the whole scenario, an antithesis of the all-or-nothing approach to an objective. And he wanted to apply it as an antidemonstrative ointment soothingly and apart from his soliloquized speech.

"It is always better to get along with people in this world, my young friend. And each one of us must try his best to do it. Don't think that because I was involved in such bitter conflicts with these men that I would not have preferred a better means to resolution. I did. It was these men that preferred to battle. And I was up for it. Don't go around pushing yourself and your objectives on others unless you have been treated with indignity like I was. That is why I, in my paid-for wisdom, have decided to treat you the way I would have liked to be treated even though you crashed through into my party. For you count too. You are a person not so very different than I was once so long ago. And I would rather have you as an asset than a liability."

"You perceive me as someone this worthy of consideration. Why? You have attained so much already. Why would it make any difference how you treated me? If you told me to go, I would just get up and go."

"Believe me, my young friend. You never can tell about a person really. You might leave here believing in a stalemate if I were to order you out, but it might not end there. Later, you could reconsider your position—you without a story, maybe a by-passed promotion on account of it. Then disappointment sets in and festers. It turns to anger and anger turns to hate, and from hate could come inconceivable retribution toward me—unjustified though it may be.

"The world is full of examples of such things. People have hurt other people for less. And consider the people who have done it. Sometimes they are the very people most would consider unlikely or incapable of doing it. The don't-judge-a-book-by-its-cover saying doesn't just speak of the sometimes hidden good in people. It could mean the devious things which dwell in us. People are full of surprises."

"Is it possible that you too might later regret doing this for me, sir? After all, you're human too. You are the guest of honor today, and my presence here now has impelled you to give that up for my lonely sake."

"I wouldn't worry about that, my boy. I have already passed the prime point of the celebration with my guests, and from this point on, it is mere blather that I am missing. Actually, you offer me reprieve. As a serious-minded man, I would always much prefer to be in the company of someone whose intent is of a serious nature. The celebration going on here today is not a one-of-a-kind type. It is an annual event marking the anniversary of my initial intervention at the Silver Mine. This is the fortieth year, but the celebrations have been going on only since this place was built. Next year, there will be another."

His last sentence had thrown him into a trance. He knew he was getting close. Another highlight in his life would come—potentially soon. But it was nothing he could lend the reporter. It was a secret kept. But in his mind, the mighty thought pervaded him, and he followed it to conclusion—that there was one great party to come, greater than all the others, greater than all that have been, and greater than all that will come after. It was an entire hope. Not wanting to betray his thoughts, Mr. Faehner came abruptly down, out of his high.

"It is time we pertained to the material intended. I have a tendency for getting off on a tangent. You came here for an exclusive, and I am willing to give it. Now, let's proceed.

"We will do it in a show-and-tell method, like I did when I was a very young kindergartener back in Elizabeth Martin Elementary School. I want to say it that way because I have always been so fond of my memories there. The school still stands on the outskirts of Lancaster City. It was built at a time when it stood surrounded by lush meadows and it had a tiny creek along its back boundary. Farm fields existed on every side, and the vista from the recess yard was one of corn and trees and cows, songbirds and butterflies afloat. It left an indelible mark on me—one that probably left me in love with nature's possible beauty.

"We will follow the portraits in accordance with their importance and arrangement although I may stray from that if I have reason to. Let's begin.

"Portrait one. This duly represented individual is my uncle, the esteemed geology professor, Dr. Rick Faehner. He was once my mentor. He was also probably the most intelligent man I ever knew. And, before you ask, yes, he was smarter than me. He was enterprising as well as smart and began a rock shop back when he was still in high school. He collected rocks and minerals from around North America and made specimens of them, cracking them down to fit into specially made specimen-sized boxes. My job was cracking and gluing them besides going around and doing the collecting. Most of the collecting was done in long trips where we would go from place to place, location to location, gobbling up all of the specimen rock we could. One trip might take us from a dolostone quarry in our state to one in Maryland and then back to Pennsylvania to hunt goethite crystals in a farmer's field. Beyond those expeditions, we sometimes just wanted to go off just for the fun of it. And that's what brought us here or, rather, there," he said, pointing a finger to indicate the vast land beyond the side window. Suddenly, he was struck by the happenstance way in which it all occurred that day, which was forever inculcated into his being. He began the storytelling in such a way as if he were reliving it himself and wanted the reporter to too.

"I was just thirteen that late August day in 1973 when . . ."

Rick appeared unexpectedly at the back kitchen door of the Pine Street home and was about to knock when he was suddenly invited to go in by Leon who was behind him.

"Hello, Sonny," Rick said affably once he realized he was noticed.

"What brings you here?" Leon asked directly.

At that moment, Pip and Mark Faehner entered the kitchen.

"What gives?" Pip asked colloquially.

"What say you boys want to come with me on a sleepover at a silver mine?"

"A silver mine! Where?" both boys asked at once.

"It's not far. As a matter-of-fact, it's right in our own backyard, so to speak. Only ten miles or so as the proverbial crow flies."

"Are you serious?" Pip ejaculated.

"Sure, I am. If it's OK with your pop, pack your things—a comb, a toothbrush and paste, deodorant if you have any—"

"That sounds like a list of the nonessential items," Pip reasoned lightly.

"Yeah, what about cupcakes, chips, and soda?" Mark was quick to quip.

All eyes were upon the boys' father as he nodded his approval. The boys bounded up to their third-floor rooms where they elicited wild shrieks of excitement while collecting a few personal creature-comfort items to take along.

Later, the boys were on their way traveling the half-hour distance through the southern countryside to the mine. They arrived in an unpredicted fashion when Rick's old Ford Fairlane made a sudden turn off an obscure secondary road onto an even more obscure tertiary road. The sun was setting, giving guise to the obfuscating terrene and the man-made objects that surrounded them as they plodded their course ever so slowly back to the abandoned mine site. An old two-and-a-half-story stone house stood in silent vigil across from the off-road entrance. A stone kiln stood symbolically of times of old. The mine entrance, half-closed by a lifetime of pluvious erosion upon the once-stationary bedrock above it, looked forsaken. This first look for the boys was a haunting experience.

"Last tent up is for the rotten egg," was the elicited motivation for the trio of experts as they unpacked their gear and erected a camp. Once the pup tents were standing, the boys were put on immediate wood-collecting detail. Usable pieces were hard to come by in the fading light, but the boys made a thorough search of the outlying woodland and returned with an ample supply. Scraps were piled inside a stone surround then lighted. Larger pieces were then placed in order on top, and soon a blazing fire was burning. Hot dogs poked by thick-enough sticks were cast into the flame and transcended into plump, juicy, pick-me-up pups. Buns, ketchup, mustard, relish, and onion bits were also on the menu.

Once the franks had been dutifully devoured by the devoted democracy of hot dog eaters, the choice had been made to go into the mine at night rather than wait until morning. Rick lit a lantern. The boys had their flashlights. When everything was ready, the boys sprinted toward the entrance one hundred feet away.

"Hold your horses there," Rick ordered. "Abandoned mines are no place to play. The both of you could get hurt if you're not careful."

The anxious boys stood at attention and waited for their slow-moving relative who walked as though he was wading through lentil soup. They beamed their searchlights into the dismal abyss and felt the mine's cool breath pour over them.

"Mines are like caves," Rick said instructively once he caught up. Their interior temperatures keep at about fifty degrees. Right now, that will feel about twenty degrees cooler than the outside air. But in the winter, fifty degrees feels warm."

With the professor in the lead, the perilous journey began. Onward they crept, one behind the other, through the narrow passage whose dimensions were roughly seven feet high by five feet wide. Along the way, Rick explained in layman's terms the layout of the mine's structural composition.

"The bedrock is phyllite and limestone each set down at different geological times. Intruded between them is the quartzite. Around these intrusions are the areas where the silver is."

"Will we find any silver splays then if we locate a point of intrusion?" the precocious Pip asked.

"I sincerely doubt it," Rick countered. The quartz veins were all pretty much played out back when the mine was in operation. But there is still silver ore to be found on the rock piles outside, if you're lucky."

"Then what are we doing in here?" Mark asked.

"Come along, boys," Rick said sharply.

They continued, then stopped about one hundred feet farther.

"Here is the first shaft," Rick announced.

On their left was a wider extent of the mine passage, possibly fifteen feet across. Its base was an enormous hole swallowed up by water.

"It's almost fifty feet to the bottom. There was a substantial amount of silver here that the miners worked to get out."

Listening, the boys carefully cast their flashlight beams into the chartreuse-tinged water with the hope of finding any object of reflection, which might signify the fact that traces of the shiny ore still existed in its depths.

"Don't get too close, boys," Rick warned. "The mine floor is very wet and slippery here. I don't want anybody falling in."

The dynamic duo took a cautious step back. In their continuing search, their minds' eyes revealed what their real eyes could not. For a time, they were intrigued. But, without much chance of finding anything, they soon gave up. After giving last looks to the watery depth, the boys moved on. As they crept forward, they took notice of a volume of fresh air introducing itself from up ahead. Rick noticed too and responded.

"That influx of air is coming from another open area—an air shaft that leads over fifty feet up to the surface. It was made for the specific purpose of inducing fresh air into the back portions of the mine."

"Can a person climb up it?" Pip inquired.

"It was tunneled by hand, so I suppose so," Rick remarked.

"Then let's suppose so," Mark declared at once.

"Hold on there, boys!" Rick intervened. "You better not. You don't know what's up there—loose rock, snakes, who knows what. I told you both before, I don't want anybody to get hurt. Old mines are no place to act out in!"

The two stalwart would-be expeditioners held back. They wanted to go up but dared not due their uncle's incessant warnings. Like it or not, he was in charge. Heads hanging, they moved on. Not too far ahead, the passage bended left. At the point where the bend began was another hollowed-out area similar to but larger in expanse than the first shaft. At the side of this shaft was a huge wooden platform, which appeared to have been built to act as a top landing. The shaft below was flooded with mine water.

"Don't go to the edge of the landing!" Rick shouted out in a scolding voice even before either of the adventurous boys had made a move onto it.

"Hey! Neither of us has even stepped on the very ledge!" Pip yelled back.

"Hey, hey there, boys. Let's be nice."

Realizing he was in a lose-lose situation, Pip declined to speak. But Rick, feeling awkward also, pressed on. In the hope of diffusing the potentially volatile situation, he sauntered past the rounded recess and continued into the mine's reach. Believing he was soon out of earshot, they opened up a conversation about how they perceived they were being treated.

"He's treating us like two-year-olds!" Pip exclaimed.

"You got that right," Mark concurred.

"He's got no right preventing us from having any fun. What's the purpose of coming to a place like this without doing any hands-on exploration? You would think, he being a person who studies the underworld would be inclined to want to get his hands dirty."

The boys were right. Their uncle had no children and as such had no real-life experience dealing with them. He had no conception of what a child was capable of at certain ages except for what had been his own experience. And that, so covered over by time, had been rendered almost useless. Rick knew this too but had a great deal of trouble distinguishing between what was his to authorize by virtue of his supreme professional title and what was his authority as it related to his relationship with his nephews. The supreme usually won. It was within the context of this mixed-up mode that the boys always had to contend with their naive relative, and it always made them mad—the bad with the good they always relented.

Reluctantly, they moved on and joined Rick in a back part of the mine. He was standing over a trickle of water, which flowed from a crack in a crevice, high, on the wall.

"Here's where you'll get a good drink," he mused.

"Yeah, if you like impurities in your cup," Pip added glibly.

"Not so," Rick countered. "This water's probably pure."

"Probably doesn't sound so good," Mark suggested.

"Well, I drank it before, and I never got sick," Rick countered.

To prove his contention, Rick moved closer to the flow, cupped his hand into the flow, and accumulated enough for an adequate taste's worth. The boys, however, were not conciliated and refused to simulate his drinking technique. Wanting to prove a point, Rick replenished his hand several more times before quitting. The boys moved on.

The last hundred feet of the mine differed greatly from the rest. Here the tunnels were piled in places by rock that had been blasted off the walls and ceiling but never removed. Clear through to the end, they had to surmount disproportionately sized stone—slabs, chunks, and nuggets lying loose on a dry dirt floor. Soon, their docile uncle caught up with them.

"What happened back here?" Pip inquired with interest. "I mean, why is all the rock still here?"

Glad to be back in the game with his precocious nephews, Rick was ready to reply. "This was, quite literally, the end of the line for the late Harvey Philly, the mine's owner in the 1890s—the last time when the property was active. Apparently, back here anyway, the silver ran out. They abandoned the lead without bothering to remove the rock. And I don't really blame him. Back then, this rock was all carried out by cart. They were really spending all their time and dime in the sunken shafts, particularly the second one. It goes down about 120 feet and even has a forward shaft in front of it. That's a lot of rock!"

"That must have been a lot of silver too," Pip interjected brusquely.

"It probably was," Rick guessed. "But there were no records to indicate just how much ore was found.

"There's indication enough for the fact that the operation was worthwhile enough to have bothered to excavate a shaft that size, especially when considering the whole hole was dug using nineteenth-century technology. Look how easily he gave up back here. Once the silver was depleted, he was! And another thing, I think, there's a chance—more than a chance—that there's silver a-plenty still in that shaft. Philly probably gave up on that too because he didn't have the technology to get rid of the water down that far. I'll bet that's precisely what happened!"

"That's quite a rendition. Too bad you'll never have the chance to prove it."

It was another bubble-bursting remark, and Pip, already angered, shook his head in disgust and left. Mark, realizing what had happened, followed. Together they zipped out of the talus piles and began retracing their steps out through the mine.

"Hold on there, boys," Rick shouted out after them.

Once they had sufficiently distanced themselves from him, the boys made comment about the experience. "Rick's a dick!" Pip said to his brother who was eager to hear something derogatory about their leaderless uncle.

"You got that right!"

"He's got that perfect can't-do attitude. I mean, that's all he says—you can't do this, you can't do that. I don't know how he ever got to where he is in life with that kind of negativity."

"Maybe he just spins that on us," Mark suggested.

Hearing that, Pip immediately whirled around to meet his brother eye-to-eye.

"Oh my god! I think you've hit on it, brother! He might not want us stumbling around onto any important ideas. Maybe he has his sights set upon this place and doesn't want anyone interfering."

Just then, Rick's chary footsteps could be heard, and the brothers shushed each other in advance of his coming.

It was late, and all seemed spooky with the dancing firelight set against the mode of huddling trees and other wildly featured growth drowning in a sea of darkness. The brothers, without orders, fed wood fodder to the deficient fire, then sat placidly around the intensified flame to keep warm and feel safe. Rick suggested a marshmallow roast, and the brothers were quite eager to comply. They spent the remainder of the before-bed period quieting down while eating toasted marshmallows and taking gulps of ice-cold Cokes. Nothing further was said by either faction about any of the discordant occurrences that happened that day.

When morning came, the brothers were up long before Rip Van Faehner who whiled away the Zs on his cherished outdoor air mattress. For breakfast, they boiled some supply water in a pan to use to make hot cocoa. And with it, they opened up a fresh box of cinnamon doughnuts to eat. Their hunger was well assuaged when Rick finally arose. The brothers had begun scattering themselves around the wooded hills searching among the indicative rock piles in hope of finding pieces containing the elusive silver. From the nearby hillside, they noticed him up and so rejoined him to inquire further as to where else they needed to look since they had found nothing.

Rick smiled to himself, satisfied that for all of his nephews' prowess, they still had to rely on his expertise to accomplish their ambitious goal.

"Take it easy," he stated simply. "We'll get to prospecting in a short time."

Taking full advantage of his one-up-on-them mentality, Rick took his time, intentionally, at preparing his morning meal. He soft-boiled two cooler-carried eggs, confiscated a few miniature doughnuts, and entreated himself to two cupfuls of hot cocoa before even looking up. Pip and Mark meanwhile had abandoned their silver-minded endeavor and went up to the pond to skip stones and wait.

"Hey, boys," Rick called out to them from below once he had emptied the car trunk of its rock-collecting equipment. Each of them then delved into the supplies, and when the exercise was over, each had a pair of heavy-duty gloves, a chisel hammer, a five-pound sledge hammer, and a five-gallon handled collecting bucket. They were off.

It didn't take long once Rick had revealed which were the more prosperous rock piles to search. Pip was the luckiest one of all. Within a short time, his bucket was brimming with pieces large and small. Many had yielded thick veins of ore. At one point, he purposely wandered over to where Rick was pounding away at some large piece of pure quartz and peered into his bucket. He was pleased to see that the perfidious professor was well behind him in their quest to find samples. He was beating him at his own geological game!

The day grew hot, and despite the overall intrigue of being in the sylvan woods and actually finding quantities of silver, the point came when everybody was ready to leave. Rick announced his readiness—the readiness everybody was feeling—and together the tired group headed out of the mine slopes and convened back at the car. Everything was packed and fitted into it. The silver buckets came last.

"Here's the best for last," Pip announced enthusiastically while he heaved up the heaping bucket to the car's extended bumper. "I can't wait to come back here and find more."

Rick, who was about to lift the heavy bucket into the opened trunk, halted his effort and replied in a pronounced voice, "No, you don't! This place is off-limits to you both. You may come down only if I decide to bring you. This is a special place, and only I have authorization to be here. Your permission lies in my say-so. I know the owner, and I know too that the only reason he allows me here is because of who I am. And he knows that a professional like me will treat the place right and not exploit it for any purposes other than enjoyment. I have been coming here since I was in college, and it has remained untouched in all that time. And that's the way it will stay. Got it!"

The discourse was over, although Pip, seriously upset over his uncle's forbidding words, continued a panoply of internally contrived rebuffs, silent guffs, in his head against his insolent leader. He reluctantly took up his place in the car, sitting in the back seat with his brother and intentionally leaving the front seat conspicuously absent. Rick didn't mind. He took the act as a sign that his stern reprimand had been taken to heart, and he was glad.

Rick's words were stabbing. They epitomized the basis for the contempt Pip felt toward him. He was standing as a god before him all the time, preventing him, forbidding him, restricting him. And for all he knew, Rick was a liar. He had devised this action on a whim. There was no intended preparation for it. No property owner had been contacted prior to their arrival. Rick was just doing as he pleased.

On the journey home, Pip appeased his tension by making mental notes of the route back. He prayed in his heart that Rick would not deviate from the regular roads, trying to disadvantage his chances of coming back alone. Roads are not easy to connect in the days before one becomes a driver, but Pip was determined, and lucky for him, Rick was not onto his scheme.

Silver Ford Incorporated

A lapse in the storytelling induced the reporter to comment on some of the detail of what he had heard. It had been conveyed so efficaciously that the newly enlisted listener's own interpolated views were brought to weigh upon it. He felt compelled to interrupt the silence.

"First things first," he blurted out. "You are Pip. Right?"

"Right you are, my boy," Mr. Faehner returned affably. "Pip was, is my nickname. It's followed me since I was a boy. Nowadays, I don't hear it often. It's a vestige from my past—a word from my childhood used only by those who used it then. And please, please refrain from portraying me in that reference when you write up your rendition of this story," he stipulated.

"Sure," the reporter said in earnest, then added, "But there is something else I would like to know."

"Shoot."

"From what you said, from almost the get-go of your story, you had this almost preconceived notion that your uncle was out to make your life miserable, so to speak, yet in the vast scheme of things, it was he that first introduced you to the Silver Mine. How do you go about weighing that enormous debt of gratitude against the way you felt about the apprehensions he had of you?"

"Wow! What a loaded question. I could spend all day answering it, but, as I have only a dime's allowance of time to me, I'll have to do so in accordance with that.

"In life, everything comes from something. But then life goes on. And the something that comes from something should not be suppressed by the something it came from. Life teaches us this. All life acts out this way. I know that all sounds a bit esoteric, so let me put it into perspective for you. In this scenario, it means that Rick led me here. I owe him that. I appreciate that. A good thing happened that day. But I had the right from that day forward to pursue my own interests with the place, and he had no right to stop me. He was like God leading me to the Promised Land, then telling me I could not enter."

"But God did prevent Moses from entering the Promised Land," the reporter added in a scholarly manner.

"But I am no Moses," Mr. Faehner refuted. "So I did as I pleased. And because I did, because I acted out in accordance with my own wishes and desires, a good thing turned into a great thing. So much has happened because of that day. The worth of it was in the worthwhile way, it enhanced the lives of thousands of people that were yet to come. And it all happened because a young boy thought to take his own initiative. And it didn't take long . . .''

The summer of 1973 was over. School began. Pip found himself doubly constrained. Weekdays, he attended high school, did homework afterward, then three or four days a week went dutifully up to Rick's to work in the rock shop. Weekends were spent either cracking specimens or going out to collect them. The stand-off that had been in place since that day at the mine had remained. Neither spoke further about it. Neither wanted to. Pip was a crackerjack rock cracker, and Rick knew it. Pip wanted to work to earn money, and he wanted to be around the rock shop and the things associated with it. It was a stalemate.

But time or good relations did not quell the yearning Pip felt in his heart to defy his uncle and return to the place, which had brought his true spirit to life. Months passed ahead. And only once winter's first furtive snowflakes arrived on the season's solstice did he kick himself for his complacency and take the necessary action to bring his abeyant plan to fruition.

In the course of the holiday days, Pip had successfully garnered the support of three close friends; and together on a torturously cold day in early January, they trekked the intrepid ten miles to the mine. They built a fire, collected samples, and toured the entreating fifty-degree underground tunnel for all its worth. Pip's pleasures were duly doubled when, almost taken by surprise, he found himself lip-locked at the back of the mine with Diane, the sister of the friend whom he had invited.

A second trip ensued the next month as a way to dispel an impending belief among high-school friends that the mine did not exist. This time a ride down and back was bummed off one of the moms, and again everything went well. But it was the third trip down that led to the charm. Warm March winds whirled about the hollow hills as Pip and his best friend Jimmy found themselves skirting past traces of overlying snowcaps and foraging under leaf litter to pry up potential source rock. It seemed a day of oneness with the wilderness when something unintended occurred.

"Hey, Jimmy, hold off on that hammering for a minute. I think I hear something."

"I think I do too," Jimmy retorted once he laid down his tool.

Keeping their silence, the boys remained undetected. Protecting themselves further, they slid quietly downslope of the sparsely wooded hilltop and sidled surreptitiously behind a stand of old-growth hickories. An amazing thing about the feature of a hollow is that around its contour, noise of any kind coming from its center becomes amplified. The slightest voice can be heard far from its source. But in contrast to this, voices made up in the hillside surround are strikingly nullified by the natural construct. The boys were safe.

The auspicious two-toned truck, olive-green with a yellow inlay, was positional to the main mine entrance and could not be seen from the boys' vantage spot. It had arrived when their backs were turned, and their whacking and cracking was so loud that a fleet of pickups could have arrived without them knowing. But the ensuing voices had been detected amid an intermittent silence, and the boys were attuned to the fact that something out of sight was going on just below. From their clandestine hickory hideout, they inched their way stealthily down through the more densely populated spread of long-lived trees until they found a spot ideal for observation. There, from a shelter of overhanging red thorns and two hippopotamus-sized boulders, the boys received a startling view of the interlopers. There were two—one was an older man who walked with a slight hunch. He had a peculiar old face, which, if desired, could be said to resemble a dried-up pickle—withered and wrinkled. On the top of his head, he had a pointed floppy hat, which, if described, could be said to belong to the scarecrow from the *Wizard of Oz*. The younger man was much taller and moved about with much more intensity. Not much could be said about him due the style and manner of his clothing. He had on a distinctive pink shirt, tan pants, white socks, and black shoes. On top of his head, he wore a style of hat too, which resembled Luther Heggs's in *The Ghost and Mr. Chicken.*

Both men appeared impatient. It looked like one or the other had just been inside the mine since their attention was pointed there, and both were carrying flashlights by their sides. The boys pinned their ears toward the fall-off and strained to hear the words being spoken. A reprieve ensued when, all at once, their voices became louder. They were perturbed and associating with each other in this accord. Their words were at once discernible and echoed up to the listeners' ears.

"That's what Ender said. He said he saw two boys being dropped off across from the house. They walked up toward the mine."

"So they've got to be around here somewhere."

"Yep, but don't you worry, Jim, we'll find them."

"Find them and finish them off. I have a mind to go up to Mr. Swank's farm and put into service old Banyon and Bay. Those two will sure sniff out those two and make mincemeat out of them. That will be one pair of sorry boys then I'll tell you."

Both boys felt tense as there was no doubt about what had been said. Banyon and Bay were obviously a pair of teeth-sinking dogs whose eagerness to get at them could already be felt despite their immediate absence. If the wild dogs were garnered to hunt them down, there was little they could do in defense of it. Their predicament was such that they needed to be out in the open with regard to leaving. Their ride off the property was coming soon, and it was too late to withdraw from what was planned. They couldn't just not show up.

Pip felt increasingly infuriated by the ordeal. He had been coming to the mine for many months now and had never before encountered any such difficulty. The property had been his playground—free from any form of intrusion. Now he had been made to feel out of place, like an outcast! But he would not go down without a fight. In a euphoric, fight-to-the-finish fashion, he got up and steadfastly approached the leading edge of the rise.

"Hold on there!" he shouted from his thirty-foot tower of rock-laced earth. He stood there in statuesque form until the eyes of the evildoers were fixed on him. A sense of supremacy overtook him that they, despite who they were, were nothing much to be considered; and he, regardless of his age and shoe size, was someone to be recognized. This sudden infusion of confidence took a second course when, without warning or provocation, he made a flying leap over the guarded ledge and crash-landed on a pile of loose detritus material below. The onlookers were astonished. He was a boy! He was only a boy! For a moment, Pip was in a daze. The jump had his legs stinging, and the shock to his body somewhat lessened his stalwart mind-set. For an awkward moment, he just stood and stared, searching inside himself for a way to improvise for his reduced courage. He swore to himself that he would not let himself down nor would he be brought down by the design of others. He would not fail!

"Look at you, fool for a boy," were the castigating words spoken by the mean-looking man wearing the bright, bold, pink shirt.

"You're not going to live long if you keep jumping off cliffs like that," came the response from the fogy standing beside him.

Pip's eyes met the old man's first, but what he expected to see he didn't. They were, despite his cantankerous appearance, soft and sublime as though they already understood each other. His words were in cadence with his eyes and moved without malice. They were not demeaning and demanded no reply. Pip's uncertainty diminished, and in a moment, he would unleash a tirade of anger still wound around his head. But then his eyes turned and met the man who opted to call him a fool. He was much unlike the other. His eyes were sly and sinister like a hungry he-lion's when he was ready to strike at a would-be meal. But Pip's eyes too were up for a challenge. He molded his own in shape and size to extend back to his gazing partner that he, for his own intent, was now ready to pounce. Luckee saw it too and remedied the potentially volatile situation by getting close enough to each of them to extend one hand each to their prospective shoulders and placate the beasts inside them.

The story was disrupted.

Mr. Faehner, inculcated by the ethereal presence of the late Mr. Boddinger, was induced to take leave of him. His senses had been struck to the core by the reminder of who he was. The storytelling had been like a séance bringing him back, back to the world of reality. He cupped his hands over his face in anguish.

"You'll have to forgive me. The very thought of that man evokes horror in me. To think of what I had to stand against back then when I was so young.

It elicits a powerful hatred in me—a hatred so powerful that it wakes up my entire being."

He was ejected from his chair like a Mr. Faehner-in-the-box and made a quick turn behind his desk to review the line-up and point out his most formidable foe. He strained his finger in a catty-cornered direction and pointed at one of the top-level portraits. The man being portrayed appeared as someone in his forties who had thin lips and was balding. His countenance was stern and authoritative, which gave the impression that he was someone important.

"Mr. Boddinger, I presume," the reporter elicited.

"What's left of him," Mr. Faehner replied. "And just the way I like him too—a figural image of a once interminably fierce person. He despised me from the first. Which in a weird sort of way, I give him credit for, for he could see into the future and see me as someone who had come to take over everything that was his. It was an unspoken truth between us. He saw in me as I saw in him attributes such as intellect, a strong will, and a zest for living, which, when given a direct course to bear, can lead to boundless opportunity and power. We knew who we were to each other and kept it in silence."

Mr. Faehner paused for reflection before continuing.

"Our litany of behind-the-scene fighting took place more in the way we dealt with each other. And it was to go on many years like this, each of us trying to outdo the other. I can only imagine what it must have been like for him, being besieged by a mere boy."

"A boy beyond his years," the reporter pointed out.

Mr. Faehner declined to comment further on that aspect of things. Instead, he dwelled on the wondrous aspect of fate and how it, and it alone, had served him, had saved him. He wrested its servile secrets from the past and brought them to the forefront of his mind.

"It was Luckee who saved me at first. He was sixty-five and had just retired from a life of being a barkeep. He liked me. He liked being around a bright young person whose life he could help create as opposed to the routine of dealing with the rounds of mundane bar people whose lives were like stale beer, without fizz or pop. He was the device that kept us at bay. Without him, there would have been no tomorrow.

"But there was an even greater portent of how things happened offered into this melodramatic one-on-one play—Mr. Boddinger's death! Fourteen years after I had first set foot on his property, he unexpectedly died. A blood clot to the brain is what did it. 1987. My vulnerability ended. In retrospect, I say that those fourteen years were nothing to wait. Time was on my side. I was so young. The fourteen-year wait was perfect for me. It gave me enough time and circumstance to find ways to stand, ready to take over as I did. I was only twenty-seven when he died. I was thirty when I wrestled the property out of the hands of his heirs."

"Did you feel sorry for him when he died?"

"He was a doomed man from the start though he did not know it. It turned out from his autopsy that he had a genetic predisposition for developing blood clots throughout his body. The one that did him in developed in his leg, was dislodged, then traveled to his brain where it blocked a critical blood flow. If he hadn't of died that day, he would have another. That's all I can say. It had nothing to do with me or my passion to control part of the world he held. As far as fate handing him the final blow and that that was the catalyst for my taking over, phooey! I had him by the proverbial balls anyway. As I already said, those fourteen years had given me ample time and circumstance to find ways to upend him, throw him off balance as it were. It was only a situational happenstance that one serious plight got him before the other."

"What does that mean?"

"Sit back and listen. There's much more to tell . . ."

To further quell the possibility of anything bad happening, Luckee introduced himself and the pink-shirted proprietor to the Faehner boy. Hands were shook.

"You are here on the very first day of Silver Ford Incorporated," Luckee announced. This is the beginning of what we hope will be a great new addition to the Lancaster County tourist trade. Visitors will come from all over the country to see the nation's oldest operating silver mine!"

Seeing that the unlikely trio was getting along, Jimmy, still hiding behind a barrier of thorn plant, relinquished his protective stand and made his way down around the mine entrance.

"That's Jimmy," Pip pointed out to the others.

By the time Jimmy got down to the others, Pip was already speaking on their behalf that they had been coming down for months now and had never encountered anyone who had anything to do with the place before.

"Well, you have now!" Mr. Boddinger slapped back like a hockey puck being shot into a net.

"So where are you boys from?" Luckee interceded in the interest of keeping the peace.

"We're from the city," Pip replied earnestly.

"From Lancaster!" Luckee shouted excitedly. "Why, that's ten miles from here. What did you do—fly on your kites to get here?" he asked with a humorous inflection in his voice.

Luckee's quick, quirky, quip quelled a crescendo of contempt that was growing in Pip, and he again attempted to entreat the party to a didactic discourse about his uncle's part in their discovery of the mine and how they took it upon themselves to come back because of how much they liked the place. Mr. Boddinger thought silly of it, having such a young boy be so capable of so much as to actually start to win him over that before Pip was done, he threw his hands up and walked away. Luckee stayed and heard him out. He was impressed and told him so.

"Don't worry about the boss. He can't stand it when anybody butts into his business. He'll get over it."

"So tell us more about what's going on down here?" Pip asked quietly.

Luckee explained the matter more. "Mr. Boddinger bought this place several months ago. It was a land deal really. He and another man traded land tracts. He gave the guy a 250-acre site over in Frogtown in exchange for the 300 acres here. In addition to the Frogtown land, Mr. Boddinger wrote a check for some large sum of money—how much, I don't know. Mr. Boddinger wants to turn this place into a tourist attraction and an entertainment facility. Someday, he wants to build an amphitheater down on the lower portion of the property and bring country-music stars here to perform. The other guy wants to develop the Frogtown site and build homes there."

"So this place is going to go big," Jimmy spurted out in a way that signaled his desire to be included.

Pip inferred the same. He considered the either-or of it. What would life be like with or without the mine? The opportunity was being laid out to him on a silver platter, so to speak. If he declined, there may not be another chance. He would have to grab on if the silver mine were to remain in his scope of endeavors. Mr. Boddinger would be difficult to deal with. Luckee would have to be counted on, on an ongoing basis to act as a go-between.

"Right now, everything's happening on a first-come, first-serve basis. If you boys wish to be part of it, you'll have to act now. I have all the authority to hire as well as fire as I see fit. And I'll give you your chance right now if you want it."

"We'll take it!" Pip shouted out for all the hollow to hear.

The boys were worth their weight in silver. They had, within them, a defining hard-work ethic that characterized the Lancaster County workforce of the time; always showing up, always trying hard, always completing tasks, and always ready for more.

Luckee was, as he said, the overseer. With the two city boys on board, his primary function now was to keep them busy while keeping the peace between them and the high and mighty Mr. Boddinger. The boys' roles were easy to define in that their personalities patterned the duties that were assigned to them. Pip, by virtue of his excellent elocution, was granted the responsibility of becoming the mine's head tour guide, which he espoused to by studying and learning all that he could about the history and geology of the area as it pertained to the operation. In a relatively short period, he became something of a genius on the subject. His expertise was attested to by every person who ever partook of his half-hour walk through time and history.

Jimmy, due his somewhat uncouth behavior and unkempt appearance, was given more behind-the-scenes responsibilities. He became the primary barn worker and groundskeeper. His duties included taking care of the two riding horses that came to stay and a sizeable herd of Sicilian donkeys, which were brought up from a farm in Maryland to be part of the tourist attraction. Late springs, summers, and fall, Jimmy would be tied to one of the riding mowers and out cutting field grass in areas of the park where tourists frequented. Later, when he got his license, Jimmy was used as a go-getter in the literal sense. Assigned to one of the Silver Ford pickups, he would, on any given day, haul trash off the property or go pick up parts for something. The advantage in this was that the boys, in off-hours, would sometimes sneak back onto the property and appropriate the truck for personal purposes.

Some duties, the ones most arduous, required the labor of both boys. These were the crack-the-whip type like clearing out all the fallen rock from the back of the mine, which the boys groaned about from first rock to last. Convinced that the backbreaking order had been issued at Mr. Boddinger's insistence for the twofold purpose of clearing out the broken rock while at the same time giving the boys an amount of work which would also break their spirits, the two would-be tonnage toilers thought up a scheme to outwit their conniving superior. Instead of implementing the proposed wheelbarrow method and hauling out the rock by hand, Pip and Jim borrowed the use of one of the stronger, sturdier donkeys and hitched him up to a makeshift cart so he could then pull the heavy loads of stone from the back of the mine to the outside. On the final day of this successfully strategic endeavor, Luckee happened to be around during the after-hours when all of this unusual activity was taking place. Still, a staunch advocate for the city boys, Luckee was upset by the undertaking but mostly because he feared for them and what might happen should the boss find out what they had done. He never did.

Other slights too, Mr. Boddinger would deliberately set against the boys; but on these occasions, the boys would retaliate in whatever way they could. Pip especially would find ways to get even. Usually, when Mr. Boddinger was on one of his fault-finding escapades, Pip would diffuse his pent-up anger by pocketing what he perceived was a commensurate amount of mine-tour proceeds due the offense. This money he saved rather than spend—first in a coffee can, then in a bank account—all for the explicit purpose of someday buying out this pugnacious man from his precious and undeserved silver mine. At nights, after the fund got going, Pip would sit alone in his own room and count it out, either by adding up the bills and change or by tallying up the bank statements while the satisfying thought that he would someday own the mine by the explicit use of Mr. Boddinger's own money inculcated his being.

There was one sacred event that founding year, which served to spur this takeover notion to an even higher purpose for Pip. The silver mine, though it was a place of business for its proprietor, was also a place for him to socialize. Every Sunday, friends and family were invited down, weather pending, to an afternoon of delights. Station wagons, pickups, vans, and just cars in general would gather outside the office trailer with some overflow on the lawn beside the 1800 house. Most came with the idea of indulgence and so brought with them the measures with which to do so. As though it were part of a schedule, the weekly foray of folks unloaded from their vehicles a plethora of ready-made party foods and ample amounts of party drinks with which to wash it down. A charcoal pit had been put alongside Silver Mine Run across from the trailer lot to keep hot food hot, and the run itself was dutifully utilized to immerse beverage containers—plastic two-liter bottles of soda and twelve or sixteen- ounce cans of beer. And my, oh my, how the beer did flow!

As part of a collaborative effort, Pip and Jim usually avoided these get-togethers, especially in their later stages of development. All too often many of the guests indulged too heartily in the partaking of the malt beverages and so were rendered into states of blatant unreasonableness as per their personality. Some became pathetically silly. Others became rude and obnoxious. Others still became downright belligerent. Once in a while, a fight or two broke out. And all the time, Mr. Boddinger, due his own level of intoxication, did basically nothing to monitor or mediate the resultant tiffs lest it interfere with his own well-deserved, self-induced state of enhanced being.

But the boys still had to eat and the all-too-enticing aromas from the plenitude of hot-grilled foods were temptations that simply could not be ignored. On this one particular occasion, it was decided that they should slip down to the food line once it looked like everybody had been initially pertained to, but before any of the heavy drinking began, but like always, unanticipated duties on both sides kept them occupied beyond what was expected.

Due to heavy rains from two nights before, Pip was busy up at the mine running the pumps, draining both shafts of their inundation of bad-weather water and monitoring the flow against when the pit levels got too low and the pumps might pick up stirred sediment and choke them. Jimmy was down on the lower peninsula, working with a small crew of tree cutters who were busily engaged chainsawing and removing cut-up parts of a hefty sycamore tree, which collapsed into the Pequea Creek during the night of the same storm. Mr. Boddinger's discount rate for rendering Jimmy's services was 10 percent, so they said. Their duties restricted them, and by the time they finally were relieved of them, the greater part of the afternoon had passed. When they did eventually convene, they knew they would be in for it.

But they had to. Chance had given them no choice if they intended to get fed. And for all the work they had performed, they deserved everything they hoped to get and more.

Coming into view from the downslope of the barn path, they hoped to move vicariously through the blended bands of boisterous bodies, pick up their allotment of food, and move off quickly while palming their placating plates out in front of them before the eyes of ogreish Mr. Boddinger detected their presence.

Oops!

"Hey, you two! How about you backing me up on a little bet I've got going over here," Mr. Boddinger shouted out from the top step of the office trailer where he was sitting.

"What do you mean?" Pip shot back in an annoyed tone of voice.

"Come over here," he insisted while all the time trying to hide a grin that carried across the entire length of his face.

"Hey, we just got our eats," Jimmy protested while looking earnestly at his plate of steaming barbecued chicken, corn on the cob, and crab.

Mr. Boddinger was a good fifty-six ounces into his sorry state as was adduced from the four empty twelve-ounce beer cans at his feet and the fifth over-half-empty one in his hand which he was delightfully swirling and swigging when they came to him. Both boys looked at each other with telltale eyes, aware that nothing good was about to happen.

Upon seeing the prestigious proprietor with the prescinded pair of adolescent boys, a pair of within earshot men quickly advanced upon the private party.

"So there are the two then," one of the burly specimens spoke up.

"You've got to be kidding," the other one replied.

"Kidding about what?" Jimmy demanded to know.

Wanting to slug him for his insolence in front of such superior beings, the first man stepped a body closer in the hope that such a move might provoke the outspoken youth further so that force could be used to quell any hotheaded ideas the young inferior might aspire to. But Pip's cooler head prevailed, and he interceded on Jimmy's behalf with a well-intended threat.

"I wouldn't start anything if I were you. One call to the cops, and you'll be sorry!"

"Hey, hey, you people. Let's not be so intense. I didn't bring you two, twos—hey did I say that right? Yes. Yes. I think so. You are both two people, and there are two groups of you. Yes." Mr. Boddinger focused his alcohol-rich mind on the matter of discerning the inveigling words he had just spoken. "Anyway," he finally went on, "I've a better proposition for the both of you both." He paused when he found himself again trying to interpret the logic of his interpolated speech. "Anyway," he began again, "what we've come up with here is a contest in the making—a canoe race to be more exact. And what we want is for you two to race you two," he said while proffering a tentative look in each of the pair's direction. "Of course it's your prerogative," he added glibly.

"What would be the conditions of the race?" Jimmy asked tartly.

"Over there on the pond," one of the burly men interceded. "From one end to the other, if you can handle it."

The fact that the competitor already knew the details of the race gave credence to the concern that something was amiss and that it would have to be discussed. Rather than refuse outright, Pip spoke up and reminded their counterparts that they hadn't even eaten a bite yet and could they enjoy a little R & R before considering such an energy-yielding exercise. In this manner, they took their plates off to a nearby hillside and sat back against its sessile breeches while they enjoyed their respite and contemplated their move.

"This thing's probably been advertised over the whole congregation," Jimmy stated hastily before stuffing his mouth with a full bite of chicken.

"You're probably right," Pip concurred. "But what the heck, we can probably beat those guys. After all, they're probably both in a state of stage-three inebriation. What have we got to lose?"

"I don't know, Pip. If we do lose, we'll be made to look like fools."

"Only in our estimation, Jim. There's not a soul around here that thinks we have what it takes to defeat those two oversized idiots. So if we do lose, which we won't, nobody would have expected any different. But what will happen is that we will kick their asses! That's for sure! Look at how much time we've spent synchronizing our paddling technique. We've probably paddled enough on these ponds to have crossed Lake Erie! And now it's show time! It'll be easy—you in front, me at the back. We'll show those guys what real skill is. And that brains can beat out brawn anytime!"

Just at that moment, Luckee, who had up until this time been off conversing with some of the regulars, began a walk directly to the boys' little nook and proceeded upon them as they continued to mollify their voracious appetites.

"How goes it," he said in a jovial voice.

"Can't you see we're still eating," Jimmy replied in a jumbled statement as he chewed on a mouthful of buttery corn.

"There's something I ought to tell you two," he spurted out without regard to the interference of their meal. "There are bets being placed on the outcome of the race. And there's a pot for the contestants. Winner takes all. So far, the pot's up to $500! Boddinger has bet against you. He even put up half of the money for the prize winnings. Aside from that, he's bet an even

$1,000. Others have bet high amounts too. So I'm just letting you know that you're not just racing for your pride. There's a lot more at stake here."

"So what are you suggesting we do? Take a fall!" Pip yelled out.

"I'm not suggesting anything," Luckee responded. "You do what you want. But if you win, you'll undoubtedly piss off the boss. And you may not get any of your winnings. He's drunk, and who knows what he'll do if he loses all that money, especially to you. He won't be able to stand it."

"He's probably so drunk he won't be able to stand at all," Pip interjected with a note of white-hot wit.

"Well, it's like I said. You do what you want but don't say I didn't warn you."

With that, Luckee sauntered off. When he came within proximity of Mr. Boddinger and his momentary bosom buddies, he was duly called over for a conference to see where things stood. Luckee gestured in a way which indicated that he was unaware of the boys' intentions.

"Well, what do you say, Pip?"

"I say let's do it. Now we have an even greater incentive to win. Just think, Jim. That's $250 a piece! That's more money than we've made since we've been here! You could buy a cycle for that! It's an easy way to fatten up the old cowhide."

"Yeah, that's if we win," Jimmy countered.

"Then let's go do something about that," Pip stated with confidence.

Once their splendid meals were over, the boys got up and strutted confidently over toward their opponents who were still convening with the illustrious Mr. Boddinger.

"I'll take it this means you're in," he said in a contractive voice.

"Let the race begin," Pip said euphorically.

An entourage of interested people began to disperse from the crowded lot and followed the participants and the henchmen across to the pond. As the spectators began to converge around the house, front of the pond, it became clear that most of them belonged on the side of the elite and all-powerful millionaire. They strayed not from his side as though they were tiny planets centered around his sun. Many of them cheered and shook his hand as if the race's outcome had already been decided in his favor. It was an audacious display of cowardice and fear. There were however some supporters of the youthful pair as few shouts went out impugning the contemptible cronies.

One of Mr. Boddinger's buddies took charge of the event. He shouted out to both sets of competitors and their constituents what would be the itinerary of the event. Like an emcee, he outlined the adherent rules in a loud, lively voice. "The race will be the length of the pond and back. It will begin and end at this sycamore tree. The first canoe back as judged by me will take the prize. Understood?"

Both duos nodded and proceeded to board their identical canoes, which were beached just aside the bended sycamore. The two burly men entered their aluminum vessel in clumsy fashion, almost spilling themselves over by not countering their weight evenly as they did. Pip and Jim were experts and knew it was best for one of them to enter while the canoe was still partially grounded and stable. The other then pushed off from shore and leaped aboard only once the canoe was going. This they accomplished in so fine a fashion that several of the Boddinger crowd became instantly alarmed—those who had put up large sums of money in favor of the motley crew.

Ahead of the other contestants, the boys were able to enjoy a brief encouraging moment with each other before the festivity began.

"Remember, Jim, the key to winning is not to give up, no matter what. These guys will probably start out strong, but they might overexert themselves early and leave a clear path for us to follow. We need to focus on continuance. Let's apply a consistent stroke and make sure we don't stray off a concise path. Breathe deep and keep your attention only on what's ahead of you. Remember, I'm the rudder. I'll dictate the variance of our sway. You best paddle side to side. And don't dip your paddle too deep in the water. That will actually cause drag and cause you to use up too much energy. And remember, don't give up!"

Soon, the novices arrived and were positioned beside the boys in perfect symmetry. The pond depiction was a cynosure for all of the onlookers who waited in wonder for the contest to begin. A few who became cynics once they witnessed the awkward display made by the bungling brutes when they attempted to board their canoe made last-minute attempts to renege on their earlier bets and instead regale the more competent younger sect of canoe enthusiasts. But all bets were off, and much to their chagrin, so were the boys once the race began.

The final announcement was made. "Ready, set, go!"

The boys took off like a dart, and their canoe established a lead with the first few strokes. Each prevailing stroke fell into and out of the water in perfect stride like a part-counter-part of a machine. Within moments, they were a full canoe length ahead and left wondering where their opponents were. But in a discerning way, they concerned themselves only with what lie ahead, for the plot lay in completing the competition and not worrying about anything else.

A revealing smile crossed Pip's face as they made an effort onward. He was duly pleased at how much all of their previous practice, which had really only been leisurely contrived, had paid off. Onward, they sailed in a straight line and by half-pond were still maintaining their one-canoe-length lead. So intense was their concentration that they were immune to a commotion that was beginning to sound from the pond shore. People began shouting and cheering as though the boys' lead was an imaginary thing. But the boys paid no attention lest they lose their sense of purpose.

Then the unimaginable happened. All at once, their canoe turned over on its side, and both boys plunged into the pond! They felt as if their life force had been suddenly shaken. What had happened? Somehow, someway their canoe had been tipped and toppled into the pond. And just like that, it was over, or so it seemed. It the two seconds he had to react, Jimmy, feeling the momentum of the canoe going over, tried desperately to lean hard to left before the hope was gone. His first reaction once he was in the water was to keep the canoe afloat, keep it from taking on water, and wade it into shore. Pip had another objective. As he was flung into the murky stillness, he twisted his head left as a last-chance attempt to see exactly what the culprits had done. And he did. The front man still held the extended paddle one-handed out in front of him—the one he had used to lean their canoe over. On his countenance was a sinuous smile. And, adding insult to injury, he even gave a one-finger salute as the young boys splashed hilariously downward. Before going completely under, Pip saluted him back by projecting his right hand high above his head and pointing an extended middle finger clearly in their direction.

The spectators had seen it all and responded to the ridiculous display by erupting into a chorus of raucous laughter. Mr. Boddinger especially was taken by the comical scene. The incident occurred while he was ingesting more beer, and as such, the prevailing interrupting laughter forced him to spit out the content of his mouth and drench the often-worn pink shirt he was attired with.

Now under ordinary circumstances, the incident would have been over. The brutes obviously had won. The illicit tactic would have worked to conclusion. But the circumstances were not ordinary. Pip's mind was a thing to be considered. The deceit had rendered upon him an extraordinary effect. He noticed, much to his instant delight, that the purveyors of their unsettling misfortune had remained in a state of stagnation. Thinking they had won by default, they remained where they were and did not move on! To Pip, this meant that race could still be won. As he stood in the water, he crossed his fingers and slowly waded into shore where Jimmy had now guided the canoe. When he reached a point near shore where they were only slightly deep, he sidled up close to his fellow racing companion and elicited to him an either-or idea that had just pervaded his thoughts.

"Either way, we win," he projected proudly. "But we have to act quickly. And remember, keep your head low. Look dejected. We need those few seconds to put us in position to pull this thing off. There won't be a second chance."

Pip's plan was a stroke of genius. In that split second of time as he stood and stared down his aggressors, he had envisioned a strategy, which might result in yet their victory. And the idea was well conceived. He believed that because their opponents resolved to maintain their stationary position, gesturing the victory sign with their fingers to the crowd on shore and congratulating each other for besting the innocent young canoeists, he and his partner might just be able to slip back into their canoe and continue the race. This time, they would stay out of reach by not moving directly in front of them. If the bullies happened to realize what they were doing, then they would implement an alternate course of action. They would simply charge into their adversaries and do their determined best to upset their canoe. Pip envisioned the extent of what would be his willingness to accomplish this. He would, if need be, get right beside them and project himself, like a missile, onto the closest person and knock them into the water! Jimmy would do the same. And there could be no retribution against them for they would be guilty of nothing more than what had been done to them.

But the best-case scenario came through. Appearing unconcerned, the boys surreptitiously reentered their canoe, making it seem like they were taking off just to be alone, away from the shorebirds who were cackling and cracking jokes at their expense. But then, just when the position was right, the boys took off. In one tremendous push-ahead, they tore upon the open water in front of them. Then, in one tedious stroke after another, they rejoined the broken race. Knowing the dread and humiliation they would suffer should they lose now, they made an effort onward as if they were being powered on by an outboard motor. By two-thirds pond, it was over. Most observers, including the two dumbstruck oafs, were quite taken by what was occurring. Nobody could believe it! They won the race fair and square for having the foresight to see beyond their predicament. And fortunes were theirs for having done it.

Mr. Faehner's enthusiastic telling of the great canoe race was over. He allowed for a brief interlude after in which he could better explain the applied meaning of it to the reporter who would invariably ask it of him.

"So you can see the race was planned. Mr. Boddinger devised it just so we would humiliate ourselves. And in front of so many other prominent people too. It was the first time he actually tried to get the better of us in such a complete and open fashion. He hid behind his drunken fools so he could never be directly blamed for it. But we turned the tables on him, didn't we! He got his that day, I can tell you!"

"What about the money?" the reporter duly inquired.

"Oh, the money. Let's see . . . If I remember correctly, we collected about $300 each—a little more than what Luckee suggested we would. I took mine and added it to my Silver Mine Fund—the proceeds of which I continued to collect for the next sixteen years, then used directly to help purchase the property. I swore revenge on him that day—that I would someday possess the money and means to usurp his position there. And I meant it!"

Party Favor

"That was quite a tale, sir. Like something out of Tom Sawyer or Huckleberry Finn. It sounds like you were quite full of pluck for someone who was only fourteen. Imagine, resolving to usurp a millionaire. To do that, you would have had to have been a millionaire yourself or better. Were you?"

"Back then, certainly not. Even when I actually purchased the place, I hadn't yet saved my first million. It wasn't one of those "become-a-millionaire-before-you're-thirty" stories. It was a lot more complex than that."

"Well, how old were you when you usurped your predecessor?"

"Ironically, I was thirty. But I didn't have a million dollars to spare. Not for anything."

"Well then, how did you manage to pay for the property?"

"A couple of things came together in my favor for that. I brought the property—the original land—in 1990. But the purchase price was only $300,000. The property was defunct, and I was in a position to take advantage of it. And I did."

"How in the world did you happen to have even that much money lying around?"

"It didn't come easy, I can tell you that," Mr. Faehner responded with a facetious smile. "It was two things really. And one was just as important as the other. So listen as I tell you and don't discount the dwelling point over the unusual event because I tell you that one would not have worked without the other."

"So tell me."

"I was a part of Silver Ford Incorporated from the very first day. I never left. It became as much a part of me that when I left on the days that I first worked there, I felt as if I had left part of my spirit behind. You can be sure that if left to me on the day that I die, I will spend my eternity as an ethereal presence there, if left to me."

That thought evoked a spiritual silence in him. They were wishful words, which had never once been spoken other than to himself, and he wondered if they sounded foolish having said them in the company of another. It was one of his precious thoughts—thoughts which were never intended for another. But the milk had been spilt, and it was time to get on with it.

"For the first nine years, I practically lived there. For the last seven, I did. Almost everything I thought, did, and said pertained to the silver mine. I was, for many years, what I had been initially—the head tour guide and anything-else-that-was-necessary person. Later, I took over Luckee's position as overseer. Luckee, by then, had lost his vitality to lead. He was in his seventies then and really didn't want the responsibilities of the day-to-day running of the place. He kept on though in a limited capacity. He was sort of like a part-time promoter of the place. He helped arrange special events and dealt with the media. He was, you could say, a silver-tongued spokesperson for the mine.

"Anyway, as far as I was concerned, I stayed on with the place through thick and thin. And for me, the operation of the place was a way to stay close and continue to find stepping stones, which could enable me to reach my dream of owning the place myself. I feared leaving the operation although I knew I was disabling my earning potential. I sensed it was better in the long run to stick around and try to compensate for the lack of earnings other ways. Because in the end, it really isn't a matter of how much a person makes that counts, but rather how much is saved.

"So I threw myself into a mode of frugality unlike any I had ever seen of anybody else. In the sixteen years between when I first came onto the silver mine scene and the day I outright purchased it, I had managed to save $113,000. In order to do that, I had somehow managed to put away about 70 percent of my entire bring-home salary! My, oh my, how my head still pulses every time I think about it! But I had to keep a low profile though to pull it off. If Boddinger had suspected for a minute that I was finding ways to keep that sort of money, he would have lowered my wages for sure, probably minimum wage for sure."

The reporter did the math and divided the sum by the number of years and came up with the answer.

"That's $7,625 per year!" he exclaimed.

"That's right," Mr. Faehner concurred. "A tidy sum too, considering I only made about $10,000 per year."

"Remarkable!"

"I don't really recommend it though. Remember, being a miser means living in misery. And you can take that statement to the proverbial bank. Believe me, I paid a dear price for it. You have no idea of the self-sacrifices I made. It's a poignant thing to recollect. In the earlier years, it didn't really matter. But later when I was in my twenties, I minded it immensely. While most men my age were buying homes and living it up, I was either living with my parents or later, living in the old stone house. I lived without luxury or freedom. Thinking about the ordeal of it, I don't know whether to laugh or cry."

"Let it out, either way," the reporter prompted.

"Why not?" Mr. Faehner concluded.

"Let's examine my mode of transportation during those years then. That in itself is a genuine example of what was my enduring hardship." In response to the memory of such a privation, Mr. Faehner let out a loud laugh and then paused to put the facts, such as they were, together in his mind.

"In 1978, I purchased my first car. It was a 1973 Chevy Vega—auburn-colored exterior with a gray interior. It had a four-cylinder, aluminum-block engine, which meant it had no get-up-and-go at all. It was bought purely to get from point A to point B. I came across it quite inadvertently one day while I was walking along in a back alley near my home. It had one of those for-sale signs on it which advertised it for only $500. I was enthralled. I had the $500, and I didn't have a car. So I responded. As it turned out, the owner had recently moved to California and had left the Vega behind. The response number belonged to a neighbor who told me all I had to do was show up with the money, and the car was mine. The very next day, I took the car out for a drive, and I paid for it.

"For twelve long years, I drove that car. From the day I brought it until just before I plopped down almost a third of a million for the silver mine property, that car and I were one. By the time I parted with it, I believe it was the last Chevy Vega on the road. I actually drove it to its final destination—the junkyard. I simply drove it in through the gate and parked it up alongside an old rusted Pinto. I left the keys in the ignition. The junkman paid me $50 for it too. Do the math on that why don't you, twelve years divided by five hundred dollars. That's how much it cost me to own that vehicle.

"That comes to exactly $41.66 per year," the reported stated firmly.

"I was the ultimate pinchpenny," Mr. Faehner affirmed. "But," he continued, "even that doesn't explain my being able to make such an expensive expenditure as the Silver Mine, does it? I had only one-third of the amount accounted for in the fund I started. And I assure you no bank or other lending institution would have allowed me to borrow the difference."

"Then how did you do it? How did you finagle the move from being two-thirds short to obtaining the obvious outcome?"

"It happened twelve years prior to acquisition. A situation arose in which I was able to solicit an enormous amount of money. But it was money I dare not make a move with—not for any purpose under heaven!"

"How much money are we talking about here?"

"It started out at $200,000 in 1978, but I didn't really have any way with it until many years later. But it sufficed. But like I said, it wouldn't have meant anything had I not taken the other extreme measures I did. In fact, we would not be here talking today if I had not had the foresight to establish myself in both terms—frugal and fortuitous."

"So where did the money come from? A long-lost relative? The lottery?"

"No. Nothing so simple." I'm afraid the explanation lies in the lines of another story—a "once-upon-a-time" version of my unfathomable life. Are you ready to be elucidated?"

"As ready as I can be."

"I'll have to caution you though against making known this telltale event. I'd prefer if you didn't cover it at all unless you can implement some skill to cover up the sensitivity of it. Here's your chance to build a rapport with me for the purpose of having a future connection to my world. The difference being a person who is privileged to come into my favor versus a person who has to sneak into a country club and hope he doesn't get caught, if you get my drift."

The reporter understood and compliantly put down his pen and paper and waited for Mr. Faehner to regale him with another alluring tale. The reporter followed him back in time and place to the days when so much had yet to be decided, when so much of what we call fate was being tossed around . . .

It was the Silver Mine summer of 1978. Already so much of the construct of the way things were had changed. Jimmy was gone. And in his stead was brought another close friend, another Jim. It had been now almost five years since the Silver Mine had first come into Pip's life, and the remnants of his adolescence were all but parted with. In its place were the whims and wilds of a young man. Things that were only once dreamed about were now certainties. Aspirations such as fast cars and women were now foremost in his mind. And although he had not yet credited his convenience with conveyance—he had not yet purchased the Vega, which would dominate his transportation life for the next decade and more—he did possess a valid license to drive, and he did have, in the context of his close association with his new Silver Mine partner, a constant connection to the use of nice cars to either drive himself or be driven in.

James had, over the brief course of his working life, funneled most of his ready cash into all sorts of over-the-road vehicles. He owned two motorcycles, two cars, and a moped, which was quite impressive for an eighteen-year-old. The car Pip liked the best was a 1966 Chevelle—red with a supercharged engine. It never failed to excite the honeys whenever they drove it around and around the Loop in Lancaster on a Friday night.

The privilege of having or having access to a vehicle with so much potential meant that their lives were not conditioned by or limited to the confines of immobility. In conjunction with having such a place as the Silver Mine to go to this meant that their frequency in coming and going did not depend on others nor was it restricted to when they were required to be there for work. With the aid of the vehicles, they came and went as they pleased.

At the mine, James had become Jimmy. Pip always referred to them as either James or Jimmy to distinguish their different time slots there. And so since James had supplanted Jimmy, he also took over his positions. He was the new stable master, grass cutter, and ready-as-you-please go-getter.

One summer day after the day's tours were over, Pip slow-poked his way toward the barn to see what his friend was up to. James was busy. He had just led the last pair of donkeys into their pens to bed them down for the evening when Pip arrived, hands in his pockets, and whistling through the side arch. His final steps inside were accompanied by a stiff breeze, which seemingly came out of nowhere. It enlivened his spirit in much the same way as a long-awaited spring breeze does after a dreadful winter. James was in a jovial mood too and expressed his vigor with a cheery salutation to his newly arrived friend.

"Hi there, oh my, friend, buddy, chum, and pal. What brings you over into this dome of donkey dung."

"I was just blown in by the breezes," he replied in recognition of the remarkable wind, which was still blowing in. "God that feels good."

"Yeah, it makes it almost breathable in here," James added sarcastically.

"You know, if you're done early too, why don't we just go out back behind the barn and wait out the last hour. God knows we do enough extra duty around here, we don't need to be filling up every last tick of the clock."

"I'm with you," James shot back.

So their whereabouts would not be detected, they climbed into the upper barn by way of a trap door in the floor, which was built into the barn for this explicit purpose so a worker could avoid any foul weather, if there was any, and still access both barn levels. James's Chevelle too was all the time parked behind the barn since this was James's daily starting and finishing place. They decided they could open up the car, listen to tunes, and shoot the breeze. What happened as a result of their intentional take-it-easy was a little more than they intended. Almost as if their minds were one and engaged in some form of ESP, they looked at one another and formulated a better way of accentuating the positive, carefree feelings they were connecting to.

"I could go for a party!" James elicited after opening up a can of Sprite he discovered while rummaging for tapes and taste-testing it for temperature.

"Tepid, isn't it," Pip interjected after witnessing James's loathly reluctance to sip any more. "So I would hope that in the event of a party, there would be a supply of ice-cold beverages."

"If by beverage you mean beer, then I'm with you partner!" James said in a boisterous manner.

"I'm more interested in the female aspect of things," Pip replied. "The beverages can be as they may."

"Don't forget, friend, beer can get those feminine juices flowing like nothing else can."

"We would have to be careful and not get caught. I don't want to lose my status here."

"You have a status here," James teased.

"Of course I do," Pip restated easily. "I've been here since the beginning."

Pip advanced through the barn's interior, then loitered over against the far wall. Every so many of the wall's boards had been built so they could be slanted open to allow air, such as was flowing, to enter into its stuffy interior. Pip peered out of one of the open slats. Down from his view, he could see different groups of tourists actively engaged in fun-in-the-sun activities. One couple was rowboating out on the pond. Another was taking scenic pictures of the rowboaters. Two young boys were busy casting lines in the near side of the pond hoping to catch bass. All the time, Pip was pondering the feasibility of what they were both thinking about.

"I know what you are thinking, James. You want to use the old stone house to host the party in." He paused before continuing. "And it's not that I'm against using it, but you know what the consequences would be if we were caught. It would be our asses on the line."

"Asses-smasses," James returned sharply. "If Mr. B happens to show up, we'll invite him in and ask him for a contribution."

Pip didn't appreciate James's attitude in taking his concern too lightly. You just never knew with a man like Boddinger. He was like a ticking time bomb, and you never knew when he would go off. It was true that as of late, he seemed less severe whenever something or someone ticked him off, but that was no security. The man had the potential to relapse with the slightest provocation. And facilitating the house without permission for the purpose of throwing a party was certainly a bit more than what would be considered a slight provocation. In fact, it was scary!

But the internal strife ended with the party prospect intact. Pip began a rundown on what would be the most essential precautions they could take to pull the party off: (1) park the Chevelle back behind the barn as usual (2) keep the party to a minimum; ideally just two guys and two girls (3) stay on guard no matter what, and (4) if we would happen to get caught deny everything and let him think what he wants. Heck, if everybody made a run for it and we all vouched for each other, we could simply say that Boddinger was crazy. As bizarre as this sounded, Pip needed to think this way to alleviate the increasing tension he felt about taking such a risk with the security of his long-term position. If it ever was to be his fate to take over the Silver Mine, he could not allow it to be jeopardized by something so juvenile as a party. If he ended up on the rock pile, then his whole life would come undone, and everything he had worked for would have been for nothing. It was an abhorrent thought.

Pip drifted in and out of these personal reflections and didn't notice when James had finished his lively speech about how simple it was really to make this party a reality.

"And you know that's true, Pip. How many times have we come down here before to just take it easy or kick back and have a few beers? And not once on all of those occasions did Mr. B, Luckee, the cops, or anyone else ever come and bother us. So come on, dude, let's get real about this thing."

Although James was right about the precedent—that they had not been caught coming down after work before—Pip was still hesitant to be persuaded that it could not happen this time. Complacency was not the hallmark of a champion. But rather than enter into a full-scale debate over his apprehensions, he decided instead to downplay his concerns. He did have an ace in the hole, and that was the time it would take to make it all happen. If during that interlude he began to feel even more uncomfortable about their chances, he could simply pull out. If it were canceled, so what?

Another week passed, and Pip watched how James's enthusiasm continued to grow. James had arranged for a tentative date—another week—and was already making preparations.

In the days leading up to the anticipated event, James had managed to obtain all of the necessary particulars, which made a party great. He stashed them all in the house cellar where they became lost in a plethora of everyday Silver Mine supplies. Luckee always purchased the Silver Mine items in large quantities by patronizing a specialty store, which dealt in selling slightly damaged goods or substances, which were near their expiration dates. The cellar was piled high with all-sized boxes full of napkins, paper towels, cleanser, and plastic utensils. Most of the items were used for Boddinger's weekend bashes. Beer, chips, soda, and various other snacks were stuffed in and among the assorted supplies and now only awaited their need. At one point, Pip asked James why he bothered to bring down the party essentials so much beforehand and why not just gather them up on *the day* and bring everything down at once, and James responded that that would be too much running around for one day.

The day of the party, the planners were most precautious. They did not act or say anything out of the ordinary that would make others believe something was going on. Several times during the day, they got together to share information about whether or not either of their bosses were suspicious of anything. They were not.

Alone at the end of the day, Pip took a time-out to make one final consideration as to whether or not he wanted to go through with it. It was a now-or-never decision and one that he had to make by himself. James, though his partner through thick and thin, did not know what was really at stake for him. Never in all of their shared experience had Pip ever related to him what the Silver Mine really meant—that it was his expected future to someday take the place from Mr. Boddinger. In fact, Pip had never revealed that expectation to anyone of importance. He had been obdurately secretive from the first about it and would continue to be so no matter *who* came along and earned his confidence, no matter *what* circumstance might arise, no matter *where* it might be appropriate, no matter *when* it might be considered the right thing to do, no matter *why* it might be in his best interest to do so.

Pip breathed a sigh of relief for the fact that he had never had the audacity to reveal such a thing to any of the Silver Mine people. His secret was still safe with him. So he paused amid the wind-swept hollow, the wooded hills, and thorny sessiles, which lined the bottom slopes and kept his thoughts. He evoked his belief that somehow, someway, someday, he would prevail upon this place of sylvan beauty and be its steward. And he would forever regard its glory.

It was an ethereal moment, and he would not give it up. Neither would he give up on the party now only a few hours away. The fairer sex too had a means of making a young man feel surreal and it, or rather doing *it* was of great significance. The difference would be in how he would bestow his best abilities to make things go smoothly.

As one final solution to the concept of the risk they were taking, Pip felt it necessary to designate James ahead of time as the culprit just in case the party took a bad turn.

"Remember, this party was more your idea than mine. I did, however, endorse it and so shall share in a part of the blame should anything go noticeably wrong. But you, you shall take the lion's share of the responsibility if we're caught. Understand?"

"And just what does that mean?" James responded tartly.

"I don't know exactly," Pip stated dryly. "But we'll cross that bridge when and if we get there."

Pip's parting words were implicating and left an air of uncertainty in the condition of the circumstance that existed between the two young men. Pip, left behind to watch over the Silver Mine situation, even wondered whether or not James would return.

It was past 5:30 p.m., and the plot was thickening. James had departed out the back way on purpose so his Chevelle would been seen leaving, but leaving without the knowledge that he was alone. Pip intentionally stayed behind and holed up in the upper barn to ascertain that everybody else of consequence would leave, and if need be, he could wave off James during his return if the coast was not clear. He paced back and forth in the heavy-duty hideout, nervous and tense. Six o'clock came, and he was relieved to finally see Luckee load up his Dodge Dart and start up the hill. The game of hide-and-peek was over.

Now it was quite a peculiar fact that neither Pip nor James, despite their relative good looks and good nature, had a steady sweetheart. This was of course due to other aspects of their nature, each relative to their unique personalities. Pip was an erudite who spent most of his spare waking hours engrossed in the lessons of literature. The Silver Mine was his obsession. He spent more time there than anywhere else, than everywhere else combined. He wanted women too, but he was more or less placated by the fact that every year some one or other young female happened to come upon him in his precious realm, and their shared infatuation would endure for the space of time she had allotted to her due her or her family's stay.

James had an even greater propensity for finding love, but he too possessed personal afflictions, which prevented him from entering into any long-term relationship. He was flamboyant and somewhat of a philanderer. He sought flirtation and attention from the fairer sex but not seriousness, not a solace of the soul. A hot car meant a hot woman or hot women as the case may be. And James was not one to play down his potential with one of the most absorbing aspects of an enjoyable life.

For people like this, whose fine art in life was only to dabble in the sensual rather than engage wholeheartedly in the sensible aspect of the male-female relationship, there was such a place to find comfort. The Loop in Lancaster was a mile-and-a-half-long stretch of cityscape where forlorn women put themselves on a sort of window-shop display, walking and stopping, along the designated route in the hope of striking the fancy of some young, carefree hot-rodder who would then pick them up and take them on a high-performance ride around town or to any other such destination as determined by their mutual attraction and consent. Those being selected from included females in every stage of maturation. Girls who were pre-teens were referred to as nubs—a way of signifying their characteristic tiny, pubescent nipple-tipped protrusions atop their chests. True teens were called twits for the way they taunted and teased the older of-age drivers with their almost-alluring bodies. More mature women, those over eighteen, were often termed mollies by virtue of the fact that they were of age and could legitimately mollify a man's direct needs if they were so inclined.

James knew the names and the games. Almost weekly, during the warmer times of the year, he frequented the city Loop and often came away with either a nub or a twit or a molly. His actions afterward of course dictated by the level of availability offered by the selection.

When he rolled into the line-up, he made several successive passes around the entire limit ogling many of the sixth-night candidates. All of them noticed his cherry-red bombshell and reacted to it with stare-and-dare enticements. Some had even started out from the curb in hope of persuading the red-devil driver to stop, look, and listen. But James had a more specific task in front of him. He had to find two available honeys to lure to the country. So he searched three times round until, as luck would have it, two all-you-could-ask-for beauties came strutting out of a convenience store sipping sodas and making believers out of men who thought that beauty was only skin deep. Upon sighting them, James whisked his wheels into the open lot aside the store and revved up the Chevelle's 350 engine to impress and lure the hotties over. It did. After a brief sizing up on both sides, the ladies agreed to go for a spin. James told them a little white lie by saying that he was in town only to try to catch sight of a friend who he wanted to accompany him back down to a place in the county where he was having a party. While he was busy conveying this to them, he noticed that they were whispering to each other how they wouldn't mind going too. So he invited them outright.

When they arrived at the mine, Pip was waiting outside the back of the barn, curious who, if anybody, would be with James. He was shocked by what he saw when the girls stepped out of the car. Cheryl was short, had medium-length dirty-blonde hair, and weighed a slender 112 pounds. Bonnie was a little shorter, had pure blonde hair, and was a mere 102 pounds. Both epitomized femininity at its best.

The candid exchange of identities went on for a short term in which the ages of the couples were revealed. Cheryl was seventeen and proved it by displaying her junior driving license. Bonnie also claimed to be seventeen, but that was accurate only by rounding up from the sixteen years, eleven months, and twenty-four days that she had actually spent waiting to be seventeen.

To relieve some of the awkward tension unavoidably present among the group of first-time intimates, James opened up the front passenger door of his car, slid in, then reached into the opened glove box and retrieved a bag of Fudgies. He tore open the bag and tossed two or three to each person and prompted them to open the gold-colored wrappers and pop the candies into their mouths. "Try them and see," he said to the reluctant ladies who testified that they had never had them before.

"They're bite-sized bits of chewy chocolate," James adduced by going first and introducing his, two at a time, into his mouth.

"Mine are all squishy," Cheryl claimed once she unwrapped both of the shiny seals.

"Yeah, they have a tendency to get that way after they've been in a hot car for hours and a day," Pip pointed out.

"Yeah, hot cars make for hot cars," James said in a weary attempt to inflect humor into the conversation.

"We get it," Pip intervened.

"So what do we do now?" Cheryl inquired sarcastically. "Where's this so-called party."

"Yeah, is this it?" Bonnie added glibly.

"First things first," James stated easily. "Let us show you two around this place a little bit."

Picking their partners, Cheryl went to James and Bonnie to Pip, the hormone-driven males, together, escorted their teen queens to some of the mainstay sights on the property. Fifteen minutes was spent in the lower part of the barn showing off the Sicilian donkeys and horses. Following that, the entourage headed up to the mine where Pip treated everybody and especially Bonnie to an enticing tour. Though he felt trepidation in doing so—opening up the mine so late—he gave it his all, knowing full well that it would be his best opportunity to show off his skill and intelligence without seeming overzealous about it.

Though Pip paid attention to the detail of information he was determining for the group, he couldn't help but be enamored by the facial beauty and magnificent body of his date. His mind wouldn't let it alone—how he hoped to make a move on her when given the chance. James too was not straying off course. Not involving himself with the interstitial dynamics of the tour, he spent all of his time and opportunity coming-on to Cheryl who was not the least bit disturbed by his bold gestures and moves. When the party exited the mine, James gave Pip a go-ahead nod, which meant that they both could expect a lot of love-making before the night was over. Along those lines, the group headed to the house where Pip exacted a key he had taken when no one was looking. He placed it into the lock, jiggled it, then unlocked the hefty door.

Once they were inside and James had pertained to everyone by regaling them with beer and potato chips, Pip pulled his friend off to the side and reiterated a warning about being on their guard, about not making too much noise, about keeping the girls in line, about not getting too drunk, and about a dozen other things. While giving his adamant stance, Pip made the mistake of speaking too staunchly and the tone of his words were picked up by their newly acquainted friends.

"Hey! I thought you two said this was your place. What are you guys talking about? We aren't breaking and entering, are we?"

"No, we are not," James spoke up abruptly.

"He's right," Pip insisted. "We do legitimately work here. It's just that by having you two here with us, we've probably overstepped our bounds. It's nothing to worry about really as long as everybody does what's right, as long as we don't wreck the place."

Pip was glad that the girls now knew of the apprehension he, especially, felt. Now, if they stayed, they would be more likely to abide by the simple set of rules and restrictions he now laid down before them. And the girls did stay. Prior to this evening, they never knew that such a place existed in the confines of Lancaster County; and even though they were not budding geology students or historical buffs, they were fascinated with everything they had seen, including their male counterparts!

So the evening went according to plan, stipulations included. The early part of the get-together was spent as a group with everybody just enjoying themselves. They passed the time engaged in light-hearted conversation of the getting-to-know-you type. Potato chips were crunched, snack cakes were munched, and Fudgies were chewed. And it all was quenched with cans of beer. And though a great time was being had by all, Pip kept up his guard, kept watch over the situation should anything go awry. He kept vigil. The lights were kept low. The music was kept soft. He pulled down blinds on the windows that had them and often peeked out.

As more time passed, the atmosphere loosened up, and the couples began to give in to their innermost desires. Flirtations turned into fondling. James and Cheryl took up a position in a corner chair in the darkened living room and began kissing. Meanwhile, Pip and Bonnie found ample body space on an overstuffed couch in the room on the other side of the stairs and started in on their own session of delight.

This went on for some unknown period of time before both couples realized they were in a do-or-die mode of sensuality. Decisions had to be made.

Each couple began to discuss it privately. Should each couple copulate where they were? Should they move upstairs to more conducive surroundings? Should they each break it off until a more suitable time and place was available for such a dalliance? What should they do?

As if connected by ESP again, both Pip and James got up from their trysting place and converged upon each other at the central hall, which led upstairs. Each knew what the other was thinking.

"Look," James said with verve," I'm having more fun than a barrel of monkeys. And I'll tell you quite honestly, I want this chick right here, right now! And I won't take no for an answer! I'm so horny I could just go crazy at any moment! I don't care who comes down here and finds us! I'm not leaving without getting what I want!"

"Now you look," Pip spelled out in a strained voice. "I'm right there with you, pal. Bonnie is just ten minutes away from giving it to me too. But we have to be cool about what's going on here. If we all go upstairs, you know that afterward nobody's going to want to leave. So what we're really talking about here is taking the chance of spending the night and then getting out of here in the waking hours of the day without arousing any suspicion from anybody who just might be around. It's a risk."

"I'll risk it," James shot back, then abruptly departed.

Pip could hear James persuading Cheryl to follow him upstairs to a place where they would be more comfortable. Bonnie heard it too and so inquired of Pip what he wanted to do.

"We'll do the same," he whispered into her ear. "But first, I'll clean up a bit. You know, get rid of the evidence."

Bonnie helped. Together, they took a five-minute reprieve from their desires and picked up most of the crumbs, cans, and clutter that signified their having had an arranged social affair in the downstairs of the house. The contrasting work did not, however, affect their mood for play. Once they were done, Pip turned off the lights, locked the door, and led his mistress back through the darkened living room to the stairs. With Pip in the lead, they stepped to the top where they suddenly stopped. Coming from the room atop the kitchen, they could hear the unmistakable sounds of James and Cheryl writhing together in ecstasy. Both Pip and Bonnie yielded indiscernible blushes while considering their friends' frenzied fornication, knowing for certain that very soon they would be imitating the same.

It was midnight when Bonnie and Pip fell off into a well-induced sleep. And the house fell silent except for the four quiet inhalations-exhalations patterned by the nocturnal interlopers as they lay naked and nestled on the bare-carpet floors. Oblivious to all else, the couples laid still until an unexpected thing happened. James, the lightest of the sleepers, was suddenly jostled from his slumber by the sound of a strange something or other coming from downstairs. He remained lying down, eyes opened, and listened. The sound was indistinguishable except to say it was apparently coming from the kitchen and had something to do with the jiggling of metal. He thought in all probability that it was probably Pip, worrywart that he was, simply rechecking the side door to make sure it was locked.

Being stirred from his sleep, he became aware of his impending need to alleviate the pressure he felt in his bladder, and he sought to relieve himself of his discomfort before further concern was placed on the mysterious noise from below. Without any concern for his own disturbance, he tread into the bathroom, lifted up the seat of the toilet, and by the casting of soft moonlight flooding in from the window, proceeded to press out a steady stream of excess yellow liquid. For an enduring thirty seconds, James emptied out a volume of liquid equal to two cans of beer; and afterward, he nonchalantly flushed the receptacle.

By then, it was too late! From downstairs came an immediate response. Footsteps thumped their way from the kitchen, to the living room, to the staircase stoop. James stood on the top landing, stiff and still, and with owls-eyes' keenness tried to pierce the nullifying darkness to see for himself just who it was. But his wait was measured in seconds as a loud rasping voice soon penetrated the incline gap.

"Who in God's name has set foot on my property? You'd better come down and show yourself right now before I come up and throw you out through a window!"

James went through a flurry of emotions in the seconds before he responded. He was perplexed when he heard the footsteps thumping toward the stairs. He was aghast when he realized who it was rather than his companion of the other room. He was anguished when he knew he was in for a lot of trouble. But he was angered by the admonishment he heard in regards to his possibly being thrown out of a window. And this became his rallying point. Without fear of consequence, he vaulted blindly down the interceding steps ready to meet his nocturnal nemesis.

"Okay, Mr. Millionaire, let's have at it," James spouted out once he landed on one of the bottom steps.

Mr. Boddinger, though infuriated, stepped back. He had believed it was the other of the Silver Mine duo who would have dared to spend the night without permission, so much was his zeal for wanting to be around. But this was James who was notably bigger and stronger and was considered to be something of a ruffian. What was this going to turn into?

Just then, another person who, up until now, had been standing next to the kitchen door in wait of what might had been a fast-and-furious escape entered openly into the living room where she positioned herself near the two intimidating men.

"Not so fast there you two!" she commanded." Let's think this thing out before one or both of you get hurt."

"You should stand back!" Mr. Boddinger shouted. "This guy can't be trusted.

"You're the one who challenged me!" James shot back." Throw me out a window will you! Just go ahead and try!"

"Enough! Both of you!"

Judy, Mr. Boddinger's personal secretary, knew both of them well and knew that each of them were fisticuff types who would just as soon settle differences with a fight rather than a discussion. She knew her influence would have to be strong if she were to keep these two sharks at bay. Sure that her interpretation was correct, she grabbed her boss with a steady hand and led him over to the corner chair where, a few hours earlier, James and his lover were engaged in intimate over-and-under-the-clothing contact. The younger James too was encouraged to enter the room. To make the mood more mellow, Judy reached for a lamp beside her and switched it on. She waited a precarious minute or more for the hotheads to cool down before any fact-finding began. When tempers seemed to lessen, she was the first to speak. Both men were feeling the sting of stupidity over what almost occurred. They imagined the embarrassment each would have had to deal with should the occurrence have escalated.

Acting as moderator, Judy decided that she should be the one to ask all of the pertinent questions.

What the younger James didn't realize was that Boddinger's coming to the house so late, indeed at all, was due to the fact that he too was caught up in a shady operation of his own. He had been out among some of his more shady constituents and had overdosed himself with wine and shots and even a sampling or two of high-grade weed. Now, bereft of his faculties and in need of an out-of-the-way place to spend some time to rejuvenate, Judy had thought to bring him to the lonely out-of-the-way Silver Mine house where nobody ever was at this time of the night. Her role in these actions were forever the same. Whenever he went out single-o as he put it, he almost always persuaded her to come. And when she did, her duty was to protect him from any circumstance, which might compromise his integrity or wallet should he let the influence of the bottle demons get the best of him. She was ever present and by his side during it all. In the best of times, she helped boost his morale and inflate his ego. In the worst of times, she was both companion and guide. In the stickiest of situations, she could always appease his meaner nature by offering him herself though not because she loved him and not because she particularly enjoyed the sex although sex was sex and it always felt good, but more because she possessed an overwhelming need to please those who were closest to her.

But this night was being spelled out differently. It was trouble with a capital *T*. Though this was, most definitely, a case where she should grab him by both hands and flee, she could not. Too much time had passed. He was drunken and fatigued, and there was nowhere else to go. They would have to stay.

The other James too, though decidedly more coherent, had obviously been sipping at the suds and may not be in a condition conducive of safe driving and therefore may not be able to go. The only reasonable alternative to either of them leaving was for them each to fall asleep just where they were, and hopefully things would be looked at differently in the morning. To begin to lull them into this hopeful state, she began talking in a soft, soothing voice.

"There, there now, mister," she said in a cajoling voice as she slid onto her boss's lap, then rested one of his arms against her breast. "And as for you," she said pointedly to the younger version of her beastly lion, "it's better for you if you let this thing ride out the night. Neither of you are in any condition to fly or fight. Tomorrow, we can sort this all out."

"No! No, no," Mr. Boddinger made an effort to say in a debilitating voice.

"There, there," Judy interceded in a consoling tone, then coaxed his hand in through two of the buttons on her blouse so he could feel the skin between her breasts and anticipate more.

"I don't think so!" James suddenly blurted out while witnessing the bizarre scene taking place in front of him. "This is all too weird for me. We're leaving."

Judy was struck by the fact that he had mentioned *we* instead of *I*, which meant that there was another he or she present in the house. Her heart palpitated for a moment as she wondered whether or not her latent lover would pick up on it. But he impugned no telltale notice to the quickly stated reference, and she breathed a sigh of relief.

"Look," she said, changing her tone's intensity, "you and whoever you are with better leave now. He'll be mad enough that one of you came here on a night when he needed to be here more. If he finds out there were more, he'll have a fit. And I won't be able to stop him."

But James was already on the go. Implicated though he was, he would not allow his new better half be subject to any scrutiny or hollering from his unscrupulous boss whether it be night or day. And in response to this conviction, he hurried out of the room and back upstairs to awaken her and make good their escape.

On their way out, James, from the vantage point of the kitchen doorway, turned to his placated tormentor and began to taunt him into making one last aggressive move. He had nothing to lose. His girl was safely out, and he knew in his heart that his time at the mine was over. Unless Mr. Boddinger, was hopelessly out of it and would entirely forget what had happened they would never reconcile with each other. Fraught with anger, he lashed out at the disabled drinker who sat slouched back in the chair, eyes a-stare, while Judy applied her brand of TLC to his wearied constitution.

James's last words out were as follows: "Hey, Mr. Boddinger, how would you like a nice Hawaiian punch," the reference of course being the comical advertising gimmick where the iconic Hawaiian-shirted cartoon character offers some unsuspecting sap a sip of his fruity drink but instead gives them a punch.

James laughed in spite of the fact that no one else cared or was listening. And he left. So inveigled was he by his own predicament-pertaining thoughts that he never once thought about those he was leaving behind. And Cheryl too so sleepy-eyed from the rude awakening she received at James's urging never once thought about Bonnie and Pip.

Upstairs, Pip's mind was unraveling. He awoke during the brief scuffle but declined from intervening. He didn't know who or how many were down there. It could have been the sheriff. It could have been an imperious back-woods thug making a move on a place they thought was deserted. There was no way to know. He determined to lay low and listen. If James was to get more than he could handle, which Pip knew he could determine by listening, he would just spring out of the upstairs like a booby trap going off and surprise the interlopers with his unexpected presence. He played out the scenario in his mind, he and his partner; two rock 'em, sock 'em, robots just like the popular action game of his youth, attacking and attacking their would-be assailants. He felt it. At any moment, another altercation would ensue. But no episode followed. When he heard his friend vaulting back up the steps, he felt that the incident was over. Then, unexpectedly, he heard the begrudging voice of Cheryl complaining of tiredness and trudging back down the steps with James. Pip didn't know what to think. He remained silent and still and waited for anything further to occur. He heard voices, then the door slam. He waited. Then the most terrifying thing of all happened. He heard the unmistakable sound of James's Chevelle as it sped out from behind the barn and onto the open road up the opposite way from the house. Whatever had taken place had been enough to force his Silver Mine buddy to leave without taking the time to even hint to his companions that something was up.

Terror-stricken Pip stuck his head out of the room he and Bonnie had chosen for their trysting place. Advantaged by his bare-footedness, he tiptoed out of the room and into the landing space. He remained aloof, daring not to make another step without first applying a straining ear in the direction of the dark descent. Time passed. Then, just when he thought everything was safe, he heard a distinct sound coming from the living room. It was unmistakable. Two people—not James and Cheryl—were becoming fully engaged in the *act*. Taking advantage of the interplay of noise being introduced from the participants, Pip quick-stepped his way downstairs and quick-popped his head around the corner of the living room wall. Aided by the subtle glow of the table lamp, he was laid witness to a sight, which would besiege him for the rest of his life. There they were, openly, ostentatiously copulating in the corner chair! Pip poked his head around the wall corner and stared. There was Mr. Boddinger slouched back in the cushions, completely in the nude, holding on to an unidentified woman, also naked, while their bodies yielded to each other's desires. After viewing the appalling sight for an enduring eyeful of time, Pip turned away and speculated in view of the precarious situation. He was momentarily stilled by the predicament.

"So it was they who James encountered. Caught him red-handed," he purported in a whisper while deciding what to do. Then he was struck by a challenging thought. Now might be the best time to leave. Now, while they're so enveloped, so vulnerable. A couple's desire to continue in the act, once begun, is overwhelming. They most likely would not deviate from it even if they heard or saw anything of importance around them. He and Bonnie could just sneak down and out and be done with it. If anything happened and they were accosted, they would just keep on with their escape.

Then he became aware of a condition, which probably rendered his idea impossible. Looking down, he noticed his own scant attire. He was clad in only his Fruit of the Looms. To make his plan work, he would have to go back up, wake up Bonnie, coax her into her clothes, dress himself, and accomplish all of this before the coupling was over. Impossible! Vexed, he scuttled up the stairs to formulate a new escape strategy.

Solaced by being once again in the protective confines of his room, Pip took the time to calm his fears and think up a new device for implementing their escape. Sitting next to his sleeping beauty, he could not help but begin to focus on her. How beautiful is a face at peace, a face without expression, a face without regard to anything or anyone. He delayed his frightful concerns for the more immediate admiration of the little princess at his side. How he cherished the splendor of that moment. How he wished it could go on. But finally, he came to his senses. His role in all of this now was to protect her, protect her innocence. He had to be her champion. So he pondered for a while.

One thought struck him as a possibility. It sounded plausible. But it would require the utmost in endurance and not knowing the intricacies of his lover's personality did not know if she was capable of it. The idea was to let her be. The longer she slept, the better. They would simply hold out in the upstairs room and wait. Stay the day. Eventually, the discomfort of the whole situation would spur Mr. Boddinger and his whore to rouse themselves and leave. Considering the circumstances, they would most likely prepare a breakfast before doing so; and the woman would, almost certainly, take a shower or at least pat herself down from the sink in the bathroom. This would take hours. But at the same time, it was unlikely that either of them would bother to venture into any of the adjoining bedrooms that were empty of beds and furniture. As far as Boddinger was concerned, he had already confronted the culprit who had invaded his building and successfully extricated him. Now all that was left was for him to find some way to save his reputation.

Then Pip was hit by a sordid thought. He and the infamous Mr. B were like-minded. What if he persuaded his woman to do the very same thing. What if he put upon her to stay the day too, so to speak. That way it would seem, to anyone paying attention, that they were just there in the course of a normal day. No one would see them coming or know when they came. And except for James, who most likely would be eliminated from the payroll, no one else would be privy to the fact that they had spent the night. James would not tell. He had no proof. And he would fear Boddinger's wrath, which might include prosecution for having unlawfully broken into the Silver Mine house. The only thing they would have to do is go about their business in an ordinary way as though it were an ordinary day.

Then what would happen? They would be trapped and essentially prisoners awaiting a fearful fate. How long could they hold out before it got the best of them? And what of other contingencies here? How long before Bonnie's friends and family became wary of her sudden, unexplained disappearance? How long before even Pip's disappearance was noticed? It seemed a risk not worth taking.

There in the quiet, there in the dark, Pip remembered the immortal words of Saul Bellow—"seize the day." His first inclination was right but just needed a modification. They would take their immediate chances and leave. While ogling his lover's voluptuous body as she lay on the floor, Pip's mind recalled the ecstasy of the previous hour's love-making. Along with it came the memory of how exhausted he felt once he was relieved of so much sexual frustration. Exhilaration followed by complete expiration! That was the answer!

He kissed Bonnie softly on the cheek, then followed through with a line of lip signatures down the back of her body until the final one rested on her other more exquisite cheek. He was hard-pressed not to proceed with a replica performance of their earlier encounter when he suddenly realized that too much was at stake to even consider it. Bonnie stirred from her stupor, looked down at him, and smiled. She was unaware of anything that had happened.

"Hurry!" he directed in a concerned voice. "You'll have to get dressed. There's been some trouble. We have to leave."

"What do you mean?" Bonnie retorted as she braced her upper body up off the floor.

"I mean that we have to go now, and there's no time to lose!" Pip stated emphatically.

"Well, where's Cheryl? And Jim?" she asked plainly.

"They're already gone," he told her succinctly, "and we have to go too. The Silver Mine owner showed up unexpectedly. James went down not knowing who had arrived. They had words. Next thing I knew, James came back up and escorted her out. I heard them take off in the car."

"And they didn't come to get us?" she asked incredulously.

"Apparently not," Pip returned glibly.

Pip waited until Bonnie was dressed before telling her the rest of the bad news. And he was doubly glad too once the last of her apparel was sheathed around her figure—so great was the restraint he had to inflict upon his animal instincts not to seduce her.

"The worst of it is, is that they're still down there."

"Who? Bonnie expressed with a look of consternation. "I thought you said your boss was who caught Jim. Who else is there?"

"It seems like the old man was on a little love fest of his own. A short time ago, he was fornicating some woman down in the living room. So I figured now would be an opportune time to leave, what with their being so physically depleted just now."

"And what if they wake up?"

"There's nothing much to do except keep going. I doubt they'll try to apprehend us. They're both very much naked right now."

With Pip in the lead, the couple, holding hands, made a tremulous descent from the upper story of the house. Once at the surface floor, Pip broke their hand-to-hand connection and raised both of his hands to rest on Bonnie's shoulder as a way of indicating to her that he had something to do alone. She resisted at first, thinking he may be leaving her entirely but then thought better of him. It was too dark to see the expression of genuine concern on his face, but his gentleness said enough for her to see through it. Slowly, he turned from her and made a chary approach toward the blank wall that separated them from the living room. Once again, he turned the corner; and once again, he came face-to-face with the identical sight of the nudists slouched out on the chair. Again, Pip didn't know whether to laugh or cry. But one thing was for sure, the copulators had not moved, or, if they had, not enough to have raised an eyebrow. It would be no threat to move surreptitiously through the house on their way to freedom.

Satisfied that the way was clear, Pip again rejoined his stealthy partner by the hand and squeezed it for a second as a way of saying that all was well and come follow me. Pip's mind was in a whirl as he seized upon the internal forces that allowed him to undertake such a peril.

Only a scant amount of night light shone through the window spaces in the house allowing barely enough visibility to see by. The ace up Pip's sleeve though was that he was all too familiar with the internal construct of the rooms they had to travel through. He led the way.

"Stay close and do not deviate from my footpath," he cautioned her with a whisper in her ear. "I can't see much either, but I know what's where."

Bonnie did not reply for fear of being heard by the licentious pair of lovebirds nestled close by. Pip steered forward avoiding all of the known obstacles in their way. His movements mimicked that of a halfback running in slow motion past the line of scrimmage, making movements side to side, front and back, twisting and turning to miss all possible defenders. Soon, the side room was behind them. Such as it was the entire first floor was all opened up. Each room was part of a four room surround without any structural separation. Only the staircase with its two support walls interfered with the rooms' connectedness. The intrepid couple now entered the room off the kitchen where stores of office supplies were stacked and packed. Some stacked brochures, pamphlets, and fliers were virtual leaning towers of paper that even a misdirected breath could knock over. But even they were no match for the fortuitous Pip who, acting as vanguard, directed their way safely through the potentially dangerous pitfall and out to the threshold of the kitchen.

Here there was light from the single soft-watt bulb near the chair. Here was the danger point. Here any action taken would have to be taken swiftly, for here their movements could more easily be detected and once detected would reveal their personages. Before going on, Pip took a minute to reflect upon and calculate their position. Suddenly, he was seized by anxiety. In his ever-thinking mind, he proposed a serious series of what-ifs to consider. What if James, who was obviously standing on his last leg here, decided to retaliate against his soon-to-be former partner and told all? What if Mr. Numbnuts over there went ahead and called the sheriff and decided to press charges? What if the truth—the whole truth and nothing but the truth—came out? Then the ruse they planned to use—that of departing quickly enough and concealed enough to say that it was none other than James and his sweetheart who got caught exiting the house for a bewildering second time—would be rendered mute. It would all come out. What to do?

He pondered the situation as it stood with disgust. There seemed to be no disparity between any of the foreseeable outcomes. Dejected, he was about to make a run for the door when something caught his eye. Hanging on the near wall was his trusty Polaroid OneStep camera. He used it all the time to chronicle his years at the mine. Recently, he had had two distinct fortunes profiling his "stilled-life" documentary. On a day not long ago, he had managed to sneak up under a beautiful red-tailed hawk and snap a magazine-worthy photo of the crafty aviator. Likewise, he came upon a red fox as it happened to be emerging from its den and snapped a photo of the amazing creature just as it opened its eyes to the day. Both were perfect and prized beyond belief. With that same thought in his head, Pip turned to the paneled wall and lifted his camera slowly, carefully off its nail hook.

"What are you doing?" Bonnie asked quizzically.

But Pip wasted no time in responding. With the camera safely slung around his neck by the strap, he quick-buzzed his better half over to the door, opened it, and hastily rushed her out. Then, without hesitation, he crept into the living room where he instantly snapped a photo of the two languid lovers.

The whole thing happened in the blink of an eye. The millionaire and his mistress, startled by the disturbance, got up, and, in the veriest of mannerisms, put on a veritable Punch-and-Judy performance as they groped around for their clothes. The split-second reference Pip made of their act became greatly enhanced when he realized that Judy was in reality Judy—Mr. Boddinger's secretary!

With his camera dangling in front of him, he headed straight for the door. Outside, he caught up with Bonnie.

"We are in dire need of getting out of here!" he exclaimed.

"Where to?" she asked simply.

"Nowhere in particular for now," Pip shot back firmly. "Follow me!"

"I'll follow you, but what if they follow us!" Bonnie said in a dire voice.

"Don't worry about them," Pip assured her. "I've got the old man by the balls and his hussy by the—! You know by now what I did in there. I snapped a "pornagraph" of those two cuddled up like they were rehearsing for an X-rated movie! What are they going to do? Ask me for it back!"

Alone in the dark, the two young escapees whirried along Silver Mine Road until they reached the intersecting highway. Rather than continue the ten-mile journey on foot, they resorted to hitchhike the remaining distance home. Within an hour, a newspaper-delivery truck had picked them up and delivered them safe and sound to Bonnie's house. From there Pip walked. His good-bye to her had been deficient considering what had transpired between them over the past several hours, but his mind was both tired and on overload. The enormity of the situation he was in began to manifest itself in him.

When he entered his home, it was early. Not even the early birds were up yet. The walk home from Bonnie's had done him some good. He reaffirmed his intentions with what he had done, and he was convinced he would win any showdown that occurred as a result of it. With nothing more to do, he slept. A few hours later, he heard his name being called out and a subsequent "Luckee's on the phone" resounding up the third-floor steps. He ignored it. A few more hours later, he heard his name again. This time he responded. It was James. He was at the door.

"Tell him to hold on for a minute," Pip yelled down the stairs.

Before going down to confront his old friend, Pip went into his clothes closet to check on the incriminating photo, which had been stashed away in a secret partition above the inside door molding. He stared at it with a rejuvenated sense of worth. It was the most important thing he owned. After dressing, he charged down both flights of stairs to meet with James who had been invited inside and was waiting on the living room couch. It was a poignant moment.

"So what happened to you last night?" Pip stated in an admonishing voice to get the ball rolling.

"I got caught, same as you," James went on. "Not only that, I was officially advised never to return to the mine again. But you know Mr. B, he won't stay mad at us forever. Especially since he has nobody else to run the place. We'll be back before we know it."

Pip did not immediately respond. He had heard what James said and the insinuation that went along with it. James believed that both of them had been captured by the bad man and sentenced to some supposed term of indefinite suspension. This was his chance. He had to let James believe what he believed. That way, the truth may never come out, and Pip would be spared any hostility that Boddinger might retaliate with. The best way to ensure this would be if Pip took charge and gave James a made-up version of what happened before he had a chance to ask any specific questions. James would be told only this once what the story was, and it would never be brought up again. If he ever talked to Bonnie, which was doubtful because she and Cheryl were not that close as friends, he would simply refute anything she said. Who would he believe?

"Yes, I heard you two going at it. I didn't know what to expect. I know that soon after you came back up and got Cheryl. Then you roared on out of there in the Chevelle. I knew that we were next, so I just bit the bullet and headed straight on down to take my medicine too. He screamed at us like a hungry lion who just had his food taken away, but we didn't stay for the show. Instead, we just hightailed it out of there and hitched a ride home.

And, oh, by the way, thanks for getting us up and getting us out of there, old pal," he added sarcastically.

"Sorry about that. I wasn't thinking," James said in a dippy voice, admitting that he had acted as a fool for leaving his friends behind.

The matter was settled. Pip had successfully inveigled James into believing, as he already did, that both of them had been terminated from their Silver Mine jobs. Pip vindicated his actions against his friend by reminding himself that it was he who got James the job in the first place and that it was James's stupidity that got them caught. If James had heard something going on downstairs in the middle of the night, then why didn't he quietly slip into the other room and apprise his friends. They could have all stayed together, the four of them, and waited out the night.

After James departed, Pip deliberately kept away from him knowing that if they spent a lot of time together, right after the incident, they would be more apt to discuss the event; and in that way, some inference of the truth may come out. Luckee was another matter. He must not know anything. Why? Because even though he was their friend, he would undoubtedly take Mr. Boddinger's side. Why? Because his position would be on the line too. And, if Mr. Boddinger suddenly found himself being supported, he would feel a surge of strength on his side and maybe even be able to convince Luckee to lie for him and say anything really. This could not be. Luckee would have to remain in the dark entirely.

The vicissitudes of the Pip, James, Mr. Boddinger, Luckee, debacle were now falling into Pip's favor. The next condition of it phased in that first evening when Luckee finally did call again and Pip was home to respond.

"Hey, kid, what happened down at the mine last night? The old man was a-hooting and a-hollering like he'd just been stung by a scorpion. He said he caught your friend down there having some kind of orgy or something in the house. What do you want to tell me about that?"

Safeguarded by the technical wonder of how phones connected only word over miles of distance, Pip proffered Luckee an inscrutable smile. It was time for the second-act implementation of his self-described once-and-done methodology, which would secure his cause. Once Luckee had expended enough breath to blow a mountain of bubbles, Pip butted in in a very abrupt manner and stated very firmly that he knew nothing and he was not about to take up an investigation of his friend for the sake of Mr. Boddinger's retribution. Luckee was left standing, like a big-time ballplayer who has just had a strike-three ball whiffed past the plate. The conversation was over.

The best was saved for last. The final serving of this hopefully triumphant triumvirate would be the pitched battle he and the millionaire would inevitably be engaged in. And my, oh my, how the fur would fly. For two further days, Pip relented from the conflict, all the time outlining the things he would say and rehearsing the way he would say them. Mr. Boddinger, like him or not, was a veritable Tyrannosaurus Rex when it came to dealing in the flesh-eating world of power and might. Several times during the evening of the second day, he put a tentative finger on the phone but each time let his apprehension get the best of him and pulled back. He felt unprepared. There was no instruction manual for blackmail!

If he did roll the dice, he would have to be ready, ready to answer any condition put to him. Mr. Boddinger would certainly be ready. He probably already anticipated what was coming and was waiting for the call. He would go into a tirade and throw verbal punches. He might even go so far as to threaten to terrorize Pip should he so brazenly wish to remain in his employ. But Pip, despite his inexperience at dealing with something so nasty, would remain steadfast. He had the winning hand, and he knew it. Boddinger had the big mouth, and it didn't matter. Then it struck him how really big his winning hand was. At first, he was going to use his picture-of-a-thousand-words to offset his boss's anger over the situation and make him take both he and James back. But the events had dictated otherwise. Only James was being implicated, and he was sure he would remain vindicated by virtue of the unlikelihood that the perpetrators and the guards would ever get together in one setting to iron out all the wrinkles in the event.

But the days assuaged his fears. He came to think that this was one of those once-in-a-lifetime chances that you hear told about. He wanted more. To trade in such an indescribably lopsided condition for only the right of job security was like buying a nickel candy bar with a fifty and forgetting the change. It was folly. More and more, Pip was induced by the thought of what blackmail really was. More and more, he became infuriated by what had almost been his undoing. He affirmed to himself that he would act more the part and take what he could get. And the best way to do this was to ask for the world. He would demand of his boss the keys to the kingdom.

In this winner-take-all mode, he set about to perfect his plan. The process would require putting into place all of the variables, which could make or break the situation as he saw it. The most important thing he could do was secure the damning evidence he so precariously held in the flimsy film print he had taken. Obviously, Mr. Millionaire would want it in exchange for any personal favors or financial recompense he should grant should he agree to bargain away the upcoming deliberations. Then it hit him—a way around that impenetrable pass—he would simply take a photo of the photo!

It couldn't have been simpler. He took the revealing snapshot and laid it flat on a background piece of large white construction paper, ribboned a tear of cellophane tape onto the back of the photo to adhere it to the border paper, and snapped several more shots with his Polaroid. These evidential mirrors-in-time he secreted away in one of his dresser drawers for now until a more suitable hiding place could be found for them.

Then he was hit by the other aspect of this greater-than-hoped-for expectation. Mr. Boddinger was a millionaire! He was not just some rich guy who you just called a millionaire as a way of expression or attributing to him the certainty that he had made it. No. Mr. Boddinger lived in the land of milk and honey. His properties included the following: the silver mine, the oil company, the quarry, the construction company, and his estate. All told it could be estimated at a value of several million dollars. And who knew how much money he had in bank accounts, in C/Ds, in investments, in other unknown land holdings. Who knew?

Figures danced in his head. He ascertained their prospect one by one. The entertainment value of it increased in conjunction with the rising amounts. What could he do with $1,000? What could he do with $10,000? The pupils in his eyes became dollar signs as the spiritual notes continued their mind dance, and he became obsessed that this one endeavor should lead him into fantasy. His intent became clear. It would be all or nothing!

The enterprise brought with it a vast amount of grief and consternation about all the things that could go wrong. Prior to making the more-than-upsetting phone call, Pip tried many times to calm his tensions. He felt as though every nerve fiber in his body had short-circuited. His systems had been tripped, and no amount of finagling could bring them back. The solution was to get it over with, and he knew what he had to do.

Pip had stayed away an unprecedented three days from the place he loved the most in life. It was all due to the fact that it took him that long to come to terms with the realization of the immensity of what he was attempting to do. But now it had to be done. It was now or never. In the space of the final day, he had designated both the time and place for the "war of the words."

At precisely 9:30 at night, Pip headed out the door of his Pine Street home and walked up the half-block stretch of similar-looking brick row homes to the corner grocery store. This time of night, Chris's would have only the occasional customer in need of some last-minute food item. The pay phone outside, hidden around the front, would be relatively left alone and so would Pip.

When he stood before the booth, dime in hand, he knew the incident had reached its crescendo. It was do-or-die time. He inserted the small coin while holding onto the receiver and trying to gain control over his thought and the out-of-control way his body was experiencing the stress of it all. His insides were killing him. All the way down from his overloaded brain, down his back into his legs, into his arms, all throughout his body, he was being besieged by the inflicting stings of nerve cells gone mad. Worst of all was his pitiful stomach, which felt as though it was host to a melee of angry jellyfish all trying to sting their way back out to freedom. But despite his afflictions, Pip was determined to go on. He placed a tentative finger on the dial pad and pressed the appropriate digits, which were burned in his memory. Once the connection had been made and the Boddinger phone began ringing, Pip felt a tinge of desperation and for a split second wondered if he should hang up. No one would know it was he who had called, and he could just go on with his life as if nothing happened. But then something did.

"Hello," came the sweet melodic voice at the other end.

"Hello yourself," Pip responded in a perfunctory manner realizing it was the millionaire's Mrs. who had picked up. "I'm calling for Mr. Boddinger and could you get him please."

"Who's calling?" she asked in an amicable voice.

"Tell him it's Pip, I mean, tell him it's Christopher Faehner. I'm one of his Silver Mine associates."

"Hold on one minute," she continued as though the call were of a quite ordinary nature.

In just under the allotted minute, another voice—a brash, haughty voice—took stage on the Boddinger phone line.

"What do you want?" were his first choice words. "I thought you had run away like your partner. He's out now, and I think it would be best for you to do the same. The same to the both of you."

All at once, a sinuous smile crept over the young Faehner's face. "So he thought it would be that easy, did he? Just tell me to leave and never come back. He probably thinks I'm on line just to beg not to be fired. Imagine the audacity of it all. Imagine him thinking of me as a fish on a hook, hoping, hoping beyond hope that the mighty fisherman might throw me back. Imagine!" These besmirching thoughts pervaded Pip's spirit, and he hurled them down below his feet and allowed them a providing place for which he could stand and be heard from. Likewise, he hurled his well-thought-out contentions right out at his nemesis.

"I'll get right to the point, big mouth. You're not kicking me out! I know what you did that night too. I have a picture of it, of your infidelity! And guess what I'm going to do with it!"

"You! You dirty, filthy—! How dare you, you punk-face—! I . . . I knew it was you. It had to be you!"

Ignoring Boddinger's querulous tone and expletory language, Pip went on with his speech.

"Now to get to my main point. I want you to do two things for me in exchange for my silence. First, I'm not leaving your employ. As a matter-of-fact, I want you to sign a pact, without contingencies, allowing me to stay on down at the mine indefinitely or until I choose to abrogate my place there. Second, I have decided that by saving your marriage I am saving you millions. And in exchange for that, such an extreme act of kindness, I want money—$200,000 to be exact. If you don't comply, I will sit down with your wife and tell her everything I know. It will be like a little game of show and tell, like when we were back in kindergarten."

The ball game was over, and Boddinger knew it. He had been royally had by a wavy-haired brat, by a precocious, pimple-faced, good-for-nothing! There were no words in any of the world's languages, which could have been useful in expressing the contempt and anger Mr. Boddinger felt at having been bested by the young Mr. Faehner.

And the world did change in accordance with Pip's expectations. Just as he predicted, his life at the Silver Mine continued, free of the possibility that he could ever be fired. And the money he exacted for his cause, a pile of bills worth $200,000, were piled away in a bank vault to wait until the day should come to summon them into being, to bear, as per their intention, the provision of rendering the Silver Mine into his heralded hands.

The story ended, and Mr. Faehner returned himself, mind and matter to the here and now. The reporter, realizing they were back to another question-and-answer period began to quiz Mr. Faehner on the account of the story.

"I dare say, Mr. Faehner, that I'm quite stricken by the fact that you were so willing to tell me such a thing—that you were involved in blackmail. I mean, aren't you concerned about that?"

"No, not really. It all happened such a long time ago. Boddinger is dead. So is his lover. And besides, there's nothing that could happen to me if it ever became common knowledge, which, of course, I do not want it to. What I did was better for the both of us. He got to keep what was his, minus the money. I got what I felt I deserved. And in retrospect, look how many lives I was able to enhance due to the fact that I took a chance in life. But please respect my wishes and do not divulge any of it. You see, I'm taking another chance in life right now. I'm trusting you."

Death as a Doorway

"So that was it. The hush money is what you began your empire with, huh?"

"It wasn't as easy as that. The $200,000 helped immensely, but there was more to it than that. When I actually bought the Silver Mine, I paid $300,000. The $200,000 wouldn't have meant much if it were not for the fact that I managed to save the other third on my own. And it took me many years to do that. When the time came, it had all worked out in my favor—all because I took that chance of a lifetime, and I lived the life of a pinchpenny."

"So what happened then? Did your old boss just up and realize that you were destined to become the next Silver Mine owner and operator?"

"No, I'm afraid not. Boddinger wouldn't have sold me the mine come hell or high water. Even if he'd been down to his last dime, he wouldn't have sold me as much as a blade of grass on the property. He was mean and spiteful toward me right up until the day he died. And that is what happened. His death was my doorway through which I entered into the realm of possibility. Without it, it may never have happened. Think about it. What if he had lived to be one hundred? I would have been in my seventies. I doubt I would have cared so much about owning the place then. Old age tends to weaken our enthusiasm for such things like becoming rich or acquiring power. All of us, at some point in our lives, seem to outgrow our dreams.

"But his death triggered another relevant realization upon me—something I'm almost afraid to admit. Up until that time, all of those years that I was squirreling away money, I had not come up with a plan, a scheme or anything really to exact a way to take over the property. I was waiting, waiting all the time for something to happen. What, I did not know. When he died, I realized the enormity of the proposition I had placed before me. I couldn't believe it. It wasn't indicative of me to be so thoughtless about something so crucial to my game plan. Maybe I felt that fate would serve me well as it had so before in bringing the Silver Mine into my life, in providing me with the interest to want to stay there, and in bringing about the circumstance of infidelity, which served as the main catalyst for me bringing Boddinger to his knees and issuing me the thrust of necessary capital I would use to purchase my dream. I don't know. It could have been the money. With it, I had reached the upper echelon and maybe, just maybe, I had become a little complacent. Having that much meant that I had other options regardless of what happened. And I suppose that somewhere in my subconscious, I knew that. I had enough money to buy a nice house outright. And have enough money remaining to buy a nice car too. I must have felt an overwhelming sense of financial security, which probably took away some of my incentive without me realizing it. But one thing is certain—his death really got me thinking."

"So what happened next after he died?"

"That's a whole another story in itself," Mr. Faehner said in a relaxed tone.

"Isn't that what we're here for?" the reporter answered tactfully.

Mr. Faehner gave the young life-learner a here-goes kind of look while searching within himself for the story parts, which, when put together, would provide for the storytelling such as it occurred so many, many years ago.

Within a minute, he was releasing it, the one true story in just the order it really happened in and in so complete a manner as to almost make them feel they were reliving it. He started off with a brief synopsis of the detail of Mr. Boddinger's untimely demise.

"Boddinger died in 1987, three years before I actually signed any ownership documents. Prior to his death, he was acutely ill, and he knew it. He had been receiving special care up at Hershey Medical Center since two years before. He suffered from some sort of blood disorder in which his blood would form clots all over his circulatory system. There was nothing they could do about it. The one that finally got him was only one of a hundred that could have. He had no chance really. His body was playing a game of Russian roulette with him, and the cylinder kept spinning and firing. Over time, his "leaves" became more sporadic, which meant either he was getting better, or better yet, he was getting worse. That question was answered in the way his attitude went from that of a jerk to that of a demon. Not only did he start to let himself go, he began to let the property fall into a state of disrepair. Things started to rot. He refused to buy new equipment: chain saws, mine pumps, a riding mower, lumber for fence repairs, the list went on and on. And he didn't care. I think he thought his neglect would drive me crazy enough to want to leave. And it almost did. Lucky for me, he didn't think to do such a deliberate thing prior to that or he may have just succeeded."

"Did he continue paying you your wages?" the reported asked sternly.

"He had to. Although in retrospect I'm surprised. Knowing he was going to die, he could have just as easily given up his pride and let the other shoe fall. By then, why should he have cared if his wife found out about any of his earlier indiscretions? Maybe he realized that either way, he was never going to see that money again." Mr. Faehner shook his head as if he were coming out of a trance. "I'm sorry. I didn't answer your question. My mind was thinking about the $200,000 again. What did you ask, about my wages? Like I started to say, he had to pay me. It was part of our stipulated agreement. Remember, he couldn't fire me for any reason, and it is unlawful to not pay an employee for work they've done. And besides, he wasn't the person signing the checks. We had a system where the checks were issued by an accountant. I don't think he bothered much with it."

In the back of his mind, there was a consternation growing about the concept of oversights. And they related to both he and the deceased. To just think how he had not ever considered just how he was going to take over should Boddinger had not died so early in life. He had not had a plan. And Boddinger, despite his ostentatious displays of flagrant contemptibility toward the stalwart young steward, never tried to run him out. How easily it could have happened. By running the place into the ground, it might have made things difficult enough to induce him to leave of his own accord. And what might have happened if he ever did call the authorities on the boys the day after the party? Photo or no photo, events could have taken a different turn. Who knew? But it was a wonder that he never really tried. How easily things could have turned out differently.

The reporter noticed the bewildered look on Mr. Faehner's face and spoke up. "You said it was his death that made it possible for you to begin the process of becoming "lord" of the land."

Mr. Faehner, coming out of his stupor, regarded the reporter with fixed eyes and an outward disposition. He was ready to go back in time. He was ready to relive the experience. He sent another here-goes look across at his one-person audience and began recanting the tale . . .

"Where's he off to in such a hurry?" Pip asked his former overseer as they stood side by side outside the door of the 1800 house.

"Don't know," Luckee responded with a dissident look on his face. "Maybe home for the day."

"Okay then," Pip concurred with a hint of sarcasm in his voice. "I thought maybe he was taking off to go up to the hospital again. Like maybe they've come up with an antidote for the sickness he has in his head."

"You shouldn't say things like that about him. He really is seriously ill you know. And for your sake, you had better hope he gets well."

"What's that supposed to mean?"

"Look, kid, I know you two don't like each other much, but you know, if it weren't for him coming down here and opening up this place, you would never be where you are today. And another thing. If anything awful ever happens to Jim, what do you think's going to happen to you?"

Luckee paused long enough for Pip to reflect on the referred meaning of his words—the warning he had given to see if he would respond.

"Just as I thought," Luckee proceeded. "You've never considered what life would be like without him. Don't hate him, kid. You have what you have because of him."

With that, Luckee hopped in the two-toned yellow and green Silver Ford pickup and sped out of the tiny parking space. Pip followed him with his eyes as he swerved up around the bended road and out of sight over the hill.

"I have what I have in spite of him," he answered back for the exclusive benefit of his own ears.

Pip listened again to Luckee's ominous words as they resounded in his brain. The words were crystal clear, but their meanings were dark and confused. And he had no crystal ball to see past them. The future was uncertain. Alone, inside and out, he attempted to sort out the confusion. At age twenty-seven, he had managed to wade his way through his Silver Mine experience with relative ease. The exceptions had been few. And the last great "happening" had occurred all of eight years ago in the very house he now looked upon. From that, he had come away clean. He looked back on that experience and realized it to be something that was supposedly life-changing. But his life had not. Despite having an ample piece of the Boddinger pie, his life had remained much the same as it had been, one routine thing after another, one mundane experience after another, all as if they were just one continuous string being laid out at his feet every day, day after day. But somehow this was different. And although the how of it wasn't yet something tangible, it was something considerable. How could it be ascertained? Pip pondered the possibilities. He speculated about the condition of it.

Boddinger's demise, should he die, should have been something of the utmost value to the thirteen-year employee who had already put up with half-a-life's worth of insults, taunts, and indifference. But somehow the elation that he expected in relation to it did not come. Instead, he found a pit growing in his stomach, now the size of a lentil bean, soon the size of a walnut. Its proportion increased with each passing internal observation.

The concept was daunting. Everything was stemmed around one indefatigable point. What would happen if Boddinger was gone? Who would be in charge? Would his service, such as it was, remain the same? Would his "till-death-did-he-part" document fashioned at the time of his boss's unfortunate affair still have meaning? He sorted out the continuing dialogue in his head and tried to answer the pertinent questions one by one.

He knew without knowing that such a man as Boddinger was he would never have considered that such a devastation should befall him, and therefore, it stood to reason that no definable recourse would have been available to set in motion should the unthinkable really occur. No person who wields so much power and influence over others ever considers themselves vulnerable to the extraordinary circumstance of dying young. So that would mean that the next person in charge would not have been hand-picked. And that left the possibilities wide open.

Mrs. Boddinger would not be in the running. Pip's thirteen-year tenure at the mine had provided him with valuable insights into the workings of the Boddinger family. He knew them all. He knew them as if they were closely related members of the Faehners or he was a closely related member of the Boddingers. They were, in terms of his intimate knowledge of them, his surrogate mother and father, sister and brothers. And he knew them in accordance of their ways. He knew their likes and dislikes. He knew their fancies and pleasures. He knew their strengths and weaknesses. He knew their sorrows and joys. He knew what made them tick, and he knew what made them tock.

Mrs. Boddinger had always been a silent partner in her husband's enterprises. She was a behind-the-scenes person who flaunted her husband's success only to those she considered worthy of her time and attention. She didn't do anything. Her days were spent in the society of her socialite friends, wasting away the hours at the exclusive Symbols of Society Country Club. And even though she would remain the grandiose figurehead of all of the Boddinger businesses, she would also remain undoubtedly a woman freed from the drudgery of the day-to-day decision-making processes that define the leadership role in such a state of affairs.

Boddinger's oldest son, Jeff, was no cause for alarm either. In all of the years since the Silver Mine's inception, he had showed no particular interest in the place other than attending some of the Sunday socials with any of his sweethearts, old and new. In recent years, he had taken a fancy toward advertising art and design; and in that light, his father had specifically set him up in business, first by buying him a downtown building in the city, next by affording him all of the advertising business generated by the Boddinger-run enterprises. Jeff had it made. He was busy. And he was busy doing the thing he most wanted to do. It was doubtful he would concede doing what he wanted in favor of doing something he had shown no real interest in. Jeff was out.

The next in line was Boddinger's only daughter, Jenny. She was two years younger than Jeff and was fresh out of college where she had studied horticulture but touted she had no intention to do anything as of yet with her degree. She lived on a little "farmette," as Pip referred to it, a very small tract of land with house and barns remaining when the more substantial acreage was parceled out to adjacent landowners, which was located only a few miles from the mine. She lived alone with an old hound dog, a few outdoor tabby cats, and a goat named Percy. Early on, she had tried to convince her father to let her goat live at the mine, but her father never allowed it realizing what a disturbance goats can be around lots of activity. "Only if the goat had grown up around the other animals would such a thing be possible," Pip had heard him tell her. Jenny was a pretty young woman, only five years younger than Pip; and he often wondered, to himself only, why he never thought to pursue her affections, which he surmised would be very satisfying against his needs. What a way to go! He would have had an heiress and a temptress all in one!

But it was not to be. Something about being closely connected to the Boddingers put a sour taste in his mouth. Coming back to the matter at hand, Pip speculated further about Jenny and her place in the portended future. She was an individualist, and even though she proudly dipped her hands in the bottomless pit of money that was hers due her heritage, she much preferred to live aside of it instead of remaining inside the hearth and home of the Boddinger estate. She rarely showed up at the mine except on occasion when she came to check up on her horses, Oreo and Dot. Though they were hers, she didn't spend much time with them, but she all the time checked in with her father to make sure they were being cared for.

As for Jenny's intervening at the mine if her father passed away, it was doubtful. For all of her beauty and for all of her love of the outdoors, she was not an entrepreneur, not even in things pertaining to nature. She may want to keep her fingers close enough to lick the icing off the cake, but she would never want to be involved in the day-to-day process of making the place a go.

Next on the list was Howdy. Though he was the youngest of the Boddinger brood, twenty, and had never really been tested in the world, he did like to consider himself "a chip off the Boddinger block." He, most definitely, would be a problem. To him, the Silver Mine was a place where he could get next to people, workers and tourists, and profess how he will someday have the power to do this or do that to the property. His father knew him to be a clod and often even castigated him in front of others. Howdy always pretended he was kidding, but the people who knew his dad knew he was not. Howdy was as his father considered him—a square peg trying to fit into a round hole.

But, with his father gone, if indeed that did happen, his father's insinuations about him would be gone too. Howdy might have his chance. That would be disastrous! The threat then would be his ineptness and indecisiveness, which would no doubt alter the competent way things were being done. He would be the place's undoing.

The last consideration was Luckee who was now old. In recent years, he came to the mine only as a person who had nothing better to do with his time and to keep an association going with his former friend and boss. Luckee's time had passed. He no longer brought anything of importance to the table. Still though, he could be considered for an interim position knowing that he could at least be relied on to keep things up and running until a more suitable person could be obtained. If Luckee were picked, it wouldn't be so bad, sort of the lesser of the five evils, so to speak.

The exception to all the other true considerations was that Pip be picked himself. This, of course, had the same probability of happening as finding intelligent life on another planet within the next thirty days. To the Boddingers as a whole, Pip was nothing more than a thorn in their father's side as he often expressed him to be whenever they found reason to clash over important and not so important matters at the mine. This, of course, was a critical error to those who would survive their father's imminent demise. Only Mr. Boddinger knew about the sizeable chunk of change he had reluctantly parted with those many years ago and how it alone could have put him into contention for buying the property should a situation ever arise in which he had an opportunity to do so.

Privately though, all of the Boddingers, with the exception of Howdy, held a secret admiration for the aspiring young go-getter. So much so that it could be reasonably speculated that if the Mrs. ever knew of his, at present, almost one-third of a million dollars, she might find the time to spend a minute or two with him from time to time. If Jeff knew of his secreted stash, he might, liking Pip's innovative spirit the way he did, even had asked him to be the one to have formed a business with. If Jenny had ever found out about Pip's fortune and especially if she found out where it originated from, she probably wouldn't hesitate to want to have it somehow near to her. To her, it still would have been her father's money; and therefore, she was heir to it regardless of the terms of the transaction. She might have even gone as far as to pursue Pip's love.

But Pip knew differently. He would never be called upon as proxy for the prominent proprietor either by virtue of his tireless tenure or by any vote of confidence from the members of the family in charge. The only way he would be placed in charge of the mine was, if after their father's death, the family members experienced so much strife over what to do with so many business concerns that it created serious internal dissensions among them, so much so that it would just be easier to allow someone, anyone, to take it over just to have one thing settled. Though it did now cross his mind, Pip decided not to advocate for himself in the cause. He would simply watch and wait.

The rest of the day, he waited and watched for anything suspicious, anything spurious, which might indicate that Boddinger may have taken the last turn in life. He even watched the sky. And as funny as it seems, he did feel a lot like Chicken Little who proclaimed to all who would listen, "The sky is falling! The sky is falling!"

That night before bed, Pip again retrieved the archival document from its clandestine hideout and examined it for detail. Holding the edifying document was a sacred act and made him feel as if he were holding something as glorifying as the Declaration of Independence or the Magna Carta in his hands. He scrutinized the written words for content and meaning, making sure there were no loopholes; exiguous language, which might cause concerns; exceptions, exclusions, points, which may be out of reference to a clause or phrase; or any contingencies, which may be based on other contingencies. In short, he had to know exactly where he stood in the safety of his position. There could be no gray matter in the situation. Everything had to be spelled out. Everything had to be black and white.

Once his confidence was restored for the umpteenth time, the legal paper was put away, and he slipped off to sleep in the quiet of his second-story room in the 1800 house. He didn't know what the morning would bring.

Partway through the night, Pip fell into a dream state unlike any he had experienced before. The stresses of the unfolding uncertainties, which he had been bottling up inside, suddenly popped out. These strains and tensions became entangled with his excitable imagination, and together they combined to create a gruesomely staged setting for a mind that was running wild: Pip found himself walking alone halfway through the mine with no purpose in mind when suddenly he heard the sonorous *sssss*, the unmistakable sound of a slithering snake. The sssss's were coming from a direction straight ahead, and in fear, Pip turned to make a hasty retreat from the underground tunnel but was seized just as suddenly by an undulant slap, which, in a matter of seconds, first turned him about then wrapped a cold tail around his waist. In an unspecified time, the serpent spiraled most of its seven-foot body around the frightened victim. Gradually, it lifted its heavy head up to challenge its foe. The captor and the captured met in what should have been an easily determined scenario of one creature's dominance versus the other's immediate demise. But it did not play out that way. In particular, the difference in which it did compared to the way it was expected was startling. Face-to-face, the true representation of each of the specters was revealed. Upon visual contact, the serpent's vile countenance, its visage, changed to that of the contemptuous Mr. Boddinger. It was no illusion! The image at once recognized the person it had seized and became simultaneously seized by fright and overcome by an inflamed sense of anger. The serpent spoke. Its words slurred together as if it had a lisp.

"Tell me why, oh, silver mine boy, tell me why you have come into the deep?"

"I have come to bear my soul upon this rock as it was my destiny to do so."

Hearing the insightful remark, one which could not be fully comprehended, the serpent began to tighten its coiled grip on its vulnerable victim. But Pip did not feel so vulnerable as that. No amount of the snake's increased effort was able to subdue him. Realizing this, Pip increased his own mind effect on the sarcous struggle. The concept became clear. This was not a life-and-death struggle. It was not of flesh and blood. It was Boddinger and Faehner fighting it out once and for all in a clash of the minds, attempting through their true considerations of each other to unlock their deeply kept purposes for wanting to possess what the other wants to possess. It was a battle of wills, and the one who survived would become the ultimate victor. Inside the depths of the darkened mine, inside the depths of their darkened minds, the titans fought on. Time was imperceptible. And in the uncertain reality whose boundaries were without borders Pip became dominant. The serpent, despite its advantageous size and strength, grew weary and hassled and soon relented. The boy, who it considered an unworthy opponent, proved to be so worthy as to defeat it. It released its stranglehold and diminished into the dark recesses from which it came. It relinquished its dominion over the boy and over all that it had power over.

Elated that his spirit had triumphed over the slithering beast, Pip raced after it hoping to ensnare it and inflict further damage to its once overconfident self. But the serpent was gone. Continuing ahead, Pip found that in its wake there came a mist where in its midst there came a presence similar to that of the serpent. Snakes appeared high and low. They too began to grow faces. From behind their facades of scale and mist, identities emerged. They were men but with countenances unknown. Each of them though seemed to recognize him. They began to chant, each in a slurred voice, similar words to that of the Boddinger serpent.

"Tell me why, oh, silver mine boy, tell me why you have come into the deep?"

Pip delayed. For reasons unclear to him, he knew he did not need to. These creatures of the mist had no hold over him. Instead, they represented only a portent of existence, a power or a presence which had not yet been revealed. They were out of time and place, and their being had not yet found its matrix. Pip castigated them one and all.

"I have come to bear my soul upon this rock as it was my destiny to do so."

The snakes vanished as did the mist, as did the darkened hollow, as did the dream. Pip awoke with a start, more frightened that he had had such a dream than by the dream itself. What did it mean? In the true dark, his heartbeats ticked away the moments. He recollected his dream to his conscious self and tried to identify with it. Then a frightful thought struck him. What if, during his dream state, he had been visited by the fleeting spirit of James Boddinger, who, as he lay asleep, fell into death and darkness and entered into his unconscious mind to haunt him, to taunt him in one last great effort. In a maddening burst of realization, he turned to the nightstand beside him and reached for the alarm clock to note the time. It was 2:00 a.m. If the next morning came with the news of Boddinger's death, he would inquire as to the exact time of his death and remember when it was that he regarded his dream. He could only wait and see.

Morning came, and it came without word of the haughty leader's death. It came without mourning. Boddinger was not yet ready to give up his ghost. And in that light, the stage had been set for the truer sense of the battle of wills. It happened in much the same way as Pip expected it too. Sensing his own end, the embittered Mr. Boddinger became despondent. He began to lose control over himself. The Silver Mine and all of his prides and joys began to lose their importance. He wanted nothing to do with things, which he would soon have no control over. He wished to get out from under everything he owned, especially the mine, which was being cared for by his illustrious enemy, Pip.

He began to let go with the Silver Mine being hardest hit by his decisive I-don't-care-any-more attitude. Being the chief financial officer of all of his corporations meant that any deviation from this responsibility spelled the slow, starving death of any business he decided to let fall. But it was only the mine that he refused to keep up with, and it was only Christopher Faehner who he refused to tell why.

As the weeks passed and the worsening influence of the intentional neglect became more pronounced, Pip decided on a course of drastic action. He would accentuate matters to the point where some of the more outspoken common people, tourists and maintenance workers especially, might speak up about their sense of being slighted. Pip's insecurities got the best of him, and he reacted with a spur-of-the-moment offensive. While mowing a section of the peninsula's perennial green, a devious thought popped into his head. Why not run the rider over a patch of jutting rocks, let the blades get struck, then stuck, then the motor might break? He'll have to buy a new one. And if he won't, he'll have hell to pay. In a few short weeks, everyone will complain. And in the meantime, I won't have to cut any more grass in the heat.

True to his word, Pip acted out the plan. Finding an obscure area of the grassy peninsula, Pip set into motion the enabling dictum. The rider was deliberately driven over an outcrop of rock, which immediately jammed the high-speed blades. The motor tried effortlessly to break past the limestone's top, which was tipped like an iceberg and holding onto its solid station by the weight of its one ton of bulk lurking just under the soil. Within seconds, the motor started to smoke. Pip fled to a safe distance down a nearby slope. Soon, the motor caught fire, and the rider was destroyed!

Proud of what he had done, Pip traipsed across the adjacent fields knowing that he had forced Boddinger's hand. Now he would either have to shell out thousands for a new rider or let the lawn acres grow wild, which would cause many internal dissensions among the patrons of the park.

Eager to report the bad news, Pip made his way back toward the 1800 house when he noticed a familiar black car parked outside the barn. It belonged to Dr. Whitten, the veterinarian. Pip checked his watch. The doctor had arrived earlier than expected. In response to the doctor's unexpected presence, Pip changed his direction at the lower end of the pond and jogged up toward the barn. He entered through a side door and looked ahead to see Dr. Whitten standing at the far end of the stalls engaged in conversation with a stern-looking Mr. Boddinger. Both noticed Pip at the same time, coming at them from the opposite direction. Before Pip could effectively speak, Mr. Boddinger, arms folded, assumed a staunch, upright posture with his entire six-foot frame and even accentuated it by lifting himself once, up on his toes, so as to convey his perceived superiority over his subordinate before he began to verbalize his discontent. Pip had seen it all before. And although his first inclination was to speak out before his pugnacious boss attempted to humiliate him with any sort of nonsensical charge against anything he had done or not done in accordance with his particular standard or liking, he hesitated on purpose so that should his high-level landlord say anything too far out of whack, he might be able to refute him on the spot and possibly embarrass him in front of the doctor. Boddinger, steeped in his own sense of himself, was unaware of Pip's well-devised, spur-of-the-moment plan and proceeded on course to put his Bigfoot-sized foot right in his mouth.

"Looks like you're late," he declared in a smart-alecky tone of voice. "I'm sorry, Doc, I've always stressed to my underlings how important it is to be punctual."

The doctor looked at the young lad waiting for him to reply. He did.

"You're early, Doctor," he said with a glistening grin.

"I know it," the doctor responded tactfully. "But I couldn't help it. Some other business I had down the road got canceled at the last minute. And I didn't think you'd mind my coming ahead of schedule."

"Don't mind at all, Doc," Pip returned assuredly. "Vindication never tasted so sweet" were the words Pip wanted to have roll off his vengeful tongue the moment he and the doctor had completed their discourse. But instead, he inveigled his red-cheeked superior with the bad news about the riding mower.

"It wiped out down on the back portion of the peninsula. It got caught up on a clump of rocks that were hidden under the tall grass. The motor's burned up. You'll have to buy another!"

Boddinger never did. The mower sat ever-idled on the back section of the amphitheater-area acres. The mower became, in the eyes of those who saw it, a monument of momentous absurdity—Pip's for ever disabling it and Boddinger's for letting things get to the point where Pip felt the need to have to take drastic action against the measure of a drastic means. Pip's only folly in what he perceived would come was in expecting word to get to his boss about the unsightly rider standing ground in view of his prized spectator arena and that something would have to be done about it. But word never came. The mower had been abandoned in too obscure a portion of the outlying area. And, as the area's wilds began to overtake it, it became even more left to its own to die.

But Pip's other intended consequence, the rapidly growing grass, was another story. Ceaselessly, it labored under the sun's hot orb to spread its spear-tipped stems up toward the life-giving light. At first, its neglect was considered nothing more than an unkempt appearance, like a man's face in need of a shave after only one day's disregard. But days turned into weeks, and the grass grew rampant and wild, and tenants began to complain. At one point during the verdant siege, Boddinger had the audacity to send one of his oil company maintenance mechanics over to the mine to sort through some of the old push mowers and see if he could get one running. That was after he had made a sojourn down through the fields and caught sight of the burned-up Big Boy rider. Keeping the unwelcome man in his sights, Pip followed him, undetected, into the upper barn and hid as he went about toying with the two old Lawn Chiefs that rested side by side in a spacious corner alcove. He tinkered with their respective, carburetors, starter cords, and highly reputed Briggs & Stratton engines until finally he made some kind of determination about their condition and usefulness then exited the barn. Once he was gone, Pip speculated about Boddinger's intent at getting one or both of the old-timers running again.

"He's crazy if he thinks that I'd be willing to cut even one square foot of the fifty to sixty acres we got of manicured lawn! Hell, he might as well give me one of those decades-older push mowers, the kind without motors!"

As with most things done with malicious intent, there are usually consequences that are unintended that go with it. In the case of the once well-kept green spaces reverting back to a time of pre-Silver Ford days, it was the opportunistic, blood-sucking ticks that began to take advantage of the recent abeyance at keeping the often-used lawns in check. They proliferated. Their numbers increased in proportion to the predicament. Acres upon acres of uncut fescue was now able to reach the apex of its growth potential, thus enabling the harmful pests to possess both the most possible and the best possible means of coming into contact with potential victims.

Ticks had always been a problem during hot summers at the mine because there were always those who ventured deep into the beyond-the-woodland thickets, which bordered the hollow hills, always in search of something; lost pets, or elusive outcrops of silver-bearing rock. But this condition of having all of the main bodies of recreational land covered over by a torrent of tall grass meant that avoiding the imperceptible creatures would be next to impossible. And it was!

Often, through the course of the midsummer days, Pip witnessed the unmistakable painstaking process whereby one unfortunate tourist after another was trying their best to remove, by whatever means available, one or more of the hard-to-remove pests. Over time, the situation worsened. The stay-over crowd—people and pets, which were frequenting the campgrounds—were the hardest hit. Annoyed at becoming afflicted on an everyday basis, they began to complain, first to each other, then to the new arrivals as they came to take their turns in the tick-laiden habitat.

Knowing the people's plight and realizing he could do nothing to assuage their frustrations, Pip remained aloof, always letting their complaints go in one ear and out the other. But in the later stages of the infestation, the complaints became more frequent and more potent. Pip grew tired of being confronted by an almost daily tirade of "ticked off" tourists. It was embarrassing. On no account could he give any reasonable explanation for the fact that the recreational lawns were not being cut. All he could keep telling everybody was that help was on the way, which meant that he hoped that the stingy overlord would come to his senses and sign the supply requisition filled out weeks ago for the purchase of a brand-new riding mower. One irate man went so far as to suggest that the park buy a few sheep to go to work on the high grass and then sell them off once the summer ended. And he was serious!

In time, the everyday occurrence of the sight and sound of Silver Mine tourists being inundated by the constant necessity of extricating ticks got to Pip. He felt sorry for being somewhat responsible for what had happened. He decided to make amends. Being an original thinker, he came up with a creative plan to help ease the tourists' travails.

On a forlorn floor space in the upper barn, there was an old canvas tent once used as a protected booth to sell local rock and mineral specimens at a "rain or shine" rock and mineral show held at the mine many years ago. It was Pip's. Now he had thought of another purpose for it. It would be a "tick tent!" The tent would be pitched on the low-lying land just below the lower pond's waterfall. The location was ideal in that it was in close proximity to the campers but out of sight from the 1800 house, the barn, and the main road. He could help the needy tourists without Boddinger finding out, without

Boddinger finding out that he had made any concessions for what they had both been responsible for in terms of causing, directly or indirectly, distress to the people.

As he intended, the relief tent was set up; and he surmised, upon its completion, that its dimensions were quite adequate for its designated purpose. Overall, the inside proportions were eight feet in length by six feet in width by seven feet in height, large enough to assemble a card table, folding chairs, and extras. Once the makeshift first-aid station was ready, Pip let it be known by word of mouth that the facility could begin receiving patients. The first few days, he checked on it regularly but soon decided that there needed to be standard times for him to offer his services so as not to interfere with his routine responsibilities. A sign, painted across both front flaps read "Ticks removed free of charge. Every day, 11:00-11:30 a.m. and again 4:00-4:30 p.m. Includes pets!"

Soon after, people and pooches alike were making the late morning and afternoon trek from their trailers, RVs, campers, and pup tents over to the first-aid station to have the parasites removed. Pip was adept in the endeavor and played the role of parasite practitioner well. Some of his more grateful patients even called him Doc to which he always smiled, approving the gesture of kindness, which also alleviated another ounce of the guilt he wore on his person.

In less than a week, Dr. Pip had already treated dozens of people, dozens of dogs, two cats, and even a pet bunny. His methods, learned in childhood, were applied as per the patient and the perceived difficulty of the eradication procedure. Probes, hot-tipped sewing needles, and tweezers were among the useful tools. Due to the high numbers of patients, Pip thought of a way of showing off his 100 percent rate of proficiency. He brought back from the barn an old tin-lidded Mason jar and used it to display the burned, crushed, squashed, and otherwise mutilated arachnids that he so successfully managed to kill. At one point, he even began to feel somewhat proud of his little enterprise and almost put up a donation jar to garner proceeds for his time and effort. But he didn't.

Although Pip had made inroads assisting the tick-infested tourists, things around the mine were not getting any better. Boddinger came less often, and though this would have seemed like something in Pip's favor it was, in actuality, not. Boddinger, despite his annoying presence, still had a crucial role to play. Bills needed paid. His haphazard arrivals usually meant that at least one thing or two would be taken care of even if it had nothing to do with getting a new rider. But as of late, whenever he did show up, paperwork, incoming and outgoing, was being disregarded. Mail went unopened. Supply orders went unsigned. Boddinger's stubbornness was coming to the point where he could have taken the place of the most onerous of the Silver Mine Sicilian donkeys.

Paper piled up on the kitchen counter where Pip, glad to add to it, wanted others to see for themselves just how contemptuous the Silver Mine boss could be. Once, when a week's worth was waiting, Pip observed Boddinger at his worst. Seeing the gulp-inducing pile of pulp, Boddinger, seized by rage and believing he was alone threw himself at the daunting paper load and tore it indiscriminately up. Pip, who had been crouched down in the living room tying his sneakers when the incident began, kept quiet and motionless except for lifting up his head to watch. Before Boddinger could make a move on him, should he afterward proceed in his direction, Pip quick-as-he-could darted for the open stairs like a hummingbird being chased by a hawk and fast-footed his way to the upper level of the house. Once Boddinger left the house and the property, Pip went back to the scene of the crime and ascertained the seriousness of the situation for himself. It was an egregious act and one that Pip would not tolerate. He vowed then and there to take the matter into his own hands. Everything would be remedied: the ticks, the poaceous fields, the perfunctory ordering of new and necessary equipment, all would be dealt with with another measure of drastic action. What, he did not know.

That evening, once all Silver Mine matters had been attended to, Pip collected some of the torn-up pieces of forms and the like and perused them one by one. While doing so, a devious though clever thought occurred to him. How easy it would be to just apply the necessary signature on paperwork like this whenever needed. It was an idea; good, bad, and both. But still, it was fodder for his brain. And it worked itself into him like a pair of hands massaging every ounce of his highfalutin gray matter, invigorating, invigorating, the concept of its good while lessening the concept of its bad. As long as there was a way to deal with things should the outcome come out bad, then the chance was worth taking, and he would take it. He searched out the house, opening obsolete files of charter tours, campground contracts, veterinary logs, and a host of miscellaneous supply-order sheets, looking for an elusive Boddinger signature. Then, after a tedious search—two file cabinets and two stacks of odd-sized boxes worth of material—he hit pay dirt! There, staring him in the face was an open folder of contracts from the previous year's stage acts. At the bottom of each one-page document was the signature of each country-music star and or agent, and alongside that was the countersignature of the one James Boddinger. He plodded through the pile in search of the most legible one but was dismayed to find that all were what he considered less than discernible. He then chose one at random and sat down at a cleared-off place at the table to practice copying the signature. Boddinger's was sloppy. It was one of those signatures that high-profiled people seemed to make as though it were special when really it was just done in haste. After a moment's reflection, Pip laughed. Actually, it would be easier to jot down an indiscernible name rather than one that would require a lot more accuracy. Boddinger's signature was nothing more than a capital *J* followed by a disconnected flow of small curves and wiggles, and a capital *B* followed by a disconnected flow of high and low curves and wiggles. There was nothing to it.

After only a brief session of practice-makes-perfect signature-style writing, Pip discontinued his work, put away the copy documents, and took the perfected samples up to the privacy of his room where he gave them and the matter another night's rest before enacting the scheme. The next day, he was up and ready to champion his cause before anything silver mine related took him away from his all-important concern. After a quick-fix breakfast of chocolate-covered doughnuts and chocolate milk, Pip took out his list of phony Boddinger signatures and reviewed them one last time to assure himself that they were indeed authentic looking, and he could proceed without worry. There could be no mistakes. If the signatures looked fake, Boddinger could contest ever having signed them, and then there would be serious repercussions. However, if the signatures—though forged—looked authentic, no accusation would hold up due to the fact that Mr. Boddinger, it could be said, was living under and enormous cloud of duress due his illness. It could simply be adduced that he signed without any real regard for what he was doing given the assiduous nature of his affliction and the psychological impact it had on him.

Either way, Pip was going for broke. It was a moment in his life when all things considered, he was not going to allow fear to tear down the ideal of possibility, which had so invigorated him. Too often, he thought, we let our judgment get in the way of our actions. Too often, a good night's sleep only renders us back to our time of indecision. We refuse to consider what our instincts tell us. We confuse ourselves by thinking too much. We become deathly afraid of the big bad wolves out there and subjugate ourselves under the influence of their power back to a safer place, back to the flock. He turned on his uneasiness by finding and filling out order forms for all sorts of new and necessary equipment, which included a new riding mower, a new backup pump for the mine, picnic tables for the campers, and even a new rowboat. While doing so, Pip, to further assuage his fears, turned on the radio. Playing on his favorite oldies station was a tune from the '70s by Andrea True. The song was playing. Just a part of it inveigled Pip with the notion to escalate his cause. In a fit of euphoric relation, he suddenly tore up the forms he had just started to fill out and started again. This time, he let himself go. Instead of the one-of-each philosophy, he had been applying to his endeavor he now began to embellish his fancy. Based on the fact that he knew the Silver Ford Incorporated fund had all of $80,000 in it he ordered to his heart's content. More! More! More! This time, it was three rowboats and twenty-two picnic tables and three new riding mowers and two new drainage pumps. Each stroke of the pen made him flit closer and closer to hysterics. He was near to tears when he annotated the Boddinger name to each of the presaging documents.

Having applied all of the necessary pseudonyms, Pip went about gathering envelopes so he could send them on their way. About the time he was done, he was startled from his final preparations by the unexpected ringing of the kitchen phone. He left his place at the table to answer it.

"Hello," he said in a businesslike tone.

"That you, Faehner," the voice replied.

"Yes," Pip returned matter-of-factly.

"Well, it happened early this morning. He slumped over at his desk at the oil company. Boddinger's dead!"

It's Howdy-Duty Time

Just the mention of Boddinger's death prompted the two participants to begin discussing the events of that long-ago story. It went without saying that a new day had dawned at the Silver Mine once the larger-than-life owner had been rendered into the ground, and the indefatigable underling would finally have a chance to unleash his restless desire to wrest the long sought-after property into his propitious hands. Mr. Faehner, still attuned to the bold-stroke chance he had taken by forging his boss's signature prior to his death, commented on an amusing afterthought he now had about the relevance of that issue.

"You know," he began, "Boddinger was a very important person, a lot more so than I gave him credit for being. He was a VIP all the way. But now, in looking at what I've managed to become and coming from lesser roots than he did, I would have to say that I think I've really redefined the meaning of what a VIP is, in fact, so much so that the very letters fail to suffice for the new effect. I think now it's time to call someone like me a PIP or a . . . let's see, a primarily important person or how about a prestigiously important person, yes. Which do you prefer? Hey, wait a minute. That's another word possibility. Yes, a preferably important person. What do you think?"

The reporter answered "preferably" although he was not quite sure whether Mr. Faehner was being serious or not. But he had something else on his mind about the story he had heard. It was an insight about the dream, and he wanted to express it.

"Mr. Faehner, the part about you being in the mine and encountering the image of the snake, I wanted to ask, those other faces that appeared after your trifle with the Boddinger snake, did you ever think that maybe they were the blurred images of the others that were to come? I mean, that they represented the men who would come in the future to somehow try to thwart you in purposes pursuant to your coming into your own at the mine?"

Mr. Faehner took a well-intended time-out to dwell on the proposed question for in fact up until now he had never included the telling of the dream in any way, shape or means. This rendition of the narrative was his first to mention it. For the briefest of moments, he reached inside of his memory and tried very hard to discern what he could not then—faces which now after having had actual contact with and connection to others who had opposed him might be identifiable. But he could not.

"That's some bit of psychoanalysis," he beamed back at the reporter. "You're something of a young Sigmund Freud, aren't you?"

"Not especially," the reporter shot back with a glint of pride in his eyes. "It was just something that caught my attention while you were telling it."

"To tell you the truth, I have never thought about it. But the theme seems right. Boddinger's was the one face I was sure of. His was the one I faced every day. The others, according to your interpretation, were yet to come and therefore unknown in the face of my dream. They were portended as evils yet to come, and I had to warn myself of their inevitable coming."

Mr. Faehner paused once the self-evaluation was over. His mind turned to the more relevant regard of story continuation. He turned his head behind him to the other snake heads on the wall and examined them each in turn, each in regard to the dream, and wondered. His eyes finally rested on the sorry-looking face of Howard Boddinger, better known during the Silver Ford Incorporated times as Howdy. Memories of who Howdy was before, during, and after his brief interim as property chief flooded his mind. Howdy was as inept as a 140-pound toad and hopped around matters of importance like he was hopping across lily pads looking for flies. And the reason was obvious. Howdy had no business sense. His father knew this and therefore did not foster his development in business matters. So whenever Howdy became somehow trapped into discussing esoteric themes relating to the money-making machines begun by his father, he instinctively jumped to the nearest lily pad whatever that might be. Once, in a discussion he was having with the highly competent Faehner boy, he suddenly changed the subject by saying, "Hey, did you know that the one ball in a guy's scrotum is for having boys and the other is for having girls. Now I just have to figure out which is which so I can plan for the time when I decide to propagate. Hey, I have to carry on the Boddinger name, don't I?"

This was Howdy. And to go along with his stunted mind, he also had a stunted body, which cramped his hefty body weight into as tight a package as could be imagined. No one took him seriously, except himself. Protected as he was by his father's wealth, he took on everything in life as if he were everything his father was. He was an heir apparent and therefore maybe even disregarded his father's disdain for anything he did knowing, just like Pip did, that soon his time would come. His cowboylike talk and his cowboylike walk probably came about as a result of realizing that anything he did he could do. Period!

But Howdy's rise to the top of the Silver Mine echelon did not come about as easily as if it were predestined. Upon Boddinger's death, the immediate family members went about as if they were all part of some giant, life-sized peanut scramble with everyone running about in all directions searching for answers, searching for that one specially marked nut who could put things back into perspective. But what the fights were really about were how to control the more profitable businesses. The Silver Mine, being administered to by the thirteen-year-savvy Faehner, was instantly placed on the proverbial back burner so the more important issues of how to run, the more lucrative—oil company, quarry, and construction company—could be dealt with more effectively. And Howdy was all but out of it. Not the slightest consideration was to be made on his behalf by anyone.

Being the unofficial outcast, Howdy pertained to the only thing that was left to him—the mine. He began to come down every day even if it was for no other reason than to make a presence. And this way, by default, he became the next contender for the prize.

Mr. Faehner pointed him out from the other portraits on the wall of shame.

"Here's Howdy!" he exclaimed in a way indicative of a talk-show host calling out the next contestant. "And I can tell you that this is indeed a superlative cast of him. The artist conceptualized him from a faded old photo I had from when I first started coming down to the mine. Nobody could have done more for accuracy without seeing him firsthand. Nobody!"

"So did that make things easier for you now that you had to deal with somebody as incompetent as Howdy?"

"In some ways yes, in some ways no. Howdy didn't have one ounce of the business sense that his father did, but he did have one immeasurable thing at his disposal—time. Unlike his father who was busy running the Boddinger empire, Howdy had nothing else to do except bother me. It made me detest him, and detest him I did for the course of three interminably long years."

"That's when you finally ousted him and the whole family too," the reported correctly assumed.

"Yes. But it wasn't as simple as that. You're getting ahead of the story. Despite the fact that I knew inevitably Boddinger would soon die because of how dire his prognosis was, I was essentially caught off guard by the changing of the guard, so to speak. I had not, for the life of me, anticipated what to do in the event of his untimely death. That's still hard for me to believe considering who I was. So I found myself in uncharted territory with no real plan of implementation to go along with what was then a testament, which had endured for almost half of my life. Howdy was atop the food chain, and I knew I was in for it one way or another!"

Mr. Faehner began to elaborate upon the foundation of the story, and together he and his listener were carried back through time—to the time and place where the onset of the transitional period began . . .

To announce his official arrival as head of the Silver Mine operation, Howdy staged something of a Sunday social such as his father had done oh, those so many years before. At the gathering, to which attendance had been made mandatory, he proffered to his people a type of commencement speech in which he alluded to the prosperous times, which would now prevail at the property now that he was in charge. It was a soapbox speech exemplified by the fact that Howdy, being a rather diminutive person, actually stood on a nailed-together, triple-stacked conglomerate of old wooden soda crates. And along with his increase in stature came his increase in ego. Howdy was neither a qualified extemporaneous speaker nor someone who could put together a well-made speech of any kind and read it verbatim so that he could dazzle an audience. His speech was riddled with old adages and the often repeated phrase "up-and-coming." The colloquium lasted for a full thirty minutes until one of the more, then two of the more, then more of the more testy individuals began to exhibit signs that they had had enough of the wordy windbag. One of the workers, standing behind the makeshift platform, turned from the eyes of the crowd and snuck off through the woods behind where the old office trailer used to stand. Another yelled out some sort of incoherent comment, thinking that any sort of disruption might send Howdy's train of thought into a train wreck. He was right! Howdy's inflated speech popped! He was left, face to the crowd, and not a syllable left in his head. So great was his humiliation and embarrassment that he actually felt a tinge of nervous movement run through his primordial tail. His coccyx—the vestigial top of what was once, it is believed, a balancing appendage in humankind—moved. Howdy, the wonder dog had had his vestigial tail laid curled between his legs like a pup that had been whipped by its master. He had been stupefied! Pip, realizing Howdy's utterly inept utility at dealing with a situation so bleak, reacted for the sake of all those vested in seeing the situation come to an end and stepped forward to take control. Someone from the crowd reacted to the out-of-control moment and shouted out for every ear to hear, "It's Howdy Doody time, folks!"

Without delay, Pip called for an end to the spectacle. He duly thanked the crowd for their cooperation in attending and told them to then disperse and go about their business. He then turned to Howdy and said in a deprecating voice, "It's over. You're done."

Howdy sighed in relief. But just as quickly resumed something of his command and shouted out to the dispersing offlookers that he was a person of the people, by the people . . . for . . . the . . . peo . . . ple. Pip turned to hide what he believed was the widest smile that had ever been put on his face. He hoped to make due like the others and head for some far-off sanctuary before Howdy had a chance to induce him to stay. But just as he was about to slip off, Howdy stopped him in his tracks with a "Hold on there, Pip!" Pip whirled around and found his belittled boss already so close that he almost collided with him.

"Pip," he began earnestly, "I appreciate you pulling me out of that jar of molasses. The truth is, is, I'm not really the best of public speakers. Not like you. Not like my father. You know now that my father's dead, it is up to us to keep this place going. And I know the secret of its success. This place made out so well because my father was like a father to you too. He may have been strictly business with you, but that was because he looked upon you like a son like me. And now that he's gone, it's just you and me, me and you. And together, that's how we will be! Yes, that's it! That's how we'll keep things together! You and I will be like brothers! Just as Dad wanted it to be! Why else would you have risked your own humiliation to face that pack of ungrateful whatevers!"

Having no choice but to take it all in, Pip listened attentively to Howdy's personal-to-him, how-do-you-do-now-that-I'm-the-boss speech. But when Howdy began delving into things unrelated to issues of hierarchy or just plain thankfulness, Pip's stomach turned sour. He and Howdy like brothers! Not likely! From that moment forward, Howdy was like a puppy on a leash. Whenever the two were together, he followed Pip around like Pip didn't know what. So often was he minding Pip's business that Pip began devising methods to keep him away. He began plotting Howdy's comings and goings to know when he was most likely to show up. Often in anticipation of his unwelcomed presence, Pip would take to hiding out in well-thought-of places ahead of his arrivals and stay as long as he could, which hopefully would be long enough for Howdy to get fed up with waiting and leave. During each of these occasions, Pip would thank God that Howdy had never opted to live on the premises in which case he would be unable to avoid the unavoidable.

So often was this scenario of cat and mouse played out that Pip's mind became preoccupied with it, and in the course of just a few weeks, he had forgotten something very important. That something came back to his attention once while he was hiding in the upper barn. It was just past lunch, a time when Howdy hoped he would be lucky at catching the Silver Mine overseer lounging around the 1800 house after a fulfilling meal. But Pip was onto him. In accordance with keeping their happened-upon meetings to an absolute minimum, Pip had, as he did on an almost daily basis, shifted his schedule so that no one but he knew where or when he would be doing anything. Howdy, after thoroughly checking the house, including Pip's private upper-story residence, came out dejected and laid down a pair of doughnuts in the parking lot dust to display his anger at again being thwarted before screeching his way up Silver Mine Road and onto some unknown, uncared-about destination. Pip watched from one of the movable slats and declared his victory to the tune of twenty-six to six for the times he had successfully eluded Howdy's detection. He chalked up the achievement on the mental chalkboard in his mind and was just about to show himself again when, much to his awe, a delivery truck came bounding down over the very hill that Howdy had just driven up! When the driver came closer to the house, he intentionally slowed down. Although he was indecisive about doing so, he then entered into the little lot where Howdy's car had been parked only two minutes before. Luckily, the trailer was only twenty feet so the swing into and around the side of the house was possible without too much chance for trouble. Pip kept a vigilant watch on the high wires leading into the house and saw that the trailer top had cleared them by a significant foot or so. Seeing the truck stop, Pip raced over from the barn and met with the driver who was then busy pounding on the unanswered door.

"Hey, mister," he announced once he skidded to a halt beside the irrate teamster. "I'm in charge here."

"Oh, you are, are you," the bulky man responded in a sardonic voice so as to display his disapproval for not being greeted promptly enough to suit his harried schedule.

"What do you got?" Pip asked in a perfunctory manner.

The husky purveyor, who after only a moment's time in the hot sun was perspiring heavily, wiped his browned brow with a polka-dotted handkerchief, then opened up the side door of the truck and retrieved a bill of lading from the seat and read from it.

"I've got aboard, let's see, twenty-two picnic tables. Yes. For the . . . let's see . . . Silver Ford Incorporated. Where do you want them?"

"Oh my god! Pip exclaimed. "I forgot all about . . ."

By offering his help, Pip somewhat alleviated the driver's upset. He hopped into the cab alongside the driver and led him to the back of the barn. There they unloaded the heavy load of new tables into the barn's spacious interior. Eleven stacks, two together, one upside down on top of the other, they were neatly arranged on the wide-boarded floor of the upper barn. After they were done, Pip signed as the receiver, and the burly man departed without an added thank-you. Pip breathed a sigh of relief. He looked ahead at the lines of assembled tables and thought about what they were in terms of why and how he appropriated them.

"They are all part of a climaxing scheme—one that I decided on to outwit Mr. Nitwit. And now they are here."

Pip remained in a state of consternation over the rest of the day. The time had come to pay the Piper for the ill-gotten gains. He would have to secure them somehow so that Howdy could not interfere with what he had done. Undoubtedly, he would find out about them. The senior Boddinger had not had time to deal with them prior to his death. They would come. And they would have to be paid for. But what to do?

The solution came to him. A few of the expected provisions would be put into use or at least put away for future use. These Howdy would be able to see and know about. The remainder, most of the cache, would be secreted away in the upper barn. To Howdy, they would be registered as purchases signed, sealed, and delivered long ago; and only now were being made to be paid for, something neglected by his father.

Over a relatively short span of time, only a few weeks, all of the ordered items arrived, all at times when Howdy wasn't around to see. Pip hid them all, all that he had deemed necessary so that their detection could not be counted as having an excessive amount of anything. Just as he had intended he would, he concocted something of a perfect hiding place for them—a place he need not ever worry about anyone finding out about.

During what spare time he had since the arrival of the picnic tables, Pip went to work devising and crafting a false side wall to the barn from the inside. There was plenty of wood. Twice since the onset of Boddinger's Silver Ford Incorporated, the huge bank barn had been partially renovated. And twice after those renovations, huge piles of barn boards, which had been replaced, had been set aside for scrap wood that could be used for anything. They were all exterior slats, which meant that one side was painted a flat, faded, yellow, which meant that in order to put them to use for this specific purpose, that of concealing the excess recreational equipment, they would have to be used with the plain side out. Not all of the barn had been boarded over with newer lumber, so that if one lower portion of one wall had the look of century-old wood, it would not stick out like a sore thumb, especially to someone like Howdy who hardly ever spent time there.

The work went smoothly. The boards were erected to match the height of the first horizontal structural beam, which was six feet off the floor. A frame was built out from the front wall, six feet out from the barn side, so the final measure of the enclosure would be an even dimension. Nothing would go on top. But to keep the curious away, far enough away to keep from noticing anything unusual about the structure, the outer wall was jam-packed with seldom-used or obsolete items. Items such as the tick tent, which had finally been disassembled and stowed away again, and old posters featuring past concert celebrities were leaned or laid in front of "the wall." Old display cases too of varying lengths and sizes once used in the shanty were now made to stand guard. All in all, when the wall was completed and filled inside and out, it could be noted that it would take quite a discerning eye to bring to it that there was more there than meets the eye! But the fraud, though so cleverly conceived and so thoroughly disguised, once it had been brought to fruition could not be as easily pretended in the context of its need to be paid for; therefore, the portent, at least, of its existence would have to be dealt with—with Howdy!

But in the midst of the deception, there were other things occurring within the Boddinger realm, which deeply affected the way in which Howdy chose to go about handling the frustrating situation. Within the crucible of power came growing confusion and consternation over the many, many matters of decision concerning the businesses. Conflicts grew. Dissensions arose. Whenever two or three were gathered, arguments broke out at the slightest mention of one or the other's belief about what-to-do or how-to-do-it matters that required the attention of a spearhead. But the spearheads, all of them, proved to have blunt tips on their shoulders. Problems compounded. All of the businesses fell into a myriad of mess, all except the Silver Mine. And in that vein, Howdy, though inwardly shaken by the perplexing stream of debt beginning to mount at the mine for things he could not find fact with, kept an efflorescent gloat in his eyes for all of his siblings to see. He would never disclose his own woeful worries in the midst of their plight. Whatever had happened in regard to the discredited accounts at the Silver Mine, he would have to deal with privately. His success or, rather, the perception of it might eventually lead to bigger and better things. He alone had control of the books and the bills. He alone had control of the access to them.

Over the first few weeks since his father's parting, Howdy received bills totaling over $70,000, most of the amount of the ready cash in the account. Time and time again, he was confounded by these interminable requests to pay for things he could not reconcile as having been recently acquired. In private places, he flew into rages proclaiming that these; this, that, and other things were all part of some sordid conspiracy developed by the constituent companies to take advantage of the money left behind. He did not suspect Pip. Having to have to come to him to explain things would in a way be infusing him with power, more so than was already his by virtue of his tenure and competency. Howdy could not risk giving him more. But he did on occasion try to inveigle him into conversations relating to some of the individual items that for the life of him he could not reconcile with as concerns their whereabouts. He was no good at confrontation and so did not try to refute any requests for payment due. If he had, it would not had gone so smoothly for Pip. Any investigation by anybody worth their salt would have uncovered the hidden items in the barn at which point Pip would simply have had to say that he had had nothing to do with putting the expended-for items in seclusion in the dark recesses of the barn. If, he perceived, that would not work as a plausible explanation, then he would of course reconsider and simply say that he was just following orders and had done as he had been told to do. Who could say otherwise?

Still though, Pip was not without his scruples. To somewhat appease Howdy's dizzying array of inveigling remarks, Pip did come forward to say that he was irked by what had happened and even went out of his way to present Howdy with an inventory list of the park's equipment, which included only a few of the missing items. To further appease Howdy's dismay, Pip introduced him to all of the items that he could afford to substantiate, namely, the new mine pump—not the backup, the new riding mower, and even one of the rowboats, which he relented about showing and secretly hauled it out of the barn and laid it on the pond shore, though he did not intend for any tourist to use it. The gateway onto it, he kept secured with a lock and chain, spray-painted white to match the boat and from a distance could not be detected. The boats would be soon put away for the season, and the new boat would be without a scratch. All of this attention attributed to the cause did a lot to quell Howdy's querulous behavior and lessen any less-than-favorable opinion he had of him.

But there were times in the early going when Howdy's less-than-favorable persona got the better of him, and he freely went about venting his frustrations to Pip or to anyone who happened to be within earshot. Once Pip caught him at it and openly castigated him for his whining while he rifled through the mail. They were not alone, and Pip hoped that he might learn a lesson in keeping his mouth shut—at least when in the company of others.

"Look at this!" he exclaimed. "The price of an entertainment permit has gone sky-high! How in the H E double toothpicks can something that is no more than the cost of a piece of paper go up like that!"

Pip, noticing the disapproving look of his guests, an older couple who had come into the 1800 house for brochures, made a wry remark on both their and his behalf.

"Why don't you just shut your yap and pay like your pap."

Having made the remark, Pip noted how easily he could have changed the line's rhyme and verse to devise a limerick and his mind went over and over it:

> There once was a sad sorry chap
> who was nothing at all like his pap
> His nerves were a-fray
> with no money to pay
> so I told him to shut up his yap!

Howdy looked up and winced at the cutting remark but thought better than to start something with Pip who could so easily win should they enter into a battle of words and wit. Pip knew too that Howdy was hardly the one who could take him on, especially in the good mood he was in as compared to the bad mood Howdy had hold of.

Howdy's real cause for his detestable mood was the fact that ever since his consternation over the books had arose, he had had to internalize every thought and fear on the matter. He could not, for a moment, let his guard down that he was involved in an inexplicable matter concerning great losses of money and unaccounted-for items while under his watch at the only Boddinger business that was seemingly doing well. And the situation worsened. Not in the sense that Howdy was experiencing anything worse. For him, his troubles in their entirety had been set into motion prior to his taking over at the mine. But what got worse were the extenuative circumstances arising on all other fronts of the Boddinger empire. The family that had banded together had come undone. Falterings and failings at the other businesses kept everybody on edge with each other. Feuds began. Fights ensued. Only Howdy seemed exempt. And only Howdy knew why. He dared not relinquish his pristine position over his rivaling relations. He walked in their midst like a king upon a mist, listening to but never involving himself in their trivialities.

Because the Silver Mine was the least of the businesses, he was never asked for the books and never made to explain for the discrepancies that nobody but he knew about. After a while, Howdy eased down from his wayward course. The mind-boggling bills, which had been coming in on a regular basis, stopped. The ones that had come were reconciled by recompense, and Howdy was relieved. And even though the Silver Mine budget had been bungled, he realized it would recover. Also, and of greater importance, was the realization that at least in pretense, he had to act the part of a person poised with the upper hand. And this role, in a short time, he carried to the extreme. Howdy, being the person who he was, the kind who indulge themselves freely but in only one level of extreme as it pertained to their particular personality, concerned himself wholly to taking on the persona of his now-absent father. His make-up included ordering special tailor-made clothing identical to that which his father wore. This assortment of pants, shoes, and shirts included the once-famous pink button-down, which the elder Boddinger donned all the time. Typical attire would be white shoes, white pants, a pink shirt with an even pinker bow tie and often a white cowboy hat. Howdy looked more like a ring master for PT Barnum's than the emblem for an enterprising business. People began to see him as something of a side show all by himself.

Howdy didn't care. For him, it was all about image, about portrayal, about perception. The one thing he could do.

About two months after the original Silver Mine owner's death, Pip began to ponder what he should do with the enormous sum of money he had swindled Howdy's father out of those many years ago. The fact was that no one but he and his former boss knew about it. The money had for all these years been lying in a safety-deposit box at the local bank where he held both a checking and savings account. Interest rates were up, and it would probably be wise to invest at least a little of it so he could make at least a little bit of money off of the money the way rich people did. Only once or twice a year had he dared to even look at it for fear that someone may see it or maybe some hidden surveillance camera might pick him up counting through the bundles of hundreds and report it to bank officials. He knew that large-enough sums of monies held or transacted were subject to report. But Pip had been smart as well as wise, and not once since he had come into the money revealed anything of it to anybody. It remained as safe and secure as the day it was slipped into the box. But now that was no longer necessary. As a matter-of-fact, it was probably better for the situation that he release at least part of the money into other venues, for if later, all the money happened to come out at once, it would be even more suspicious. He had to act. Over the period of another week, he perused bank brochures and made random calls, anonymously, to find out about yields and rates of return. Once he had gotten all of the pertinent information, he decided to take out two certificates of deposit, which were yielding 13 percent. Both would be issued in the amount of $20,000 and would yield over the course of the issuance—eighteen months—an additional $2,600 each. The rest of the money would have to remain in the vault. Some of it, over time, would be very slowly, very carefully, added to the existing accounts. In a time frame of a couple of years, a doubling or tripling of interest money would probably not raise any eyebrows. His bank books would play out a scenario of a thrifty working man with a penchant for saving all of the income he could.

But while Pip was busy resourcefully administering to his Silver Mine future, Howdy was busy boring his way into the everyday operations of the once-smooth-running attraction. Soon, he was thrusting himself into the spotlight of every activity, tourist or trade, as they occurred. Often, he would humiliate himself by act or word or sometimes just for being a pink-shirted, pimple-faced, cowboy-hatted, white-shoed Humpty Dumpty look-alike. More often than not, people, sensing he was someone whose bark was worse than his bite, would stand toe-to-toe with him and remark as they would to the given situations, embarrassing him repeatedly for daring to be present at such a time as was important to them. Howdy, in response, began to carry with him at all times a little black book, which he would always keep in the pocket of one of his pink shirts for all eyes to see. He would, in times of personal crisis, get out the book, open it, and make clear and precise annotations about any altercations, debates, or candid interviews he would have with any of the personnel. Even sarcastic remarks made from a distance or thought to have been made from a distance merited a written word.

But Howdy fooled no one. As believed, the little black book was an object of intimidation used solely for the purpose of purporting his power over people. Proof of it was that in a very short time, everybody's name had been added to the blacklist, some with asterisks beside their name, and not once had anyone been reprimanded for slighting the little lord. Pip's name in particular appeared twenty-seven times as was evidenced when one of the workers inadvertently found Howdy's book and showed it off to each individual he came into contact with before giving it back.

Pip laughed in spite of it. To him, the twenty-seven strikes, enough to wipe out every chance held by the opposing side in a regulation baseball game, proved to him just how powerful was his purpose there. Howdy thought about him all the time and knew he was one with the place, knew that he would never leave, knew that he would hold on no matter what, forever, to what was precious to him.

But Howdy never knew the depth of it. The extent of Pip's desires—that he not merely have control of the operation, but that he someday usurp the Boddinger family entirely from their long-standing presence at the Silver Mine—never entered his head nor had it ever entered the heads of the other family members. Only his father, now deceased, could have made such a speculation based on his esoteric knowledge alone that Pip did already possess enough of a money potential to make it possible. To Howdy and any others who cared, Pip was nothing more than an enthusiastic individual who wanted nothing more from his life than to continue to enjoy his obsession. Nothing further could be garnered from knowing the outside of him. But nothing could be further from the truth. Pip was sly. Who would have ever thought someone so capable of remaining so steadfast for so many years toward such an exclusive goal? He had already sacrificed half his life toward this end—an end which had no end in sight. At times, Pip felt like he was in a boxing match of a hundred years ago when rounds went on and on and on until a winner was decided by knockdown or knockout. There were no time constraints in either those olden bouts or these. Only the partner had changed.

Howdy's mistake lay in the way he considered it. To him, Pip was a layman, overzealous, yes, but a layman nonetheless. He was content being there and being in charge as much as he could be given the fact that his last name lacked the proper consanguinity to give him true deed. And Howdy believed, despite his own personal disliking of Pip, that the two shared a better rapport than that which had been shared between Pip and his father. So of course they stood to get along better too. And because they would, Howdy would continue to hold sway over a successful operation. He would continue to take credit for the way Pip ran the place just as his father had done.

But something came undone in Pip after James Boddinger's untimely death. Time! The purpose that had driven him all this way all these years had become a second revelation. Proud that he was of his indefatigable certainty that he would someday walk away with the Silver Mine deed in his pocket, it struck him just how long he had waited just to get to where he now was and where he was, was a place that had not been established by any mode or fashion of his own doing. What had happened had happened out of nowhere. Thirteen years had elapsed in all. Eight years had gone by since the money deal. And in all that time, all those years, Pip realized that he had done nothing, nothing to finalize his ultimate goal. It burned in him just how little bit of time he had devoted to conceiving a way to actually take ownership away from the Boddingers and give it to himself. He was appalled!

The only way he could get the Boddingers to give up on the mine was to have the place fall into hard-enough times that they would want to get out from under. And Howdy would have to be made the scapegoat!

Pip's interactive plan began. He knew that over time the Silver Mine accounts, though depleted, would invariably work their way back up due to the efficient way the place was run. Howdy would simply become complacent and rake in whatever the operation would bring him. That would be a stalemate. Learning from the elder Boddinger, Pip sought to bring about the Silver Mine's demise by deliberately keeping the fund money low. Boddinger did it by keeping the money earned from filtering back into the everyday operations and thus stifling progress. Pip would intentionally keep the monies earned from even getting to the fund and thus make it appear as if the dollars were being mishandled.

The first thing he did was to alleviate his apprehensions about all of the objects in the upper barn. One by one, he made deals with other faraway parks and campgrounds and sold them. Most of the owners and operators had already heard of Mr. Boddinger's death and thought nothing of doing business exclusively with the Silver Mine foreman. Most of them knew of Pip's reputation. Most of them also knew that no other member of the Boddinger family had ever had much to do with the mine, and therefore why wouldn't it be necessary to do business with someone obviously much less connected to the place? In all, Pip reclaimed almost the entire $70,000 originally put out even though several of the items were kept. The money was placed in a special place—the safety-deposit box. Pip was no thief. The money would be kept for the specific purpose of someday reincorporating it back to the mine. In addition to confiscating the money from the barn objects, Pip thought to further his initiative by then confiscating other collected monies that were within his facility to do so. No receipts were ever given for mine tours, which, depending upon the time of year, amounted to anywhere from $100 to $1,000 daily. Pip began to pocket this money, which meant literally each day his khakis were stuffed with an entire assortment of bills and coins that had to be exchanged at one bank into larger denominations, then put into the safety-deposit box once monthly for safekeeping. The campgrounds too became a target of convenience. Although those that came, came mostly through the special PO box or through a special number, which both led to a tiny out-of-the-way office in the oil company and therefore were subject to all the procedural paperwork, Pip did think of a way to take advantage of the situation by entirely circumventing the proper courses. It would not proffer any money to him, but it would prevent the campground from taking in all the revenue it could and hamper the operation that way.

Pip's plan was simple. Using only a miniscule amount of the tour money, he placed an ad for the campground in several out-of-town newspapers, inveigling potential customers to call into the house number before such and such a date and receive an unheard of bargain if they should decide to facilitate the park before such and such a time. It worked! And no one was the wiser. The fees he collected, he added to the till. At times, the campground swelled with sometimes as many as one-third of the park's patrons, paying as little as one-third of the required amount. There was, of course, a risk in doing business this way. If the lucky patrons ever began telling others of their unusual benefit it would, no doubt, create dissension among the crowd, and maybe word of it would get back to the Boddingers.

The months rolled on this way with Pip secretly squirreling away as much of the proceeds as he thought he could get away with without risking his job. It made Howdy, once the PT Barnum ring master, now the caducous clown.

Now the stage had been set. The operation would slowly fall, at least on paper, into the red. Howdy, with his myopic view and understanding of how things worked and reluctant to express any real concerns to his family circle, would be unable to rectify the situation and therefore would do little, if anything, about it. He would go on, holding on to hope that whatever had gone wrong would go right. And for a time, Pip allowed things to go on that way, essentially allowing Howdy enough time and space to hang himself. Slowly, by attrition, Howdy's aegis, the protection afforded him due Pip's veritable ability to run the place like a genuine genius, wore away. For Pip, the experience was an amalgam of mixed-up feelings. He was both elated and fascinated to see Howdy finally made to experience some of the hardship that came with command over such a vast operation, and yet he was also quite upset and worried at watching the place become so mismanaged that it wouldn't take much more than a nudge to make it go belly-up.

But it was necessary, and Pip had to do his part by dropping the ball and letting Howdy play the game by himself—win or lose. Over the course of the duration, Pip kept a watchful eye on the worsening condition of the business. He gained access to the Silver Mine accounts by virtue of the lackadaisical way Howdy kept order. Monthly statements, formerly kept secured, were now left lying about. All one had to do to seek out private information relating to the funding account was to rifle through the ever-present pile of papers strewn across the kitchen counter in the 1800 house and discover what it was one wanted to discover. Pip did too. Prior to Mr. Boddinger's death, he had had limited access to the information in that he could request it if he adduced a reasonable need to see it. Mr. Boddinger never minded. To him, Pip was the second-most important person there and the second-most important reason for the Silver Mine success. He was no real threat. And for as long as he lived, it would remain that way. Pip would always be in second place.

But Howdy was not his father's son. He was utterly inept and totally lost when it came to managing money and people and the park. Without Pip's helping hands, he was helpless. And though partly afraid to see things come so undone, Pip finally managed to overcome his self-doubt and stand tall in the belief that he had to do what he had to do regardless. As hard as it was, he would have to fall too—that is, until the dark days were over and he could come into a new light.

Howdy's bungling had no precedent. Things got away from him as easily as water flowing over a dam. Money. It was slipping through his fingers faster than he could count. By the year-end statement, the account had a balance of only $12,690 as compared to the previous year's end totaling five times that amount. By the end of the following year, 1988, the account was actually in the red. It now stood at $2,650 with a debt load of over $4,000, bringing the overall balance to a negative $1,350! This brought Howdy to his knees. He was in a constant state of consternation, and he ran around every day like a chicken with its head cut off. Pip feared the worst. He knew that Howdy still had probable access to other Boddinger funds and that in desperation might try to misappropriate some of that capital into the failing account. Determined that he had not come all this way for nothing, Pip devised another devilish deed, so to speak, against this bad apple whose seed had indeed fallen far from the proverbial tree. He would notify Mrs. Boddinger anonymously about the financial difficulty and allow her to confront her son and see what happens. Two days later, he had a letter completed and mailed it, along with the most recent account statement, photocopied, as proof of what he was attesting to. It read: "Dear Mrs. Boddinger, It is with great sadness that I must relate to you a matter of grave concern. It appears that for the past two years, your son's inability to deal with matters at the Silver Mine has left the place in ruins! The accounts are now in negative balances despite the best efforts of the staff to keep the place running. Discrepancies in the books indicate that monies are being handled poorly. Please look into this matter promptly as creditors are now beginning to inveigle their lawyers on what action to take regarding payment on services and property. Please advise."

The letter was left unsigned, leaving her to speculate just who it was who audaciously attacked her son's relating performance as business head of the Silver Mine. Pip hoped though that once her anticipated wrath about that had lessened, she might then get to the more relevant issue of how in the world her Howdy had managed to make-believe things were going so good when all the time they were going down the toilet. She blamed herself. She knew how her husband had felt about Howdy as he so often protested his having anything to do with any of the Boddinger enterprises. Now he had been tested true. Her initial reaction was her motherly inclination to bring the matter to bear, scold him for his deceit, and warn him that this would be his last chance to make things right should she let him further his initiatives there. But the matter got out of hand. Howdy's siblings found out about it, courtesy of Howdy who had inadvertently misplaced the letter, which he had demanded to see hoping to be able to ascertain the identity of the secret author. They scorned him ceaselessly for his lying and deceit for making them feel of secondary importance when all the time he was faltering behind their faces. Even under threat, things didn't get better. The pressure got to him. Soon Howdy was flapping around every day like a fish out of water. And it didn't take long for Mrs. Boddinger to pull the plug. She did it, sending baby Howdy down the drain along with the bath water.

The Silver Mine employees were let go. The property was promptly put up for sale with a California holdings firm. Why a firm so far away was never to be ascertained. Pip found out because representatives flew in from the far state, and he was the one who received them and gave them a tour of the land they had been authorized to sell. He further knew it was true when he got word that Howdy had been kicked out, so it was sadly said, from the Boddinger estate. It was reported that he left one day with little more than the clothes on his back and took up housing in a rented upper room at the Frogtown Inn. Pip, out of curiosity, verified this often recanted tale by once in a while going over to the inn and seeing for himself Howdy's little green Mustang II, which he had had fixed up over the past several months, probably with the last of the Silver Mine money. Howdy never showed his face again at the mine, not even to relate to others that he was once a person of the highest priority there and counted as a member of its history. Pip was probably why.

Just as he had done in the act of bouncing Howdy off his throne, he acted alone. Anonymously, he penned a letter of the greatest importance to the representatives of the California firm, informing them of his intent to purchase the Silver Mine property, which they had hardly begun advertising to prospective clients and the like. Pip's proffer attenuated their taste buds' desires to go any further with the process. He told them that he had the stipulated amount in cash to pay for the property. The sum offered was $300,000! No delays. No mortgages. No liens. No collateral. It would be a straight cash deal, and it was all just waiting for them.

It was doubtful that Mrs. Boddinger would refuse such an offer. It was more than the original amount her husband purchased it for, and she owed nothing for it. The Silver Mine was not a moneymaker either at least not like the other businesses were, or, at least, had been. She needed money. Although she still held what was considered a vast amount of wealth, she was altogether lacking due her other businesses' languid performances. Rather than forfeit those once-lucrative enterprises, she very desirously elected to sell the Silver Mine and use the proceeds to pump up the others.

She accepted Pip's lucrative offer without ever knowing who it was she was selling her husband's beloved Silver Mine to. Everything was done between attorneys and Pip. Once the deal was done, Pip imagined how aghast she must have felt realizing that it was he who had bought it. He imagined how utterly throttled Howdy must have felt once he found out. But Pip didn't spend much time or thought on the subject of their coming to terms with such a revelation. He had now, after half-a-life's ambition, realized his dream! He was now the proud owner-operator of his beloved Silver Mine!

Mr. Faehner stood up from his chair and breathed in a sigh of relief just as if he had only now again accomplished such an improbable task.

"It gets me right here," he said, pointing to his chest. "Every time I recall in detail the difficulty of those days. How it was that I believed in myself enough that I never waned from my purposes. I'll never know. If I had to face it all again, I don't know if I would have prevailed. So much of my life force was spent in it."

"Oh, you would do it again I'm sure," the reporter snapped. You are you. And you would have found other ways of accomplishing it had not things happened as they did. I'm sure of that. As a matter-of-fact, it all could have been easier. Even if JB lived, you could have found a way to have come to your purposes. Why not? You could have married his daughter. You could have acted more like a son to him even if pretended. You could have let things stand with Howdy at the helm of the good ship *Silver Mine*. Leaving the status quo alone would have kept you in command. If you humored him, he just might have found out how much easier it would be for him to let go of a place he could not deal with. There is never just one solution to a problem. What do you say?"

"I say it all sounds rather interesting. But I was never one for beating around the bush with people. I rather prefer standing up for what I believe in regardless of what it means, regardless of who might not like it. I prefer to be honest with myself, with others, despite where it might lead me. And that's how I have always been."

"You're telling me you never looked at a situation and wanted to take the easy way out. You have never looked for help?"

The Cuz!

Mr. Faehner reseated himself and clasped his hands upon the desk as a way of indicating he was ready to begin telling another story. But before he did, he again set up a background for it in accordance with his assertion that he had always been a go-it-alone kind of guy.

"My times at the mine go way, way back into my early adolescence, back to when I was a boy. And like most boys, I was aware of my young age and lack of experience in the world. And actually there were many times in my inexperienced life when I called upon the certainty of others to come to my aid. My two brothers helped me, hand over fist, whenever I needed them. My friends too were there for me in many instances of need and circumstance. But the Silver Mine remember was a place of special importance to me. One that I dared not let open to the wilds and whims of others. I had dreams about what I wanted with it, and dreams are not to be left open to other people's interpretations.

"But I also realized the importance of having an advantage in a situation too. I did use Luckee to my advantage as a way of avoiding, whenever possible, having to have direct contact with JB. I also, from the earliest times had, not one but two, Silver Ford confidants to help me get along. Both were, of course, dismissed but through no fault of my own. Each of them lacked the maturity that I possessed at such a young age."

"Yes. You told me of how the one friend was extricated due to the party. What happened to the other? How did he meet his end?"

"He was the Cuzze, that's what we called him. He was my original partner at the mine. He came with me on my first ventures down, not counting the original time with my uncle Rick. At first, he was like me. He was enthusiastic about the place. But in time, he got bored. Jim was a person who thrived on excitement, and as time went by, he slipped into a real melancholy, what with the sedentary dullness of being in the country all the time. For him, the daily routine of feeding a barnyard full of donkeys and horses and shoveling shit every day became depressing. He needed more. But he was up against it with someone like me around. I rarely relented to any of his high ideas, and when I did, I did so with extreme caution. Believe me, this guy was a lot more risky to have around than the next James was. Like I always said back then, if you ever put one of those mood rings on a guy like him, it would go through every color known to man. Jimmy was a moment-to-moment person of the most profound order. You never knew with him. Most people kept their distance from him once they got to know him. I brought him with me to the mine originally because of his proximity to me. We were, by all accounts, best friends back then, strange as it should seem. But I did have an ulterior motive for keeping him around once we got started. He was a distraction. I figured the best way to keep old JB off my back was to keep his attention on something else, in this case a someone. Jimmy was perfect for this. Like everybody else the Cuzze encountered, James Boddinger was kept in a constant state of disarray by his antics. All in one day, you could love him, hate him, like him, and want to kill him.

"Yes, once I sensed the difficulty in dealing with such a stern man as the Silver Mine proprietor I had no reservations about keeping someone like Cuzze around to take the brunt of any heat JB might throw at us. But, of course, as was inevitably what was to be expected, Jimmy's affiliation with the mine was doomed to failure. Never one to be bound to restrictions, Jim had too hard a time regulating himself, his actions, in regard to what was expected of him. Due to his blatant lack of respect for authority and his ceaseless not-knowing-what-to-do-with-himself due to his boredom, he often set himself up for conflict and reprimand. It was in this mode that he so often found himself riled in conflict with the powers-that-be that he was spurred to take even greater chances with his association with the place. Jim believed, I believe, that there was an alternative ending to every situation and never the one that could most likely be expected. In this mind-set, he spelled out his own doom. And I, I stood by and watched and even shoved him a little forward you could say. But in retrospect, I can perfectly say he got what he deserved. He wanted drama and excitement in his life, and oh boy, he got it."

"You have enticed me to the point of excitement now," the reporter said with expectation. "Tell me, in exact word and detail, what happened to this miscreant. Any story about someone you describe that way has got to be good."

Mr. Faehner complied. He introduced the reporter to the one incident which set into motion the downfall of his first partner. His reminiscences were of so complete a nature that together the walk down memory lane was sufficient enough to make them feel as if they were both caught up in the experience. Never before had words brought forth such context and meaning as to inveigle such listeners out of time, out of place, to a setting of distant view. But this story did so . . .

"I told you. I told you!" Jim shouted in a commanding voice once he successfully unfurled the black bearskin rug out in front of the shanty's pot-bellied stove. "Can you imagine it! Can you imagine it, Pip! Just think, we get some dynamite chicks down here all alone, and we can have fun with them, in front of a roaring fire, on a floor made of black fur. Won't that be the ultimate in sexy!"

Pip glanced over at the floor and watched with amusement as his work partner made a spectacle of himself by lying on the animal rug and acted all the animal by pretending to be involved with a member of the fairer sex while writhing and whirling around, arms folded around to his back, make-believing they were the arms of his chosen one. He continued at his "floorplay" until Pip spoke up.

"If you and whoever you're pretending to be with decide you want to be alone, just let me know. I'll be done here in a minute, and the both of you can go on doing whatever it is you're doing."

"Oh, shut your fancy mouth!" Jim countered. "You don't have anything to say because you're the one who can't get any! The closest you ever got to having real sex is when you kissed Annice at the pool last summer. Pity you!"

"Actually, you are right," Pip conceded as a guise to guide the conversation away from the standards-of-passage-for-teen-age-boys speech that he was sick and tired of being lured into every time Jim brought up the issue of the contrast of their abilities to seek out and seduce sexy young girls.

Jim was dumbfounded. He was ready to pick a fight using the one principle he was superior to his academic buddy in. But Pip would have none of it. He continued his activity, adding a knapsack's worth of silver specimens to the for-sale portion of the display cabinet, then applying price stickers to them individually. Once they were all aptly displayed, he affixed made-up values to each one by judging their size, shape, luster, and thickness of silver. Jim got up. He knew the serious nature of his longtime friend, and he knew that if Pip was preferring to be serious instead of sassy about defending the pretense of his still being a virgin, then now was the time to strike—to entice him into one of his wayward schemes—with the notion that that particular status quo need not be any longer.

"Hey, dude," he said in an affable voice. "Let's, the both of us, be what we really are—two virile, good-looking men looking for love. Let's forget about all the reasons why we shouldn't and instead focus on why we should."

"Why we should what?" Pip asked sternly.

"Why we should have a party!" he exclaimed. "Right here in the shanty! Can you imagine how intense that would be! Having two hot chicks down here with us. Can you imagine!"

Pip pondered the possibility but only to himself. He admitted without saying so that that would be a thing most specially desired in his bleak, fantasy-only sex life. His mind went into thought about how, party-specific, that idea would be if it were brought to fruition. Jim guessed what was circling his mind and minded not to interrupt the flow of cajoling thoughts as they served up his intended purpose in his friend's juicy brain. He kept still.

It was true. Jim was phenomenal when it came to sweet-talking members of the opposite sex. He exuded pheromones to the point where most females, captured by his presence, walked away from their initial encounter with an expression on their faces of "phew." It was an ephemeral moment unlike any other. Pip knew that if he gave his subordinate partner the green light to go ahead with the tentative idea, then the chances of it actually materializing were profoundly favorable. It probably could happen just as he or Jim imagined it. And it was the bearskin rug that provided for it. It alone was the catalyst for activating Jimmy's weary persona. Over the many months they had been at the mine, Jim especially had been lulled into a state of lethargy by the constant routine and drudgery of day-to-day work. Thinking about it, Pip realized that there had been no reprieve for either of them. There was nothing to break up the monotony. For all the thousand of hours they had spent attending to the relevant issues of their work, there had been nothing done just for them. That was appalling! Since the first day they had joined forces to help make the place something special, it had been all work and no play! No way!

What a way to rectify things a little, Pip thought, as feelings of perceived exploitation inculcated his being. The influence he felt was stinging. What he inferred from his friend's expressed desire to do as they pleased as a way of appeasing the apparent imbalance of work to play now rested upon him in such a way that he was glad to have it, glad to have had it said, and glad to be in a situation to do something about it. In regard to what to do, he felt almost a certain stigma about it. The decision about what to do rested entirely on his shoulders. Since the earliest days at the mine, Pip had been put in charge of whoever else worked with him. In this leadership role, he had succeeded in bringing about the best results in building up, then maintaining the most efficient schedule of tourist-related activity ever thought possible. This recognition he had earned through the process of, time and time again, having come up with the best possible solutions to all of the expected and unexpected problems that had occurred during the start-up and continuance of the nascent operation. And now, after repeated performance, he was considered an expert at everything he did, period!

For the time being, he did not wish to become embroiled in any squabble with Jim should he caution him about acting on a whim, though deep inside himself, he knew that he too was stirred to the highest anticipation. Instead, once he was done categorizing and cataloguing the silver specimens, he excused himself from the company of his companion and made a brusque retreat from the shanty. Alone, he made a steady streak toward the barn so he could be by himself to consider what he should do. Today had been a day when their afternoon duties had been switched with Pip working the barn and Jim giving tours. Trading places once in a while assured Pip that Jim never became inept at dealing directly with the public.

In the barn, while putting out the last of last year's winter corn for the horses and donkeys, Pip weighed out both their wishes against what he knew was only his caution should he decide in favor of the proposed night to remember. He got serious about it. Up until the moment he departed for the day, he went over and over all of the necessary steps they would have to take to make it successful. This meant avoiding all of the pitfalls that usually accompany teens whenever they decide to let themselves go in a relatively unrestrained environment. Left to himself, he came up with a plan, a plan he hoped would both enable and protect them in view of the circumstance.

That night, he put his thought to paper by comprising a tentative list of rules, which he would expect everyone to follow in accordance with his approval that there should be such a party. He mulled over each and every stipulation before assigning them to the official treatise, then took the time to type up the document on clean white paper. Having made it into such a fine thing, Pip decided to then make photocopies of it so that everyone in attendance could have one. Satisfied that he had done well, he arranged to meet with Jim that very same night and share with him what he had done. He expected Jim to be elated that he had decided for it regardless of the related regulations. But what he expected, he did not get.

They sat together face-to-face in the third floor of Jim's home, a place he had made all his own, when Pip handed Jim one of the extra copies. Jim went into hysterics serving out commentary and laughter as he read the scripted passages both out loud and to himself. Before he finished, the phone rang; and he picked up, still in the middle of a slap-happy, laudable gesture of unrelenting mirth. Once he became aware of who was on the other end, he calmed himself down enough to engage in the ensuing conversation. It was a return call he had made to one of his many interested intimates who he had called upon to invite, along with a friend, to come to the only recently conceived and only moments before confirmed, commandments notwithstanding, Silver Mine party.

Assured that the party, at least in theory, had been approved by his by-the-book leader, Jim immediately went to work getting his specially selected "pick" to agree to "come"—*come* having of course a twofold meaning. She agreed also to bring along one of her best friends, one best suited for Pip. Jim turned to Pip and pressured him into naming a date to which Pip reluctantly—realizing it was too late to negate the idea and wanting to get it over with—related that the upcoming Saturday would do.

Then Jim decided to have some fun at Pip's expense. Realizing that his friend was a man of his word and he would not capsize any boat he had made to float, Jim turned on him by turning him into the girls by beginning to read the humorous document over the phone.

"Okay, ladies, the party's on. But first each of you has to agree to the terms of this proposal so that everything works out. It says; number one . . ."

Pip, outraged by Jim's unkindly act, grabbed the document when he had, by his own close proximity to the phone, become aware of the jovial response being issued forth from the two imbued females, laughing and making comment at the other end of the line.

"Hey, Cuzze! Knock it off!"

"Knock what off," Jimmy responded passively. "You're the one who started all of this ridiculousness!"

"No!" Pip responded in an admonishing tone. "I was being serious. This whole thing should be taken seriously. You'll be the one who'll be made the fool if something happens and we end up in some kind of trouble. The real trouble is that you never take things like this serious enough!"

"You act like we'll end up at the end of a rope if we get caught doing this. You're crazy! The worst that'll happen is that we'll get yelled at and maybe suspended for a while. And besides, I don't intend on letting that happen."

"Then why all the attitude, huh?"

"Would you just calm down, Faehner. You get so high-strung over the simplest situations—things that haven't even happened. Let me be the first to tell you, you need this worse than anybody."

"Need what?"

"Need"—Jimmy quick-covered the phone so the girls couldn't hear— "____! There now you made me say it. And it might just have scared it away."

Jimmy returned to his conversation, which, during his brief abeyance, had been continuing one-sidedly. Pip relented from instigating Jimmy any further, realizing that what he had just been told could possibly be true, if the girls had heard Jimmy's crass one-word summation, they could just decide not to come. But Jimmy was expert at smoothing things over. He responded by convincing his would-be date that she would be in for the time of her life if she should come and, in a much lower tone, regarded to her friend that Pip, regardless of anything else he was, was a virgin and therefore should be considered safe to be around.

"Anything that happens between him and her," he told his party date once they were in the middle of a private moment, "will happen as a result of her desires."

Disturbed by the uneasy event, Pip retreated further and further from the phone. Putting his faith entirely in Jimmy, he instead tuned out from the disconcerted experience by tuning into the entertaining sounds of music. The Fischer stereo, tuned to one of the premier rock stations with the volume pitched high, began blasting out hit after hit of their favorite '70s sounds. Listening to Zepplin, Floyd, and Aerosmith, Pip found just the right mix to soothe over his frayed nerves and embarrassment. Though he was detached from hearing the words of the ongoing conversation, Pip knew that nobody, but nobody, was better than Jimmy at swaying members of the opposite sex over to his view. The party would most likely be a go.

Another aspect too of his earlier encounter had Pip's head in a spin. Though the voices and noises he had heard from the girls were one's of jocular ridicule, they were nonetheless voices of enticement. Ears do not deceive, least not when they are called upon to connect the sound of a voice to the impression of the person they are being issued from. And the sweet, melodic sounds of the voice of the person he was intended to be with were as music to his ears. With them as his all-defining colors and textures, he went to work painting a perception of perfection of his soon-to-be-unveiled mystery date, who would in the flesh undoubtedly exceed his own fantasy-driven expectations. With this angel image carried around with him, Pip, contrary to his earlier assertions, collected up his hastily written, needlessly contrived rules and tore up the copies into portions the size of confetti, then flung the black-spotted paper bits into the trash receptacle in his room. The pendulum now swung on the side of free love with caution left lying; its antithesis, its victim.

Over the course of the next few days, everything of importance to the success of the party was readied or set in motion. Parental permission to spend the night was granted to each of the party-going elite, each under a guise of their own unique invention. Supplies were garnered and, for the most part, sneaked down into the shanty for safekeeping. Unopened bags of potato chips and pretzels were left in large paper grocery bags and stashed in a corner of the back room alongside the cooler. Inside the large cooler were placed canned soft drinks—colas, root beer, orange, grape, and lime, enough of a variety to please everyone. Unbeknownst to Pip though was Jimmy's inclusion of a few extracurricular items, which he had managed to slip in unnoticed. Hidden way, way deep in the huge open ice were two six-packs of beer, which would have otherwise been forbidden. It was Jimmy's way to keep things a secret whenever they might create controversy. Then, when the time was right or when it was too late to make things right, he brought things, illicit or ill-conceived, to bear upon a given circumstance and then just explain them away as best he could. And whether they made sense or not never mattered, for once they were done, they were done, and anyone who didn't like it could just lump it.

There was another, even greater secret, Jimmy carried with him on the night of the party. He had bought a certain quantity of high-quality Columbian Red-bud marijuana from a dark-sided friend, one with whom he frequently and without Pip's knowledge smoked the mind-numbing weed whenever they got together. Pip would have been appalled if he had known Jimmy was turning into a pothead, let alone give him grace enough to smoke it freely on the mine property. Jimmy knew too how Pip would have felt. Beer he had an answer for if it was contested that he had been the provider, but pot had no reply. Whatever he did with it would have to be done on the sly, either by himself or in the company of only his female companion.

The day went unheralded prior to the highly anticipated evening. Pip and Jim left the mine as they usually did with Luckee, who drove them this time, unusually, to a drop-off point in the city other than their block of Pine Street. There they quickly darted into the apartment house of a mutual friend whom they had previously paid to convey them back to the mine with their dates who they would pick up on the way. Soon, all three had filed into the pickup's cab and were making a rapid go of it across the city streets until they came to the designated meeting place along the curb of a city park, where the girls and their belongings were packed into the back. Each of them had thought to bring along a little something of their own inside a knapsack.

In an unlike manner, Pip did not invite either of the two "hotties" to take his seat up front in the cab. Jim didn't either but did so in accordance with what was his manner. Pip rather was daunted by their beauty and was rendered helpless in their first-time presence to act, react, or feel as he normally should.

The ride back to the mine was like no other. Pip turned time and time again toward the back and watched in disbelief how the two hair-tangled teens seemed to take it all in—the discomfort, the lack of consideration in allowing them, instead of him and Jim, to sit up front in the protected compartment.

Pip's introduction to the two pretty girls back by the truck had been nothing more than a quick exchange of greetings coming from all directions, but at the mine, things quickly progressed. On the way down, Pip's intended had already let out that she was totally into him with his cute, clean-cut looks and physically in-shape body. Once everyone was out of the truck and the driver duly thanked and on his way, Pip at once ushered his companions up the old mine road and out of sight of Silver Mine Road. Though it was only just past six, the November sky was already darkening, and a cool, almost cold, dusky air was settling on the hollow. Pip took note of how the two newcomers seemed so inappropriately dressed for the certain time of year it was when warm days turn to cold nights as soon as the sun went down. Thinking of a way to open up a conversation about anything, he made comment of it to which both girls aptly responded by informing him that they had thought to carry extra layers with them, but that the available protective apparel was for the moment inside their knapsacks.

Once the company of teens arrived outside the shanty, Pip stepped up onto the long porch and opened the Slaymaker padlock so everybody could enter. Pip went through first and quickly turned on one of the overhead lights. Next, he made his way across the room and over to one of the far walls where he glanced at a wall thermometer, an old-time Nehi soft drink advertising thermometer used in its heyday to facilitate the outsides of gas stations, garages, and store fronts. The temperature read a brisk fifty-eight degrees, which meant that it was in everybody's best interest that a fire get started in the pot-belly stove as soon as possible.

Jimmy did the honors. Plenty of wood and kindling was available for use as supplies for the winter had already been appropriated during the past several weeks. Within minutes, a hearty fire was blazing, and the temperature of the room as well as the room's occupants went up. Several times while stoking the orange tongues of flame, Jimmy looked sideways at his Silver Mine pal and smiled a self-congratulatory smile in connection to the fine job he had done in getting such a fine duo down to their domain to have some fun. Pip restrained himself from smiling back as he was all the time being looked at by both of his new friends.

Acting the part of a gracious host, Pip made short work of first offering, then bringing his guests sodas and snacks. Jimmy, once he was satisfied that the fire would last, thought to get some music playing. He knew that once he got the music playing, he could get some bodies swaying. And he was right! For the next solid hour, the sounds of the seventies held sway over the four dexterous rockers. As the hits kept coming, the party rolled on in a manner that only like-minded teens could appreciate. Then suddenly, the course of events changed as the reign of the one disc jockey fell to another, and the music style changed to appeal to a more subtle, subdued group of listeners. Slow music was the theme. Jimmy's instant reaction was to curse the radio station up-and-down for being a bunch of sissified assholes and throw his hands up high in the air in disgust. The initial slow song played was the sensational "Wildfire" by Michael Murphey—a song about a wild horse's longing to be free. The song's enchanting melody mesmerized Pip and his dance partner, so that they allowed themselves to be captured by it as though it were meant exclusively for them.

Jimmy, however, was upset. He liked the song for its more literal context and meaning. The advantage he derived from it was to use its seductive power to help persuade his date into wanting to experience something of what the song was all about in a more applicable way. Privately, he invited his partner to participate in an all-out thrill by saddling up one of the Silver Mine horses and going for a ride. This, he believed, would score him enough brownie points so that later he could end up eating the brownie! Pip was none the wiser. He and his date had become so infatuated with each other that little else mattered beyond the reach of their arms and the length of their stares. When Jimmy and his girl exited the shanty, it was with little regard for the others whose minds as well as bodies were in a state of rhythmic slow motion.

Out the door and out of sight, Jimmy felt free—free from the far-reaching perception of his Silver Mine partner. Finding exhilaration in the open air, Jimmy thought to further his potential chances with his fairer-sex friend by openly inducing her to partake in a little recreational smoke. He introduced her to the Red-bud, which he had hidden in his front pocket by reaching in and pulling out the baggie it was contained in, then extricating one of the rolled joints for her to see. Before lighting up, they strolled out of sight to a location up behind the shanty, far enough away so that they could not be detected from any of the windows even if somebody was purposefully looking for them.

Outside, the night was changing. A contrast was taking place in the form of a cold Canadian air mass, which was invading from the north. With it came the collision of the settled and disturbed fronts, which, when set to do battle, created an eruption of the upper atmosphere and touched off a rare November snow.

A fury of flurries burst forth from the sky as the fast-approaching cold front mixed in with the stationary air and uplifted it, creating huge sky pillows atop the supernal dome. The sight of the frosty flakes sent shivers of both a cold night and a special delight to the two awed spectators as they stood in sight of the spectacle of dotted white made even more spectacular by the fast-influencing effect of the mind-enhancing THC now possessing their beings.

After finishing the joint, Jimmy led his female companion away from the shanty and its environs.

"Hurry up," he shouted, though his voice was somewhat muted by the stifling flurries. He broke stride, quitting her side, and raced off ahead of her once they reached Silver Mine Road. "Come on. Don't be a slowpoke! It's safe and dry in the barn."

Once they were both sheltered, Jimmy wasted no time in leading Oreo out of his stall and provisioning him with saddle and harness so that the couple might take him out. Though Jimmy's date tried to caution him about taking the horse out in the inclement weather, Jimmy just ignored her. He continued his purposes as though he intended to ride with or without her, which made her feel somewhat of a party pooper and therefore more willing to throw caution to the wind and go along with the foolish endeavor.

"Look, I don't need your consent to do this. You're either with me or without me. I don't care. I get enough of that constant care from the king of all constant caregivers—Pip! Now are you coming or not?"

Oreo did his best to keep up with Jimmy's demands to gallop when he could in the open fields above the barn, but often he slipped and slid out of step due the wet insecure ground. But Jimmy was relentless with him. He wanted their experience to be profound as he had promised, for how else would he end up getting what he really wanted—his girl's desires expressed on him like he was the saddle she wanted to mount. The horse would have to come through come hell or high water!

Then a fearsome thing happened. Oreo, jaunting across the snow-struck, open-field path, which led back toward the barn, suddenly struck a patch of ice accumulated in a worn-out rut, which his one leg happened to catch while he was intentionally avoiding another. At once, he lost his balance and whooshed across the iced puddle. Now both his legs were smartly stretched out in front of him, awaiting their first chance to find a firm footing amid the punctuated tufts of dried weedy grasses lying dormant all about. Unfortunately, his momentum carried him swifter and farther than expected and when he finally did catch onto a bit of foundation soil he did so with only his right limbs. Immediately, all of his weight and the weight of his passengers surged into the unanticipated landing. Oreo's single leg buckled under the excessive stress, sending him and his mounts flying to the ground. The two two-footed creatures were thumped to the hardened earth but were relatively unharmed by the accident. But the four-footed equine did not come away unscathed. The unfortunate fall had forced all of the pressure being exerted into his leg into the area where his body could most easily lock it up—his knee joint. The load of force caused by the shock of his leg trying to stabilize itself caused the joint to fracture and the leg bone to come out of its socket. Oreo whinnied in pain as he lay on the snow-encrusted surface. Jimmy, though not an expert on the afflictions and maladies of horses, did suspect that Oreo was more than just a bit shaken up by the tragic experience. He did pretend though, for the sake of his riding partner and a little for his own self-vindication, that the horse was no worse for the wear, just startled perhaps, and would only require a nice prolonged rest to adequately recover.

"He'll be good as new come tomorrow," he projected once they had led him, wobbling and whining, back into his stall. Sensing by her empathy toward the horse, pertaining to his needs by tenderly stroking his head as he lay down on the straw, Jimmy sought to undo the rift he perceived was growing between them. He would not permit her concerns and affections for the hurt horse to release her from what he regarded were her obligations to him. He looked intently at her, her face, her figure, and refused to let go of his real purpose.

With quixotic words and touches to her body, Jimmy tried to quell the disparity, which was causing them to separate from each other. At one point, he had her stand up; and using both his hands, he began atop her head and, in an artful manner, used each hand to travel down each side of her body—her head, her arms, her sides, her waist, and even her legs. It was enticing. But just as suddenly, Oreo whinnied again and the spell, which had been so magically laid out was broken. Immediately, Jimmy's girl reacted by bending down over the fallen steed and began applying, similar to those she had just received, touches of the gentlest nature to hopefully lessen his ills. Jimmy watched helplessly from behind as he tried to think up a way to outsmart the situation. He was upset and nervous, and he reached into his pocket to retrieve the baggie. Without a word of conversation to even try to inveigle her to smoke another one, Jimmy proceeded. He took another roll from the commodity bag and fired it up. After taking three hits himself, he passed the burning bud to her, which she dutifully took and readily smoked. The sight of her compliance sent shivers of renewed hope into Jimmy's lion-sized loins. As the two less-than-innocent bystanders kept the faith as it were by camouflaging their degrees of guilt behind a vapor of pot and ash, Jimmy sought to advance his real cause further by attempting to temporarily relieve the horse of its misery by inducing it to partake of the ritual. When he was back in possession of the mind-numbing and therefore pain-numbing substance, he readily fitted the lit portion into his holed mouth and blew out, shotgun style, a steady stream of smoke into the horse's nostrils. The horse, subjugated by his injury, did not retaliate. Soon the horse was hooked. Another joint later, the horse was in a stupor comparable to having been injected with PCP, a powerful animal tranquilizer. Now Jimmy was ready.

Having put the horse temporarily out of its misery and having put his one-night mistress into a stated high, Jimmy sought out a refuge where he could best relieve himself of his pent-up, animal-like frustrations. He lured his sweet-nothing into one of the adjacent animal stalls—one which was empty—and proceeded to cope with his needs. Without ceremony or performance, Jimmy exacted himself on his female as though they too were barn creatures, and doing it in a stall was a perfunctory act of copulation without love, care, or concern. Jimmy tore at her excitedly until every article of her clothing, that which separated her outwardly from the animals, was shed upon the freshly strawed floor. He groped at her flesh voraciously, letting his instincts go wild, and assumed upon her with every fervent touch and feel, his complete dominance over her. She was his, and he would have her.

From outside the occupied stall, the other animals too became quite aroused at the tryst that was taking place. They, although of a dumber lot, recognized the familiar grunts and groans emitting from the stall's interior as sounds of excitement and became agitated by it. When the couple climaxed, the donkeys went into a bit of a frenzy, kicking their hooves against the stall walls and shrieking. Then it was over. Jimmy had taken her in a way not unlike that used by the donkeys. Depleted, the couple collapsed, sending both their bodies crashing onto the thick bed of straw.

What took place inside the shanty while Jimmy was having his fun and adventure was the complete antithesis of how the barn couple behaved when deciding to venture into the adult world of expressive love. They took their time, making the most of every sensation. Words could not describe the savoring, the completeness of every moment, of every feeling as they fondled their way into adulthood for what was literally an encounter of virgins. After paying only brief attention to the fact that they were not altogether alone, enough to have Pip go over to lock the shanty door from the inside, they presented themselves each to the other at first fully clothed, then in various stages of undress before standing before each other fully naked and fully ready to explore what up until now had been only an illusion.

Amid trembling hands and trembling hearts, Pip exacted his passion for this most beautiful girl in so masterful and complete a manner that it brought tears to both their eyes. Though his inclination due his youthful disposition was to take her quickly, Pip regarded the act as something far more intensely designed than what the final stroke can accomplish. As they lay bare on the bearskin rug while before, during, or after, they regarded the one thing which makes the act so special, the oneness that comes from meeting and completing each other in a manner that makes needing each other the most important thing in the world. Through it all, Pip professed his heartfelt desire, time and time, again to his lover, "I love you."

After what seemed like hours, Jimmy and his stall mate arrived back at the shanty. The door had already been made accessible again, so neither one came back with any suspicions that their virginal friends had dared to attempt any sort of the same activity that they had recently participated in. But suspicion arose on the other side in that Pip was almost certain that, given the duration of Jimmy's disappearance, it could not have been anything good that he could have been up to. A faint odor of smoke too resided on

Jimmy's clothing, which Pip immediately detected but declined from making any insinuations about given the circumstance that if that's all he had been doing, then at least it would not lead to their undoing.

But that situational assumption did in no way summarize things in the way they eventually played out. Two days later, someone reported on the fact that Oreo, the handsome white stallion, was refusing to leave his stall and, as far as the amateur observer could determine, was injured in his one front leg. Pip was among the cast of onlookers when the veterinary doctor was called out to investigate.

"He's healthy as a horse," the doctor said in a jocular voice after his initial examination was completed. "Except for that leg there," he added with a frown. "I'll have to take x-rays to be sure, but I believe we have some kind of a fracture along the joint. Looks like this horse took a mighty big spill of some kind."

The looks all around landed on Pip who flung them off by reminding everybody that the health and welfare of the barn animals was the specific duty of the one Jimmy Cuzze. He would have to be questioned on the matter.

Reluctant to admit what he was responsible for, Jimmy led the others on something of a wild-goose chase by pretending that his guess would be as good as theirs in regards to what really happened to the horse. But Mr. Boddinger would have none of it. He was angered by the fact that the pending medical attention and treatment would add up to potentially thousands of dollars, and someone would have to be made to be responsible. And even if no one had taken the horse out for a foolish ride, on the day after the light snow perhaps, it could still be considered an act of neglect should the horse have escaped the barn and ventured out on his own. And since Jimmy was responsible for the adequate care of the animals, he would have to bear the responsibility for the accident. And he did. Jimmy was suspended. By the fact that he didn't put up much of a fuss, Pip correctly deduced that he was somehow directly responsible for what had happened. Oreo, though, was never the same. His leg never completely healed, and he spent the rest of his life as a conversation piece in that people would wonder and ask what had happened to him.

The storytelling stalled at this point as Mr. Faehner's vivid recall of the once vibrant horse caused him to feel the contrasting sorrow of the from-that-day-forward again, which lasted, unfortunately for him and the magnificent steed, many long years before he lied down in the field of eternal rest. Mr. Faehner appeared like a clam opening up his shell, allowing all that was currently connected to his life into his open-and-close reality once more. The reporter, though far more interested in things other than the plight of Oreo, thought it prudent to ask at least one question about the unfortunate creature before passing over to other more interesting topics as depicted in the tale.

"You seem to have a great deal of compunction for the horse. Tell me, were you the only one? Did your boss ever shell out the money to fix him up properly?"

"I don't recall whether or not I mentioned it before, but Oreo was technically not a Silver Mine horse. We were his handlers. He, along with the other horse, were the exclusive property of Mr. Boddinger's daughter. She lived only a few miles away but didn't have enough barn or space for them to live the life she intended. Though they were purchased for her by her dad long before she was old enough to move out of the estate, they were supposed to leave the mine when she was able to take care of them elsewhere. That never happened. Too bad too, or that tragedy would have never taken place. That horse wouldn't have spent half his life wishing he were dead. But anyway, back to your question. I believe, judging from just how seldom seen the little Ms. Boddinger was, that she lost interest in the horses early on. Who knew why. And as far as her old man went, he looked at things through green-colored eyes. Having the horse around at little cost was no big deal. The tourists liked him. But having to expend hundreds, potentially thousands of dollars on him just to get him back to being a horse that the tourists could look at, was something altogether different. The value of that horse plummeted when he became such a huge liability. And I'm sure Boddinger would never seek to force his only daughter to come up with the loot to help."

"Why not make Jimmy come up with the cash? After all, he was the one being held responsible for the horse's condition?"

"It's not that simple. Remember, at the time, Jimmy was a minor, which meant he could not legally be held responsible for anything. The business had to assume any and all responsibility for anything he did. And another thing. There was simply no way to prove that he ever really did it. He never admitted it. The girl he was with that night never admitted it. And no one else, except for the horse, was privy to what happened. And unless the horse was of course the famous Mr. Ed, there was no way to ever get anything out of him."

Mr. Faehner gave the reporter the beaded-eye stare in the hope that he had gotten the joke about the talking horse from the situation comedy, but probably due to his young age and lack of interest in watching late-night old-show TV, the joke never got him. Rather than explain the detail of it, Mr. Faehner dropped it. The reporter, however, focused on another aspect of the explanation as to who knew what about the incident and in response to that he did what reporters do best and examined yet another possibility of the contention he had heard.

"What about the girl you were with that night? Surely, she must have heard something of the story from her friend after that night. Did you ever hear from her? Did you ever seek her out to find out what you could from her? Or was she just—and forgive me for saying this—a one-night stand?"

Mr. Faehner's response dumbfounded the reporter. Hearing what he had to say in regard for the other female present that night put him in a state of consternation as to why such a relevance had been previously placed on the aspect of the white horse when such a revelation was waiting to be conveyed and might not have been had not the adequate question about the girl in relation to the horse been asked.

"What happened between her and me that night was magical. Neither of us ever forgot it. Years went by without seeing each other. What we did, we did far too early in our lives. Had it come just a little later, it would have been the one thing that led to another, and we would have stayed together then. As it was, there was a long-enduring wait while each of us grew up. But the memory of that night never left us, and the day came many, many years later when we rekindled our love. And since that time, she has never left me. Connie is my wife!"

The reporter was shocked, so much so, that he dropped both pen and notepad onto the floor in front of him. He retrieved it, then righted himself back into the chair to await, yes, another validating statement about such a thing that sounded like it belonged in a fairy tale.

"Yes, it's true," Mr. Faehner confirmed proudly. "She came back to me after what seemed a lifetime. And it made me think. Those two young lovers who shared such a profound experience grew up to be the exact same people they were that night. The essence of who they were never changed, never faltered, never failed. A murmur was created in their hearts that could never be extinguished, and the love that once was, was once again."

"I think you got a little past me there," the reporter contended.

"It's this," Mr. Faehner continued. "Connie coming back to me after all those years proved something to me about people. People never change. Not in the sense of the core person they are. From their earliest years, through their adolescence, up to their young adulthood, and throughout the remainder of their lives, they remain who they were when they were at any time before in their lives. Connie came back to me because in being true to herself she realized that we were meant to be together. And I found in her the exact same person whom I loved so dearly during that all too brief dalliance one night long ago.

"And it's true about all people too, although you're probably not old enough to recognize it yet in the people you know. But as for me, I've seen it a thousand times already. Take Jimmy Cuzze, for example. The crux of his character in the story was his innate live-for-the-moment style of living. He carried it with him all the way through his life. He was reprimanded for it time and time again at the mine, which, by the way, he was finally let go of for attempting to grow marijuana plants along a secluded hollow ridge, and later in life, as his transgressions grew from the trivial to the more odious, the repercussions did too. He finally met his untimely, ultimate demise at age thirty. He was killed by his fiancée's friend down in New Orleans, but that's another story. And the moral of the story is that you can learn to count on those around you based on what you already know about them, even if what you know pertains to some dalliance you had with them way back when you were young. If you met a damaging person, then you'd meet a damaging person now. If you met an encouraging person, then you'd meet an encouraging person now. Stand by this belief, and it will help you in your estimations of how people will affect your life."

Selling Silver

At that moment, an interruptive ringing of the desk phone ensued. Mr. Faehner paused until the third ring to consider whether or not he wanted to answer. He tried to interpret by the day, the time, and what pending affairs he had involvement with, who it was, or what the matter was about. But he could not. Only by making the connection could he come to a conclusion about a call, so unexpected, coming at a time when a prearranged festivity was taking place and all or at least most of the people he did business with were within close enough proximity to him that they could, if they desired, seek out his person. Those who had been instructed to make contact with him over the course of the afternoon should something so serious as to require his immediate attention—at this point in his thought he was reminded of the reporter, the very reason he was where he was—had been instructed to make his contact by the use of his private cell phone, which was currently resting in a pouch clipped onto his pant's belt.

Whoever it was and whatever it was about, it would be no perfunctory matter. He decided to pick up. The conversation was lasting. Several times, Mr. Faehner looked up from the receiver and signaled to the reporter that he expected the discussion to last only another minute. By the seventh index finger up, the reporter slouched back into his Italian cane chair and began perusing his earlier notes, making annotations, altering words, and embellishing meanings of the exiguous material he had previously put together.

He did however pay what attention he could to the interesting discussion taking place in front of him, though he could only interpret for himself what the person on the other end of the line was saying.

Thinking that it may have some level of either related or unrelated importance attached to it, the reporter considered it wise to then turn to a clean, clear page of his notepad and began issuing down words and phrases from his end of the conversation as they caught his attention. The first words to arouse his curiosity were, curiously enough, the introductory words. Whoever was speaking to the esteemed billionaire did not seem to know who exactly he was and had to be told, yet this was the person, a man by all accounts, who had placed the unexpected call to Mr. Faehner's private office phone. How then could he not know to whom he was speaking? Part of it went like this: "Hey, I was not that much of a smartie. Was I? Although I wish I could have seen myself, the way I acted back then. I'm all too sure it was worthy of the silver screen. So despite all that, that spilt milk, you are willing to hear my proposal, and you can without a doubt do something for me . . . What's that? You're, you're eighty-three now, wow!"

When the ambiguous call ended, the reporter was relieved to find out that he was about to be filled in, in relation to it.

"Sorry about the delay. He's an old man, someone I actually did business with when I was very young. He's hard of hearing now, and I didn't want to be impolite by rushing him off the phone. After all, I was the one who initiated our contact. He was just responding to a personal letter I wrote several days ago. I wrote it on a whim really, never really expecting him to reply. Heck, I didn't even know if he was still alive yet, let alone still involved in the business. I looked him up in the phone directory. But you know, sometimes names and numbers are kept current in directories for a while after someone's deceased for matters of keeping the pertinent documents coming."

"What sort of business is the gentleman in?" the reporter questioned plainly.

"His name is Mr. Goigle. I don't believe I ever knew his first name. And his business as it is, is selling silver!"

"Certainly, he's involved in the one thing that really rocks your world then," the reporter stated assuredly.

"Certainly so," Mr. Faehner concurred. "Old man Goigle is a businessman from way, way back. Even before I had any interest in it. He's been in the business, let's see now, more than fifty years as far as I can determine. He's the best in the business. And whenever you do business, always stick to the best, the experts. That way, you'll never be led astray. This guy has a fetish for the shiny stuff. But he doesn't mine it. He only deals in it, you know, buying, selling, trading, sometimes hoarding it by the tons just so he can unload it in little bits and pieces when the marketplace price has reached a premium. He helps manipulate it."

"What do you need him for?" the reported asked bluntly. "I mean, certainly by now, you have the power to overlook someone like him for whatever he can do for you."

"It's not about power. He's not my enemy. Although at one point in my life you could certainly say he vied hard to become a part of my everlasting sanctuary of faces I have depicted on my illustrious wall there. But once the riddle that developed between us was answered, it came to my attention that my uncle, not old man Goigle, was responsible for the problem. So anyway, I kind of left him off the hook. You know, I didn't burn every bridge I left behind in life. As a matter-of-fact, if I think about it I believe I had ongoing relationships with every one of them, that is, if they wanted one. That's one thing you have to come to terms with in life—people get mad at one another from time to time. And it's no reason to go around abrogating relationships just because they faced you down. Remember that."

"So what is it, precisely, that you want this Mr. Goigle to do for you?"

To answer back precisely as the reporter so pointedly worded his inquiry would mean to jeopardize a matter of great privacy for now, and importance, so to respond, Mr. Faehner deferred the matter to a realm of indifference and with some difficulty said, "I'm . . . I'm . . . expecting to blow out some of the rock up by one of the electrical pylons. I'm expanding the back road there to have easier access to the above-hollow ridge, and I think I may blast into some silver. Near the pylon is an area where silver rock has been picked out from the exposed layers of phyllite and quartz. So in case I find myself buried in specimens, I would just as soon be alleviated of the burden of cracking open potentially hundreds of pieces of rock and silver to make a few bucks. So I thought it best to be done with the whole enterprise in one enactment. That way, I'll be happy and so will Mr. Goigle."

The lie, as it were, sufficed to quell any suspicions the reporter may have had that there was more to the story than that. And before he could ask anything further, Mr. Faehner began to soliloquize about his past dealings with Mr. Goigle so as to prevent any further solicitations, which would force him to tell more lies—something the esteemed entrepreneur disliked doing.

"Back in those days, my uncle was quite the entrepreneur himself. He was the most ambitious person I knew. Besides running the rock shop, of which I was an integral part, Rick often busied himself or, rather, us at supplying wholesalers like Mr. Goigle with mostly second-rate rocks and minerals for them to do with as they pleased. Rick's intricate knowledge of the outlying geology of any area within a day's drive of home made him the go-to guy when it came to finding localities to extricate bulk material from. And my, oh my, did he know it. He controlled the specific localities like they were special preserves in which only he had the authority to go in and out of. He confided in no one. I learned about them only because I bore the same last name, of that I'm sure. If I had been anybody else working in the rock shop, regardless of my special talents and abilities, I can tell you assuredly, I would not have been allowed to venture into those places, private oases, where the only entrance pass possible was a Ph.D. with the name Richard Faehner on it.

"I never forgot any. There was the goethite field just outside of the tiny village of Silver Spring directly west of Lancaster. There you can find huge oxidized pyrite crystals lying scattered in the topsoil, loose after heavy rains or if a field was plowed. Not all of them are big. They come in all sizes and are colored every shade of brown. I don't know who it was we supplied them to, and I don't know what he did with them. Then there was the secret stream in Strasburg where you could find amethyst crystals. Can you imagine that? Gem stones right here in good old Lancaster County. I can't blame Rick for keeping that place under wraps. If the word of it ever got out, every rock hound and lapidary enthusiast in a hundred miles would have come to seek out those precious purple peaks. But Rick was careful not to disclose the locations of any of his private reserves. Sometimes he intentionally misdirected some of the harder-nosed jobbers who tried and tried to get him to admit where some of the more valuable material was coming from, but Rick eluded them by telling them lies. He would give them an alternate location. For example, if he collected blue quartz from some secret location in, let's say, Perry County, he would provide the inquisitor with another valid locality. Let's say, in Juniata County where they could then, if they desired, go and explore for more. Because the alternate localities were always ones, which did bear the same rock, mineral, or crystal, the persistent fool would be satiated without ever knowing where the real specimens came from.

"One of the most sought-after places was the Cedar Hill Quarry close to the Mason-Dixon line. It was a veritable treasure-trove of serpentine-based rock and minerals. Rick researched that quarry for years and even wrote his dissertation on the quarry's geologic history and composition. He even discovered a new mineral there. There were two variations of it. They were deemed "blue one" and "blue two." To prove that they were truly a new mineral species, Rick had to synthesize them, grow them from crystals in a laboratory by placing and organizing their constituent compounds in a foundation of chemicals, solutions, pressures, and temperatures in a timed culture. Then, if all went well, you'd have a new mineral to add to the world of known minerals. Rick worked hard at it too. He used the research facility at his alma mater, Penn State, to conduct the experiment. I went with him on one occasion too on a day when he had time to check in on the progress of the growth process. In the months following the completion of his research and development, he prepared a scientific paper on his discovery, ready to reveal his new mineral. He was going to name it after himself, call it Faehnerite. But then something inconceivable occurred. Much to Rick's complete and utter chagrin, he caught wind of a publication recently put out in the geological community about the discovery and successful synthesis of an identical new mineral found and worked on in Japan. For the longest time afterward, Rick's anger over the catastrophe was irreconcilable. I was extremely disappointed too because it was such an exciting thing to be involved in. My last name too would have been borne by the new blue mineral.

"Anyhow, back from being sidetracked, I meant to tell you about the real relevance of the quarry in relation to Mr. Goigle. He was interested in the talc found in deposits all over there. Talc is known as soapstone to those not closely associated with the earth sciences. On the Mohs scale, it's listed with a hardness of one, which means it can be quite easily shaped, carved, sculpted, smoothed, and buffed into objects of art and craft. People make pipes, jewelry, figurines, and miniature statues from it that they then sell in shops and at rock and mineral shows. Talc is abundant and cheap. And it's of little or no use to the quarries. It's too soft to use as roadbed material, so it's mostly cast aside when large deposits are broken into. But it's perfect for geology professors with both the aptitude and appetite for making money.

"Rick had special privileges in Cedar Hill Quarry. His erudition of the quarry's formation gave him insight into the distinctive layering of the serpentine, particularly, where specifically to blast for the harder material, where to blast for the picrolites, another serpentine-based mineral having other commercial values, and how to avoid delving into the deeper pockets of asbestos, which the quarry was not equipped to deal with given its scarcity within the quarry deposits and its problem as a potent irritant toward the workmen whenever they did blast into a formation of it. Simply put, it was Richard Faehner, and no other, allowed the prestigious position of facilitating the quarry on days off, which meant that he, and no other, was privileged to come, collect, and carry off what he could any Sunday of the year without receiving ongoing permission. And Rick took advantage of it too. Often, we would pack up the van with sledges, pry bars, and burlap sacks and make the fifty-five-minute drive to get there and spend the two to three hours breaking and bagging rocks.

"The serpentine we used for the Pennsylvania mineral box. The picrolite was used on individual-sized cards and sold to the Franklin Institute and the Academy of Natural Sciences. Rick only collected the dark blue-green specimens of it. But the talc or soapstone was collected just as randomly as it was found. And each day we went, we brought back bulk bags by the ton.

"It was through these soapstone dealings that I became associated with Mr. Goigle. We would supply him several thousand pounds of the soft rock per month in the good-collecting months, and Rick would receive several hundred dollars of relatively free money for both his and my efforts. I was given only the per-hour pay for the collecting trip as if I had been back at the rock shop cracking rocks. My pay at the time, I believe, was only about $1.65 per hour. So you see, a five-hour day would only get me a measly $8.25. Sometimes Rick would stop at the Freeze and Frizz on the way home, and we'd buy ice cream, that was my bonus. Looking back, it's hard to believe anyone, including me, would ever have worked for such a low pay, but I was just getting started, and so I was easy on myself for putting up with it. I have to admit though, I did enjoy the job, and it did start the ball rolling toward a lifetime of nature-specific dictums. Where would I have gone without it?

"So I took a chance. Once I became ensconced at the mine, I took it upon myself to do a little wheeling and dealing with the prodigious-minded Mr. Goigle. I approached him in person at his little shop out on the old

Lincoln Highway. I took the bus. I told him that if he was interested in getting his hands on bulk silver from the mine, I was interested in providing it for him. He was, of course, totally surprised by the whole thing, I mean, with me being just a boy as I was, coming to him, a man of the world as he was and attempting to talk him into having a businesslike association. But I stood by who I was and what I was trying to do when at first he reacted in a stand-offish manner. I remember it so clearly. In a composed manner, I countered his adverse reaction by giving him my credentials as they related to the Silver Mine—that I had already been an associate there for nearly two years and that there was no one else in the whole wide world who could offer him a deal anything like what I was proposing.

"After what I considered a mediocre attempt to unnerve me, perhaps to see if what I was proposing was true, he relented and began asking questions pertinent to the business end of the situation. Looking at me, standing only half his height, I'm sure he wondered wholly whether or not I had the wherewithal to pull off what I was intending, but I think as we spoke my confidence, and my competence came shining through as they usually did in all things Silver Mine related. There was of course one thing I was somewhat concerned about, and that was getting away with it—from the perspective that I was taking this up by my own initiative. I was giving myself the authority to appropriate samples of silver from the private property where I worked without revealing to anyone else what I was doing, without permission. It was a gamble. On paper, it looked like an impropriety, but I rationalized it by reason of example. There was no standing order not to do it. The tourists who came were allowed to take away as much as they could find as long as they paid the simple fee of $10 per day to hunt through the remaining piles of rock strewn across the hollow hill. And I had always been allowed to collect what I wanted, either to fill the display cases in the shanty or to sell alongside it on the counter marked "For Sale". Basically, I had always been able to do as I pleased without any restrictions. So, as long as the status quo remained that of a finders-keepers type of environment, I felt somewhat free to do as I pleased too.

"I knew I had old man Goigle by the balls, however, when it came time to begin negotiations on the prices of the silver. His tentative style suddenly changed to that of a highfalutin businessman. His true expressions were revealed—that he was, the entire time, salivating at the mouth at the thought of being involved in such a potentially lucrative venture. He became effectively like the bridge troll who threatened the Three Billy Goats Gruff when they tried to cross his bridge without paying the toll. Having gone off on a tangent about it suddenly made the usually didactic Mr. Faehner feel somewhat silly, especially when he noticed that his listening partner's expression was one of bewilderment over the symbolic analogy."

"You, you've never heard of the story," he said with a lowering tone which indicated he too conceded that the influence of the tale, and indeed the tale itself was something hardly heard of any more. Thinking to himself, he responded aloud, "I . . . I . . . can't truly recall whether that was one of Aesop's fables or one of Hans Christian Anderson's tales. Possibly neither. Now that goes to show you that even I'm not so keen any more about the subject either. You know, I don't believe most children read nursery rhymes any more."

The reporter never responded except to indicate by his remote indifference that he knew nothing of the once-popular fairy tale. Mr. Faehner felt it too. The difference that had been their experience, his an inclination to hold onto a memory so dim and the young person seated before him without memory at all. It was a profound moment. Here was the exact proof upon when in time one generation's last influence regarding a slice of their popular culture finally slips away. It happens to everything eventually. There's hardly a book, a song, a poem, a story, which survives successive generations. Most of them die out when the last person left alive who experienced them dies. Happily ever after does not mean forever as we like to think it does.

Mr. Faehner shook his head as a way of clearing out all the esoteric thought. He would take up the matter another time. "Anyway," he began again. "Back to the story. As I was saying, when it came time to begin discussing the financial aspect of the matter, old man Goigle turned into a snapping turtle, no analogy intended. We haggled prices for a while as he conducted the routine business in his shop. Between the occasional phone call and the occasional customer, we slowly came to terms about the worth of everything related. But I knew I had the upper hand. Simply put, he had no silver, and no other way to get it except from me. And as we both knew that soapstone was soapstone, we also knew that silver was something else altogether. He would be exclusive! Nowhere else was anybody else able to get hold of the precious metal, put it on display, and proudly get a price for it, the Silver Mine excepted. By the time we were done, both of us were content with what we expected.

"In only two short weeks, my part of the negotiation had come to fruition. And the extra time and effort I exacted to meet my terms really was not a lot. It was during the approach of the slow time of the year when fall slides into winter and the number of visitors begin to dwindle that I found for myself plenty of free time to go scavenging through the talus piles left long ago by the turn-of-the-last-century miners. Tourists pick through them all the time, but only a few are smart enough to realize that these rocks have to be opened up if you hope to find any silver in them. And I never told. They were of the mind that if there was silver present than the silver would present itself. What a fallacy! So in every pile of thousands of rocks, I knew I would come up with a decent amount of sellable silver. And boy did I ever!

"Every day, I accumulated more and more until finally I realized I had nothing to convey them in, and I immediately appropriated a few empty Coca-Cola crates from a local mom and pop grocery up the street from where I lived, and I was in the business! The first tally was an exceptional haul, and there was so much good stuff that I paused to look at it before deciding that a deal was a deal, and I had to keep up my end of the bargain though several of the really exceptional pieces I put away for myself to add to my collection at home, a collection I might add, I still have as my own.

"One late evening after everyone else of consequence had departed for the day, I took out my hidden stash of shiny ore and laid it on top of the display case in the shanty. There I tallied up the value, in terms of what Mr. Goigle had promised to pay, of the priceless pieces. The agreement we had come to was intact and measured the amount of the per-piece payment by the size of the piece itself. They were categorized, by the size of the piece as compared to the size of an average man's fist. Half-a-fist-sized pieces he would pay $2.50 for regardless of how much silver was streaked across the rock's surfaces. The rate for a full fist-sized piece was double that. Any pieces bigger, regardless of how much bigger, would be worth another times as much. That meant $2.50 for small, $5.00 for medium, and $7.50 for the large. Not too bad for something I could procure in my spare time and while being paid!

"The transfer of goods for money had to be conducted strictly off-property. This was a clandestine operation to be sure and had to be done without anybody else finding out about it. Because of that I determined it was better to conduct these secretly performed transactions as few as possible within a given period of calendar space. Two weeks, I decided was the best interval of time in which to gather an appropriate amount of silver and issue it to Mr. Goigle's store. The two-week interlude seemed the perfect space of time and circumstance to allow me to find and facilitate a worthwhile volume of the valuable raw material.

"The arrangements I made were for every other Friday evening after school, after homework, and after dinner. Nobody would miss me once these three major things had been attended to and my declining involvement in anything beyond them wouldn't matter nor wouldn't seem suspicious due to the seldomness of my intended extensions toward other matters. Transportation was the hard part. Though I had recently turned sixteen, I had no license or car. I would have to rely on someone else. And it would have to be a someone else who would comply with my requests without giving a heck about what it was I was really up to. But I had the perfect candidate, Dave. He was sixteen also, but already a driver of distinction. He was fortunate in that, though he did have one older brother, John, Dave lived with the royalties often afforded to that of an only child. John was eleven years Dave's elder and as such had long since established his independence from the household. To top that off, Dave's grandfather, John, resided with Dave and his dad. This dual effect served to double Dave's leisurely lifestyle. He had money and privilege coming in from all directions. In the transportation department, this meant that Dave had reliable access to three different vehicles. And believe me, he indulged himself in the bosom of his family like no other person I have ever since known. He had, at his immediate disposal, a 1974 Vista Cruiser belonging to his mom; a 1975 Oldsmobile; and his prized mode of vehicular travel, his dad's cherry-red 1975 Chevy pickup. The variety allowed Dave to pick a vehicle in accordance to his mood, and it was a real treat to be escorted around in any of the three.

"Dave liked to drive and probably would have provided me with ongoing methods of transportation based solely on that, but I knew him as a fellow who could be easily distracted and therefore might abruptly abandon me on one of my planned excursions, so I had to sweeten the pot so that we would be in harmony about my expectations of his services. Dave would have to be cut into the deal, at least from a financial perspective. My offer, he accepted without reserve when I first approached him about it. Initially, he declined as I somewhat expected because I understood that he was only thinking about the here and now and not the future. I refused to accept his no-compensation and what-are-friends-for argument, knowing fully and surely that the day would come when he might have felt slighted or just simply he had something better to do. I proffered to him the sum of $20 an outing, plus a contribution to his gas tank. And in addition to that, I told him we would stop in any convenience store along the way where we could purchase any assortment of soda and snacks as we desired—my treat. All in all, it was a sweet deal, and Dave was no fool when it came to taking advantage of things offered him. In fact, he was an expert and could have written a book about the subject.

"So we had our deal—Dave and I—Goigle and I. And things went smoothly. My first take netted me a whopping total of $260! Wow! That was as much money as I made for working six weeks in the rock shop and about four weeks working at the mine. Plus, I didn't have to pay taxes. I remember I had totaled up the value of the transaction prior to arriving at Mr. Goigle's shop wanting to impress him that I was all business-minded, like him when it came to actuating a business affair. There were thirty-seven specimens. Wait here a minute! I still have the original slip!"

Mr. Faehner, tickled by the fact that he did indeed have in his possession the original slip of notebook paper in which he had totaled up the intended sale of first-sold silver, got up, and moved briskly from his chair to a distant two-drawer file cabinet across the broad room. He rifled in its drawers fluttering folders until he happened upon an age-old file fixed way in the back of the top-tier drawer. He opened it, glanced briefly at it, then returned to the desk and seated himself as before.

"Here," he said in a self-satisfied tone. "Look."

The reporter took a look at the forlorn document handed him with its tattered edges and yellow-stained appearance and wrinkled texture and evidenced the facts he had listened to while Mr. Faehner picked up his oratory. "The situation as it stood was a win-win-win one, a veritable three-way tie for first-place finish. Each of us got out of it as much or more than we conceived. Everyone was happy.

"Then something happened. It had been only two short months since the inception of the business dealings with Mr. Goigle when suddenly, and without the slightest inclination, things went spinning into a downward spiral. It had nothing to do with me or Dave. It had nothing to do with the silver, its content or delivery. It happened one evening after we had just completed our fourth transaction. Mr. Goigle, noticeably upset, informed me that for the time being, he could no longer take any more silver. I was dumbfounded. I paused as I awaited him to explain what it was that changed the mutually satisfactory situation, but he proffered none. Then I prodded him about it in such a way as to indicate that I might not leave without hearing some kind of reason for the changed relation. I followed him around in the shop from place to place inveigling him with all the why's and wherefore's of our pact, but he consistently attempted to avoid interaction with me. Finally, Dave, who had been patiently waiting for me outside the shop, entered and called upon me to hurry it up. Again, this time in Dave's presence, I asked Mr. Goigle as to why he decided to abrogate out agreement. Noticing Dave, his size and stature, and realizing there were two of us now, Mr. Goigle relented at least enough to purport a lie just to get rid of us. He stood up straight from behind a counter and stated that the changed condition was due to something unintended. It was simply a matter of supply and demand. One of his main bulk buyers for the silver had taken ill and could no longer accept the responsibilities involved in purchasing and receiving more of the ore until he was well.

"I didn't believe him, and I told him so to his face before departing with Dave. Out in the truck, I pondered the whole situation further. There was no topical answer for it I knew. And I knew that it would take a powerful amount of creative insight to figure things out. There was no one to call who might elucidate Mr. Goigle's true intentions. From the beginning, it had been just the two of us, him and me. And I was no mind reader. But what I did have was an uncanny sense of figuring people out when they were up to no good. And I used it as best I could to try to break the seal on old man Goigle's secret.

"I began an internal discussion with myself, thinking better than to bring Dave into the heart of the matter. To him, I simply said that we had just had a little tiff over prices, which was true in the greater sense that there would be no more—prices offered or prices paid. I began to speculate. The very first thing that came to my mind was the possibility that the old man was beginning to get greedy over the matter. He had been selling the silver pieces like they were pieces of candy. Nobody stops buying M&M's or Reeses Peanut Butter Cups once they've acquired a taste for them. And nobody would stop buying silver from a supplier who sold it at a good price right after they had just gained access to it. Nobody! It made perfect sense to assume such a thing. This was probably his way of letting me know, in no uncertain terms, that the standing agreement would no longer suffice if we were to continue doing business. I tested this theory by placing a call to his shop some short time later pretending to be some local rock and mineral enthusiast who had heard recently that specimens of silver ore could be obtained at some obscure shop out the Lincoln Highway. I didn't even admit to knowing the name of it. I told him I checked out the yellow pages and came up with the only shop on the eastern highway, which seemed to have anything to do with the commercial trading of things related. I made it seem quite inadvertent. My voice I disguised by holding a chocolate chip cookie in my mouth, which made my words sway and kept me from using my more adept language skills, which I have a hard time not using in instances where I feel like letting someone have it.

"But the result of the inquiry offered no real solace up until the very last statement made by the propitious proprietor. He claimed, after an ongoing appeal, that he might be coming into more of the ore sometime soon. It sounded evasive, but I wanted to put the matter to further testing. Days later, I called again, this time camouflaging my identifying voice by pinching my nose slightly with a clothespin. I introduced myself as someone else I knew and asked about the silver that I had been hearing about. He offered the same response as before saying that maybe he might be able to get a hold of more. I wasn't about to let go. A third time I called, and this time I even told him I knew me, had met me through a mutual friend, and I had directed him to the shop as a way of acquiring pieces of the precious rock. Goigle seemed assured. He was more confident than before that he would be coming into some soon. The third time was the charm. The reference I had made about knowing me paid off. It loosened Goigle's tongue, and he went off on a tangent about how he expected to have the best pieces at the best prices yet. He then made the biggest mistake of his life. He mentioned my uncle. He said that if I knew young Pip Faehner, then I would probably be interested in hearing that the silver that he was speaking about was to come from none other than the highly reputed Dr. Richard Faehner and that I could trust him implicitly to bring forth as he always did the highest quality items ever seen.

"For a moment, I felt disturbed, like some part of me had been rubbed away, like a butterfly's wings after having been pinched by a curious child who captures it momentarily to admire it, then lets go.

"Then, the butterfly is left with a little less fluff, a little less charm, a little less dignity. My uncle had been implicated. My imagination was let go to wonder how it had all transpired.

"Not for a moment would Goigle divulge his tedious relationship with my esteemed uncle. They had after all been tied to a reciprocal, though uproarious, association which had endured beyond a decade. Down through the tedium, Rick, above everybody else, had come through time and time again for the hard-nosed entrepreneur. First, it had been the rock crystal, which Rick had had permission to dig up near a research facility outside Carlisle. The natural crystals, once used in experimentation, had become obsolete once artificial crystals were being produced on site. Rick, due the prestige of his profession, asked for and received the OK to collect a few of the thrown-away, gem-quality stones for his own. With permission, he collected crystals by the ton and over the course of several years sold them for a ton of money. This Rick had told me about. Next came the Swatara Gap fossils. Back in the day, the exposed-shale fossil site was a veritable treasure-trove for collecting some of the earliest known trilobites, starfish, and other marine arthropods. My favorite was Orthocerous, a bottom-dwelling cephalopod, which had a long segmented tail. Cryptolithus, yes, that's the name. I was thinking about it since the subject came up. That was the name of the site's most popular trilobite. They were tiny in size compared to other species but intriguing nonetheless. We found hundreds of them. I kept a few. Here, let me show you." Again Mr. Faehner leapt up off his chair as if he had been jolted by a bolt of electricity. He felt the same, and it elucidated a memory of long ago when he had been challenged to a duel as it was of electric chairs, which were once a part of the event attractions of entertainment offered by the Youth for Christ organization during their highlighted Scream in the Dark, Halloween, events. This time though, the Faehner in the memory now knew what it was like to be shocked, at least in theory.

Once up, Mr. Faehner moved to another faraway cabinet, opened drawers and sorted through the collected contents of each until the reporter heard the scoring "voila!" From what appeared to be an old-styled watch or jewelry box, a white exterior with a thin trail of gold-laced trim around the edges, the proud bearer extrapolated from its interior, bedded down on a billowy bed of cotton, a quarter-sized piece of gray shale. Near its center was the remnant, still complete, of the famous Ordivician trilobite he had just laid claim to, Cryptolithus!

"Here it is," he announced proudly, then showed it, while boxed, to the captivated reporter. "See," he continued, "it pays not to arbitrarily throw away old possessions. You never know when they might come in handy. You might not have believed me if it were not for this little guy. Look at it. Isn't it a beauty? This was one of the ones I deliberately pocketed while excavating the site with Rick. God knows that if I had not, Rick would probably have persuaded me to give it to him for him to keep, no doubt. But you see it pays to think of yourself too. And I for one was a person who did."

The memories that had opened up for him did much to soothe his soul. The electric chairs experience, though completely unrelated to the current unraveling story, injected a jolt of humor in him and humor, as we know, comes from the inside and interacts with us at a core level, which does much to alleviate any adverse tendencies we might be experiencing. The adventures made collecting at Swatara Gap gave something else. It reminded him how he had bested Rick another time, another place, when his overbearing uncle would have taken advantage of his then naive look on life. The Cryptolithus was his because he made it his!

With the new source of humor coursing through his demeanor, Mr. Faehner was now capable of facing the discerning truth of how his own relative must have conspired to defeat his silver selling. His temper now tempered, he faced the truth down to its last whim and word. And traced, through indulgent, inspired innuendo, the compact that once came into being by the two men who sought to supplant him. He rendered it as though he were reading pages of a short story and in so doing wanted to capture the style and mood of it as it may have occurred.

"I can imagine it then as it was just as I have a thousand times in my days and a thousand times more in my nights when dreams take over and our minds make our minds face the realities we sometimes suppress. The esteemed professor walked in arbitrarily to the little, out-of-the-way shop. He did that all the time. He walked into places he fully intentioned to do business with, but he all the time acted as if his presence there was by some misguided act, and all he really came in for was for directions to some place he really needed to get to. I think with his Ph.D. came the ability to make other people think that he was someone whom they were, by chance, lucky enough to find themselves in the immediate presence of.

"I can see how he happened to mention that he had just recently returned from a highly profitable collecting trip down in the county then happened to secure a prodigious amount of rocks and minerals from the heralded and hard-to-get-into Cedar Hill Quarry. And while poking around the hard-to-do-business-with shopkeeper would happen to mention that he wouldn't mind taking a look-see at the haul and would especially be interested in getting his hands on some more of that nice soapstone that he had so appreciably gotten those not-so-many weeks ago. And then they transacted. And somewhere along the way of doing business, Rick just happened to see a select piece or two or more of the standout silver ore just recently come into the shop or being kept as a piece or pieces of personal souvenirs, enough to entice other patrons into questioning whether or not they could acquire some.

"There's no doubt about the fact that Rick's expertise would leave him no doubt about the ore's origin. I can envision him now with his arms all akimbo standing there as if some personal insult had been flung in his distinctive direction. He would have immediately challenged the validity of the circumstance. That the silver mine, a place he had long protected as a private sanctuary, had now been raped! That its virginal hollow hills had now been ravaged and ransacked by some loathsome creature! And the loathsome creature was me! Inwardly, he would testify to this unimaginable circumstance while outwardly he would exhibit a passionate scowl on a terrified face and growl and grumble with every word spoken. I had committed the ultimate sin again! I had excluded him, my mentor, from my purposes, from something indulgent to me, which he and he alone had the credit for bringing into my life. How could I have possibly dared to do such a thing, to perform such an indescribably abhorrent deed?

"And who would be implicated? The shopkeeper was by virtue of the fact that he had hold of the evidence. He had possession. And possession as we know is nine-tenths of the law whether it applies to the vindication or the detriment of the person or persons involved in any given situation. So I can't say that I blame him for giving in to Rick's grievances. How else could he explain away the silver. He knew that Rick knew. He knew that he knew everything there was to know about anything geologically related in the county. If he had even attempted a pretense, a cover-up about me, about the silver, Rick would see past it. And probably end, for all times, his business relationship with him.

"And that was something worth considering. All in all, they had done business for nearly ten years already. And a substantial amount of goods and money had passed between their hands. How could Mr. Goigle deny that? How could Mr. Goigle defy one of the hands that fed him? No, I couldn't blame Goigle for that. Given the weight of that particular circumstance, I probably would have done the very same thing.

"For me, basically it was over. It had lasted only a few scant weeks, and I had garnered only a scant thousand or so dollars, scarcely enough to consider the operation a success. But it was a learning experience. Looking back on it now, I believe I could have, if I wanted to, circumvent the circumstance. I could have put away numerous more cash-sized samples of silver, possibly to wait out the bad vibrations between Goigle and Rick. Because if you think about it, Goigle and I could have continued doing business on the sly, so to speak. He and Rick didn't see each other that much that Rick would have been privy to the ongoing operation if Goigle would have been more secretive about it. Things could have blown over. Or I had the option of seeking out other venues for the ore. I could have. But I waited. And in so doing, all of the negative connotations of what could go wrong began to seep into me. That's what happens when a person with a predicament has all the time in the world to think about it."

Rick's Trick

"Waiting was the hardest part. And the waiting was done under the condition of the worst possible guise—silence. After three attempting phone calls, I stopped calling Mr. Goigle. Our business relationship had hit a dead end. I knew that. And besides Rick, there was no one else who knew anything about what was going on. And he was never going to approach me about the matter. We both knew where we stood when it came to doing our own thing in regards to the silver mine. We had had it out years before when he found out I had begun to go down there on my own without his knowledge. He was really one to hold a grudge, and I knew there would be no point in me initiating a mediation over the matter. But despite this, despite the fact that I knew the matter was over conversationally, at least I did not feel it was over altogether. And I was right!

"While I waited for what I didn't know, I prepared a proper defense. If anyone should point-blank me as to why I did what I did, I would have a reply. And not just a reply but a reasonable response. And more than a reasonable response, a rational explanation about how I could have legally, morally, ethically, sold something that technically didn't belong to me. It was easy. As anybody who knew me knew I was extremely proud of the fact that I had come to the mine before Silver Ford did. I existed in that place before them. And I spouted it off to everyone I could if they so speculated before me about it. It was a question like the chicken and the egg. But this one had

an answer. Which came first, the boy or the silver mine's incorporation? And
the answer is, the boy!

"If asked, I would justify what I did by simply saying that all of the silver I
sold to Mr. Goigle was silver I had uncovered in my earliest expeditions down
to the mine. Who could say otherwise? It had been noted by everyone who
ever went with me that I was enthusiastic about having my own collection.
And it's true that I did. Although my own collection consisted at that time of
only about thirty pieces. I only kept the biggest and the brightest of what I
had ever found. It was enough for me. I thought myself strangely fortunate in
one regard, that is, if I had continued selling silver in the quantities that I had
started selling it in, then my contentions could have been called into question.
As it was the timing of things gone awry was to my benefit. The quantity of
silver rocks that changed hands was below the stage of unbelievability, below
the level of speculation that I was lying to cover my butt. It could have gone
either way in their belief anyway. But I would have won. All the evidence
was in my corner. I could substantiate that I had collected on my own before
Boddinger became owner of the mine. I could have come up with my own
people who could and would corroborate my story. But all the same, I was
left hurt by the experience. I felt like a child who had gotten his hand caught
in the cookie jar by his mother and was awaiting final judgment by his father
who had yet to come home.

"Some months later though, I did run into Mr. Goigle. And when he
turned around and saw me, he instinctively threw off the whole matter by
claiming in an aura of castigating humor that I was too much a minor to be
a miner. Joke.

"Yes, I definitely believed something bad was about to occur. Rick would
tell my father and put into question my character. He might have related
to him how he had lost faith in me, possibly hoping that my father would
rescind my privilege of working at the mine. That plan had a chance too,
considering the way my father was. But that never happened. Rick, as it turned
out, was up to something more. He had come to realize over the years that I
was as stubborn as him. He had no other choice. Since he couldn't stop me,
he would have to top me!

"I would have argued with him if he had given me the chance. The same
argument that I had used before when he first found out that I was visiting
his pristine playground without his permission. And that was that Silver Ford

Incorporated would have come into existence with or without me! If you think about it, that was a very rational explanation for why he should not have been so upset by the whole thing. But Rick was a little mental about things he considered his private affairs. No amount of rationalizing would have worked on him. And now it was worse. Now, not only had I tread on what was as he believed his sanctuary, I had gone further by purposely exploiting that hallowed ground for my own profit, in a way beating him at his own game. I was profiting off of his profession, trying to be Professor Pip.

"For a period of time, nothing happened. I stepped constantly in and out of fear and readiness. I was steeped in consternation. There was no way to know what was going to happen next. If Rick became a tattletale, I would be ready for him. And it would be dealt with on my terms too. I would want to face my accuser, one-on-one, and have it out with him. I would bring out all the pretermitted defects, flaws, and indiscretions, which capitalize him and the way he does things. After all, he is the one who brought me to the mine in the first place, and I'll bet without the direct knowledge or permission of whoever was then the landowner. Let's see him squirm his way out of that. Let's see him wind his way out of his tangle of previous laid down impropriety.

"It was twenty days into December when the culmination of everything being made came to climax. It was a week-ending day when I was jolted out of my coming complacence by a sight I had never deemed possible. The day was abnormal as it was with the temperature out of flux with the season. Contrasting the sixty-degree weather was the remnant of a heavy snow, which had fallen only a few days before. I was at task on an unassigned duty, a mission of mercy. One of the younger donkeys had inadvertently been kicking up in the soft snow and had somehow interrupted the hibernation of a poisonous snake, who though most likely docile at the time of encounter warmed up quickly enough in the bright midday sun to strike out at its instigator. Evidently. I became aware of it by investigating the high-pitched squeals being made by the injured animal and then noticing its awkward movements, always leaning away from the left. God forbid, I leave an injured animal in the field and let something worse happen to it, so I was leading it back to the barn along a briar path when I came into view of the bewildering sight. Lucky for me, I was obscured from plain sight all the way down the barn hill by the thick-growing briars and bushes filling in the landscape everywhere outside the thin-line lane. I had escaped immediate detection.

"After escorting the impaired ungulate to an uninhabited stall and then applying a soothing ointment to its wounded leg, I made for the upper reaches of the barn by playing a real-life game of chutes and ladders. Nearest to me was the corn chute behind the middle stalls, and I shimmied my way up its interior until I could reach up to a ladder that began halfway up it. The ladder's extending part was blocked from use by the chute casing, which was fastened to it near the approach of winter so tons of stored winter corn could be easily accessed. After an adroit climb, I made my way over to the front wall where I attached myself to one of the moveable slats, and I pushed on it, out, and braced it with a catch. From there, I stood and stared hawk-eyed across the territorial span in a state of disbelief, hoping that maybe all I needed was to rub my eyes once, maybe twice, and the impression of what I thought I saw would either disappear or turn out to be something other than what I thought it to be. But my focus proved otherwise. With pinpoint accuracy and blue-sky, sun-shining clarity, the apparition remained just as it had been during my first moment's notice. My mind sought to analogize it, and I conferred with myself to do so. I felt singularly stung by the abhorrent sight as though I had been bitten by a poisonous snake, like the donkey, but my snake's venom having a little more punch. And my snake's strike had the ability to reach me from a much further distance.

"There they were standing next to each other, two entities never meant to be in the same place at the same time. So out of whack. It was like seeing a Stone-Age man and a Bronze-Age man meet for the first time. My uncle was there in his doplic slouch, his stomach a-bulge, all 210 pounds of his body shifting and moving into and out of equilibrium. He wore one of his twenty or so pairs of khaki-colored shirts and trousers—Rick referred to pants as trousers—and was motioning with his free hands to Mr. Boddinger to look off into the distant hills. Mr. Boddinger listened attentively. He was clad in one of his iconic pink shirts, tan pants, his often-worn corn-colored hat with the red midstripe around its rise, and a pair of dark-shaded sunglasses, which when thinking about it looked rather silly considering it was on the cusp of winter.

"At one point during the discussion, Rick stood up, so to speak, out of one of the many slouching positions that had accompanied his many little speeches and many little listenings up until then. He was attuning himself to act out his importance in ways that made him feel like he was more a part of what he was doing. He followed up his erection by firmly clasping both his hands together behind his back, which gave him an air of authority and from that point on would stare straight ahead at whoever it was he was talking to as a way of captivating them. A dual of the minds would ensue, and from that point on, any opposition to his proposals would mean a direct insult to him, his credibility, and his profession as a whole. The situation was becoming overloaded. Whatever happened now would be big. Things would end entirely good or entirely bad, there was no other way with Rick.

"It made me sick standing there knowing what I knew about each of them. I would have liked to run over to them and expose them, one to the other, with the truth about who they really are. My desire to do so swelled the longer I contemplated it. Turn the farce face-to-face into the desired, behind-the-face to behind-the-face. It could have been a meeting like no other! But it was my own indecision that cost me the chance. For not long after Rick had made his move the two self-made men parted company. Whatever covenant had been contrived for their purposes had been sealed. And judging by the way Rick departed, all casual and calm, he had undoubtedly got his way.

"I contemplated what to do. For the time being, I was content to pretend that nothing had happened as it concerned me. One thing was for sure, my old Silver Mine boss did not appear to be the least distressed by my uncle's news. He did not immediately search me out. So it stood to reason that I was not in trouble for selling silver!

"Later that day, I caught my first inkling of Rick's sudden appearance and the reason behind it. Luckee mentioned it. He stated simply that my uncle had arrived earlier in the day and spoke privately to Mr. Boddinger and that they had made an arrangement for Rick to begin making surveys on the property to mark some kind of geologic formation. That was it. And though Boddinger had been a bit wary of allowing it and wondering if it would affect me, he came to some kind of understanding with Dr. Faehner. Confirming my belief that by Boddinger's earlier reaction, that of an interested listener, Luckee made no mention of my being in any trouble as concerns the illicit trafficking and trading of silver ore off the property. My heart gleamed about that. I was in the clear. My reputation would remain untarnished. Thanks.

"How smart was Rick really when it came to gaining a perspective on others, on me? He knew his presence there would not have gone unnoticed. Maybe he was just trying to flush me out. Have me think that he might have told all but was clever enough to have had Boddinger agree to cover it up by playing dumb in the hope that I might crack—crack in the sense that I just might confess or crack in the sense of cracking up. These were serious considerations. After all, Rick was far older and wiser. And he did have a Ph.D. in his pocket. So I considered my defense again, my tactic of believing that all of the silver I sold had come from a time previous to my involvement with Silver Ford. Again, I waved off my fears and apprehensions. My position was strong. There was no way to disprove my contention.

"And I kept that position through the remainder of the day, the weeks, and the months that came. A considerable amount of real time passed while the episodic event lapsed into memory. My apprehensions faded along with it. Though try as I did to pinch both my bosses for more of the truth about why my uncle had come, I elicited not a spec more of information—Luckee, probably due to genuine ignorance, Boddinger, probably due to arrogance. But after a considerable while it just didn't seem to matter any more. The matter was closed. And nobody walked away the winner.

"Then instantly, just like before, everything changed. I was again jolted out of coherent thought and rhythm by the sudden sight of the so-called erudite's blue Ford resting lonely in one of the uppermost fields just above and just beyond the 1800 house. For the second time, the incidental sighting was inadvertent. Rick had again successfully vied for and received access to the property for reasons unknown, at least to me. The vision was palpable to me, and I felt compelled to do more than turn my back on it. I had to find out what he was up to, and I could not allow anything or anybody to impede my resolve to do so.

"The occurrence was rendered one day in early summer. I found myself accompanying a small group of mine-tour patrons up to the top of the hollow hill directly above the main mine and shafts. It was an area well known to contain obtainable pockets of silver ore. I didn't take everybody there. Only those who were enthusiastic enough during the mine tour that they actually enticed me to want to do more for them, or were so nice to me that I felt the desire to do more to make their trip more special, or maybe they had treated me to a generous gratuity and I wanted to give back something in exchange. Anyway, it was a special privilege for anybody to be taken to the rise, a privilege that only I could decide upon. And I favored few.

"The pit where the exposed strata lay was located on the underside of the high-pointed pylon, as it was known, one of the many strategically positioned electrical towers, which were strewn across the property and carried high-intensity current all the way from the hydroelectric dam miles away on the Susquehanna river. The pylon could not be undermined, and therefore I was forced to play caution when allowing anyone to access its underside to break away samples of rock and mineral and possibly put it in a continued state of instability and collapse. God forbid that someday the high tower come crashing down during a storm or some other natural calamity, and I be made to be responsible for it by having allowed the multitudes to come in and pick away at the embedded foundation over the time of my watch over it.

"But as I was saying, I was up there one day minding the business of allowing my special-select group ample opportunity to search out the miniature quarry for its easy-to-find pockets of silver-laden quartz when suddenly and for no special reason, I decided to climb up from the pit and grab a bit of fresh air, which always seemed to be in supply on the summit of the rise. For a moment, I looked down on my fellow searchers and even envied the way they so enthusiastically went about their silver-finding expedition, expecting and then discovering the sought-after element without exception. Then I looked up, up at the prevailing sky and tried to discern whether or not the weather was going to turn on us that day and possibly shake down the earth on which the volatile tower stood and commence with the all of the danger associated with it. The next thing I knew, my eyes had been drawn to the spec of deep-colored blue that was my uncle's familiar vehicle. Needless to say, it was truly an out-of-the-blue experience.

"My immediate reaction was one of feeling protected by the advantage I had. I knew instantly that I could see him, but he could not possibly see me. I had the upper hand. Whatever would happen as a result of my seeing him would be my decision and no one else's. This gave me reprieve. But I did decide to take action. I excused myself from the party and made my way back down from the rise, down to the shanty, which was for the moment unoccupied by either guest or attendant. From behind one of the display cabinets, I grabbed a pair of high-powered binoculars then sure-footedly moved back up through the mine-side hill by-passing the top section area where the loitering bunch of prospectors were still amassing their individual fortunes. From a clearing not far away, I lay patient, listening to the group's incessant noise and all the time watching the area around my uncle's far-off car for any kind of movement.

"I put into service the visual-enhancing apparatus once I discovered how to use them. Up until that moment, I had never previously placed a pair of binoculars to my face. They were Luckee's. And he used them exclusively for watching woodpeckers at the famous woodpecker tree, an old half-dead locust tree, which sat just opposite the main mine entrance sipping water from Silver Mine Run all day with its one lone root, which still reached its banks, keeping it alive. Almost every day that Luckee frequented the shanty, he could be seen training his eyes on the spectacle of feathered black-and-white birds with red-crested heads as they fluttered around the tree, making merry of the pecking they did. He allowed everybody who asked to spy the whimsical birds so that most people who came left with the experience of having watched the special air show through the enhancing, up-close imaging brought on by the magnificent magnifying glasses.

"I clicked in the magnifying positions one at a time, realizing that the given proximity of Rick's location and distance would probably not require the full capability. The modality in which the terms of attuned acuity were expressed needed no clarification for my part. The first number followed by an *x* told the number of times the object will be magnified. The second number indicates the diameter, in millimeters, of the objective lens. The third number told how wide an area can be seen from its farthest distance. How I knew this was beyond me, for I had never been much of a Boy Scout; and before Luckee, I had never known anyone who owned a pair. But somewhere along the way, I must have read something on the subject and came away with the knowledge and skill to use them.

"The first click-in was 7x, so I tried that. The view I was attempting to reach, some 150 yards distant and blurred, was brought into focus so much that I could depict what kind of weeds were growing outside the spot where the vehicle rested. 10x made the view seem as if it were only a few yards ahead of me, and I could have seen a lot more if there had been a lot more to see. 12x gave me such a keen sight of the scene that I felt I was viewing it through the eyes of an eagle. I could read clearly the numbers and letters of Rick's license plate, which I was familiar with and concluded without any doubt that that was him.

"Just like before, I was faced with the debate of what to do. What would I gain if I simply observed him? Yeah, he was obviously doing something that was geologically related. But what did that necessarily mean? He couldn't object to it if I decided to go and meet up with him. After all, he was where I worked. Wasn't he? I thought about that. I wanted to encounter him. But what would I do if I did? What would I say if I did? And what would he do if I did? And what would he say if I did?

"Moments later, he came into view. It was like watching a silent film and trying to discern what was going on without words. Rick had risen up from the side hill and trekked back to his car for materials and supplies, off-loading the many pieces of equipment he was carrying. It was ironic that I so vehemently protested his presence there since he was the one who had in the recent past brought me into the realm of the land of silver. Thinking about it, I realized that he had been coming to the place since probably before I was born! But I could not afford to be put into jeopardy regardless of any other consideration. Rick had to be dealt with—the sooner the better. Tired of viewing his clandestine operation from a distance, safe and sound, I arose from my secluded branches and marched across the high ground toward his position. I knew I could no longer sit idly by and wait and watch as Rick exacted his unknown purposes upon the place that had become a part of my everyday experience. I knew this second coming would not be the last, and I had to find out what I could about it."

Mr. Faehner elaborated on the past in such a pressing manner as to bring about a complete change in the way it was being perceived, enough that the depictions of time and place became an invitation to the past. Concepts turned into reality. Descriptions became visual illustrations. The way had been made, back to the time of the actual experience.

Young Pip Faehner advanced intrepidly upon his uncle's nascent camp, which he had spied from across the property divide. Decided as he was with the outright style of his approach, he did have second thoughts about his audacious behavior once he had broken the perimeter of the trampled weeds between the blue Ford and the woodland ridge just a few yards beyond. He had a just cause for wanting to flee. Pity the person who dared to be an interloper into his esteemed uncle's privacy. But he had been through all that before, and in this case, the table was somewhat turned. Wasn't Rick really the interloper here? Wasn't he?

It was apparent from viewing the old car that Rick's recent ramblings, to convey equipment from the transport vehicle to some unknown destination were over, witnessed by the fact that the car was relatively empty of all essential cargo. Another chance. But Pip remained steadfast and at ease. Rick's motives for being here had to be determined. What was the old saying "Keep your enemies closer than your friends, for sake, forsaken"? No matter. The meaning was clear.

The next thing to do was follow his advance through the steeped tree-lined ridge, from the point of his observed comings and goings, and work his way to wherever Rick had stationed himself. It was not going to be easy. Rick had left behind no traces of evidence as to indicate even which direction he had taken into the dim-lit, tree-topped terrain. Intuition took over as Pip made his way over rock, over root, searching for any telltale signs that Rick had plotted a course previous to his along the same footpaths. Knowing that his uncle was a practical man in all matters, Pip assumed correctly that Rick's secret station would be found higher rather than lower on the side of the 150-foot-high hill. There was no word in the English language to accurately describe a hill this size. The term hill in no way justified its dimension or presence. And the term mountain seemed an exaggeration of its approbation. It lay somewhere in the middle. So it was not a remarkable thing to suggest that Pip did experience a great deal of difficulty in locating his quarry despite the fact that he had been through these woods a number of times while off exploring, especially now that all the deciduous hardwood and softwood trees were in full leafy-green composition. But despite the apparent obstacles, Pip carried on. His duty was to find and find out about his uncle.

He searched the high and low of the ridge's upper reaches, waywardly, through the vast array of large and medium-girth trees until he thought better of his ostentatious display, then toned down his pace in consideration of the caution he had earlier thought to use. Chary were his footsteps now so that not even a woodland Indian could have detected his movements through the dense landscape. Slowly and carefully, Pip kept on, creeping along the slanted hillside as though it were on a pattern of terraces. He made sweeps, great distances long and short distances wide, searching for any traces of Rick's hole in the woods.

His persistence paid off when, rounding an abutting outcrop of rock, he came into his uncle's makeshift camp. Rick was not there. He made a quick perusal of the camp before then looking out in all directions as was possible for any sign of his return. Nothing could be seen or heard from the surrounding area, and Pip breathed a sigh of relief that he had at least made it this far without being detected. Now to learn what he could. Besides a folding table and chair, Rick had with him several simple provisions of food and water and quite a few piles of papers and maps, some rolled up, some completely unraveled and held open on the table with indigenous stones he must have located nearby. Pip crept up closer to them to find out what he could. Though he was by no means a cartographer and possessed no authentic credentials as an expert in geography, he was able to discern by deduction the general application of the maps. One was noted 56-57, which Pip assumed correctly meant 1956-1957. On it was a geographical and geological breakdown of the entire silver mine property and its immediate adjacent properties in all directions. The map was a survey made by an old F&M professor, Dr. Fetterer. He had done a complete topography, a profile of the land indentifying all of the above-ground rock and mineral deposits and similarly identifying the very same deposits extending underground, those that were proven by all of the recorded mining extrapolations and those whose depth and declaration had only been suggested by virtue of the known variables of the formations.

Silver was the key interest to the aforementioned professor. Tracings had been made on areas of the map, which indicated, according to old mining records, precisely where large deposits of the precious ore had been found up until the time when the water table had been breached. By that time, all of the mine's minds had been paying exclusive attention to the lowest region of the second shaft—and little else. For months or maybe years, according to the pick-and-shovel technology of old, the mine's central focus had been salvaging all the silver from this lone location—in a tunnel opening over one hundred feet below the surface. There had been no geologist on hand to come up with other possible sites to bore into or to survey the above-ground rock and soil to see if any geologic condition existed in conjunction with the known formations and could suggest that some investigation should be made.

But it had not been Dr. Fetterer who was claiming this contention. This theory, extrapolated by means of his extensive research, was now the exclusive idea of the one, Dr. Faehner. Scribbled on the map's surface were considerable notations about size and distance. Projections had been made concerning the two carrying beds; phyllite and quartz, and how they were in occurrence in the mine and how they were most likely spread out in all of the outlying underground. This had never been done before. No one had ever considered that the ore deposits could be found in places other than the main mine area. The sense of what Rick was attempting was startling! He was trying to either prove or disprove that another or other deposits of silver existed within the same locality!

"Oh my god!" Pip spelled out in disbelief. "He's trying to usurp me by bringing about the coming of a new day here! He'll get credited with being the only person ever in the history of the silver mine who had the smarts enough to find out, to think to find out, about what else may be hiding here."

Suddenly, Pip was rattled out of his contemplative stare. A sound was heard off in the not-too-far distance.

"It must be Rick!"

The tiny platform ledge Pip was on offered no escape unless you left the way you came. And Rick was too close. Any attempt Pip made to go back and even detour into the woods would be detected. Were there any alternatives? Up until this very moment, Pip had not intended to escape; in fact, his plan had been to meet up with his uncle and just go from there. A quick perusal of the immediate area offered no solution to the predicament. His options were limited. If he was not going to meet him head-on and he was reluctant to run, then he must hide, if it was possible. He looked around. There were several large-girthed trees that he could hope to hide behind, but that seemed doubtful, realizing that he would have to maintain perfect silence and stillness while balancing himself against the lean of the steep, steep hill. For a split second only, he thought to lie face down in the dirt and cover himself with fallen branches and last fall's leaf litter, which still lied brittle and decaying over the forested floor. Then a better idea hit him, and quickly, with the short time that was left, he climbed up the nearest, largest tree. High up, he positioned himself for the inevitable return of the professor.

He didn't wait long. In only a few brief seconds, Rick reared his ugly head from the nascent path leading up to the makeshift camp. Pip gulped three times to suppress a cough, then held his breath as long as he could to ensure a piece of quiet as Rick, traveling with slow, heavy footsteps, centered himself around the midst of his belongings and relieved himself of the various instruments he was carrying. For Pip, it was sheer blind luck that he had not been detected upon Rick's approach. The angle of the walk-in, up steeply, and the forward position Rick would have been in, certainly was conducive to his being discovered. But luck is always a partner with circumstance, and in this case, circumstance was that Rick was a person who frequently walked with his face in a downward cast and did so this time too. Though he was now only a short distance below, he did not discover his foe positioned in the tree directly above his head. But even though Rick was not attuned to things particularly above him in the more literal sense, he was not oblivious to things which were out of the ordinary. And it did not take too long to notice.

Though mostly all of his personal provisions appeared to be much as he left him, it did not escape his detection that there was now an included item, an item which in no way could have been mistaken for his own. The binoculars! He seized them where they lay, on a slab of stone along the back wall of the rock-drop behind him. Upon noticing them, he snatched them up and examined them for data, especially personal information implying ownership. There was none. Realizing at once that his camp had been interfered with, Rick went immediately back to his notes and maps and made sure that nothing had been taken. Nothing had. Then a second, more substantial realization hit him, that was that the person or persons who had come upon his hillside retreat had somehow, or for some reason, left behind a piece of their own possessions. And why would they do that? It occurred to him, whoever came and went would probably be back. Perhaps they had left the binoculars behind only to explore other parts of the larger spectrum of hills and rock without the hindrance of field glasses swinging off their necks while negotiating the erratic, this-way-and-that nature of the slope.

Always one who, at the slightest indignation or the perception of one, was eager to pounce on the alleged provocateur, Rick attended to his besieged imagination as to how best to deal with the situation. He delved out a handful of punishments in his head before settling on the one that most aptly fitted his annoyed character.

"The punishment will fit the crime," he stated aloud once he was sure of what he was going to do. "Those pesky kids will learn the hard way not to invade another person's privacy. What once was found will now be lost." And with that, Rick set off on a long-distance walk to some far-off location to purposely lose the left-behind item. He was not a finder-keeper and would never think to steal them. Nor was he about to play participant in the role of recovery and return the glasses to the nearest authority, in which case would be the silver mine attendants, possibly his nephew, Pip. Rick also did not have it in him to destroy other people's property, so he could never have broken and discarded them. Rick's way was to administrate to those who have infuriated him using methods, which symbolized his superior position in its process. He would role-play with people, he being the put-upon fatherly figure and they being the defiant little one who needed discipline but also example. In this case, they would learn that interfering in other people's business would cost them their prized possession. The lesson being that there was always something to lose when you stick your nose out too far ahead of your body.

Self-satisfied that his determination in the case was with merit, Rick set off on his trek to his yet undetermined place where he would fling the field glasses off into a bush or hang them from a low-lying tree, anywhere where he was sure they would not be retrieved, at least by the person who lost them.

All the while, while Rick was pertaining to his little glory, Pip remained wrapped around the thicker-than-he-was branch of the overhead tree. Unfortunately, due to his peculiar circumstance, he had no choice but to listen in as his uncle alluded to his all-powerful purpose and position. Then when Rick came up with the artifice of taking the object off into the woods and deal with it rather than wait and deal with the person, in this case him, Pip became so bemused, thinking up a connotative analogy to the amusing scene—that of Hansel and Gretel, when their poor woodcutter father led them off into the woods to enter into their own fate through no fault of their own and left them. "I could just see him doing that to a real person," he interjected into his own thoughts as he almost fell out of the precarious perch. He was lucky. Even though his hands would not fit entirely around the circumference of the thick bough, it did have deep-cut grooves in its bark, which gave him an ample amount of staying power. But what did happen unnoticed was that he had lost a part of his grip and in that split second that he did he shifted off-center on the top of the limb. To maintain his tenacious hold, he pretended he was a Pliocene tree sloth and that holding on was first nature to him.

The sloth in him served him well for when Rick trudged off onto his wild and wacky adventure, he was still hugging the tree for all he was worth. But just after Rick's last movements could be heard from a far-off distance, Pip lost his equilibrium; and in one swift motion, like a sloth being shot down, out of a tree, he plunged full-body onto Rick's project table. The table broke in two. The precious maps and everything pertaining to the proofs Rick was working on were sent scattering to the ground. Pip looked up, forlornly at the branch that had seconds before offered him such an enabling position and asserted, "Newton's law, Newton's fall!"

The poignant memory of toppling out of the tree brought Mr. Faehner back to where he was, back to the future. The painful ending even made him wince as he recalled the stinging left shoulder, a severe sprain, incurred from the fall.

"So what happened next?" the reported asked in general, hoping to hear a tie-up to some of the story's context.

Mr. Faehner knew what he was asking. He did not want to be entertained any further about the field glasses, which were looked for but never found by the younger Pip despite many desperate years of searching. Though the glasses themselves held no real intrinsic value to him or the mine, it was the quest to find them that piqued Pip's interest since they had been left loose on holy ground. The reporter also did not want to hear anything further about Rick's and his relationship—what happened between them as a result of Rick's camp being obliterated. He wanted to know about the one thing which he was not going to find out about—not yet.

A Break in Time

That couldn't be. Secrets are best kept when they are being kept by the smallest amount of people keeping them, the fewer the better, in this case fewer being one—for now. And this in itself was quite a burden to bear for the eminent empire builder, who, win, lose, or draw would experience very little detrimental effect should others find out the certain something or other he was safeguarding. It was difficult though playing one emotion off another just so an old reputation could remain spotless. But he figured it would be worth it in the end. And so, tempted as he was to disclose the bit of private information he had regarding his long-ago episode with his uncle, he remained equivocally reserved over the matter. But he knew things were not as simple as that. There was another side to this equation. The reporter, now sitting directly across from him, had been entreated to the meandering tale and was, he was certain, enticed by its implications. Something would have to be said, something would have to be done to properly satiate his ravenous appetite—to know, to learn, something of what resulted on that long-ago day in that faraway camp. He would have to be pleased, appeased before any of his stoicism left him, before words were slipped.

He went over the excuses in his mind to clarify them, possibly modify them before spouting them out across the bargaining table to the youthful personage who was ready to receive them.

"Suffice to say, young man, each of us kept from the other all that had happened and walked away from each other with our own exclusive knowledge about what had taken place. The exception of course being that Rick didn't know it was me that had infiltrated his expeditionary camp and wrecked it. But what he was actually up to, I could only hypothesize about. I believe he must have come to some conclusion about what he was trying to find because he never returned. And usually he never gave up. Whatever he wanted to discover, he did; and whatever he wanted to do with his discovery, he did also. You just had to know Rick."

Cleverly, Mr. Faehner had claimed that Rick's quest, filled or unfulfilled, had remained with Rick which was true. And he hadn't divulged any specific information about Rick's expectations, right or wrong. The identifying word had not been mentioned, silver had gone unspoken. He paused, wondering if his little jaunt off the information highway had been favorable enough to distract the reporter's zealous little mind. Fate intervened. The silence was broken by Mr. Faehner's cell phone come-to-life. Since the previously placed "intruder-on-the-premises" call, the phone had been left activated. Its interruptive jingle now announced another caller's intent. Obliged to respond, Mr. Faehner reached for the small handheld device and answered it with a perfunctory "hello." The conversation was brief but important. After putting the tiny voice box away again, Mr. Faehner exhibited a look of consternation on his countenance. Thoughts about what to do prevailed upon him, but all the while, he felt an inward relief about the fact that once and for all now the tendency toward the telling of the silver secret had been rendered mute. Mr. Faehner, still considering his options, spelled out his dilemma for the benefit of allowing the reporter to have a say-so in the situation. He began.

"Something's come up. Something that requires my immediate attention. Something to which I should respond to too in person. You can either stay or come along, if you want."

"What's going on?" the reporter asked directly.

"That's a loaded question," Mr. Faehner replied honestly. "If I were to tell you everything of the situation, it would take some time. As it is, we best get going. I'll fill you in on the way. We need to take a short drive down to the tiny town of Pequea. My presence is being requested in a matter that concerns me greatly. I'm trying to get rid of a little eyesore down there, and it's been a real nasty one to gain control over. What happens today just may be the end of it."

Feeling Mr. Faehner's exuded confidence, the reporter at once exhibited a desire to accompany him. This would be a chance, no doubt, to see firsthand how a man such as him can step into a bad situation and make it right. He elicited a very pronounced acceptance, and they were off. Before actually leaving the prominent office room, Mr. Faehner excused himself and placed a well-intended call to one of his attendants informing him to inform several others, including his wife, that he would be leaving for an undetermined amount of time. That done, he issued a second call, this time to his chauffeur, apprising him of his intent to leave the property posthaste. Seconds later, a second incoming call came, which he promptly responded to. It was his wife, who wanted a personal explanation of where he was going and what he was going to do. Their conversation was brief and to the point and in no time at all reached an effective ending, which told that he had successfully satiated her curiosity. "You're the hostess with the mostess."

"Everything's settled, so let's go," Mr. Faehner advised once he was off the phone. He checked the time. The interview had now lasted beyond one hour, a sizeable chunk of his day considering it was being held opposite his own party. They were off. The reporter followed the man-of-the-hour-and-a-half out of the inner sanctum and into the front hall. There they went halfway down the dimly lit corridor until Mr. Faehner made a sudden unexpected halt in front of an obscure side door. Upon entering, the reporter found himself transformed into a hidden little world—a garden bounded on all sides by building two stories high. The shape of the garden was elliptical in the nature of it though the surrounding structure was made of straight-lined angles. Allowing his secret-garden guest a full appreciative view of the seldom-seen-by-others sight, Mr. Faehner came to a momentary stop so they could both gaze upon its wonder. Along its thirty-five-foot midsection, the length from door to door, was a laid out path of beige-colored concrete stepping stones, which each had within them a pattern of mosaic artwork—pictures depicted by colored stones embedded into the mortar. One such scene was of a blue dolostone pond with little feldspar goldfish set to appear as if they were swimming freely in it. Another was of a green serpentine field dotted across with shaped pieces of calcite to depict little white flowers growing in a meadow. In the center of the beautiful courtyard was one flowering mimosa tree now vibrantly arrayed in its warm-weather presentation—globular heads of pink and white flowers, hundreds of them. Around its base was a circular stone bench made from the same material as the walkway. Above their heads was an open-domed sky, which allowed an ample amount of light and air to fall into the four-sided atrium. Hedges which ran along all sides gave it its circular shape, and they too were fully bloomed; hydrangeas—purple, pink, and blue in hue.

"This really is something," the reporter remarked once he had gained a compliant perspective of the secluded garden. "Do you visit here often?"

"Not as often as I would like, but it is my sanctuary, the perfect place to step into when chaos abounds. When I do come in, I can forget about my world for a while."

Then, to keep them moving, Mr. Faehner quick-stepped ahead from the center-point place from which they were standing, the reporter in tow. Exiting the garden through an opposite-end door, they entered into an adjacent hall, skinny compared to the one they came from, moved down a part of its length, then made an abbreviated stop before a left-side door, which appeared seldom used by virtue of its out-of-the-way location. The door was only knob-locked, and all Mr. Faehner had to do to open it was to twist his wrist while holding the handle. Both men had to shield their eyes from the burst of bright light that entreated them once they crossed through the threshold.

Already the limousine was waiting.

"I didn't know we were going to be riding in style," the reporter chortled as he proceeded straight for the back entry door.

"No, don't," Mr. Faehner said in a light admonishing voice. "Wait for the driver to open the door."

Not used to and knowing he was not used to the etiquette as such was involved in the kind of lifestyle Mr. Faehner was accustomed to; that of the rich and famous, the reporter immediately backed away from the long silver-and-white vehicle. Seconds later, a neatly attired gentleman, if you could call him that, emerged from the vehicle's driver's side front and walked briskly around the idling stretch to where the two passengers waited. He greeted them in accordance to their standing.

"Good day to you, sir, Mr. Faehner. How are you today, sir?"

The nicety, having asked as to the general welfare of his boss, was said only as a gesture of kindness and without the expectation of reply. Realizing this, Obe opened Mr. Faehner's door, then turned to the young reporter and nodded a simple "sir."

Once seated comfortably inside, Mr. Faehner gave Obe instructions as to where they were headed. After acknowledging his orders, Obe raised up the sound-proof, heavy-glass partition between him and the passengers and started off toward Pequea.

The men in the back were face-to-face, enjoying the spaciously laid out interior complete with soft-piled carpeting, leather-upholstered seats, a mini bar, a VCR, and a TV. But not so caught up in his immediate surroundings, the reporter's eyes were sullenly cast into the forward compartment where Obe was attending to the tendencies of the road in front of them. Mr. Faehner noticed how his eyes were glued to the forward man and observed, first inwardly, then outwardly, the probability of what had drawn his companion's stare.

"You're face has the appearance of a sturdy pear dangling from a fruit tree but within a larva is growing whose protestations are beginning to manifest itself in the whole being. I fear that if the impression endures any longer, the fruit may fall from the tree."

Not wishing any sort of schism to grow between them, the reporter owned up to the obvious impression he was wearing on his countenance though he was altogether surprised that it had been so easily detected.

"It's your servant," he said in a diminished tone, applying along with his concern an application of pity. "He's a sorry sight."

The reporter's words were not of condemnation nor were they spoken in a disorderly way. To anyone looking at him, physically, he was a sorrowful sight. And anyone who did not know him would think him like a slave of old, a ghost from the past, awakened into future service and servitude. Obe was a colored man though that could be said of everybody who ever graced God's green planet. His skin was dark as though it had been dipped in a vat of popsicle chocolate and permanently dried on. His face was withered and wrinkled, partially deformed, like a dried-up raisin. His movements were slow and deliberate due to the lasting effects of long, untreated illness and ailment. On his face was a pasted smile, which he wore continuously as though his life depended on it. Under it, one only imagined how he really felt; but in keeping his smile, he kept his condition of life, and that, of course, is always the priority.

Since the partition glass was up and its sound-proof effect in place, Mr. Faehner felt the desire to expound upon what he knew was an often-held view of the forlorn-looking facilitator.

"I won't throw the old saying "you can't judge a book by its cover" at you, my young friend, but I will dare to say that, believe me or not, that gentleman sitting up there is undoubtedly the happiest person I know."

"Him! You've got to be kidding!" the reporter snapped, letting his reflex get the better of him without thinking.

"It's so!" Mr. Faehner shot back. Obe's been in my employ for all of thirteen years now. He came to me unexpectedly. Once I came in off a flight at the Philadelphia International Airport. I dillydallied around after the landing to the tune of appearing outside the terminal fifteen minutes late for my ride. The limousine I had arranged for left me stranded, blaming me for my indifference, which technically was true but, nonetheless, did not wait any longer than what the service deemed necessary. Their by-the-book attitude left me without a carrier and them without my services ever more. Obe, up there, rescued me. He was at the airport that day plying for trade himself. He would when he could rescue people like me who had been left behind for one reason or another, like maybe someone forgot that they had promised someone to do an airport run for them, or maybe someone's car already waiting at the airport lot wouldn't start. Anyway, old Obe would be there waiting. At the first sign of trouble, he would go out and flag a person down and offer them his services. Sometimes he would get the call, sometimes he would not. He found that if he remained all the time pleasant and kept those bright whites open for business, there was a greater tendency to get people to say yes.

"Obe noticed me when I came out of the main entrance. I knew I was late, but I still fully expected my ride to be there. And rest assured, I had already decided I was going to tip the driver extraordinarily well for my tardiness. And I had already prepared my apology. But when I saw nobody there in the line-up of limos, my heart sank. I always used the same service, so I knew which carrier to look for, and no one had been inside waiting for me with a placard or who may have known me from prior experiences. So I knew rather quickly that I had been abandoned.

"Obe came over as I stood on the sidewalk, my head shaking, my eyes downcast, and inquired as to my perceived predicament. I denied it at first that I was indeed in a dilemma out of apprehension and fear that he may have been a "taker" as I call them, those who try to take the ultimate advantage of others in stressful situations. For all I knew, he would have loaded me up and headed for the inner city and then really taken me for a ride! After my initial refusal, he left. I made phone calls but to no avail. Nobody was around, or they were tied up and couldn't come and get me. Remember back at that time, I only had about one-third of the fortune I have now. And favors, you will learn, increase proportionately in accordance with wealth—those that are rendered unto you. When I emerged from the terminal again, Obe again inveigled me. I gave in and gave it a shot, but I insisted that I keep my two bags of luggage in the back seat with me, that way if I needed to jump and run, I could.

"So Obe brought me home, all the way to Lancaster. I pitied him, a little. Here he was a man of meager means and sustenance willing to drive me all the way back, 130 miles round-trip, in his old broken-down Buick. Lucky for him. The duration of the ride made me realize that there was something special about him, his candor, his willingness to help others, despite what was thought about him at first glance. I began to feel like it was one of those once-in-a-lifetime chances to do good for someone. And I believed it too in what I was doing, after all he didn't know me from Adam. For all he knew, once I had brought him into my element, I could have turned around and threw the screws to him—not paid him at all. What could he have done about it? No, there was something more to this guy than meets the eye, I knew. I paid him $100 to be exact, twice what he asked for, but I also invited him into my service that day. I gave him my name, address, and phone number and told him that I had decided to begin keeping a personal driver. He didn't hesitate a minute and promised me that if I gave him just three or four days, he would be at my place. He said he would live in his car if he had to just to get the job. I told him that that wasn't necessary and that I would arrange to get him an apartment and pay for it as part of the exchange of services. He's been with me ever since."

"But what does that explain about his being the happiest person you know in the world?"

"It doesn't. But I don't often get the opportunity to tell anyone the "Obe Tale." Too often people look at him the way you did and then look away. But you tried to look into his being, his character, and attempted to determine something from it. True, you pitied him much the way I did, and you thought the worst of him just the way I did, but you also came to some instant perception that there was something of a higher nature about him, so I wanted to be the one to tell you that was true.

"Humbled though he seems, I reiterate my contention that Obe there is a truly happy person, happier than me, happier than you. And how is this possible? After all, if we go by the "what-you-see-is-what-you-get" theory, then how could a man with so much physical detriment possibly look at life except through the eyes of misery. I'll tell you how. Obe has exceeded the highest expectations of himself that he ever thought possible and found a place of solace in that. He never wanted more. He was even happy when he was busy every day inveigling airport people, like me, as to whether he could service them somehow. He doesn't hear the susurrous sounds like you and I do."

"What does that mean, Mr. Faehner?"

"That means that he doesn't hear or pertain to the everyday sounds within ourselves calling for more, more, more of everything like we do. He doesn't strive to be better than himself. He's content with his place and position in life because he's happy, for when a person is truly happy, it's hard to be discontented."

"You mean then that he's accepted his lot in life regardless of what it's been or what it's come to."

"No. It's more than that. His contentment doesn't come from acceptance alone. He appreciates himself for exactly who he is, which means that regardless of what his situation in life is, he is nothing more, nothing less of who he wants to be, which is himself. I know it sounds like semantics, but the reasoning couldn't possibly be any clearer. Obe is happy simply because he's Obe."

"Oh, I think I get it. It's kind of like the old saying: "A person is as happy as they make up their minds to be.""

"No, it's more internal than that. That saying implies that a person can look at life in any of its many moods and simply put themselves in an alternate state, if the mood was bad. And quite frankly, I think that's a lot of hooey. I believe it's better to be true to your feelings, but that's another subject. No, true happiness, I believe some people are born with. It's true that all of us possess the ability to learn to appreciate things in life—and we all do—but Obe there is one of those rare people that have it within their souls to truly appreciate life for what it is, being alive and having a life to live. It's something the rest of us understand but only from a distance. I believe happiness—the ability to live happily—is something that has to be inherent in us from the beginning."

"Does that mean you have to be born with it?"

"I really don't know. But I suppose it probably helps to have come from someone who had the gift. Who knows?"

"You don't think he could have become that way due to his being deprived of so much for so long then."

"No no no. You're missing the point. It's not something that comes out at certain times in life, like after the experience of a tragedy when a person afterward comes to a certainty that the life they are living is really a precious reality. That's a life lesson that we all learn sometime in our lives. But that's not what I'm referring to here. What Obe has, Obe had, always!

"Happiness doesn't just occur at certain points in our lives when we need it. It's either there or it isn't. It's not something that can be searched for and found. It cannot be doled out to us by what life brings. Others cannot fill us full of it, and we cannot fulfill the needs of others by giving it to them. It comes from within us. And it is within us at birth. What we have of it, we have of it. It can never be taken from us nor can we give it away. Happiness dwells within our soul. And the irony of this is that if we fail to realize this, we can never be happy with the happiness we have!

"I too have looked at my life in accordance with this and found that this is true. The base line of my life's happiness has never really changed even though my life has. In fact, my life has changed much more dramatically than Obe's has. And through it, I have found myself to be no different in my true identity of myself as it is contextually perceived in regard to being happy. In the essence of myself, I am not any happier as a person now than when I was at any earlier point in my life. Things are better, no doubt, but not me. I have the same manner as a person as I did when I was a boy. That despite everything I achieved. Money doesn't bring happiness. Remember that. How can I say that? Because I remember who I was. I can recall when I was a boy of around eleven or twelve, and I made a living going around the city streets selling soft pretzels for a nickel a bag. I earned about five dollars a week, and I felt happy—at least happy in the measure of my ability to be happy. Then I went to work with my uncle in the rock shop, and there I learned all about rocks and minerals and made decent money for the time, maybe thirty to forty dollars a week, and I was happy. Now let's look into my Silver Mine beginnings, the time of my life. I had found my destiny, and I knew it. I was happy to be a part of it, but no more or less than I had the ability to be. Then when the day came and I became owner, you would think that I, having fulfilled a dream, would be happy ever after. But I wasn't. I wanted more. For a person like me, happiness can never be the ticket because I can never acquire enough to satisfy myself. So I compensate for it by acquiring other things with replacement value. But it is no real recompense. Oh, it's not that I'm unhappy, mind you. I feel it when I have arrived at something—self-satisfaction, contentment, realization—but they are temporary remedies and are not lasting. So I've given up. I know now that true happiness can never be intended. It can be hoped and wished for but never bargained for. And deep, deep down inside ourselves, I think most of us know this. That's probably why we sing "Happy Birthday" to each other every time we come upon that celebrated day every year. We're wondering whether that person we're singing to is truly happy, and knowing they're not, we hope we can improve their deficient state by providing them with a sufficiency of words and adoration. We know it won't help, but we try nonetheless.

"So don't feel so sorry for that man up there with his diminished appearance and hard-luck past, for he has surrounding him a protective coat that emanates from deep inside, an aura of happiness."

The country club was now five miles behind and the trio of travelers were stopped at the main thoroughfare in the town of Little Conestoga. Traffic up and down the stretch of secondary highway was heavy, and because there were no traffic lights at this or any other intersections in the vicinity, the limousine, like everybody else, had no choice but to wait one-at-a-time for openings to occur once the stop-sign position had been attained. This suspension of movement caused the vehicle's occupants to pay closer attention to their immediate surroundings, forcing them to concentrate on things other than what had been in their minds. Nearby, across and to the left of the roadway, they were now third in line of attempting to negotiate, was a local mom and pop grocery, the only store within miles. It was called Mom and Pop's. Mr. Faehner knew the store well and had been a patron of it since his earliest days at the Silver Mine, back at a time when Mom and Pop weren't quite yet the mom and pop of anybody. But forty years going had changed that, and Mom and Pop now were mom and pop five times over with grandkids to spare.

They were considerably likeable, and Mr. Faehner's mind began to run over many of the many memorable instances when he had interacted with them, one or the other or both, whenever he frequented their tidy establishment. Touching off his fond memories of them made him want to see them again, and he debated for a moment whether it would be prudent to do so considering what was pending. But then he thought up a reason that might require it—his guest. The reporter sitting next to him was no longer just some want-to-be who had come down for the day following his duty. He was now, by special invitation, his special guest who was being given the opportunity of a lifetime as he saw it. And in that capacity, he should be afforded special treatment wherever applicable.

The lengthy limousine was next in line to intercede the highway, so it was a now-or-never consideration as to whether or not he could request that they make a stop. Always quick at making decisions, Mr. Faehner pressed down on a little black button, which activated and lowered the partition glass between the driver and the back.

"Let's hold over there at the store, Obe. I want to go in for a minute."

Obe obeyed. Three minutes later, the silver-white limo glided gently into an off-side parking space alongside the two-story, white-board house whose spaciously interiored downstairs had been completely converted into a store over four decades ago. When the limousine came to a stop, Mr. Faehner quickly got out and invited the reporter to accompany him into the store. On their way past the car, he tapped ever so lightly on the driver's side window and waited for Obe to lower it.

"We're going in for some eats," he said in affable voice, taking on the intonation of a country person. "Is there anything I can get for you?"

Obe paused as he did whenever Mr. Faehner approached him on a more personal level, wondering if it would be proper for him to further the engaging conversation. Often, he left it alone. But today, already he sensed that something nice was taking place for his typically overburdened boss, and he felt happy that he was being included in it.

"I wouldn't usually trouble you sir," he began sincerely, "but today of all days, I've got me a tempting desire for one of them there chocolate-covered ice cream bars I can never get enough of. And it sure is a fine day for it."

"Enough said," Mr. Faehner responded sharply, realizing that if Obe was to be given even the slightest window of opportunity, he might renege out of consideration that he had been out of place accepting such an offer. Hurriedly, the two would-be patrons made their way over to the store steps and climbed up. For Mr. Faehner, it had been quite a long time, two years perhaps, since he had made his presence known to the two old storekeepers. He was ashamed of that. It had been a silent vow, made all those many years ago, in which he affirmed to himself that no matter what, he would always find his way back again and again to the two wonderful people he had built such a rapport with. Over thirty-nine years now had elapsed since he first set foot inside the Main Street store and into their lives. He recalled vividly how they took him in, believed in him, when he candidly revealed to them his candied ideas about someday owning the silver mine property. All the way through, they supported his cause and applied their own brand of logic and reasoning to his assertions that this could be, would be, accomplished. If the silver mine was his home away from home, then Mom and Pop certainly had been his surrogate parents away from his own.

His reflections were surreal and made him pause for a moment while standing before the entryway. The reporter, not knowing what to make of the marked hesitation paused too, maintaining his secondary role in silence, sure that his esteemed mentor was experiencing a sentimental stitch in the fabric of time. The whole day had come to that. Together they had been delving into the past, story by story, and not just in a superficial way. The events had come clear almost as if the reporter had been taken by the hand and whisked back into time. He felt as if he had been witness to the events already expressed to him. And he wondered now if he was about to be led into another realm of the past, another place in time, which may relate to the very place he was standing.

Mr. Faehner, about to pass through the threshold of the store also felt as such the identity of the past as though if he passed through the threshold, the doorway, he would be cast back in time. He would be that boy he once was, that boy who still so strongly held presence in him. He backed away, afraid that if his current assertion was true—he being as he was, not who he was now, and all that he had accomplished would be back to being a dream. It struck him that this store had been one of his secret wishing wells, and the storekeepers had been like fairy godparents to him. Everything he had ever wanted that was oriented in the southern end had been wished for—openly in this place—and had come to fruition! It came to him. He would make use of it again. The realization began to grow in him, and he began rationalizing what he intended to do against all of the pervading nay-saying thoughts that started to inveigle him. There was no denying the present or the past that had gotten him here. They entered.

Very little had changed since the days of old. The store looked the same. The lone improvement that the store had ever experienced was the diamond-laid, black-and-white-tiled floor that had been put in in the late 1970s. And even that Pop had protested adamantly about, insisting that a good wood floor would last forever. But Mom had, over the course of many intervening months, managed to persuade Pop into her way of thinking that for the sake of breakages and spills, a floor can be more readily mopped up on a smooth-surfaced floor. Mom and Pop's interpretation of improvement mirrored the often-heard adage—"If it ain't broke, don't fix it."

A young Pip Faehner had been privy to many of the lively discussions held by the storekeepers prior to Pop's eventual acquiescence. It was no wonder how they had managed to keep the store going all of these years. Their overhead was only the little bit of electric needed to keep the refrigerated cases cold and a few cleaning supplies, which they got at cost. Other than that, the floor had been their only extravagance. Modern-day convenience stores, which had all but wiped out the old-time groceries, didn't stand a chance against the likes of Mom and Pop and their exaggerated sense of frugality.

Mr. Faehner perused the aisles for old times' sake. The reporter remained by his side, intrigued by the store's old-fashioned quaintness. In his own hometown, there remained but one store similar to this, but he had never frequented it. Then, out of the blue, Mr. Faehner was spotted. The soft scolding words rained down upon him by Mom who had left her position behind the register to come out and intercept the man who had always promised to keep coming back.

"Well well well, if it isn't the prodigal son returned!" she shouted once their faces came in contact with each other. Remembering him as the boy she had watched grow up for the last thirty-nine years, she instinctively raised her right hand to high heaven as if she were intending to threaten him as she would her own son if he had dared to alienate them. Mr. Faehner feinted to cover up from the aiming arm by guarding his face with both his hands, while all the time guarding against exposing the true smile that was growing on his mouth.

"Hold on there, Mom," he finally uttered in pretended protest. "I've come back. I've come back to—"

While explaining on about his prolonged absence from the proprietary, Mom turned her back and left to get Pop. As she did, she continued to pop off lashing remarks aimed at reprimanding the remorseful-sounding man to whom they had been endeared to for so long. But to Mr. Faehner, the lashes sounded as words of lavish praise, for he knew that for Mom and Pop only a considerable content of caring on their part could bring about such a response.

When Mom returned, her face—once a bust of stone replete with a look of contrived contempt—was now putty, softened, and sad. Pop, following up behind her was the first to make a statement. "What'll it be there stranger?" he asked facetiously.

"Hi, Pop," Mr. Faehner responded, smiling. "I told Mom already how sorry I am for neglecting to come in, in all this while to see you. But I've been all so busy lately, you know, and you just plain forget."

"Plain forget nothing," Mom said sternly, feeling a second surge of reproachfulness. "Don't go about trying to make excuses for not having the decency to stop in and say hi from time to time. You don't live but a cow's walk-a-day away from us!"

"Hold on there, Mom. He's not the boy you're remembering him to be anymore. He's a grown-up man with responsibilities that neither you nor me can comprehend. Now go on and fix him up something special that you know he likes, why don't you."

"Actually that's true, Pop. I would like for Mom to fix me up one of her home-made ham and cheese sandwiches. And one for my friend here too. And an ice cream pop to go," he shouted at the flustered woman who's emotions were stirred up—one-third mad, one-third sad, and one-third glad.

While Mom traipsed off to put together two of her sandwich specials, Pop began to put together an offering of peace for the way Mom had acted.

"Lucky for you, you came when you did. If Mom's really this upset over not seeing you for the time it's been, I'd hate to be you if you'd waited any longer. But you know Mom, and Mom's got to have her way sometimes. Why, look here at this floor. She kept after me for a year till I ran out of wax to put in my ears."

But there was nothing to conciliate as Pop may have thought. Rather than be offended, Mr. Faehner felt flattered. He knew in his heart that

Mom's touchiness came from a good place inside her, and he was glad that she, that all she really wanted was for him to be around to appreciate. "Say no more, say no more," Mr. Faehner kept repeating in his mind, watchful of Pop's presentation and knowing that if he gave it any further inducement, Pop would be standing on a soapbox for as long as he could keep his balance on it. The best thing that could be done was to take Pop off into another direction, get his mind off something that was so dear to him—defending Mom's honor—and on to something else. He had his own woe to get off his mind too, one that had plagued him since his loitering on the porch. And the timing couldn't be more right. The reporter, enticed by the expectation that he would soon be having his appetite appeased, had followed the lady store owner over to the counter where she was busily slicing up thick-carved pieces of home-made bread to hold together the made-to-order sandwiches that had been requested. Mr. Faehner took advantage of his and Pop's one-on-oneness and decided to bend his nonwaxed ear about something on so grand a scale that even telling someone like Pop who always minded his own business—and yours as his—if that was the intention, seemed a dare. But the disadvantage of not telling him certainly outweighed the advantage, if history had anything to say about it. Mr. Faehner knew. He knew. Everything he had ever hoped for, he had hoped for in this place. And now could be no different. The Silver Mine, the country club, the estate, all of the land deals he made acquiring thousands and thousands of southern-end acres, and every other enterprise of magnitude and importance had been first wished for and spoken about here in this docile little place. Who would have thought? How could it be? Were Mom and Pop his real-life guardian angels whom fate had connected him to to watch over him and guide him? Were they? It didn't matter. The continuity of the matter, of how it had worked, stretched out over thirty-nine years and scores of opportunities could not be ignored. He began without transition.

"Here's the thing, Pop—," Mr. Faehner said but then was interrupted.

"Come and get it," Mom elicited from her far-off counter once she had completed her tidy little task.

After paying for his sandwiches and ice cream bar, Mr. Faehner bade Mom and Pop a fond farewell and promised, by crossing his heart and hoping to die, that he would never let another such interval of time pass between them as long as he lived!

On to Pequea

Outwardly, Mr. Faehner was not a man of distinction, that is, he did not possess any superficial characteristic, which made him someone to take notice of beyond a first glance. Among a crowd of people, he would not be picked out as the person he really was—a man rich and powerful. By his looks, he was very ordinary. And that was not meant to mean that he was without appearance or charm in the way he was featured. He was. If a woman was attracted to him without knowing of his fortune, she would usually yield to her feminine instinct—that he, by virtue of his ordinary shape, size, and swirly hair was at least someone worthy of a little attention. In contrast to this, he too did not possess any outward characteristic, which could be considered unusual. There was no part of his facial feature, which would compel an onlooker to cry out that there was a hideous creature about. There was nothing ugly about him, head to toe. And by virtue of this, this ordinarily ordinary man had the uncanny ability to place himself before the public without being recognized as the person who had been for so long a time in the public eye.

But the same could not be said for the vehicle of conveyance that he chose as his preferred mode of transportation. The silver-white stretch limousine stood out wherever it went. Its lengthy size and high-gloss finish, dazzling white, was enough to draw stares from everyone within sight of it. Up close, one's attention would come to focus on the laid-out trims, headlights, window casings, wheel trims, taillight sets, all traced out in sterling silver. Spectators who saw it from near or far were awed by its unique beauty but never by the man whom they would sometimes see entering or exiting it.

And so it was this day too when Mr. Faehner and his follower walked out of the country grocery, each holding on to the remaining part of one of Mom's home-made sandwiches and approached the refulgent car. They were not in the sights of the few that watched. But there was one person who caught notice who did care about the man behind the car, and he was very much interested in making his notice known. He eye-balled the luxury limo as it, first remained idled while its occupants ate, then pulled up through the otherwise-empty parking lot to face a turn on the highway. From his den across the roadway, he waited in anticipation to see which way the limo was intending to go. He crossed his fingers and hoped. To the left, he would pursue; to the right, he would not pursue. He readied himself. When the alluring limousine pulled up to the highway, Obe signaled left, which to the onlooking motorcycle attendant meant it was time to get up and go. He tossed aside the open-ended wrench he had clutched in his fist and hopped aboard his own "king of the road." After carefully negotiating the black-and-chrome Harley out the back of the converted garage, he began a run across a series of backyards behind the highway where the luxury vehicle was now traveling. To Mike, the route he had chosen to run, he still considered a shortcut because behind the houses, he did not have to obey the posted thirty-five-mile-per-hour speed limit; and therefore in a distance of less than a mile, he could overtake any vehicle, which might have had a head start on him. When he finally pulled out onto the roadway, the limousine was still in sight only a short distance ahead. Mike increased his speed in successive bursts accelerating to over sixty-five miles per minute—or so it felt like—and was front-wheel to back-bumper with the pursued vehicle in no time at all. Obe, believing that the biker behind him was just riding on impulse and only wanted to momentarily intimidate the slower-moving car before taking off, thought better than to possibly provoke the situation by taking off himself and decided to only maintain the proper speed and hope the lone rider would leave them be. But another mile down the road, the situation was still the same. Stressed out by the uncertainty of the reason why they were being hotly pursued, Obe now decided it best to decrease his speed in the hope that his action would annoy the intrepid highwayman. Glancing back, Obe could not see that the adamant rider had been using his right hand to signal the car over. But from inside the car, Mr.

Faehner noticed the purposeful slow down and thought to question the driver as to what condition had caused it. He lowered the partition.

"Obe?" he said, expressing his perplexity.

"We got's trouble," Obe replied in an odious tone. "There's some crazy person out there behind us, trailing us on a motorcycle, keeping so close he could probably reach out and touch us. I done all I could to get him to go out around, but he won't give up. What's you want me to do, sir?"

Concerned for the welfare of the others, Mr. Faehner first undimmed the rear window to get a steady view of what was happening.

"Pull over, Obe," he directed his driver in a less-concerned voice once he had had opportunity to observe the outside disturbance directly.

Obe complied. Having never been in a similar situation while driving Mr. Faehner's limousine, he was unsure of exactly what would be expected of him other than bringing the slowing vehicle to a halt at the side of the road. What role would he be expected to perform? A protector? A proxy? An intermediary? Once the car was stationary, Mr. Faehner was prompt in telling his spooked attendant that his services would not be needed outside the vehicle. The reporter too was ordered to stay inside. Both men did. But the cost of doing so went against everything their gut feelings told them. They ached to open their mouths and be the harbingers of what would surely be misfortune. Sensing their by-the-looks-on-their-faces upset, Mr. Faehner paused once in the middle of his evacuation and reassured them that he knew what he was doing.

"I'm not an anile person, I can assure you," he stated firmly. "And besides, I know this fellow, and I think I know what he wants."

With that said, Mr. Faehner shut the side door and ventured, hands in his pockets, toward the rear of the limousine where the lone biker was waiting.

"What's up there, Evel Knievel?" Mr. Faehner sounded out in a jovial voice when he came to where the rider had stopped just inches behind the stationary limo.

Anyone, other than someone who knew him, would never have thought to approach Mike Zoig in the casual manner that Mr. Faehner now did. Mike was a burly man, whose watermelon-shaped head was capped with curly, blond locks of hair. He sported a similarly curly, similarly blond goatee, which accentuated the overall manner of his face in a way which made him look like the Cowardly Lion in the *Wizard of Oz*, although no one had probably ever dared to make that comparison to his face. He looked forty and at the peak of his abilities, which made him someone who instantly garnered other people's respect and fear—the fear made so by the ever-present, surly disposition he carried both on his countenance and in his attitude. But not to Mr. Faehner. To Mr. Faehner, Zoig was the quintessential manservant, always striving to please him, always willing to go the extra mile, if at all, he could. They were not strangers to one another as the others in the car assumed. Mike was a local, born and raised, and had many years past met and gotten to know the esteemed billionaire, back when his fortune was counted in only millions.

Mike knew a good thing when he got into it. His previous dealings with the quintessential rich man proved that. From the first moment they met, Mike had always strived to be the quintessential brown-noser in his company. And Mike had profited from it immensely. Now was no different. By having gained the rich man's confidence already, Mike was ever on the alert to the possibility of becoming involved in some sort of association with the hand that had fed him so many extravaganzas, perks, and privileges—in fact, the only extravaganzas, perks, and privileges he had received in his life. Mike was ever a fruit ripe for the picking.

Although Mr. Faehner was none too happy for having been flagged down in broad daylight by the intrepid cycling enthusiast, he was able to cast aside the vexed way he was feeling because of the certainty he also felt knowing that Zoig would have never done something so brash unless he had news of the utmost importance to reveal. Their conversation was succinct. Mike started out sketchy though just to be sure that Mr. Faehner was indeed willing to listen despite having been intervened upon so unexpectedly.

"So sorry for surprising you there, Mr. F, but I saw you over there at Mom and Pop's, and I wanted to surprise you with the good news I have regarding our little enterprise. I'm excited to tell you that I've been watching over the woodland as we agreed."

The one-sided conversation came to an abrupt end. Overhead the sky, which had for some time now, been gathering itself into a thick gray veil, erupted. Droplets of rain began falling from the cloud blanket overhanging them, hitting Mr. Faehner on his head and Zoig on his helmet. Mr. Faehner, largely unprotected, except for what of a shield he could make with his hands over himself, grimaced over his plight—getting his new suit wet—and sought to conclude the get-together at once.

"Got to go," he announced abruptly. He turned to leave but almost as suddenly stopped only a footstep away. He turned toward Zoig and without pause retrieved from his pant's pocket a newer leather wallet stuffed with cash. Reaching into the wallet, he quick-picked two crisp $100 bills, folded them, and handed them over to the cycle man.

Mike, overwhelmed by the amount of the offer, smiled profusely at his benefactor and offered him in return countless adulations. The limousine then pulled away to skitter along the wet roadway, and Zoig skirted his way along the backyard bike path back to the shop.

Back in the limousine, Mr. Faehner was met by the inveigling eyes of both his companions and felt compelled to address something of the meaning of the unusual event, which had just taken place. If not, he knew that both their curiosities could fester, and who knew what that could lead to.

"That, curious creature, was Mike Zoig. He is someone whom I became acquainted with many years ago. He is indigenous to the area having been born and raised right here, in illustrious Little Conestoga," he added on with an inflection of humor. "Since our initial encounter, he has grown rabbit ears and red-hawk eyes to zero in on me whenever I happen to occasion this quaint little community. And though my excursions are few and far between, Mike usually manages at least to be seen by me in the hope that I'll throw a bone his way. It impresses me the way he goes out of his way to "catch" me."

At this point in the explanation, Mr. Faehner began to express a look of deep reflection as though his thoughts were exclusively on Mike and the many instances of circumstance he had had with him. But really it was a ploy to put an end to the conversation as it was without giving any room for rebuttal. Onward, they commenced down the lonely road, other drivers having yielded to the bombardment of penny-sized raindrops falling from the low-domed sky. Obe pressed on. Amid the contrast of the verbal quiet and audacious display put on by Mother Nature, the conversationalists were all adequately distracted enough that the all-important discussion of Zoig soon lost all meaning. Concentrations now focused on the natural world—the nature of the rain.

So far, Obe had navigated so good. He continued to traverse the saturated countryside assured of his abilities to maintain a good connection to the course. But ten minutes more toward their destination, the penny-sized rain turned to nickel-sized hail; and Obe, without pause to seek advice from those

CHRISTOPHER L. HAEFNER

he was escourting, began an immediate search, both visually and in his mind, for a place where he could safely stop until the onslaught let up. Nearby was the entrance to the Pequea Park, a recreational campground and picnic facility owned by the local electric utility, PPL. Obe made for the opening on the left-side roadway, high beams up and wipers in furious action swiping streams of icy water left to right and right to left to gain what visibility he could given the dire circumstance. Moments later, the limousine stopped with the motor still on so adequate power could still be provided to the car's comfort controls.

Together the trio of trapped travelers resigned themselves to the fact that they were there to stay until the duration of hail and heavy rain eased up. To gain a more appreciative view of their surroundings, Mr. Faehner activated the undimmer control next to where he was seated and immediately all of the limo's back windows became clear to view out. To the left was the creek a short distance away. Across the creek was the larger portion of the park where basically everything park-related took place. The segment that they were situated on was seldom used by visitors as it encompassed only a few land acres in the vast totality of the recreation facility. Across the creek the park appeared abandoned. Any who had been frequenting the picnic grounds or playground had long since retreated from the threatening storm. The only proof that the park was in use was the telltale parked car of the park's ranger sitting idly beside an outbuilding. If he, or she, was there, they were inside it.

And the rain came down, more so than any of the detained passengers thought possible given the sudden appearance of the inclement weather.

"We are in what I call an airium," Mr. Faehner announced in a jovial voice.

"What's an airium?" the reporter asked in advance of Obe's "a what?"

"It's like the opposite of an aquarium."

"You must mean a terrarium," the reporter quickly interjected.

"No, I mean an airium," Mr. Faehner stated firmly. "It's not a real word, mind you, but I mean to say it anyway. The English language though very profound does not yet have within it every possible word. And this is one of them. I know it sounds kooky, but it has meaning all the same. We are here contained, trapped really, within the confines of the air and space that keeps us. It's simply that."

Noticing the silly look on the reporter's face, Mr. Faehner made further comment about his made-up word.

"Suffice to say . . ."

Halfway through his testament, Mr. Faehner side-glanced out of the window next to him and noticed the rapid rise of creek-level water. Already the Pequea was struggling to keep the copious volume of increase within its boundaries. They, stranded on a portion of the park where they could not find refuge by advancing to higher ground, would become inundated by the swollen creek's flow should the swell grow greater. It would be prudent, despite the current driving conditions, to leave their little sanctuary before the forces of Mother Nature took over. Aware that their overall safety would be put in jeopardy should they continue to hold out on the beside-the-creek flood plain, Mr. Faehner prevailed upon his driver to exit the park part at once and risk the hazardous road instead of waiting to be overcome by the creek's wrath.

Obe complied, and their interrupted journey resumed toward their intended destination. Slowly and steadily, the stretch car eked along, carrying its occupants in a manner more suited for sightseeing visitors. The rain still fell heavily, and its impression upon the Pequea path made it seem, to those observing, like being in another world—a world where rain would never stop, a world where water could encompass everything if it so desired. Being the sort of person who was good in a crisis, Mr. Faehner thought to even out the odds they were facing by gaining a relative perspective on the impending doom as it was. Using the television set, which was mounted on a framework beside him, he operated the media-capturing device to try to see if any of the local stations were pertaining to the climaxing storm. Checking his watch, he was glad to see that the time was right for the weekend update of the acclaimed *Weather World* forecast. The regularly scheduled Monday through Friday broadcast of Pennsylvania's weather was often repeated on the same PBS station, Channel 33, on both weekend day afternoons. And now was the time. And even though it would not be a current, up-to-the-minute forecast, the predictions that had been made relative to the system now plaguing the Pequea area might be valuable enough to gain a perspective on their overall situation. The enormity of the storm—what could be expected—might be ascertained. After tuning in to the broadcast, Mr. Faehner saw that a line of potent storms had indeed been predicted for the southern regions of both York and Lancaster Counties although the way they had been spoken of, in so perfunctory a manner, was in no way indicative of the severity of things being experienced in the here and now. The contrast between what was predicted and what became reality was huge. He was about to relent, turn off the channel, and just hope for the best when suddenly one of the prominent weather professors came on-air—live. The forecaster's "break" into the prerecorded program was a syndetic sign that something serious was occurring. The spotlight was on the very region they were traversing. Radar showed that an intensifying storm was centered directly overhead and would be moving due east, trekking at only five miles per hour. In its wake would be left an enormous amount of precipitation—up to four or five inches in most places. The announcement was ominous. Mr. Faehner's first thoughts were of the impending wreck and ruin that would be brought to everything and everyone in the storm's path. Travelers on the road would incur hardship with the less fortunate involving themselves or being involved in accidents. Mom and Pop's would invariably become a way station for the weather-weary. Turning his thoughts further east, he came in mind of his own beloved properties. The Silver Mine would be inundated by the immensity of water that was sure to fall on it. The ponds would flood, probably up to the paths that surround them. The mine itself would receive a proportion of water enough to keep the pumps running for weeks to come. The 1800 house basement would receive substantial seepage. In all things would be nothing short of a substantial mess for weeks.

In reaction to his besieged mind, Mr. Faehner lowered the television's volume so he could still see but barely hear the reiterating statements. Snatching up his cell phone, he then quick-called the Silver Mine office and made contact with the attendant on duty, warning him of the impending approach of the terrible storm. "Make sure the mine pumps are operating at the first sign of trouble. And take one of the auxiliary pumps into the basement of the house. There's sure to be problems there." Next on his last-minute itinerary of phone calls to make was the all-important call to his sweet wife who, although completely comfortable and safe in her Silver Hills haven, would worry without end for the safety of her husband knowing he was out and about in such a nightmare of a storm. "I assure you I'm in a good place," was all he told her, not wanting to further her concerns for him needlessly.

Having attended to the matters of his own personal interests, Mr. Faehner again turned his attention to what was happening around him. The one-car procession had now reached the park's end. From this point on on either side of the creek, the wilds of the land took over. Hillsides steepened. Runaway streams, now spewing forth like turned-on fire hoses, erupted from everywhere along the rocky clefts and ledges. Also, along the hillsides, embedded in the rich green and gray were a multitude of hillside dwellings, some considered by those who still occupied them "home sweet home." Others unoccupied by their current or former owners were considered "home sweet hovel." The latter's condition had been a matter of fate, a fate which had never been forgotten.

The aftermath of Hurricane Agnes in 1972 had left behind legacy. That legacy was one which would never be forgotten by those who had experienced it. All rain-producing events since were measured against it. And would be until the day when an even greater event surpassed it. Agnes was one for the ages. And she was different too than what most people would expect having heard of her devastation and effect. She had not come in fury as it would be supposed. She did not lay down a torrential day-and-a-half's worth of downpour as most hurricanes do should they manage to spin their way across the northern latitudes of the interior United States. By then, they are dwindling, dying. But Agnes did not act that way. She came in what was actually late June, unusually early by the standard of recorded years, and she dawdled. In fact, she could not escape. Pennsylvania became her prison for the majority of one week, a locked system that for the life of it had nothing coming at it to knock it out of state, of country. So Agnes remained, and she spent her remaining life on the residents of the Susquehanna Valley. And in that measure, that of her expending herself, selflessly upon the poor, defenseless Pennsylvanians, she did things that other, more potent, remnant hurricanes did not. Rain gauges gave the amounts as records were recorded and broken day-to-day. But the story of dear Agnes was not written in inches annotated in a recording book. Her story lied in the actuality of what she did to the people whose lives she changed. Lives were lost. Livelihoods forsaken. And all because of an unfortunate glitch in the way nature usually deals with its mighty forceful storms. The truth be told, Agnes had lost most of her punch by the time she landed on the Pennsylvania midlands. In fact by meteorological standards, she was actually a hurricane—category zero. Weather centers tracking her had downgraded her to a typical tropical storm long before she cast her practically weary winsome shadow upon the state. But like any unwelcome guest who has overstayed their welcome, she was made into something far worse than what she was. Agnes became the "herricane" of hurricanes for generations to come.

Absent the swirling, hurling winds, which usually accompany even a substantially downgraded tropical storm, Agnes's claim to fame came due to her desire to remain over the gently rolling hills of central Pennsylvania. Mr. Faehner compared in his mind the contrast between the consequence of the severe storm he was encountering and the memory in his mind of the devastation as measured in quantities of precipitation, of the storm of the past. The storm currently letting up outside his window had probably emptied a saturating three inches of water across the areas it hit. He did the math. Per acre that would come to about 81,000 gallons—enough to flood the creek right up to its banks, maybe a little beyond. All over the current storm path, flash flooding would occur—a nuisance really. Damage would be minimal. But Agnes on the other hand had unleashed at least four times that amount, in certain places more. As per the equation, she delivered an astounding 335,000 gallons, per acre across the parts of the state where she stayed, and stayed, and stayed!

The misery she left behind was beheld by all. They knew she would be the one against whom all others would be tested. All around the state markings were instituted commemorating Agnes's destruction. And there arose among the ranks of the discordant people a certain pride in having been part of her history, of having endured and outlasted her. And in observation of this, prideful Pennsylvanians posted the progress of Agnes's prowess. Flood levels, marks, some etched into buildings' bricks, some highlighted by spray-painters on trees and bridges made memorials of the once-in-a-lifetime event.

But these purposeful little reminders were not all that remained of Agnes's fury. And these, remainders of another kind, were still to be evidenced all these forty-one years later. Cross-creek from where the limo now trekked stood the outlying seclusion of the Pequea people—homes set apart from the cutout district where entire tiers were leveled into the hillside above where the hefty Pequea creek spilled into the mighty Susquehanna river. These smaller but numerous domiciles were built with the idea of being alone, apart from the strained living condition of the nearly 300-person-populated town. These arranged-for-privacy dwellings were strewn out, a mile or so distant from the point of confluence of the two waterways. Here, amid the rustic woodlands, peace-seeking land-loners could live free from the hectic lifestyle featured in the closer-than-they-liked town where the distance from one neighbor to another was less than desired.

Looking across the swollen creek, Mr. Faehner came to terms with the concentrated appearance of the once-pleasant-looking suburb. Most of the homes lower to the creek were hovels. They were long since abandoned by owners who fled during the two-generations-past event. They were in ruin. They would never be rebuilt until taken over by someone who possessed no memory of Agnes or was naive enough to think that something like Agnes would never come again. And there they remained in ruin. The wreck of the flood water, which had reached over twenty feet above the current bank-high creek and the deterioration of the over forty years hence, had rendered the once-prominent structures into dilapidated shacks though they were not forlorn. Despite their lacking, they became places of frequency for itinerant indigents who, in their wonderings, happened to stumble literally upon them until, that is, their inevitable discovery led their closest inhabitant to place a call to the township officer to have them duly kicked out. Another use too was found for the more hospitable hovels—that is, they became places where overnight parties could be conducted without fear of retribution. These were mostly local teens and twenty-somethings who learned of the long-since-abandoned abodes by discovery. In their youth, they made play things of them, holding up in one or another during a winter snow or making use of their utter privacy and bringing first-loves into their hidden spaces to experiment at love-making. These once-in-a-while dalliances although frowned upon by the populous, especially when the music got loud, were for the most part tolerated. No one knew if someone they knew would be among the group should someone decide to call upon the peacekeepers. And so, time stood still along the quaint Pequea hills. And the row of low-lying hovels remain. Their testimony is one of pride. What is left of what they once were—exemplified by their continuing state of decay—shown off to any who dare to ponder their display.

In light of their experience, of having dodged the pounding rain, Mr. Faehner pondered for a moment whether or not he wanted to make the others in his company privy to what his experience was when Agnes was making the news. He had been part if it too. His experience had been that of a twelve-year-old boy, who by the third day of the epic flood, began venturing off, either alone or with companions, to see for himself just what it was everyone was talking about. From his west-end-of-the-city row home, he began making journeys toward certain places of interest—places that would have been cool to see flooded. In three days, he made nine trips to see for himself to what extent things were turning into because of the excessive precipitation. They were methodically made trips too, for in those days, *hype* was not an overused concept with the media, and the renditions made on the round-the-clock news outlets were depicting fact and not fiction. Had the young Faehner boy been privy to the existence of the silver mine property at the time, he no doubt would have trekked the ten-mile-or-so distance to see—the ponds, the house, the run, the creek in a state of liquid liability.

But such as it was, the adventures remained closer to home and included places he considered a more reasonable walking distance from his city's west-end residence. Intriguing was to see the everyday coming-up of water levels in the old west-end quarry, the Maple Grove Swimming Pool, Boas Fruit Market across the Little Conestoga Creek from Maple Grove, the intervening Columbia Avenue, which became, at the point where the highway bridge crossed over the creek, a pool in itself. These places, their workings, became points of reference to all who witnessed them, their daily inundation, deeper and deeper, into the oblivious Conestoga who knew them neither as friend or foe but only did as Mother Nature prescribed.

Memories. Life was so full of them. They could be brought up either when times seemed relevant or not. When each time something of dramatic proportion occurs, we often think and wonder when something similar will happen again. We expect it once it—whatever it is—happens. But too often life has a way of showing us just how insignificant we are. Events, that form and shape our lives, often, are not repeated, and like the cross-creek cabins now passing into oblivion, we too pass along through the all-too-brief realm of our existence without further eventful realization, without renderings, good or bad, without again feeling as though we were picked as to be part of something special. And once we're old enough to have felt that time's passed us by, we begin to yearn with our heart's innermost desires to be part of that something once more. Nostalgia. No. It goes deeper. Life is about experiences first and foremost although most of us don't begin to recognize this until most of our time is spent. Who recalls the day-to-day living even if it encompasses us with comforts and pleasures? Who recalls the relaxation, the lazy days spent without purpose or consideration? Who recalls anything of them? They are just split-second realizations, yet they are culled from endless hours of derived situation. It is the events in our lives that renew us whether we like it or not, whether they delve us fortune or destruction. And Agnes was one of them. And love her or hate her, she was a mark in time.

The half-hour storm carried east, its fury being spent now on places in the distance. Having done no permanent damage to the locality that had just been under its threat, it would be forgotten. It had laid down no credence upon which to entreat it as anything formidable. It would remain without credentials, without consideration, without a name. The limousine's speed picked up a bit in response to its diminished state. The journey was near complete. Just a farther two miles was the town of Pequea. Obe pressed on the accelerator just enough to prove he could be depended on as a facilitator who desired the same thing as what was expected of him.

Coming out of the dark creek hollow, the silver-white vehicle entered into the bottom end of the tiny community. Here, where the now-roaring creek emptied into the mile-wide river existed what was once the nascent beginnings of the thought-up town. Here and there were a few of the turn-of-the-last-century, three-story, brick-and-board homes in which still lived some remaining ancestor of the few original unintended founders. Near to these first-to-be-seen dwellings was the town post office given license and operation during the 1940s, a decade after the town had boomed from what was once just a scattering of residences into levels and levels of vacation cottages erected into the lesser restrictive incline areas of the river's sloping backdrop. Also too was the marvelous Pequea Hotel built in the late 1940s by a son of one of the original town founders to house those who came but without accommodations of their own. Nearby the hotel stood the ever-popular store with no name, which literally it was. The old woman who currently owned and operated it for the past thirty years had never bothered to put a sign up giving it a name, a reference point. Neither had her parents whom she inherited it from after they had had it all of another forty years before. Opposite the store with no name, across the old town road, was another notorious town site, the three-in-one; garage, gas station, fix-it shop all run by the same proprietor. Beyond these town traditions, the old town road carried on on a gently upward slope some short distance. Along the Susquehanna side was one huge parcel of level ground set aside since the town's beginnings for use as a parking facility. Word was that nobody knew who owned it. Neither the township nor any of the townspeople had ever laid claim to it, had ever restricted it, or had ever acted on its behalf. At the point where the parking lot ended, the old town road turned sharply then traced its lowest course on a parallel route 20 feet higher up from the riverside stretch. Along this elevated extent had been built the oldest of the added-on terrace cottages. Most were in excellent condition due their select position on the often-viewed, seldom-visited mountain. More boats than cars passed by them, ready to pass judgment on how they either added or subtracted from the overall pleasantness of the scenic landscape. The road rounded out from one end to another creating tier after tier where cottage after cottage had been cut into the mountain. From the second tier up, each terrace took on a unique identity derived mostly from how all second, third, forth, and fifth-tier comers had decided, by their own volition, to emulate the put-into-place taste and variation of the first-comers. Ginger-bread houses dotted the second tier. Scaled-down Cape Cod's sprang up on the third. And it went like that all the way up to the top tier where lookout dwellings looked like oversized birdhouses with high-peaked apexes where extra rooms built atop the top floor all vied to gain an appreciative view of the wide river spaces hundreds of feet below.

To enter into this land of milk and honey, one had to first find their way up and over another of the land-marking makings of the tiny-tiered town—the singing bridge. Built during the town's boom period the all-steel structure loomed large at the entranceway, cross-creek, into the town. The span, erected some 100 feet from the actual merge of the silty creek water and the clearer river water crossed over a point where the difference from one side to the other of the confluent waterways was at its greatest expanse, not quite an ideal spot when deciding to put up a costly point A to point B jumble of metal. Places farther back the creek would have been much more suitable, much more simpler when considering something such as cost-effectiveness and convenience. But to those who knew the town, knew its history, the answer was clear. The connection had been built at the place where upon both sides of the channeled creek dirt paths had once been. Probably, though there was no evidence to prove it, the indigenous peoples—the Susquehannocks—once had an archetypal archway set across the deepening dim. The old town road upon which the original town had been laid out upon had really been part of a system of Indian trails, which traversed the entire county and beyond in both directions. The town founders, so to speak, had done little more than pick up where their predecessors had left off. If one could look into the past, one could see the thousands of prehistoric people who once inhabited the glorious river hills and who freely wandered its banks in accordance to their own daily needs.

The singing bridge was once one of many which dotted the Lancaster County landscape. Built at a time when Carnegie's influence could be felt far and wide across the Commonwealth, the sturdy steel bridges were erected, size and shape depending, across every expanse of open water. From tiny tributary runs to the hundred-foot crossing at the Pequea-Susquehanna confluence, deals had been sealed in steel to build the essential bridges across the lands' divides.

But time had taken its toll. And one by one, they fell to both the pressure of modernization and what Mother Nature had doled out as part of her signature service. Agnes alone had destroyed many of the remaining metal tributes in one swoop. Of those that somehow survived her immediate wrath, her influence was brought to bear in the way she undermined the structural integrity of the bridges' foundations. During the heaviest part of the flooding, these bridges had been bombarded by hundreds of tons of debris, which literally, by the force of the raging waters around them, acted as picks and shovels to undermine the sediments on all sides of the foundations, leaving pockets and pock marks where cavities, unseen, developed. Bridges weakened and collapsed years after the high-water event, too late to change the condition, the legacy left by the lady who was in no way ladylike to the people of Pennsylvania.

"Hear that," Mr. Faehner addressed the attentive ears of both the other passengers. "That's music to the ears."

The heavy stream of dulcet tones vibrated through the car compartment almost like a consistent hum.

"It's the last of its kind in the county," Mr. Faehner commented with an air of authority. "The last of the singing bridges."

"What does that mean exactly?" the reporter said, acting upon the slight made by the so-sure-of-himself billionaire.

Mr. Faehner responded without notice of the annoyance present in the reporter's tone, so dulled over by the low-pitched frequency of the melodic metal music.

"This bridge is being dismantled very soon. By me. I purchased it from the township, and I stand ready to demolish it and put in a newer, safer one. This bridge is past its prime. Its barely two-lane passage will be made into a four-lane wonder. Currently, it stands as an impediment to trucks and emergency vehicles who might try to pass it. Quite frankly, I submit that it's been nothing short of a miracle that no serious accidents have ever, in fact, occurred on it. I'll admit though it is an eye-pleaser. I'll be sad to see it go."

"Then why let it go?" the reporter asked in a direct tone of voice.

"I just told you why," Mr. Faehner shot back in reply.

"Why not just disassemble the thing and refit it somewhere else, somewhere where its old-mode style won't be detrimental to those who use it?"

That thought that had never crossed his mind struck the middle-aged entrepreneur like a strike of lightning.

"What a brilliant idea! Why, there's a dozen or more places I could stage that beautiful eyesore! Raze it down just to raise it up! Now there's a clever way of making the most out of a bad situation."

Wide-eyed, he looked across at the reporter and stated honestly, "My friend, you cut me to the quick. I must be losing my touch for not having thought of such a thing myself. Though I will definitely incur more of an expense at first for doing such a foolish thing, I think I can find a way to turn this lemon into a pitcher of the finest lemonade. Yes, I think I can. The bridge will become a lasting memorial to a bygone era instead of just a memory."

More of the sky's cloud clutter broke open as the limousine proceeded slowly across the metallic span. Open to view at the opposite end and made more refulgent by the cast of golden light was the sight of a clearly marked paint line and letters clinging to one of the structural support beams about midway up the tower line. A full fifteen feet up from the bridge's surface, someone had taken the trouble to scale the tower beam and make note of the rise of the infamous flood. No doubt from memory they had been able to observe approximately where the height of the high water reached, then after, thought to memorialize it. It read like an epitaph: "Agnes of 72. May God have mercy on us!"

The Peq-Way

Advancing beyond the soon-to-be-supplanted singing bridge was the grouping of plain-view brick-and-board structures that comprised what remained of the original town of Pequea. Due to the size and shape of the outfitted buildings, it was easy to tell which was which in comparison to each other. The three-in-one shops all had their bay areas open, and each compartment had within it several to many relative objects displaying which particular trade was being plied inside. The store with no name had, as any place of central business would, an easy-to-access public entranceway, a flight of wide wooden steps leading from a small adjacent parking area right up to a set of double-wide doors, which were now standing double-wide open. The post office had pasted to its front window, a hand-painted depiction of Mr. Mailman, the likeness of which left a lot to be desired. Offset from the store was the Pequea Hotel, a four-story, twenty-four-room, lavishly decorated facilitation, which although decades past its pride and glory years still could be considered, by modern standards of appreciation, of at least a three-star rating in its overall provision of accommodation. Even Mr. Faehner had stayed the night on a whim just to spend the night. And from that day on, the history of the hotel had changed. Forever more, the townspeople would spout as others had done for other famous people that "Mr. Faehner slept there."

The Faehner mark of approval had done much to infuse new life into the sleepy structure and the town around it as well. Every time he showed up, no matter what the reason, revenues shot up over 40 percent for the next three or four weeks. And word-of-mouth was quick to carry the news. Already a buzz was beginning to circulate from the mouths of the people, waiting to be attended in the post office, the garage, the gas station, the store with no name, and inside the hotel as well. Within hours, this news would spread, like a plague, to every inhabited house and hill-hovel in the outlying community. There need be no proof other than to say, for Mr. Faehner's infrequent cameos were well known. He did little to remain anonymous while in the midst of such a well-thought-of community. The inclination of some of townspeople was to, rather than approach a man they considered unapproachable, paint his name along with the dates of his comings on the sides of the single line of telephone poles, which lined the old town road in then out of the town. But it had never as yet been done.

As procedure dictated, Obe guided the limousine onto a spot alongside the hotel's closer side, a side specially designated for Mr. Faehner's convenience whenever he decided to frequent the town landmark. Without delay, the trio exited the vehicle and made way toward the front entrance of the establishment. Before actually entering the building, Mr. Faehner turned to his entourage and requested that for purposes of intended expectation they all act as one, meaning, that he required that they, despite whatever happens, maintain their silence and follow any lead he gives them. They agreed.

Other than to say that he was meeting a client of sorts, the reporter and the chauffeur knew nothing of the person they expected to see or what the meeting was about. Suffice to say, they didn't need to.

Bob Drayton, a sluggish man of about sixty, was a man who was once considered, at least by his own interpretation, a big shot in and around certain communities in the southern end. He was at one time the owner of two thrifty sporting goods stores—one in Willow Street, which was located about seven miles east of Little Conestoga, and one in Oxford, which was located twenty miles south-southeast from the first store. For a decade or more, Bob's stores prospered; and Bob, due the person he was, pretty much flaunted his success in the way he spoke, in the way he dressed, and in the way he let it be known that he was someone who was somebody. Bob's comeuppance, if you want to call it that, came in those later years when first one, then another, Big Box stores began arriving, close enough to even his stores' rather remote localities that they began to feel a negative impact from them. Bob, although loaded by his own standards of monetary self-importance, could in no way compete with stores who had budgets in the billions. Little by little, soccer ball by soccer ball, badminton racket by badminton racket, Bob's stores lost out to the cheaper, more convenient Big Boxes. In the end, Bob declared bankruptcy although in reality that had been done as an easy way out, a way out of paying much of his business debt. Bob had, over a lengthy period of time, hidden away a sizeable amount of money that he had simply siphoned off from the daily capital. In short, he would raid the cash reserves without receipt and allocate the "run" money right into his pocket. His intent was to wait out a term of time and then auspiciously return, entering into another type of best-suited business, and become prominent again. But Bob's comeback was never to be. He became a shell of his former self. His overly inflated image, sustained by the model of lifestyle made possible by his entrepreneurship had been ostensively popped. Aware that his credentials had been seized, Bob became something of a fugitive from his former life. He sold his buildings and home and secreted himself away in the birdhouse tier of Pequea. There, with the money he had siphoned off of his failing businesses, he put together a fortress of solitude, a place where he could be forgotten about for a while, while he dreamed and schemed of becoming something of his former self again. To do that, he had over a period of about seven years bought up several adjacent high-tiered properties all in a row—one he fixed up quite considerably on the inside. To viewers on the outside, Bob's one domain appeared ready for the bulldozer; but inside, it was quite sturdy and quite nice. Altogether there were four adjacent properties, three of which he reluctantly rented out from time to time. But Bob's secluded life up on the precipices of Pequea had with it one insurmountable problem—water or rather the lack of it. Although the town possessed a huge community cistern, which drew in water from a nearby trickling rock, which when it rained splashed tons of water into it, the cistern's facility could not do much for the highest-point dwellings. The pumping system, which ran from the well, was insufficient to carry water up to points so far away. The answer would have been to have had a secondary supply well installed halfway up the steeply terrained hillside and from there carry on as a pumping station. But the concept could never be carried out. None of the lower-tiered owners ever relented to converting their properties over to the idea. So the uppermost dwellers were left to fend for themselves, which didn't bother many of them as their properties were used basically as vacation getaways and water to be used only short term, for cooking, drinking, and showers could be provided by themselves, brought down with them for one of their "escapes."

Bob, because he was permanently there, required a better solution to his solution-deficit problem. He had tried by implementing a well-water-delivery method of his own device. Fifty feet higher up on the hill than his home, he dug something of a hole in the wall, which he drilled out, tediously, with the extensive use of a generator and pneumatic drill, the prominent Wissahickon Schist, enough to place a large water-storage tank in or against as one would say. By holing out three top sections of the holding tank and fitting funnels atop them, Bob hoped that during longer-lasting rain events, an abundance of atmospheric water would collect in the collecting tank, enough to keep him sufficiently supplied with water he would need for the basics. Once the hold tank was adequately receiving water, it could then be used to send water to the house down the hill. By using a valve, gravity-fed water could be turned on and off into the house as desired for the purposes of cooking, washing, drinking, or cleaning. But the system had a glitch to it. It relied on the principles of what it could get, precipitation-wise, when it could get it. And too often, deficiencies in the week-to-week or month-to-month averages of rainfall meant that the well-intended, above-ground well was not always capable of supplying even the essential amounts of counted-on water. Because of the inefficiency of the system, Bob continually went without water for days, weeks, or even months at a time. Because his system never really got going—he never as yet faced the complications of winter with its ever-present cold, its ice-inducing sting—he didn't fully realize he was working with a system that was a nine-month-on, three-month-off reality.

Officially, the two men of means had never met though each was sure they could recognize the other if they had to, such as the reason they would have to now. Mr. Faehner, despite his always being in the news, as it were, still went about in relative anonymity due his common looks. Mr. Drayton, whose visage was once splashed on roadside billboards all over the county, was now only a former image of who he used to be and hardly a soul who knew or kept company with him before would know him now. So here the two would meet once the threshold of the hotel was crossed.

As darkened as the ground floor lobby of the grand hotel was, it was hard to tell if anything was going on outside. The windows were drawn and sashed with heavy curtains so that guests could reflect only on the eye-catching, turn-of-the-nineteenth-century design and content of the affluent interior. Mr. Drayton, feeling the acute sting of nervousness and intimidation, paced frontward and backward between two of the front hotel windows, periodically peeling back the stiff curtain material and peering into the scape outside. His anxiety peaked minutes before his called-upon meeting took place, and in reaction to it, he administered to his own relief in such a way as he frequently did whenever the stresses of the world served to unravel him. Determined to go ahead with it, he backed himself—so no one was looking—into the nearby men's room and entered the singular stall. After latch-locking the stall door, he quick-swiped a wad of toilet tissue and, holding that in his left hand, held the padded paper to his eyes and cried. Next he heard a light tapping on the room's door. Outside standing was one of the two collaborators he had brought with him for moral support. One had been his accountant when he ran his old business. The other had previously been a legal advisor. Neither he had seen for years. Each had been paid a sum of $50 and a meal for their appearance here today.

"Hurry, I think it's them," were the words issued forth from outside the thick-wooded door.

The aggrieved Mr. Drayton stopped short at the entranceway and tried to get hold of his jitters before going out to face the inevitable.

Meanwhile, Mr. Faehner and his ensemble entered through the heavy-paneled doors. Here he confided with his chosen companions and made them privy to some of what was expected to happen.

"Look, this guy is a real pain in the butt. He can get vociferous or worse when he doesn't get his way. He's even been known to throw things at people before. Stick by me until I ascertain his disposition or effectively knock him down a peg or two. Then, if I decide to deal with him alone, or at all, you two can just go about your business. Take a stroll around the hotel. It's really a first-rate place."

After acknowledging the Faehner plan, both Obe and the reporter fell into their perspective supporting roles and followed their leader into the main room. The stares were ever so intense between the huddled groups when glaring eyes fell upon glaring eyes. There was a perspicuous air of elemental emotion that presided over the groups as the individuals sized up one another trying to figure things out about each other. But for their efforts, none could come away with any real idea about who was who in the world, except between the group leaders. They knew a lot about each other, which was all they needed to know.

Though contact had been made, at least superficially through a prolonged duration of facial observation, neither of the two leading men made a motion to immediately approach the other, neither did their constituents. Already it had turned into a private parlay for power—a head game. What ensued over the next two minutes would have appeared radically hilarious had any of the onlookers known the extent of disparity between the two staunch characters in terms of their individual portfolios. Mr. Drayton was leagues below the esteemed Mr. Faehner and had always been so even in the days when he was taking the south end by storm. He was, and always had been, a cream puff when compared to the likes of Faehner.

Too late to make the first move without undermining his stand, Mr. Faehner pretended by looking away or by occasionally looking noncommittally toward the intended target, not to care. This not-to-care demeanor was actually intended to dare his opponent into taking action.

Too late now to make any move without compromising his wrongly perceived notion that all things were equal, Mr. Drayton quaked in his shoes about what he should do.

The dilemma was solved by Mr. Faehner's desire to either end things as they were without mitigation or to compel his rankled opponent into taking action. He carried the farce forward by carrying on an ostentatious display in which he played the part of a person readying to resign their position and inveigling the others in his company to do so too. Lifting both arms high in the air, he then brought them down around the squared shoulders of each of his companions and acted as though he were headed for the door that they had only recently come in. To Bob Drayton, this meant he was put in a now-or-never type of situation.

He responded promptly. Throwing aside his perceived presentment of power, Mr. Drayton began promoting himself conspicuously to his opposition. His regard came as "Hold on there! Hold on there!"

Mr. Faehner whirled around toward the caller with a mask of consternation on his face to face-down the bothersome little peanut. But still he did not acknowledge him. Mr. Faehner kept his eyes above the head tops of those closest to him and those closing in on him as though he were busy scrutinizing faces and places far-off in the distance. Only when Mr. Drayton had practically bumped into him did Mr. Faehner finally announce in a somewhat annoyed voice, "Mr. Drayton, I presume."

Of course they had met before although not in a social way and not in a formal setting. The context had been one of jumbled confusion. It had been during one of the bridge sessions held at the local supervisors building in which Mr. Faehner, obligated by process and procedure, had to appear before the board and interested residents and again attempt to propose and persuade them into approving his project—his benevolent project, the project with which he hoped he could use to win over all the leading naysayers who didn't want to see the length of one man extending himself to the point of owning every last house and property in their beloved little town. By taking on the bridge, it appeared that here was at least one kindhearted gesture, one selfless act, in which could be attached no private gain. The townspeople had been led to believe that the motivation behind Mr. Faehner's desire to acquire the singing metal was one of pure benevolence in which he would incur the prodigious costs at loss so as to help the town, help the people. The fact that he had an ulterior motive, one in which he would be defiantly helping himself never occurred to any of the people ever present during one of his sessions.

Only in his mind was the concept of the something-else he was trying to accomplish known. Its possibility was so far removed from the scope of consideration that no one could have possibly concluded it. But Mr. Faehner knew. Many miles up the river had begun another unknown project, one which would be linked to the removal and rebuilding of the bridge. No one knew yet the reason why Mr. Faehner insisted that in order for him to carry on such a lofty task, he wanted the right to move the bridge back-creek from its present location. He had portended, in the lone statement he had made on it, that it was for reasons of having the bridge founded upon the closest known resource of solid bedrock, not in the breakage where it now existed. But in truth, it was to have a larger docking area, which could someday accommodate a flotilla of bigger boats.

Only once during one of his self-representing meetings had a voice of dissent raised above the crowded hall and shouted out, "And how much will be the toll across this privately paid-for bridge?"

Meanwhile, both sets of associates lump-summed themselves around their perspective leaders like spectators at an arena. Except for the two men in charge, no one knew anything of the others—their names, occupations, or rank in society. Drayton's group, two slightly elevated societal men, believed falsely that anyone having anything to do with such a person as Mr. Faehner must themselves possess a great deal of importance. This was exemplified in the courteous way in which they vied for and then introduced themselves to their counterparts and in doing so made certain to give up something of their credentials to authoritate their feelings of self-worth.

Though both of his companions certainly looked the part of people who might hold certain high levels of esteem and degree, Mr. Faehner interjected on their immediate behalf and interceded their introductions, succinctly and without description, to the awaiting audience, much to their chagrin. He wanted to keep them in the dark, and for the same reasons, they wanted to get out of it. He believed too that they believed that no one, lacking credentials, would be admitted into the company of one of the most uncommon men in the commonwealth. Without including their areas of expertise openly, he knew that in their minds the sky was the limit. And Mr. Drayton did not let it go by unnoticed. Anything he said in the company of the unknown professionals could come back to hurt him someday. He sought to alleviate his concerns and summoned up the courage to speak up about it.

"It's not polite to go on without us first getting to know a little something at least about—"

"Look! Mr. Faehner said admonishingly before all of Bob Drayton's points had been made. "You asked me down here for something more than an examination into the finer points of etiquette as they relate to the proper method of professional introduction. And that, may I remind you, was done in as just an impolite manner. How dare you expect me to walk out on a party being held in my own honor to come socialize with you and still after several tedious minutes not know why?"

Mr. Drayton's feeble attempt to humiliate the man he hated most in the world ended in his own humiliation.

"My advice to you, Bob, would be to spill your guts about just what it is you think is so seriously important to send for me in such a rash manner as you did."

Mr. Faehner's harsh words and brash attitude gave Mr. Drayton all the sense of things to come. There would be no debate. The ultimatum, as it pertained to his personal crisis, would be decided in a way that heavily favored the richer, wiser man. There would be no sympathies delved out this day. The great Mr. Faehner had spoken.

And Mr. Faehner was in no way a dummy when it came to realizing the debacle Mr. Drayton was facing. He knew the gist of it. Having already spent days dealing with other owners, he knew that many of them had experienced the same travail that Bob Drayton was experiencing. The old pumps drawing water from the community well did not have the power to reach the upper tiers efficiently. He would plead like the others had pleaded to have a resurgent system put in place so he could live in peace in his high place atop the hill. But Bob knew too that no one before him had had the luck of convincing the hard-boiled man into softening his stance when it came to anything Pequea related. One by one, the dwellers of the hillside community sold out, were eradicated from their homes, all in favor of having a new community supplant the old one. Hardly a home still stood after deed had exchanged hand for succeeding that would be a home by home refitting, which usually meant having the domicile bulldozed to the ground. Only seven out of seventy-seven, counting Bob's, had managed to elude the wrecking ball, which in this case meant eluding the thick wad of ready bills Mr. Faehner always had handy when it came time to knocking the next noble landowner off the shelf. They were like lollipops, which could be licked to the stick without any effort. All any of them needed to see was that fistful of dollars ready to be flung in their direction. And Mr. Faehner was wise to do that. He came with his cash each and every time: $15,000, $20,000, $30,000, all laid out before them, each in turn. Most had never seen so much of the treasured green in all of their lives before. And the allure seemed to set them on fire. All of a sudden, they could begin to rethink their lives. There were other places they could go to live. There were other things they could do. Mr. Faehner knew that money, actual cash, could do things that checks or promises could not. But Mr. Drayton could not be enticed as easily. In his dire straits, during his businesses' decline, he had secreted away gobs of money, gobs enough so that at least he could afford to spend the remainder of his days—he was only sixty-one—living comfortably, comfortably meaning other than the day-to-day living with, dealing with, the ongoing aggravation of having an inadequate supply of water.

Drayton had thought to safeguard himself financially to take care of himself but did not possess the finances that would be necessary should he have to, or intend to, ward off an onslaught of legal maneuvers perpetrated by the persistence of the powerful southern landowner. Any sizeable amount taken from Drayton's inadequate supply of dollars and cents would seriously deplete it and render him incapable of either reinvesting in some promising business future or force him to do the unthinkable—get a job!

The small talk was over. Drayton's persona, in the course of only a few fleeting moments, had been reduced from that of an unduly perceived hit-and-run man to that of a person who had been the recipient of a hit-and-run. Now with his ego squashed like an ant at the heels of his own feet, Drayton felt ready to play out his last hand. The inflection in his voice took on the tone of a filial son who wanted only to please. Ever self-conscious of what others perceived of him, Drayton became aware of the effective stares around him and began inveigling his formative foe to follow him up to his hilltop home so they could then deal with the as-yet-to-be-disclosed circumstance that had called them together.

"Come, come with me," he pleaded. Then to his constituents around him, he announced, "Go, we're done here for the day."

They returned to him their $50-smiles—the amount each of them were paid for their appearances—and simply walked away, glad that their afternoon expectancies had come to a close so soon. Then, having turned back toward Mr. Faehner, Drayton, now unencumbered by the weight of what he believed his paid-for partners believed about him, stood before the haughty billionaire and, in a manner made to be as obsequious a showing as could be displayed, bowed in an ultimately desperate act of humility and deference. Rarely had the once-important Mr. Drayton ever humbled himself before another so ostentatiously but rare was the kind of man he now had to face. And he justly believed, who around him—should they infer the worth of his diffidence—would do any different in view of who they were to this man.

Though fully aware that Drayton had turned to tricks to try to get what was wanted, whatever it was, Faehner nonetheless pretended too to be somewhat moved by the length to which he was being shown respect and given treatment. In a manner befitting a father who had just forgiven a son, he spoke out in a soft but stern voice, "What is it you want from me?"

Excited, Drayton began making awkward motions with his hands as though he was proceeding to, but keeping from, placing his hands directly on Mr. Faehner as an expression of wanting to show him his appreciation but then realizing he had better not indulge his fantasy that they were, at this time, sharing a oneness in spirit. From there, Bob led Mr. Faehner toward the hotel's doors intending to exit and together go up to his plateau. Mr. Faehner, having agreed to go-it-alone with the nauseating little man, nodded to the other members of his party a parting gesture and proceeded out of the hotel.

"Your chariot awaits you, sir," Drayton said dryly once he had reached his vehicle, which was parked on the side of the building opposite the silver-white limousine. The chariot referred to was Bob's thirteen-year-old Cadillac with its egg-white shell and egg-yellow insides, which Mr. Faehner looked at with amusing eyes—one big egg. As Mr. Faehner stood, hands on his sides and staring, Bob scrambled over to the driver's side and electronically unlocked, then opened the side door. He portrayed, although somewhat whimsically, all of the proper mannerisms of a professionally trained chauffeur, one who could be hired by kings and queens of the modern-day world. There was something about it, something innate about this man in his character role, which revealed that he had been born to be subservient but had somehow missed his calling. Mr. Faehner approached the opened door and allowed Bob to attend him as he eased his way into the "egg." Unbeknownst to Bob was the mile-wide smile plastered to Obe's face as he watched the made-up spectacle from one of the curtained windows on the pertaining side of the lobby.

Out in the car, Bob thought it best to continue without delay. He had been blessed to have gotten this far, and any disruption could cost him his chances. He began whisking his special guest up, up the tiers to reach his home in the sky. To ease his own tensions, he turned on the radio and tuned in to one of the easy-listening channels. He played the music just loud enough for himself to hear, daring not to increase the volume in case his passenger disapproved.

Disapprove or not, they ascended, the tentative twosome, up, up, up to the highest reach of the cliff-top top, where Bob had his perch of precariously positioned birdhouse dwellings. While on the way, Mr. Faehner took special delight in noting the scores of getaway homes he had over the recent past developed into something a lot more than they had been. "Out with the old, in with the new," had been and continued to be the prevailing code with this modern-day venture. And the conversions had not been made without adherence to what was considered by all a special regard to the long-established charm and character present in the riverside town or village or community or whatever else it was considered.

Its original layout of homes built upon or, in some cases, built into the natural level of tiers had remained intact although in most cases the newer homes had been modified as larger than what stood before it. But the most concerned point was that the institution of keeping copy houses, or look-alikes, together on the same tier was kept. This had been the settling point as to why the community had not opposed the Pequea project. Because of it, Faehner had been left to deal only with the individual owners as they were and on an individual basis. And deal with them he did. Most departed shortly after having the bundles of strapped cash thrust at them. Others opted to stay upon the condition that they pay for the new home at the stipulated price. Those who opposed the either-or of it and instead arose in dispute had only to have another bundle of money cast their way, and they were ready to pack their bags and bake a pie for the benevolent businessman.

The calculations ran through his head of all that had transpired, and the numbers acted upon him like a potency of medicine, each a dose of self-induced painkiller, cash values valued as milligrams. And the numbers were high. An average of slightly less than $28,000 had been paid out for each property acquisition and likewise an average of slightly more than $28,000 had been netted as profit for each one. In all, slightly more than $2,000,000 had been made so far in the Pequea dealings, enough to have made the project worthwhile, at least on this side of the bridge. The calculated cost of the new bridge would wipe out the savings made on the other side of it, but compensation would come in the light of an even newer venue. Still, the one to come depended upon the one being done, so the initiative had to go on.

Getting to the top the oblong egg rolled to a landing spot between the first two of Drayton's birdhouse homes. Not wanting to be kept in the confines of the irritating car, Mr. Faehner exited the vehicle in haste. In the few seconds of wait before Bob got out, he took in an appreciative view, a bird's-eye view, of the spectacular landmarks below; the dotted rows of neatly arranged terraced homes, the mile-wide river whose color was said to change every day—one day steel, one day white-tipped blue, one day aqua, one day chartreuse, one day a combination of every complete color. The river's colors were a story all by itself. Today's colors were such that the avid contemplator was soon to exploit. Today, the river was a raging blue-gray-green made furious by the sudden influx of drenching rain that had just lifted it out of the doldrums. While entranced by the river's relentless awe and beauty, Mr. Faehner heard a call from behind him, and he responded by turning abruptly around and having to look upon the harried "hatchling" who had just emerged from the egg.

Before Mr. Faehner could respond in word, Bob had begun cajoling him to "follow me, follow me" up behind the house. It was a path of loose soil and rock, which led up a short but arduous distance from the house level, and both men managed the climb with a certain amount of alacrity. Reaching the destination spot first—the cutaway Bob had etched out of the rock hill—Bob stood before the partially exposed tank and prepared, in the few seconds left, the points of speech he had to make. This one-time-only speech had to be made as efficaciously as possible if it were to do any good for the reason it was intended for.

"See. See here!" he pointed out a finger to specify. "Look at that, will you. We just had a rainstorm that would have filled barrels instead of buckets and look, look at this!"

Mr. Faehner gazed ahead at the purposefully dug excavation, the bulky dropped-down holding tank, and the something-or-other type of contraption splayed out over the top of it in a way which was meant to collect rain water into its three centered holes and remarked, "Just what is it you're trying to show me?"

"Show you? Why, look at this," he said and insistently placed his pointed finger on the side of the tank to a point so low he had to crouch and reach. His finger stopped at a barely perceptible watermark, a meniscus, and, with evidence at hand, declared, "There's hardly a day's worth of water in it," he complained.

Bob paused, holding off, holding his forthcoming pleas in abeyance, hoping to hear some kind of sympathetic reply, a "sorry about that" or a "that's too bad" would have done nicely. But there was no response, not in word or motion. Faehner's countenance was cold and calculating, at least from Bob's perspective. He was as hard-boiled a man as could ever be imagined, insensitive to the plights of others. Suddenly, all bets were off. Pleading would do no good. The thing would have to be decided on the up-and-up. The case made would have to be made in the light of truth. Things said would have to be said about what each man perceived about the other and the other's intent. Things had to get real. Bob would begin. As he did so, his confounding lack of confidence got the better of him and in a last-ditch effort schemed to better his chances by staying put in the hillside hole and exemplifying his cause by appearing to be down on his hands and knees, so to speak, while relating his case. From five feet down—the depth of the pit, the depth Bob had buried himself—he began, "You and I both know—"

"Save your breath, Bob," Mr. Faehner interrupted after listening in an amused stare to several long minutes of the man's speech. "I know exactly what you're getting at, and I can tell you that my plans are unalterable, and they don't include the likes of you maintaining, if you can call it that, your little hilltop hovels here."

Taking exception to having his home referred to as a hovel, Mr. Drayton broke away from the conversational path and defended, with pride and prejudice, the provisional allotment he had made for himself atop the Pequea pinnacle. "Now look here, Mr. High and Mighty, I'll have you know that what went into making these homes livable was quite a lot of time and effort."

"You call this time and effort," Mr. Faehner countered as he turned to examine the forlorn facades facing him from the back. "Why, I built better backyard forts as a kid. You might as well face it, Bob, you're going to have to leave unless, that is, you have decided to come to your senses and pay up to have your properties upgraded to the newly established standard. Then you can live out your days in peace and contentment in a house that will be worth your while. It's your prerogative. Other than that, you will inevitably just be pushed out of the way. I'm not investing anything into a new pumping system like you and some of the others want just so you can continue living up here."

"Then just how, just how do you expect anyone else to go on living up here even after you've managed to displace me and the others?"

Bob's remark had cut Mr. Faehner to the quick. What Bob didn't know was that "the others" he referred to had already been taken care of long ago. Though two other families still lived in their still-undone homes, provision had already been made for them in that they had agreed independently to pay for the adjustment that would be forthcoming. In essence, they had sold out to Mr. Faehner; and in the coming months, they would move out temporarily until their newer Faehner homes could be built. For the first time in the many, many, months of the long extrication and implementation procedure, Mr. Faehner felt uneasy. To the end, Mr. Faehner had counted on Bob's reclusive behavior in favoring him from Bob ever finding out that he had recently leaked the news about the new water retrieval system, which was currently being put together. The other two higher-up families, both of whom Mr. Faehner felt somewhat sympathetic toward, had been enticed, even encouraged to remain where they were by virtue of having confided in them that his new water system would solve all of their water woes. It was not expected that Bob Drayton would ever find out about it. Up until now—now meaning only the past ten days—the new water plan had been kept secret. Mr. Faehner had for the past ten months been constructing, in congruence with fast-paced buying and selling of the Pequea properties, a private pipe line, which when complete would forever feed the promontory town with enough clean water that it would never be without it again. Twenty miles of laid-down pipe had been set, submerged, just below the silt surface of the meandering Pequea creek. Rapid as the flow of the Pequea was the pipes would never freeze, and the concept of placing the pipe in the body of water was nothing short of genius. The cost of doing so was only one-tenth of what the cost would have been had the pipe line been laid underground down through the many private and public parcels of territory, which ran from the Little Conestoga Pumping Station to Pequea. The Pequea is a relatively undisturbed waterway in that in most places it runs through private property, mostly farms, and its overall depth is too shallow to allow any watercraft, other than canoes and rafts, to recreate it. So in all reasoning, any below-the-silty-bottom construct, in this case a pipe line, should remain intact for an undisturbed period of time. Not even another Agnes could upset it, at least in theory. Come drought or deluge, Mr. Faehner's pipe line should, by all reasoning, remain in its place and its beneficial resource always be just a turn of the tap away. But this was something Mr. Faehner had no intention of ever telling Bob. This man he despised through and through, knowing full well of the slight-of-hand tricks he had pulled at his former businesses, how he had misappropriated a ton of money, hiding it away from creditor and associates alike up until the businesses were lost. Bob turned out to be a despicable man in Mr. Faehner's view, and no special consideration would be made on his behalf. The question could not be answered, not even attempted, for the slightest slip of the tongue could forever foreclose the forecasted certainty that Bob, given his disposition to always run from trouble, would not push for a fight when push came to shove.

It was time right now. Another day could not be spared against the outside chance that Bob might, might seek out the sympathy and condolence of his neighbors and perchance catch a word about some new pipe line that's soon to reach the Pequea town.

"Bob, you're going to have to go," was all Mr. Faehner finally spoke to the disheveled little man. "We've been through all this before, and there's no other way. If you refuse me this last turn, I'll have all your properties condemned, and you'll be thrown out then without any of the money I've already offered. As a matter-of-fact," he announced with an air of supreme authority, "today is *the* day, the take-it-or-leave-it day. It's all up to you. The papers are right down in my car. The money too. You'll accept and sign right now, or I'll apply, first thing tomorrow, for the condemnation of your homes. A simple inspection is all it will take. We both know that."

Before Mr. Faehner could say any more, Bob popped up and out of the hole and after making a feeble attempt to brush away the loose dirt which had soiled his only good suit, he looked up at the venerable billionaire and knew that his hands-and-knees approach had now failed. Flustered and unsure what to do, Bob, acting indignantly, brushed his way past the man who would have him expunged from his hilltop haven like a cockroach being swept off a porch and headed hurriedly down the nascent path toward his soon-to-be-no-longer home. Mr. Faehner followed. On his way down, he cell-phoned Obe and apprised him that the intercession between him and Mr. Drayton was for all intents and purposes over, at least when considering whether the power of persuasion would have, could have, or should have made the final decision any different than what it was. In conjunction with this final, fatal rendering, Obe was further instructed that when he did appear up on the precipice, he was to bring, out of the locked compartment in the spacious trunk, the old tired briefcase as Mr. Faehner so lovingly referred to it so as to turn the situation entirely in his favor. After receiving the cell call, Obe looked at the reporter who looked at him and by innuendo, the fact that he had not been instructed otherwise, planned to accompany the summoned driver, limousine, and briefcase up to the proposed business station.

Mr. Drayton, after a precipitant dash back down from the surface tank, made for the best in his line of properties, the place he called home. There he embedded himself temporarily from the consternation and regret over having failed to reach any compromise with the hard-headed Mr. Faehner. What to do? Uncertain as to how the overtaker would react, Bob fled to an upper-story window, and using the wooden floor as a prie-dieu, he viewed on bended knee the goings-on behind the house, watching intently as the billionaire first blew his nose, then affixed his yellow tie, adjusted his belt buckle, and brushed off his pants, all in preparation for, he was sure, rendering some final blow. Bob felt so, so vulnerable as if he were the one remaining spore on a dandelion fuzzy about to be whisked away by the wind. The sky in his mind turned tenebrous. Moments later, Mr. Faehner was on his front porch standing vibrantly, standing as though he was a king overlooking his kingdom, and he was.

The limousine pulled up beside the forlorn-looking house, and Obe went immediately to his second assignment. The reporter got out too, reticent in doing so, and remained by the vehicle. After flashing a quick look in Faehner's direction and recognizing that he was being beckoned, the reporter then made way over to him. Meanwhile, Obe's compliance brought him to the others only seconds behind the reporter. His part though he knew from previous experience was over, and once he delivered the inconspicuous case into the hands of the capable reporter, he retreated to the vehicle to wait. For the next several moments, only Mr. Faehner knew what was about to happen. He looked at the shock-eyed reporter and entreated him to the mystery story.

"Come, you'll see firsthand of things such as I have to deal with on almost a day-to-day basis."

With that remark, he strode over to the front door and pounded on it. The reporter, in tow, moved along too but remained beside the proximity of the enclosure's entranceway, a bit worried that something bad might happen. Faehner noticed.

"Don't be concerned about this guy. He's a lamb. If there was a trap door to this place, he'd have been out it and racing madly away from here by now. As it is, he's moments away from realizing that this is his last chance to get out while he still can, to take the money and run, so to speak, and trust me when I say I know he's good for that."

"What exactly are you doing?" the reporter asked pointedly, having only the slightest inclination about what may be transpiring in front of him.

But before Mr. Faehner could reply, the brass knob half-turned, and its locking mechanism clicked open. Neither of the men moved upon the opening until there was heard from a short distance inside the prevailing room that an invitation was being extended to them. Slowly, cautiously, the testy tycoon nudged the slightly ajar barrier further and further open. He did not cross over the threshold and enter until he could see Bob and see that he was simply standing beside a lamp table, hands in his pockets, and beads of sweat trickling from his forehead. Tracking into the room also came the reporter, who stood beside and to the rear of his esteemed companion. At his side rested the attention-getting, smaller-sized case. Attention-getting because as the story had so often been told among the gossipy guild of townspeople, that when the case came out, so did all the remaining will and desire of the person holding out.

"I'll state very emphatically, Mr. Drayton. I did not come here to listen to you whine about your lack of adequate water. Nor did I come here to listen to you beg me for help. I also did not come here to settle any terms other than what was first proposed to you many months ago. The offer remains the same—$50,000. No more, no less. $20,000 for the house we're standing in and $30,000 for the others as they stand. It makes no difference to me what they're worth to you or anybody else who might have an interest in them for what they are. They're all being razed. And in their place will be put, probably only three, new homes. Your best bet is to take what I've got to give you and run, something you're good at, something you've done before."

The insinuation that he had taken from something and run sometime before stabbed at Mr. Drayton. But of course it should be so that a man such as Mr. Faehner should have suspected as much. Business is business. And in the end, the ethics of business are such that a man will do anything to protect himself financially, no matter what. Help himself. But what to do now? Bob could, if he wanted to, rescue himself from the situation and accept Mr. Faehner's long-standing offer and put up the majority of the money he stole from his former businesses and be placed in one of the new Faehner homes. But that would mean exposing himself, albeit these many years later, of the fact that he had misappropriated monies from the past. To all of a sudden come up with such as enormous amount of money after living like a poor hermit all these past years would certainly raise a cloud of uncertainty about where it had come from. From it, implications might gather. And these strands of gather might grow. And grow they might into something bigger. And the something bigger might get bigger. And the something even bigger might get . . . Mr. Drayton had to shake his head to take it off of the path, the path of uncertainty. The inward streak of assuming thought came to a halt when he noticed, for the first time, the case.

He was had. There was no way out. He knew himself better than anybody. There was money in the case, a lot of it, just like he had heard in the rumors of the recent past. And he was no match for it. He would be swayed just like the others. It was a moment of truth. Conflict stirred. How could it be that it all came to this? How unlike anything expected. Defiant outer layers were all being unraveled, and at the innermost point of his self, his self came to bear. No longer concealed by the layers, the true Bob came to bare himself in the light of the situation. The context became clear. They were competitors in the ring, the arena, the town. But the fight would not go on as planned, for no one would put together two who were so unalike, two who were so unevenly matched. Bob would take the payoff. Bob would take the fall. But he would not go out without a last word, without contempt.

"You're a crumb, Mr. Faehner, for having so little consideration of others. For having to extract every last ounce out of a person's flesh just to please you. For having . . ."

In the very middle of Mr. Drayton's impact speech, Mr. Faehner unfolded his obdurately folded arms and summoned for the reporter to bring forth the case. The case, once it was with its owner, was duly opened and the contents, straps of machine-counted cash, were conveniently stacked along the corner ledge of the coffee table. Along with the bundles of money came a document, which had been folded into three equal parts.

After relinquishing the case upon request, the reporter removed himself from the center stage and took up an inconsequential position to the rear of the chief negotiator. Though now apart from the unfolding spectacle, the reporter felt a part of it. He understood the gist of what was occurring though few words had been spoken about what was really taking place. And he had participated in it. How intrigued he felt! How connected to the life and times of the buoyant billionaire he considered himself at such an identifying moment! It was all so surreal!

"It's all there, Mr. Drayton, in green and white! You can count it if you like. The agreed-upon price and payment of the settlement just as had been described to you before."

"What! What agreed-upon price? Why, this is outrageous!"

Though completely outraged by the audacious act and thoroughly ravaged by the contempt being shown to him, the clear loser, Mr. Drayton's lips were quivering at the sight of the sum ostentatiously sitting on the table in front of him. He could not pretend otherwise. He was captivated by the prospect of being able to take it, make it his own, play with it like a toddler would—an occupying toy placed in a crib. Was it real? Was is really real? Or was it Monopoly money? How much cash?

"Like I said, it's all there. A total of $50,000. Twenty for the place where we stand. Thirty for the others. The offer is nonnegotiable and final. You'll take what is in front of you, or you'll get less later if you decide to put up a stink. Less for every day you delay. So the choice is yours. You're at the top of your gain. Take this play and learn to walk away. Play another hand, and you'll do nothing but lose, of that I can assure you."

It was all out in the open now, basically a take-it-or-leave-it scenario. Entranced, the reporter tried to imagine what it would be like to have been either man—Mr. Faehner, holding all the cards, or the hard-swallowing little pip-squeak. How would he have acted in either man's place?

The sight alone of the money was enough to entice the last-handed Drayton into signing the conditional surrender, but his enticement was enhanced when the aroma of the new money began to form a detectable cloud of inducement in front of him. He was hardly a match for it. Within moments, he leaped for the money and reaped all the bundles into his anxiously awaiting arms. And that was that.

Once outside, the reporter commented on the incident and tried to induce Mr. Faehner into commenting back about the worth of what really happened.

"Is he another one for the wall?" he then asked with an inflected tone of mirth.

"No, I save the wall for the ones who almost made me fall," he reported back facetiously. "This guy, he's, he's a tick. A little hard to get at but gets gotten nonetheless. No, I'd catagorize him as just another chalk-check on the blackboard of life."

The Ferry King

The Drayton debacle was over. Outside, Obe, on stand-by, felt relief when he heard the entrance door open and saw his fellow companions make their way out. He hurried over to Mr. Faehner so as to escort him to the limo. While doing so, he extended his right hand toward the case, which was then turned over to him to place back in the vehicle, back where it came from. The reporter, meanwhile, helped himself back in the car and sat in wait, expecting to be returned promptly to the Silver Hills Country Club. Obe, after stashing the case, dashed back to the back door nearest where Mr. Faehner stood. He supposed he was waiting deliberately to be extended the proper courtesy and be propositioned, door opened for him to enter, door closed after he did, by his attending chauffeur. But Obe, despite his preemptive measure to assure proper assistance to his superior, was rebuffed from the very first. As he stood back of the wide-opened door, Mr. Faehner refused to react. Obe looked, first to see if he had offended his ordinarily easy-to-please boss in any way, but then to notice that his immediate attention, his boss's, was anywhere but concerned about entering his own vehicle. The reporter noted too that the time it took for everyone else to get in and get going had come to a standstill. Head-bent from his side-seat position, he considered the situation. The gnostic pose Faehner had on was one that could not, should not, be disturbed. Mr. Faehner was in communion with his thoughts. He was postured toward the river, his eyes seemingly fixed on the torrent of water, white-cuffed and raging.

His mind was in a spiritual place, one of those never-intended places that grasp then envelop us unexpectedly from time to time. It was a place that one dare not be shaken from, so holy is its state upon us.

Though it was true that Mr. Faehner appeared to be in character of someone who had been cajoled into some transcendent state and though it actually may have started out that way, his mind was now working, applying thought and reason, to a soon-to-be reality. He was intensely projecting ahead at some distant future, a future that would be connected to the disturbance now taking place out and below him on the commanding waterway. He dared not speak of it in the moment, and the others knew not to dare to invite him to too.

The minutes seemed like hours, but finally Mr. Faehner came to. Some sense of self-satisfaction had come to him and carried him back from his strayed apprehension. He addressed the others to "not mind me" and promptly took up his place in the luxurious inner space in the limousine. His mind and attention went back to the business at hand. And the order of his first thought was that his last holdout had, at last, sold out, and that all things considered, it had been relatively easy as compared to how hard it could have been.

Obe drove on, down from the elevated slopes of the terraces to the level old road, which led to the town. Continuing on, the singing bridge awaited. After that, there was a split possibility. The option was to either go back the way they came, along the narrows of the Pequea Creek or follow the old river road, which hugged the Susquehanna for miles and miles of scenic distance, past little forests and meadows, through other little towns, over overlooking high tops on the road, and through all of it passing alongside picturesque riverside farms. Obe knew well Mr. Faehner's penchant for opting to take the long way round on days when he'd nothing better to do or days such as this when he was in the finest of moods and needed such devices to satiate his ever-present desire to get more out of life. In regards to this, Obe lowered the glass partition between front and back and asked the all-important question while it was still pertinent to do so.

"Sir, would you prefer to go back the way we came, or would you prefer another route?"

"No no no," Mr. Faehner shot back immediately as though the very same thought and implementation process had gone through his mind, and his answer was as ready as answering to himself. "No," he reiterated. "Let's go back the way we came. We're not going back to Silver Hills directly. I want to stop off at the Silver Mine and see firsthand what our little "Agnes" did to the place."

The reference was, of course, lost on the two now-informed associates. As a young boy, Mr. Faehner had lost out on the opportunity to view firsthand what the wrath of the remnants of Hurricane Agnes had done to the Silver Mine property simply because he had not yet become acquainted with it. Now, every chance he got, whenever a sizeable storm had dumped its precipitous contents upon it, Mr. Faehner never hesitated to rush over and see what it might have looked like those days back in '72.

The aspect of wanting to do so sounded absurd. Who in their right mind would, as an expectation, want to see a place so dearly cherished devastated by an inundation of atmospheric deluge. But he did. And why? Because he always knew that despite the devastation felt by the rest of the county, the mine had survived. Though also inundated by the flood waters of the time, the natural aspect of the mine property, the hollow, centered into which is the little run, which runs through the land extent, top to bottom, then splashes into the Pequea Creek, allowed for the quick expulsion of all of the excess water before it had a chance to swamp any of the low-lying ground. For days following the event, the mine must have been a virtual underground stream flowing steadily days-on-end from its gaping darkness out, hole, to hollow, to run. Certainly just one year later, when the then young Faehner boy first set foot on the silver mine's property, there would have been some exiguous evidence that the surfeit surface water had overcome the area. Ruts, cutaways, surface swell, would have pocketed the land. But there had been nothing. The quick-draining hills and swift-carrying run had kept the land from becoming a soak. But still he wondered.

With this ideal of satisfaction already in his head, Mr. Faehner was able to sit back and actually appreciate the wonder of seeing the effect that the little storm had just produced on the waters of the now silty Pequea. Freed from the concern that the mine had taken a bad hit, he relaxed and took in his right-by-the-side-of-the-road view of Mother Nature's little temper tantrum. The Pequea Park was now partially flooded, in some places almost to the road on the side they were traveling. Along its submerged banks stood the only living things made to withstand such unintended wrath. Poised imposingly on each side of the swollen creek stood grand old sycamores, one after another, along the covered banks. Tree to water, tree to water they stood, standing out remarkably in the midst of their scenic splash, made so by virtue of their mottled bark, thin and patterned with a variance of light splotchy patches—whites, off-whites, gray. The huge trees who made home here along the creek were most likely busy, their roots sucking up the copious nutrient-rich drink so their branches could then burst forth skyward adding to their already gigantic size, making them even stronger.

Throughout the entire journey back, Mr. Faehner kept his mind in the world of big and little Agnes and was taken aback when at once he came to realize that the journey had reached its end. The vehicle, the while traveling on Goods Road, suddenly emptied out onto Silver Mine Road at the intercession at the western extent of the Silver Mine property. The limousine was just about to cross over the tiny bridge which passed over a run similar to Silver Mine Run in size, in shape, and in direction of its flow. Whenever Mr. Faehner traveled over the small paved bridge, he strained to look down its tree-parted width to see, if he could see, any of the local white-tailed deer, which frequented the woods nearby. But the time of day was wrong, and he understood as he watched that it was unlikely he would detect the movement of any of the careful creatures.

The limousine rolled on, up the back-hollow hill, then down the back-hollow hill before turning sharply right into the tiny lot beside the 1800 house. Mr. Faehner was first to get out, ever so concerned about being back on his beloved property that he seldom, if ever, waited for his faithful attendant to accommodate him with a door-opening ritual. His eyes first peered on the massive stone structure turned darker by the saturating sheet of water that had, only a short time ago, enveloped it. It was striking. Water, still finding its way along the intricately laid tiles of rooftop slate, still dripped from its top corners and spilled in timed drops to the ground. Next view was the pond, which, though filled to excess and taking on more, was doing a good job at dispelling the unwanted fluid at its spillway. Its current capacity had breached its customary boundary, but its waters had not, and would not, reach the level of the encircling pond road. A lone old sycamore downslope from the house was now about one-third trunk-sunk in the pond's stretching reach but as is the nature of all of these thirsty trees it seemed not to mind. In fact, its thick boughs and thinner branches seemed more bended up than was usual as though the tree was appreciative of its sudden ability to drink in nonstop. From a certain distance back, it appeared that the tree's limbs were all smiling, all curved in that certain contour. The happy-face tree, after all, was a living thing, and who's to say what trees were capable of?

In his mind's eye, Mr. Faehner viewed what was happening up in the hollow hills, up by the mine. He knew that the land was protecting itself in the ways it always did. The tonnages of water that had hit upon it were being dutifully discharged—in currents, cascades, spillages, and swooshing swoops down out of the hollows, and making way across time-defined passages to the swelling run whose short-lived action it was to carry the deluge to pond, to the run again, and on to the Pequea only a short distance beyond. All was as it should be without exception.

Getting out of the stationary vehicle, the reporter commented as to the whole, letting out that he felt they were now all part of some complicity in being somewhat insensitive, if not rude, about being tardy in their return to the festivities that awaited them.

"Won't people start to be mad about how long you've been gone? And won't they become even madder if you stay away longer?"

"No, they won't," Mr. Faehner replied in a nonchalant voice. "They," he began, "have tables full of food, shelves filled with wine and liquor, and a hogshead worth of beer."

"A what's head?" the reporter beamed back profoundly.

"A hogshead," Mr. Faehner reiterated expectantly. "If I remember the meaning correctly of that old-time colloquialism, it should relate to a quantity of beer equal to about fifty gallons."

"That's certainly a lot of beer," the reporter admitted.

"Now to get on with what you were saying," Mr. Faehner continued. "They," he again began with emphasis, "have each other too. They certainly don't need to see me standing around acting all enthused by every little consideration thrown my way. And besides, most of them know me well enough to know that my life is made up by these incessant little annoyances. They know that at the drop of a silver dime, I could be off without any expectation of my return. Being interrupted and interrupting others has become part of my lifestyle. It's something that will never change up until the day when I cease all future business dealings. Then I'll have the time enough to stay and play out any of my involvements."

The response was satisfactory, and the reporter inquired no further as to his speculation. Mr. Faehner also attested to this by turning his attention once again to the storied old house, still spitting remaining raindrops off its stone-domed cap, the way it had done for all of 213 years now. "Happy birthday, old house," Mr. Faehner said with an accompanying smile. Then, in relation to his appreciative meandering, he reacted by reaching in his pocket and removing a set of brass keys. Once in hand, he picked through their order to find the one belonging to the blue-painted door he stood in front of. He inserted it and turned back the latch until the door lock released. Turning back the brass knob, Mr. Faehner announced for his constituents to hear, "Welcome to the 1800 house."

It was an open invitation. All were being offered to come inside, but Obe with the wave of his hand declined and in turn decided instead to take up a position on a nearby bench, which overlooked the pond-turned-lake. There he sat patiently and awaited what he was sure would be a considerable length of time. Anytime Mr. Faehner was in his element, he knew that time would inevitably stand still as he proceeded to enthrall his listener, especially a new one, with the profusion of Silver Mine stories that have accumulated over the past forty years. Obe had heard them all, and if by mistake he had missed one, he knew inevitably one day it would catch up to him. So instead he became part of the profile of the new afternoon. He arranged himself in the middle of it, deliberately closing his eyes against the bright warming rays, to feel the special effect of the heated light on the thin-layered lids of his eyes. There, in the quiet of the day, he imagined he could hear the living tree quenching its unending thirst, quaffing up huge volumes of life-sustaining liquid from the overwhelmed reservoir. In his own appreciation of it, he, like the tree, smiled too.

Meanwhile, over at the house, the painted door opened then closed without notice. Once inside, Mr. Faehner, while still one step ahead of his guest, cracked an open smile as he paused from further comment in wait of the question he knew was coming.

"So why do you call it the 1800 house?"

"To give it a quick-and-easy reference," he replied matter-of-factly. "Since its inception, it's been so many things other than the structure you see. At one time or another, it has been a house, a storehouse, a first-aid station, an office, an artifact museum, a party place, and on and on and on."

"And what is it now?"

"It is a house, a storehouse, a first-aid station, an office, an artifact museum, a party place—"

"I get the point," the reporter interjected.

"Quite frankly, it's because my predecessor and I never quite knew what to do with it. And actually, it's worked out quite well having it be all these things at once. It's quite nice to be able to come to one place and be able to take care of all of your needs. Come, let me show you."

Immediately, the reporter could see that as had been just reported the house, well, the kitchen anyway, appeared to be fully functional and in use regularly as surmised from the stack of dirty dishes clinging to the edge of the sink, the carton of cracked-open eggshells on the small counter beside the stove, and the small box of chocolate-covered doughnuts sitting lid-up on the huge rectangular eating table just off-center of the spacious room. Always the considerate host, Mr. Faehner offered to his guest any of the food items hidden or revealed that might be to his liking.

"These chocolate-covered doughnuts I go crazy for," he recommended by personal testament.

"No, I'm good," the reporter replied, indirectly referring to the fact that it had not been long since his respite at Mom and Pop's where they had stopped when they were in Little Conestoga.

"OK then," Mr. Faehner responded once his gesture had been waived away, "that'll mean more for me."

Never far from being hungry for the special treat, Mr. Faehner sought out the ostentatious lid-lifted yellow-and-white box, opened it fully, and began consuming the delectable doughnuts, devouring them in a way that did make it seem that he was crazy for them. While the doughnut-starved leader indulged himself with the treats, the reporter at once began, first around the kitchen, then into and around the next room, to wander and wonder at the things that filled the house-of-many-meanings. There were objects of curiosity everywhere, a compilation of many tastes and styles, of pieces new and old, of things of relevance and not. At one point in his meandering, he came upon and switched on the overhead light due the dim view afforded to the room by the room's only window. Instantly, things became clearer. The room, like the house, was an eclectic mix of purposeful and purposeless objects all put together but without defined order or specificity. In one corner was a rounded antique cherry table on whose tabletop center had been placed a white-laced doily. Centered on the doily was an old Emerson radio, the kind styled in the shape of an oval that was all so popular in the middle of the last century. Catty-cornered from it, almost in the opposite corner, was what appeared to be a 1990s twenty-one-inch color television, which, because it was dusted and clean, probably worked if it had a digital converter. Bending down, the reporter got a good look-see at an antique doorstop standing in front of an unused but useable front door, which had long ago been abandoned. He reached for it, lifting it, feeling its heavy weight. Close, he could see what it was by size, by shape, by structure. It was a cast-iron wooly mammoth about the size of a football crafted in intricate detail revealing elongated tusks and linear flows of coarse wooly hair along its thick body and strong-stumped legs. The believed-to-be original paint still stuck admirably to it, brown, an unlikely real-life color considering the primordial icebox the creature roamed in. Concentrating still on these imaginative ramblings, the reporter's senses suddenly became attuned to the paced advance of the other two-legged creature there in the dwelling with him. He turned, his face angle-up, to meet the approach.

"Having a high time of it, I see. Like I told you, this house is a paradise for anyone interested in anything. It has it all."

Letting go of the iron mammoth, the reporter shot up from his crouched position on the floor in so swift a manner that Mr. Faehner would have believed it if he were about to be told that the iron-cast figure had somehow suddenly come to life and moved while still in the grasp of the curious looker. The alacrity of movement characterized by the action made the midlife'd Mr. Faehner take notice. It punctuated the profound difference in their ages—just how hard it would have been for him to perform the very same act, more like a stunt. His body quivered in response to the perceived phantom aches he knew he would be experiencing if he had been the one who had popped off the carpet like an exploding kernel of corn. Reacting to his own weird brand of psychosomatic pain, Mr. Faehner began rubbing the joints of his arms and legs as though he were relieving actual discomfort. The reporter meanwhile moved on.

Venturing into the next of the four corner rooms, he found himself surrounded by a suffocation of boxed and paper clutter. The only way through the room was to walk along a bended path piled on both sides and beyond by stocked stacks of boxes and half as much loose-leaf, all of a pertaining nature to the operations of the Silver Mine, past and present. Tiptoing through it, the reporter made note of the various months, dates, and years written all over the boxes' sides and posted on paper bundles. The bold black told the stories of old; stories thirty-nine years in the making, stories older than the reporter's life. Catalogued by year, the closed cartons contained documents, reports, ledgers, all pertaining to the many years of the mine's operations as a tourist haven. From 1974 to 2013, Mr. Faehner had kept the tradition alive, of keeping the day-to-day operational paperwork in the room of records in the 1800 house. Of course the priority papers of the past twenty years had all been transcribed into computer data and filed away electronically.

The last of the four corner rooms was unlike the others in theme and purpose. It was shelved to the brim with nostalgic and historic items all relating specifically to the time since the mine had been reopened. When Mr. Faehner finally caught up to the curious guest, he noted with interest the interest he was taking in the artifacts that decorated almost all of the available wall space. The Silver Mine owner, once Silver Mine worker, could not help himself. The boy that was inside him came out at once and wanted once more to do the telling, to tell the tales of the plethora of preserved objects in ways which meant the most, most because coming from him they were still first-person perspectives. It was a joy to do so even after thirty-nine years and several thousand renditions, and Mr. Faehner applied the same amount of eagerness and verve to the rendering as when he was young.

"This old thing here," he started off with, "was pulled up from the first pit in the mine, which of course you haven't seen yet. It was part of an old system of wooden ladders used by early miners to get down into it. Somehow it survived. Seventy years in a watery grave, and it remained intact. Go figure. The mine water must have some sort of quality to it, which retains the integrity of wood."

"Maybe because the water is cold all the time, and less microbes were present to disturb it. Most rot on things that were once living is the result of biological breakdown caused by molds and fungi."

"My, aren't you the eager mycologist," Mr. Faehner replied in a facetious tone before answering him seriously. "But you know, you might be right. I never considered that before. As a matter-of-fact, I've never had the temperature of the shaft water measured. It's probably in the forty-to-fifty-degree range.

The air temperature in the mine itself is a constant fifty degrees Fahrenheit, so the water would have to be that or colder, and that doesn't make for the creation of a very good microbe soup, does it?"

Mr. Faehner was captivated by the thought, the thought of something new, something new in relation to the silver mine. The esoteric idea set him off. It got him going on something of a tangent, and he began in earnest delving into the minutest of detail about the next and the next and the next item on display. He came to the old carbide lamp found during the first exploration of the air shaft. "It was probably placed purposefully up in the overhead crevice where we found it to be used in case of emergency if all other lights failed. It could have been retrieved without too much difficulty as a backup source of light. They probably had candles hidden too and matches in much more prominent locations near the back portions of the mine. Miners are a wary bunch, overly concerned about their safety, in the days before when their working conditions were necessarily a high priority of the proprietor."

Piece by piece, article after article, Mr. Faehner conducted his little lecture until finally the reporter, through his own initiative, uncovered a light cloth draped over a easel standing in the section of the room closest to the kitchen. Without any fear of reprisal, the reporter uncovered the stand and revealed what was underneath. For the first few moments, Mr. Faehner seemed unconcerned, caught up in his current discourse about how the early miners had had rock removed from the underground by the clever use of donkey-pulled carts. "Donkeys of course because their size was a good fit in relation to the low-ceilinged, narrow-passaged contours of the silver-rock realm. And let's not forget . . ."

All the while the curious reporter continued his concentration on the display. He had discovered unwittingly the charts for Mr. Faehner's latest, greatest, southern-end adventure, something that was for certain connected to his elongated stare while looking out over the river from the precipice of Pequea. On the board in front of him was a sophisticated map of the Susquehanna River, which showed an up-to-date detail of the river's currents, depths, and the many just-below-the-surface croppings of river rock. The provision of the map detailed a specific section of the waterway, the dam-to-dam in-between, which included the frontage of Pequea's second-coming community. Pinned to the map were tiny red arrows, which outlined particular passages both down and up the river from a designation point right where the Pequea Creek's confluence met with the mightier mile-wide flow. At the point of designation were a construct of red dashes marking a perimeter around a recognized spot—the Pequea marina. The site of the outline, though, was at least twice the size of the existing structure and accompanying environs. That meant, the reporter concluded, first in his head, then with an expressive elicitation, "You're going to demolish the old marina and make way for something new, something on a grander scale!"

The outburst took Mr. Faehner by surprise, so engrossed was he still at his renderings and remembrance. He turned and took notice.

"Your eyes are like crystal balls," he returned as he advanced toward the man and the map. "Your interpretations are quite correct. In the very near future, I mean to convert the old marina into something quite extraordinary. Right now, it is adequate only for the accommodations of smaller recreational and pleasure boats: pontoons, outboards, runabouts, and the like. What I have in mind is for the facilitation of something much bigger, much better, than the ordinary boats that are kept there. What I am going to bring"—and he held off bringing up as if to heighten the suspense—"are ferryboats to the Susquehanna deep!"

Again, the conversation was suspended as a way of awakening all of the imaginative recourse in each of them to visualize, in their minds' eyes, the yet-to-be-realized coming attraction.

"It's all; the bridge, the homes, and the ferryboats, a way of making the old town whole. A revitalized town needs a way of staying that way, or else it would be doomed to extinction once again. Money needs to flow in and out of the community. And I need to provide ways to accomplish that. I have, I feel, the responsibility to infuse more than just a rebirth to the area. Once I have given it life, I must give it a way to go on living and breathing. The ferries will provide that. Out-of-town tourists and local sightseers alike will flock there just as they did the Silver Mine once they had reason to. Hundreds a day will come spending money on the floating giants, at the hotel, at the grocery store, at the gas station, at the garage, at everywhere money can be spent, all to enjoy a spectacular day aboard the *Ferry King* and the *Ferry Prince*. That's what they will be called. There will be two, only two, one slightly larger than the other, so that during low-level periods, I'll have at least one ship that can skip over the many low spots, which line some portions of the river."

"You mean, due to the displacement of river water, the lesser boat can venture out more safely during times of low flow?"

"That is essentially correct."

"What will they look like?"

"They will be look-alikes. One, like I said, a similar but smaller version of the other. The *King* will be made to accommodate about 200 passengers, the *Prince*, roughly 75, not counting skipper and crew. Both, though, adequately sized to put the operation on a paying basis."

"But what will they look like?" the reporter reiterated, anxious to get a more descriptive view of the concept being given.

"Regrettably, I have no visual aids," Mr. Faehner conceded. "But imagine if you will the old-time ferry steamers that once plodded the muddy Mississippi back when Samuel Clemens, er, Mark Twain was a boy."

"Er, I know who Samuel Clemens is, was," the reporter interjected for the sake of his own recognition.

Mr. Faehner chuckled, interpreting the young man's interpolation for what it was, a way to indicate his enthusiasm for the description.

"What they'll be essentially is two life-sized, steam-powered boats." And he added proudly, "They'll be run quietly, efficiently, and cheaply by coal. Anthracite from the provinces of Pennsylvania's coal country, which, he continued getting to the point, burns so cleanly in these newfangled furnaces that the only emissions from the fires will be the boiler-generated streams of steam trailing high and behind the boats. "Yes, everything's being done with principles in mind. The original, the *King* is already under construction. The son, I'm leaving on the planning table for now. It's prudent, I think, to go one at a time. Test out the waters, so to speak. I've leased a site of by-water land up from the town just below the Safe Harbor Dam. That's where everything is being done."

"So you're going authentic then," the reporter edged in just to continue being part of the conversation.

"And why not," Mr. Faehner replied presumably. The project is being attended to by a great group of skilled boat builders, craftsman, all! They were all former workmen of the longtime defunct Trojan Boat Company from right here in Lancaster County. How fortunate for me. I inveigled only one former foreman. He did the rest, found them all. Most are beyond retirement age now but most willing and able to ply their special craft one last time. One fellow, in particular, even suggested that he be captain of the first vessel. It's extraordinary really how nothing quells the needs and desires of the true men of the sea, be they actual seamen, those who go off to sea or seamen like these, who build the vessels for those that do. Either way, they've got that pining, which supersedes all else, to never give up the ship."

"So will he be made captain of the first ship?"

"He will in the sense that when the *Ferry King* slips out of its dry dock, he will be the one wheeling him on his nascent journey down the river to Pequea. That should appease him even if I decide not to pick him to captain him. They'll all savor that special trip. For the first time in their lives, they'll be given the chance to take what was theirs—their craft, their skill, their infinitely measured processes—and take it upon the waters and waves and see for themselves just what they've accomplished."

"You sound like a banner saluting the boat builders of America," the reporter said in jest. "But I couldn't help but notice your unusual characterization of the ferries. You refer to them in the masculine context. Why? Isn't that a contradiction to the cause? Haven't seamen from time immemorial imparted upon their seafaring vessels names of or symbolic to the fairer sex?"

There was a moment of silence as Mr Faehner established in himself the implication of what was presented to him. He mulled over its aspect.

"I guess I won't be able to call it a maiden voyage then," he mused. "But no matter. I think that that tradition-of-old had more to do with the uncertainty of whether the brave seamen would ever come home again and how the parting of such long journeys made men's hearts show, through ceremonious testament, just how much they did desire to find themselves someday back in the arms of their loved ones. But seafaring is not so perilous in our modern age, and thus the reason behind the tradition no longer exists, so I don't feel it would hurt to dismiss it in this case. These ferries will never be gone long from port, and they will never meet their wreck and ruin on a river that's barely deep enough to hold them up."

"The way you speak about the boat builders, it all sounds so altruistic. Is there really a profitability here to make it worth your while?"

"There is always profit derived from things that are worthwhile. Not always money. But there again, I've responded with an altruistic answer. I suppose, more and more, I'm turning into a benevolent old man, nothing like the ruthless character I was once purported to be. It does make life sweeter, though, to be able to be kinder, nicer, toward others whose lives we influence. I like it. To get to your point though, you assume that the costs of a project such as this may not be worth it in the end. To tell you the truth, I have not yet calculated the net worth of this substantial undertaking. You tend not to do that if you know that a certain dalliance such as what this is to me can neither make or break you. The investment, albeit in the hefty range of over $1,000,000, may or may not come back to me. I think it will. But regardless, I won't be deterred. Even if I lose it all, I won't become destitute. If these ships sink, I will remain afloat."

Mr. Faehner's eyes closed for a moment as his mind became focused on the aspect of altruism that had just been regarded. Inwardly, he had been stirred by the feeling of it, of genuine compassion, of seeing one's dignity rise up in one's self without complaint and form expression. So seldom in a person's life does this happen that it tends to take one by surprise. The inculcation brought out sentiment from the past, a long ago, faraway past. Mr. Faehner took the moment, received and perceived what came out of it, and prepared its rendering in as able a fashion as he could.

"And I quote," he finally stated, "lead the world to a better place," is what my grandfather told me on his deathbed. And though I was only five, I took that advice to heart, at least I must have, for I felt the desire to do so all through my life. I was perpetually considerate of its consideration. But only now, now in these finer years have I had a chance to prove to myself, to my promise, that I would do so."

He examined his conscience openly.

"I have always in my past done things for others when I did not have to. Little things. But little things mean a lot. And now, given the opportunity, I am doing more. And the proof of it is just as you've said—that I don't really know, don't really care that I profit from it. And even if I don't, I'll have still given out an excess of joy and pleasure to people I don't even know. And if that isn't doing what's right, then I don't know what is."

"That's as efficacious an account of someone attempting to exonerate themselves from something as I've ever heard," the reporter shared in as just an idyllic manner as he had just heard.

The echoed meaning of the reporter's words were not lost on Mr. Faehner despite the soul search he was on. He responded in as perfunctory a manner as he could as though he was embarking on a conversation about his dress; his choice about which pair of shoes he selected to wear for the gala, which was ongoing just a look away from the stone house where they stood, steeped in ideals and ideas.

"I'll have you know, young man, that I've never been, nor have I ever been accused of being a robber baron. I have nothing to atone for as others may have, those who have managed to extrapolate from life riches such as I. If you're second-guessing me, that maybe I do know that I eventually will make yet another pile of money from this new watery escapade, then I salute you, young soothsayer, for your future cast, for you are honoring me really by predicting my success. And if you're right, then how can I help it, for success really does breed success. The rich really do get richer but through no fault of their own. It simply gets simpler. The more you have, the more you have to do with. And also, the more you can afford to lose or throw away as the case may be. For me, throwing away $1,000,000 would be like you throwing away, let's say, possibly, $100—a loss you'd certainly regret, but one you certainly could handle. Likewise if I'd give money away to a cause or a charity. The portion of what I can spare, if in proportion to your worth and what you can spare is relative to our individual holdings, so what is as to me, is as to you, seemingly great, but only the same on the condition of percentage."

Mr. Faehner smiled broadly for seldom did he get to give out wisdom to someone he viewed as so receptive to the things he said. Neither did he feel the slightest upset toward the impressionable lad for having tried to get to him. It was not his fault that he grew up believing in the stereotypes concerning rich people—that they got where they are by relegating all those who stood in their way.

Mr. Faehner, satisfied that he had handled the reporter's insinuation well, went back to business. To demonstrate this, he moved forward, more toward the map, and picked up a pointer that leaned against the stand. It wasn't unlike the kind school teachers used to point out places on maps in geography classes and in so doing made each of the recipients feel somewhat more attuned toward the subject material.

"Look here," Mr. Faehner demonstrated at the onset of his lecture by utilizing the effectiveness of the attention-getting pointer-tip's tap when striking the heavy-textured cartograph, "these red markings are the indicators. They represent the point-to-point process of where the ships will roam."

The reporter followed with his eyes, as an astute student would, the lines of fixed red dashes as they were spoken about and depicted by the intensely interested teacher. He began by motioning to the harder-to-see up-river location, where, come next day's dawn, a scheduling of long-ago-displaced boat builders would be convening to perform their highly coveted though two-year-at-most, jobs, phasing into reality the dream that Mr. Faehner had initiated. The anticipated launch date of the *Ferry King* would be met "come hell or high water" as spoken by the confident crew.

Totally absorbed by the project's prospect, the reporter put in a rally from the earlier offense he had committed when he purported that Mr. Faehner's intentions about the project might have been spurred on by remaining feelings of some old guilt rather than for the pure sake of altruism.

"You keep referring to your ferryboats in the vernacular, I mean, in general terms. Even if you intend to keep them guised in the masculine form, why not give them a more meaningful moniker? Why not *King Kris,* spelled with a *K,* after you? Or how about naming the first ferry after your grandfather who guided your sense of being so civic-minded? What better accolade could you give back to him?"

It was wisdom. The words were like inspiration. And Mr. Faehner used them. After dwelling on them a bit, he responded in kind to the testament he had heard.

"There's no way for me to one-better what you just said," he said approvingly. And isn't it fitting that my grandfather's name was Leo. So that's what it will be, *King Leo,* like the lion who's king of the jungle, my Leo will be king of the waterways!"

The display continued. And for a short period of time became something of a didactic discourse. This interlude included a brief explanation of the history and function of the end-to-end dams—the Safe Harbor and the Holtwood. During this time, Mr. Faehner remained staid in his nature and discourse, didactic and without opinion as he released information. "The fact that we have a dam-to-dam system to work with is what makes this possible," he went on with in a perfunctory manner, "the lower dam swells the level of the river's water between, making channels deep enough during normal or near-normal conditions to hold up bigger boats such as the ferries. And our little town of Pequea just happens to be ideally located to have such access to it."

Pointing to and tip-tapping certain spots on the map, Mr. Faehner regarded with intricate detail many of the deeper river channels of which he had just spoken. Like an expert mathematician, he detailed their certain lengths, widths, and depths— standard, and when influenced by high and low flow. He used his handheld pointer as if it were a magic wand and revealed the intransigent locations, the underwater hiding places of the channel rocks. He explained too how each of the ferries would be equipped with intricately designed charts, which will identify the exact placement of the meddlesome stones. Then he went on to regard the extent of the river trip itself, explaining that from end to end the voyage was approximately 14.5 miles long, and with the ship's swing to come back around the entire trip would be about thirty miles. "By time," he said, "it would be about a two-hour tour."

"A two-hour tour, a two-hour tour," the reporter expressed in a timed melodic voice almost as if it was done on cue.

The words set to music, of course, referred to the theme song of the old '60s comedy "Gilligan's Island" and went on to tell the tale of the fateful ship, the *Minnow*. Mr. Faehner, having actually grown up watching the iconic show as compared to the reporter having only seen it occasionally in syndication, made the connection to it instantly and, only a split second behind, upheld the reporter's humorous intent by first grinning, then laughing out loud at the antical remark. Once the laughter had ceased, Mr. Faehner was apt to point out that these ferryboats, his ferryboats, would suffer no such fate as Gilligan did.

"I assure you, young man, that my ships will arrive safely to the quay at the marina after every trip out. Make no mistake about that."

"I do not doubt it," the reporter responded in a more serious tone of voice.

Then, forgetting entirely, the earlier slight against his character and the light-hearted jest about his ferryboats, Mr. Faehner concentrated on the matter at hand, the safe, serene, and scenic journey that his two-boat fleet would soon be taking. From his centered attention, he began an efficacious account of what the journey was like, for the journey he had taken several times before. He had seen it; pristine, primordial, the river, the lands it touched in its many splendors. Though only from the back of a racing outboard at various times of the previous year, he had taken in fully the offerings, the visual arrays that the river kept. There were valleys between 200-foot hills, where gentle slopes of green-blazing grass came and merged with the water's edge. There were places too where the cliffs came right on contact with the river's side, the sheer rock wall, eternal. And in warm, wet weather, these monoliths would tear down digested ground water in long glistening trickles, which would make the mountain sparkle. And so too as the cold approach of winter drew near these cascades would turn to ice. Icicles, 100 feet long, would form against the rock wall sometimes to last until winter's last. In some places too where the mountains bowed down in height were vast mingled areas of precipice and tree. Here, a wonder of wandering wildlife visited frequently, undisturbed. Here, while at dusk and at dawn, small herds of deer came to graze undetected on sweet clumps of sessile grasses. High up above the promontory would fly, wing-spread, mated pairs of hawks; swirling, searching, the placid pools, the rapid ranges, for river-sourced fish. The esurient couples were ever watchful for a catch of catfish or bass. Farther below were crop islands; small by-the-shore outcrops of rock and soil solidified by deep-rooted shrubs and weeds where occasionally an observer could catch a glimpse of elusive red foxes, which frequented the tiny water landings to sleuth for the many salamanders and skinks, which skulked amid the creases and crevices of the anchoring boulders. Farther down beyond the crop islands was an area of calm where the water was noticeably deeper, made so by the nearby presence of the Holtwood Dam. It was here that an even grander display of aerial beauty took shape. Just below the mile-wide dam was the home of many nested pairs of the great bald eagle. "In the midst of their realm, loads of people will be brought amid a river station; a series of connected, sunken poles, where the ferries can stop so the spectators can spend some precious time appreciating the sky spectacles. It's the perfect solution to a problem that's persisted since the start of the eagles' reintroduction into the area decades ago. There was simply no real way for people to come and view them in their habitat. The environs in which they live are too wild to get through. The land is inaccessible. Ninety-nine percent of it is privately owned. The rest is too obfuscated by natural barriers for anyone to attempt getting through it. The thing that some people try to do is foolish. The real die-hards trek on down to the bridge about one mile below the dam. There they dare to go out onto the road, unprotected, and cling to the bridge's concrete side while duly doing their best to observe the aerial acrobatics of the "baldies" and keeping themselves from getting killed by the infinite number of everyday tractor-trailers that zoom across the county-to-county bridge at high rates of speed. Braving the river and rock below the dam is even more dangerous than the highway. The river runs in rapidly moving torrents between huge high boulders, broken chunks of the mountain, fallen over the centuries.

"Each of the ferries will be equipped with high-powered binoculars so that every man, woman, and child can have access to them. It's kind of like giving them an eagle's-eye-view of the eagles themselves. They will come, one and all—anglers, outdoorsmen, conservationists alike—to see the mighty birds."

Mr. Faehner then took a moment to breathe, epitomize, and elicit the special way he was feeling.

"Oh, how I can picture it, a sparkling sunny day, a light breeze blowing, standing perfectly still on the side deck of the *King Leo*, taking in their movement, their beauty, their inherent belonging, and becoming part of that belonging."

Having elicited the newly described eponym for the grandfathered boat, Mr. Faehner felt a surge of gratitude toward the one who had suggested it and gestured to him. "You'll have to come back sometime as my guest and come with me when I take out upon the *Leo*. Bring your girlfriend or wife as the case may be. Call me in advance though, you know how I can be called upon to do things other than what I intend."

The Hell Riders Part I

Straying a little from the ferryboat conversation, now ending of its own volition, the reporter became distracted by the sight of a forlorn-looking object sitting next to him, top-spot, in an open box, which had been filled so full that the box's flaps had been taped up so as to accommodate extra material and what-not all relating to the Silver Mine's past. He reached for it, surmising correctly its identity. Picking it up, he realized he was holding an old, worn, outdated motorcycle helmet. Palming it firmly with his left hand, with his right hand, the reporter felt over its dulled rounded surface. Coated in black, the top of the helmet had been artificially branded with a large orange and red fireball. Coming out of the flames were the fiery words—Hell Rider. Upon connecting to the insignia, the reporter exercised his free fingers over the shaded letters as though he were blind and reading Braille. From the corner of his eye, Mr. Faehner at once detected his young friend's fixation on the curious object and decidedly came to his aid.

"I see you've become acquainted with the Hellmet Riders. That's H-E-L-L-M-E-T spelled with two Ls. That's what I called them anyway."

"Tell me about them?"

Hesitant with words, Mr. Faehner extended his hands toward the relic signifying what he wanted. The reporter relinquished it. For a moment, Faehner stood silent and began fondling the helmet in much the way the reporter had been doing. The more he did, the more the helmet's intrigue seemed to influence him. Finally, he gave into it. Finally, he spoke.

"The ignoramus, to whom this belonged, is really not worthy of my time or attention. But, admittedly, it is a fascinating story. One that would bode well for yours, that is, if you are up to the task of putting something together from all of these short stories I've been revealing to you. By the time we're done, you're probably going to need a whole section of the newspaper to cover what we've done."

"Don't worry about that," the reporter answered assuringly. If there's too much for the original allotment of print, I'll convince my editor to let me run a series of it. He'll agree. Most of these stories have never been told. This is prime material here."

Hearing the young man's enthusiasm, Mr. Faehner could not help but insist of himself to carry forward with the story. Closing his eyes, he began looking into the past to summon up images that once were life. It came to him. Images that once were, were passed on into a new day. In his mind, they formed forms of his former self. "Come to me, come to me," he cajoled to them from their distant state. And they came, and they came leaving no recess of his memory undone. And once brought forward, these memories became certain, so certain in fact that in each listener's mind a motion picture played out, displaying the events as if they were being played out, moment to moment.

"Looks like they had a good time again last night," Kye, the older of the Leckner boys, pointed out to his younger brother, Tye, once he had reached the upper pond's rim and spotted the numerous burned-out campfires and the associated trash: assorted personal objects, cigarette butts, cellophane wrap from cigarette packs, a black comb which inadvertently fell out of someone's pocket, and a few foils from Hershey's Kisses.

Tye, who had raced up to the pond side too, took a moment to catch his breath, then commented, "Who's it going to be? Who's going to tell Mr. Faehner?"

Kye, menaced by the expectancy he had heard in his brother's voice that it would be him, responded by declination, intimating refusal with a twist of humor and wit. "Not I," he said, referring to the series of responses issued by the barnyard animals in *The Little Red Hen* when they were called upon to do something they did not want to do.

Tye, who had from childhood on acted out this comical bit with his older brother whenever they entered into a dispute about which of them was going to be the one to do something that neither of them wanted to do, engaged his brother in the folly, if only to waste a few moments before coming to terms with the difficulty at hand. "Not I," he responded in kind.

"Not I," Kye returned quickly.

"Not I," Tye remarked as if on cue.

"Not I," Kye declared suddenly.

Tye reacted admonishingly and moved toward his brother as if to initiate a boxing match.

"Not fair," Kye reacted, knowing that Tye, though one year younger, was vastly stronger.

"Then how about an arm wrestle?" Tye replied, furthering his hope that a physical contest could be used to solve the dilemma.

"No, I don't think so," Kye responded while for the first time trying to come up with a suitable solution to their predicament.

"Then we'll do it together," Tye remarked, noticing for the first time just how concerned his brother was by the frown on his face. "Don't fret about it, brother," he then added quickly, "there's strength in numbers."

Joining forces, the newly positioned Silver Mine tour guides jumped out of their self-doubt and flounced off of the pond rim, bounded down the short rise, and began racing toward the front of the mine. As usual, it was turning into a competition, and each boy began picking up pace once they had reached the level surface of the juncture in the road just outside the mine entrance. Then, unexpectedly, Kye stopped dead in his tracks. Out of the corner of his eye, he caught sight of some splotch of discoloration, an object that was in contact with the still-yet-closed bars guarding the silver mine entrance. Without regard for his brother, who was now quite a distance down and around the sharp curve in the road which marked the line of sight to the gates, he bounded toward the bars. Before reaching for it, he gave it a discerning look. Obvious to his eyes was a black-strapped motorcycle helmet dangling from one of the many pointed spires of the black gate. Painted over a sizeable portion of the front-face side was a huge fireball with flames of outlining red, orange, and bright yellow. Scrolled along the flames were the fiery words; "Hell Rider". Emanating from the helmet was a foul-smelling odor, which, when enhanced by the frowzy odor wafting out from the mine, combined to make the helmet completely undesirable to touch. While contemplating what to do, Tye, who had long since realized he was running aloof of his brother, made it back to the point where they had separated and, surveying the immediate area, noticed his brother's figure standing in front of the barred entrance of the mine. Without words, he then raced over.

"What are you looking at?" he asked in a bewildered voice even though he too then plainly saw the object of his brother's fascination. Sensing an even greater apprehension in his brother's eyes, probably due to the fact that there would be even more to report on, Tye without admitting why, began examining the gate's lock as to whether or not the mine had been trespassed upon by the night-riding interlopers. He connected his hands to the bars and yanked, attempting to ascertain if the security line had been compromised. Nothing appeared out of place. The two gate halves swung out and in just a little as they normally did. It appeared right. Satisfied, Tye quit on the gate, then summoned his brother to come, follow him.

"Time to face the music, so they say," he proclaimed bravely. And let's not forget to bring the souvenir," he added firmly.

"Why, so we'll be spanked even harder?" Kye responded facetiously.

"Two against one, just like I said," Tye remarked as he had when the pond discovery had been made. "Besides, Faehner's a pretty smart guy. When he sees that we've found evidence, which points to who's coming down here at night, he'll be alleviated somewhat, I think."

"Hey, anyway, I've heard he's much better to deal with than the original owner was, Boddinger, wasn't that his name? I'm glad we weren't around when he was here. He was a real tyrant, at least that's what people say about him. This guy's new, but he was once just like us. He came up through the ranks. If anyone can understand the quandary of all of this, he certainly can."

"Glad to hear you talk so simply about what we're about to go through, brother. So here, you can be the one to hand over the helmet."

Though certain doubt still lurked in their heads, the boys, joined together by will, began run-walking down the road, which led to Silver Mine Road. Once they arrived at the glen where the original operations trailer had been, meaning they were in eyesight of most of the pertinent places where the exulted Mr. Faehner might be, they slowed down to a trot and then began to stride, side by side, in perfect unison as though they were some two-headed creature. Coming out onto the road, they picked up the feint sounds, signals, orders, being shouted from a distance, like those maybe heard by a defensive safety from the opposing quarterback twenty yards away. As the boys drew nearer in the direction of the plank barn and behind, the volume increased noticeably, and the voice being heard became more distinct. It was none other than that of Mr. Faehner. Striding up alongside the barn's side, each boy gulped down his fear as a way to make ready for the inevitable—whatever that would be. Almost as an omen as they were about to round the corner to the behind-the-barn scene, a family of highly irritated yellow-throated buntings began swishing and swooping in their path, flustered by the incessant harsh commands being elicited in the heart of their home.

The boys came into view and were spotted. The reciprocal eye contact struck them down. The two-headed monster they imagined themselves to be became elfin in size. The encounter was at hand.

Mr. Faehner was standing, hands locked behind him, in the back of one of the Silver Mine trucks, the open bed as his platform. He was calling out to a small assembly of day-hired workers there to perform a once-in-a-decade-or-so duty—cleaning up the long stretch of the Pequea Creek of accumulated debris: fallen sycamore branches, old tires, tossed-away shoes, camping gear, even the rotting carcasses of dropped-dead deer, which were illegal to hunt and kill in the park. Shot outside the park, they would sometimes manage to "escape" long enough and far enough to lie down and die in the protected wild of the Silver Mine sanctuary. Because of the associated risks involved, regular mine workers were seldom, if ever, called upon to perform this precarious duty, risking life and limb in the splotchy, deep-pocketed, sediment-carrying creek.

Noticing the boys' approach and noting profoundly that they, surely after a careful consideration, had decided that the news they carried was worthy of both their time away from their perfunctory duties, Faehner quickly ended his didactic instruction. Without further consideration to the crowd he had only moments ago been so interested in, he about-faced them entirely and directed his sole attention to the abbreviated advance of the Leckner brothers who had stopped in their tracks still twenty feet away.

"Come closer," he instructed while still maintaining the high-standing, hands-behind-the-back persona as if to convey an opprobrious effect on the boys to be questioned.

The brothers did. And as they did, Kye issued forth from behind his back the purposeful helmet, allowing it by its sheer presence to tell much of the "what the hell" story without elaboration or comment. No mention was made alluding to their belief that the Silver Mine property was being placed in more and more jeopardy by the continued overnight presence of the motorcycle gang. No mention needed to be. Mr. Faehner's reaction was immediate and stern. He was an obsessive-possessive when it came to all things Silver Mine related. The property that he had strived all his life to obtain meant the world to him. Down to the most minute detail, he worried over things. It was as though he still coveted the property from afar. If a lightning bolt happened to strike down a tree, he was overwhelmed by its loss. If a section of weathered phyllite suddenly collapsed over the front of the main mine entrance, he would undoubtedly collapse too in spirit. If an abysmal sky let loose a tempest, which overspilled either of the property ponds, he could be counted on to throw a tempest himself, a temper tantrum of a degree directly proportional to the damage caused by the inevitable charge of unnecessary water, which would create cuts and ruts in the back rises of earthen containment, which had to be packed around the bottom ends each time such a thing occurred. That was Mr. Faehner.

The enemy was anything, anything that moved against him, his beloved Silver Mine. But this now was an enemy of greater difference. It did not come all at once, inflict its damage, then let Faehner alone to pick up the pieces. This enemy came as it pleased, as often as it pleased, to do as it pleased. These were creatures of the night whose nocturnal comings and goings were as elusive as dark clouds sneaking across a night sky, concealed by the elements. They came unannounced and could never be anticipated. Any expectation of their that-night arrival would always end up in disappointment. When one would consider a certain Friday or Saturday night upcoming to be one of the nights they had chosen to exact their purposes, they would simply not show up. And then would the Monday after the weekend. There was no way to catch them unless one was willing to literally camp out in the hollow hills and lie in wait for that sudden unexpected appearance.

They were an older sect, not bound by authority of any kind. They were not of the age when parents or school attendance would have regulated much of when they would be free to do as they pleased. They made up their own minds about that and maybe even plotted their trespasses in such a way to distress the Silver Mine owner, knowing that such randomness could never be dealt with or overcome, for surely they knew fully that their presence was unlawful but didn't care. And the fact that they rode motorcycles yet made them all the more difficult to deal with. The speedy two-wheeled machines they used to infiltrate the mainly accessible property lines meant that they had the upper hand in that they could come in from practically anywhere and, if detected, could promptly flee in any direction, and unless one would be in pursuit of them in a like vehicle, it was unlikely they would be, could be, apprehended. All of the road barriers in the world meant nothing to a rugged bike. Mr. Faehner ascertained these thoughts. What to do? These were thinking beings he was up against, thinking, that is, relative to what he could be dealing with—a woodsy bear or a robust deer coming around and messing up the property. How to outthink them?

He pressed himself for answers, and possibilities came to him, each one carried through to its utmost conclusion, each one's utility or futility as he put it in his head. The idea of a watchdog he had already contemplated—a dog of the right type, big enough and mean enough to act as a deterrent, could effectively be used to keep away unwanteds. However, there was one major drawback to this plan, which was that a dog of this size and demeanor might, with or without provocation, attack anyone it perceived as a threat, regardless. And even if the dog attacked someone who had trespassed onto the property, they in fact could sue; and as it is written into law, every dog owner is responsible for the actions of their dog. These miscreants could end up taking him for a bundle. No, a dog wouldn't do.

In all of the previous years, 1973-1990, the Silver Mine had never had to be protected by a private security force. Was now the time? Mr. Faehner was reluctant to go this course. Thinking about it, he realized that such a thing could have prevented him from ever becoming a part of the place. Had he ever had the bad luck to encounter a security force when he first began his boyhood ramblings here, without the consent of his prestigious uncle, he would have surely been found out and most likely forever banned from the place he considered his heaven on earth. Just the mere thought of just how easily that could have been the case gave him shivers. He could not bear to think that all that came about could have so easily just as not. Though he tried, he could not deter his thinking about it and pondered it for a period of time. Fate had been on his side, and he wanted fate—no, needed fate—to be on his side still. There were other more significant things that had yet to be decided, and he had to believe that the stars were still, and yet to be, aligned in his favor. And if one thing fell out of place, it might signify a realignment of the stars, and if that would happen, it could mean that things yet to be decided might not go his way. At this critical point in his mind-meanderings, he determined not to go further. He shook his head to help free his mind of the matter. As he did, a resolving thought surfaced in his head and he decided instead to pertain to it, for it, once again gave him his purpose. It had happened as it happened, and no amount of speculation could change that. His purpose here had been intended, for any other person could have come along when he did but didn't. The stars that had been in his favor so long ago still had to be because their particular purpose had not quite yet been brought to fruition, for nothing as substantial as bringing an obscure thirteen-year-old boy into the realm of the mine just as it was to come to something after seventy-five long years of wait and then to cajole him to become part of it, and then to provide him with the amazing opportunity to take it for himself was just beyond coincidence, just beyond it! And the rest that was yet to come; the part that had been his initial hope had indeed been the concluding part; of fate, of the stars' markings, of the reason for it ever happening, to find, where under the elusive hollow hills existed, the once highly touted and once highly sought-after treasure-trove of silver, concentrated tons of it, that first captured his imagination those seventeen years ago.

But enough of that now. The precious property had only recently come into his possession. There would be time enough now to find out if the thing he believed in most was true. His mind though, in the recesses of his mind, always battled back and forth about it whenever it found a venue to do so and the concept of just how easily he could have been averted from ever being a part of it all bothered him immensely. He feared this failure and had to remind himself whenever he struggled with it that someday his final aspiration would be determined.

His mind warped back to the present and the relevant issue at hand. Unlike the way his thoughts would always become mired in the premise of whether or not he was worthy of his ultimate intention, when it came to making decisions about things more ordinary, Mr. Faehner never faltered. Already he knew there would be no watchdog. There would be no private security force hired to maintain order. The next consideration was a little more feasible. He could alert the local authorities—the sheriff of Little Conestoga—apprise him of the confounding situation, and hopefully be able to convince him to afford the Silver Mine a bit more protection than the once or twice a month when the single patrol car would take a drive through part of the property. This the sheriff or his deputy did out of duty due that the mine was included in their jurisdiction. But in reality, they were obligated only to pass by the property edges, along Silver Mine Road, not go in. Enticing them to do more on a routine basis might prove difficult, except if they could be made to feel special for even being selected to perform such a task. To be associated with the up-and-coming Mr. Faehner was a privilege. To be in his good graces would be an honor. Having the local law enforcement officials do a little more for him than what was already expected might solve the problem. The deputy, or sheriff, laying in wait some late, unexpected evening, could unravel the riddle as to who exactly they were dealing with; and with a gun in hand, the mysterious motorcyclists wouldn't be so apt to flee once they were sighted. The speed of a fast cycle was no match for a fast bullet.

Stepping out from the backside of the huge barn, Mr. Faehner took in the view of everything around him, juxtaposing the new difficulty at hand with the configurations of the land in front of him. Looking left toward the lower end of the pond, below which was the immense campground portion of the property, he came to a certain conclusion, which made him breathe a sigh of relief. One word summed it up for him—occupied. The Silver Mine was in its seventeenth summer season. Its popularity was such that half of all the campers that annually frequented the park were repeaters from the past. Many came year after year once the weather got nice. A few even kept their favored spots year round and stayed, or visited, for weeks at a time, even in the coldest of winters. So usually there were people around, people whom he knew well and had a vested interest too in keeping the mine free of unwanted disturbances. So it was unlikely that the nocturnal nincompoops would waste much time attempting to take over the peninsula and adjacent areas. It wouldn't be long before they were spotted, observed, and identified.

Next, he turned his view to the 1800 house. Correlating again the specifics of the problem, it came into his mind a time when the blue-stone structure did house, at least temporarily, a person whose job it was, at least in theory, to hold down the fort, so to speak—a caretaker. Early on in the Boddinger days, Luckee, the old overseer, convinced a methodical Mr. Boddinger to take in a former friend from the bar he owned. His name he couldn't remember. It didn't matter. He was an intruder himself in the young Faehner's estimation, but brought in nonetheless as a decoy to make outsiders believe that there was someone in charge year-round on the property. He was an artist somewhat and meant to earn his keep by plying his craft in whatever ways could be applied as concerns the artistry needed to enhance the newly opened tourist destination. He sculpted fist-sized pieces of green talc brought up from the well-known Cedar Hill Quarry, thirty miles to the south. He made objects relating to the Silver Mine operation: donkeys, miners, mine carts, horses, deer, foxes, bullfrogs, and even a carbide lamp. Once he even sculpted a figurine of Mr. Boddinger and presented it to him as a token of appreciation for allowing him to live there. He also painted murals on the wood-paneled walls of the shanty, the made-to-purpose museum, gift shop, mine-tour office, situated right outside the main mine entrance. On the hewn pine-board walls were depicted life-size scenes of eighteenth—and nineteenth-century Silver Mine mining operations conceptualized by known historical fact. Among them were pictorals of early Conestoga Indians carving out pockets of the easier-to-access silver veins exposed in outcrops of surface quartz. Other depictions showed miners picking out the main floor passage, following trails of glittery ore deeper and deeper into the subterranean strata.

Aside from those two more profound attentions, he made a few signs and arrows, which were used to point the way from various strategic places along the nearby roads for the purpose of making it easier for people to locate the hard-to-find locality. But he, for whatever you thought about him, his talents, didn't last. And Mr. Faehner entertained himself with a long laugh when he summoned up the image of the spoiler he had been in ridding his precious property of the nuisance.

But back to the principle of the story. There had once been a person who presided in the house. There could be again. This time for the exclusive purpose of maintaining discipline, a caretaker who would care for things, just as Mr. Faehner would, would he be the person selected for the task. He had to think of another person, another salary—$20,000 at least. Was it worth it? It didn't hardly seem so. After all, it appeared in all probability that this would be a temporary situation. There had never been any trouble like this before—a thing Mr. Faehner could assuredly say since he had been here since the beginning. He decided no, but if problems such as this continued into the future, he would reconsider it. He then thought about the boys—Kye and Tye. If, during the summers and weekends out of the busy season, their hours were extended, extended to include permission to sleepover on the property, they could surely be his eyes and ears when he wasn't there. They of course would be advised as to what to do should they unexpectedly come across the notorious gang—run as fast as they can to the barn phone and call both the local law enforcement officer on duty and him. Like he did before them, they knew all the ins and outs of the place and could never be caught if chased, at least could not if they applied all of their skill and knowledge aptly once a pursuit of them began. The chances would definitely be in their favor to successfully elude anyone who would strike out after them. But perhaps he was putting too much faith in the fact that he was comparing their decision-making processes to his. They did not possess the same amount of enthusiasm about being at the mine as he had and therefore may not have acquired the same level of connection to it, meaning, that they had never taken the time to learn of it, its intrinsic nature, its intricate patterns and outlines, hiding places, quick-paths, back-tracks. Knowledge of these things he attributed to himself may not hold true to them. He declined. The boys were untested and did not have the savvy to come out ahead in a situation like what could occur if they were left alone to deal with it.

A perspiration collected on his brow not induced by an increase of the day's temperature, and Mr. Faehner sought relief by taking the short walk down to the Silver Mine Run bridge, kneeling down alongside the closest stone setting and, casting the emblematic helmet aside in a nearby clump of pond weeds, dipped his cupped hands into the cool water and splashed his face with it. Repeatedly, he did this attempting to free his mind of the impending trouble. The run water did much to relieve the stress that had been building in him since the hel-l-met, as he now considered it, came to him. In his refreshed state of being, he sought to gain a new perspective on the pending problem. Quickly, he picked up the head protector and jogged over to the side of the 1800 house. There, without care, completely irrespective of why he did it, he flung the helmet like a soggy doughnut into the thick-stemmed branches of a row of half-century-old rose of Sharons. Due to its unintended trajectory, straight up and then straight down in, the object dropped onto one of the bushes where it angled and bunched together tightly with other branches of and not of the same plant, affording a splendid catch-place for the intrusive object. Despite its size and discrepancy in appearance, the helmet was well hidden by the abundance of leaves and pink-and-white blooms attending the bushes while in their fullness of season.

Unburdened, Mr. Faehner began another jog, this time across Silver Mine Road, into the glen adjacent to the bridge and then up Silver Lane as he now referred to the original unnamed road, which led directly to the mine area. At a point just beyond the century-old kiln, half-distant to the main mine, he darted off onto a remnant trail up into the hollow hill. He was a man on a mission. And to carry out his self-appointed task, he carried with him everything he had—his past, present, and future. His intention was perfectly clear to him. He would traverse these hallowed, hollow hills with the hope that by studying the structure of the intricate hillside, he could find a way to outwit the unwelcome interlopers the next or the next or the next time they attempted to come on the property unnoticed. The best way to do that would certainly be to identify them, who they were and what exactly they were up to. Someone would have to lay in wait, somewhere up in the lofty hillside at a selected, secluded spot, without being seen, so that they could see, who and what Mr. Faehner was dealing with. With the same alacrity and speed he had once possessed, he swayed this way and that across the lopsided slopes, examining every dip and drop, every tree stand and rock crop to find that perfect station from which to begin a repeated surveillance in the hope of carrying out this purpose. From these points of predicated purpose, Mr. Faehner, while remaining in the pose of pretense, acting as if the gang members were within view, observed what was below—pond, shanty, mine entrance—imagining how easy or hard it would be to see what was going on. He fitted himself from one advantageous spot to another until deciding upon the one or two winners. It occurred to him spontaneously that he himself could probably do the job. Why would that be so far-fetched an idea? No one would know. And no one else's safety would be put into jeopardy. What a simple solution. But he declined. There comes a time in a person's life when they better understand their limitations, or better yet, as in the case of Mr. Faehner, that privilege prevails, and some things are better left to be done by others. There are certain people whose spirits never age as the body does, and Mr. Faehner was one of them. Thirty was not thirteen though he often wished it was.

Having located the one or two potential positions from which the potential someone could secretly spy on the random raiders, and having reconciled with himself that it would not be him, Faehner leaped and bounded out of the woodsy setting so adroitly that he seemed like an indigenous creature who belonged to it. He came out at the point where the pond began to swerve around its side, mine-side. This was where a long dirt road, hardly used, made its way up, up to where the wooded extent edged into field. Here, the rudimentary road led up to one of the several electrical pylons on the property. The road was access to it and therefore could not be closed. It could, however, be restricted. This was an idea, an idea which could be implemented as long as the electric company knew about it and had access past it. Mr. Faehner felt elated. All of this had come to him just because he had put himself in condition of it. He had opened himself up to possibility just by believing in it. The ritual, the splash of run water, always seemed to satisfy whatever it was needed for—little miracles.

He trudged up the dirt road until he reached the top and looked things over. What he was proposing was simple. Strong steel cables would be strung across the road at several strategic places putting up barriers, forcing the interlopers off the road, making their infiltrations onto the property far more difficult. All of these rudimentary roads would be effectively cut off this way on the opposite hollow hillside, opposite Silver Lane on the other side of the run, everywhere where old paths, trails, and partial roads existed these barriers would be erected. The only way around them would be around them, that is, unless these motorcycle maniacs possess the skill to actually vault three to four-foot-high steel cords. God forbid they splash miracle water on their visages and bikes and then make a run at them. Then they might be unstoppable. Because of that rather out-there thought, Faehner thought harder as to where to place the stopping fences. If he placed them on even ground, they might just do the undoable. Better to place them in spots along road turns or amid washouts on worn sections to aid the prevention even further—make it as hard as possible for them to do the seemingly impossible. Not being a man who delayed actions, Mr. Faehner went even further with his plan while still in this initial phase of doing something about it. When it got late, he summarized the day; the boys, the buses, and the tourists were gone, which made it entirely possible for him to temporarily vacate the property without worrying about making a final check on the mine, shanty, the barn, the 1800 house. Glancing at his watch, he discovered he had been traipsing through the wooded hills for hours and was struck by how quickly the day had gone. Inspired by what had been accomplished already, at least in form and theory, Faehner, wanting to keep the momentum going, pointed his body and spirit in a direction of further development.

After sprinting down out of the area where the electrical pylon towered, Faehner landed on the encircling pond road, which at its furthest extent from where he now stood edged the boundary line of the upper end of the property. Adjacent to the mine property this direction was a centuries-old Amish farm. This property, although only a scant sixty acres, flourished by the hands and hard work of the Old Order sect. The house and barns were always in a state of well-being. The crops were always plentiful even in years of drought. So easy was it to draw water up to the smaller hollow hillsides from the run, which picked its way right through the middle of the land before spilling into the first of the two Silver Mine ponds. The Plain People who worked this land, the Beilers, had been on the farm since the days long before any silver had been mined on the lower portion of property now known as the Silver Mine. During the 1870s when the real mining operations began, the Beiler ancestors watched and mused at the activity and hoped that the situation would run its course before too long a period of time. Very little contact had ever been made between the so-close neighbors, very little had to be, for they were like two little worlds out of time. But now, Mr. Faehner, for the first time ever, endeavored to breach the little Amish world beyond. And his reason was purpose.

At the backdrop of the upper pond, Silver Mine Run meandered through a relatively level area of grassland marked by water pockets and sparsely distributed trees, saplings mostly. A barbed-wire fence defined the outline of Beiler property, and to successfully enter into it, Mr. Faehner had to scale one of the sturdier sycamores and lift himself up and over the jagged obstacle. It was the first time he had ever transcended the upper property line, and it struck him as strange that he, even in his youth, when he was his most adventurous of all, had not done so. Perhaps it was the fact that the occupying people, the Old Order Amish, were ever-present on the property, except of course on that once-in-a-while Sunday when the family would depart entirely, on their horse-drawn buggies on their way to some distant church member's farmhouse for services—an all-day event. Or perhaps it was the fact that he respected them, their way of life, their way of minding their own business, and that in all of the years since 1973, he had never witnessed any of the

Beilers, even out of innocent curiosity, strolling onto the Silver Mine land. They were the exemplification of eximious neighbors.

Mr. Faehner felt like he was stepping into a new world when he thudded onto the lush little knoll, which underlied the sycamore's base, a moment marked in time. He likened it to as much as what an early world explorer felt like when stepping foot onto a new island or continent, so much was his appreciation for having finally done it. For a moment, he stood tall and still and surveyed the road to his ambition. No longer apart from the unknown land, he was now a part of it; and in this new vein, he began to think in accordance with it. His mind now merging with his new surroundings, he began to pick up on the particulars of the life and land of this new place. In particular, he now thought it peculiar that the grassy grove he was now present in was so lush, so green; for after all, the Amish owners certainly had a plentiful number of grass-grazing ungulates—horses, goats, cows, enough to keep even the wildest and most remote corners of the farm manicured in the style as having it done on a regular basis and by the personal intention of the property overseer. But a few steps into his purposeful journey, Mr. Faehner discovered the reason why the small solemn sanctuary so filled with growing things remained untouched by so many prospective creatures. It was not a rejection. Not far-off in a forward direction was the reason why all the goodies were left alone. Ahead, a few more steps, over ground which was becoming apparently softer and softer with each footfall, was another almost-invisible-to-the-eye fence. This fence was made of the thinnest wire imaginable, hard to detect even with the most acute vision, be it bird, beast, or human being. He noticed at its base line a tiny spread on both sides devoid of the hardy green growth that was beyond it. He surmised, and accurately so, that the thin-wired fence might be electric. But how was this possible? The Old Order Beilers, like all of the Old Order sect, were selectively cut off from the implementations of the modern world.

To avoid getting shocked by the current-charged fence, Faehner searched for some way to gain an advantage over its perimeter. Making use of another sycamore, one with a sturdy low-hanging branch, he grasped the limb and again, swung his body ably over the obstruction. The moment he had obtained a safe landing, it struck him how ridiculous he must have looked, a grown man such as he was swinging from the trees like Cheetah in a Tarzan movie. Unavoidably, he began to laugh. The inner boy in him certainly was in control of him this day. But his mission had to be completed, and he rose up from his squat position and headed in the direction of the closest farm structure, the barn.

The Beiler barn was not a bank barn such as the Silver Mine barn nor was it as big because it had never had to care for the size of crops and animals as compared to the days when the Silver Mine property was exclusively a working farm itself. Mr. Faehner followed the run for a tiny stretch, then turned away from it on the side he was walking. Not a soul could be seen of animal or person. He traipsed across a slanted meadow, sloping gently away from the red-painted barn some further distance, his eyes keeping careful watch over a ground tainted with cow pies and tiny pop-up ponds. It was nothing short of a grand-scale obstacle course—the most difficult he had ever experienced. At various points, he felt like he had just competed in and completed a little kid's game of hopscotch, without picking anything up.

Finally, he arrived at the side of the barn, and he heard, with a strained ear, a considerable amount of clucking coming from somewhere inside. He followed his ears upside, back-barn, then in an open bay. Next, he routed himself, past buggies, harnesses, and farm tools to where suddenly there appeared a long side of a man-made pit. Coming upon it, he peered over the edge and was confronted by one of the eeriest sights he had ever seen. In that first split-second view, he encountered a Beiler whomping off the head of a now-befuddled bird running about in a craze on the dirt floor as though still alive and trying to retrieve its chopped-off top. There were two other chickens in the pit, both dead. The executioner's work was done. Ten seconds later, the last bird to die went lifeless. The elder Mr. Beiler looked up at the stranger looking down upon him. Neither recognized the other. Seeing the robust old farmer staring at him while wielding a blood-dripping ax prompted the now-anxious, uninvited guest to speak quickly on his own behalf.

"I'm so sorry for interrupting your . . . your . . ." And his mind went blank over how to categorize such a frightful sight. "I . . . I'm Mr. Faehner, your neighbor. I wanted to intro—"

Sensing and speculating what the spectator must be thinking about him based on what had just transpired, Epheram Beiler shot his eyes straight at the woebegone onlooker and sought to set things right.

"Don't be afeared at what you just seen," he stated in a judicious tone. "It ain't for us to say. God made the world the way he made it. It ain't for nobody to think any differently neither. Killing chickens, cows, and pigs is done for the sake of keeping God's best creatures alive. And by keeping alive is the same as praising. He gave us this here life to keep after as the best we can while we're here. So by killing things so's we can eat and keep our health, so's we can keep praising on Sundays, we're keeping faith with the Almighty."

Epheram, encouraged by his praise of God's well-intentioned ways over the living and the dead, spoke openly to his unfamiliar neighbor.

"So you's that boy that come here all those years back and started back at looking for the silver again. When I was a boy too, I heared all about it when the first time it was when they started taking the silver out of those hills. Sorry thing too. So you're looking for more, eh?"

Though Mr. Beiler's facts were not entirely straight, Mr. Faehner held no desire to debate the matter for reasons that it made no difference whatsoever whether the Beiler family insight reigned true. And it made no nevermind to him whether or not the Beilers held religious credence in the swing of an ax when their birds or beasts were brought to slaughter. Instead, he needed to interact in a business negotiation. His idea was to get the help of the Beiler boys and their demonstrative father to set up his road barriers cheaply. If not, and he really didn't want to go down this road, he could bring up the matter of the dirty little secret—that they were utilizing power from a modern-day utility—electricity to keep their farm animals from straying off the property. Now wouldn't that be devastating, getting the word out on that? A hypocrisy! A sacrilege! To him! He'd receive an admonishing worthy of the wrath of God or, even worse, a shunning by the local Amish community. That would teach him to go against the principles of faith.

Epheram was no fool. It had already crossed his mind—the things that the illustrious Mr. Neighbor had discovered and was putting together into thought. And he then spoke in terms of the unspoken. Very quickly, a tentative agreement was reached, sealed with a fistful of bills and the promise of a fistful more once the project was completed.

"I'll pay half up front and half once you and your boys have completed the assignment," Mr. Faehner contended.

Three days later, first-light, the men and the crew of Beiler boys, of which there were seven, met atop the silver mine hill next to the pylon. The supplies—several knotted strips of inch-thick steel, eighteen six-foot poles, screw-in fasteners, and digging equipment lay across the base of the electrical tower. Mr. Faehner reminded Mr. Beiler of the location of each site where the steel cords were to be erected, pointing out that each spot had been tagged with a bright orange flag.

In addition to putting up the protective steel-cord barriers, Mr. Faehner also made it possible to close up all the main entrances. At each of the four entrances, metal gates were installed, which had to be manually unlocked and swung open each morning and manually swung closed and locked each evening. The only exception to this was made on the lower portion peninsula where campers had to have the freedom to come and go as they pleased. But this allowance was not a real disadvantage in what was trying to be achieved in that the perpetrators so far had shown no interest in advantaging themselves to this part of the property.

Over the next several days, Mr. Faehner smiled more and more as he watched the gates and steel-cord barriers go up around him. And much as he hated to see more man-made materials being placed all over his precious, pristine property, he had to admit he did feel more secure having it. His philosophy ever since day one—the day he first arrived—has been to keep the property whole, pure. The Silver Mine was so beautiful a place that it should never be prevailed upon.

The Hell Riders Part II

Thinking that the protective measures already taken might suffice in keeping out the unwanted, Mr. Faehner adopted a wait-and-see attitude before initiating any further action. His own workmen who had put up the road gates and the Beiler boys who had put up the access-blocking barriers had both done a good job. For days after the installations, Mr. Faehner visited all of the sites, looking for any signs of disturbance. There were none. After two weeks' time, Mr. Faehner had been lulled into a state of belief that the motorcycle gang had gotten the message, maybe by means of having had one of their own come upon one of the blockades. But this wasn't the case. The interval of no intrusion was nothing more than random. Then one night, they came. Quite upset at practically running into the stretch of steel planted up by the pylon, the gang reacted by cutting ruts into the soil beside it—making their mark no doubt—then out of nowhere, one of them found an old discarded piece of plywood and used it to set up a ramp with which they could jump the obstacle. Mr. Faehner admitted to himself that he had never thought of it, of how simple a thing it was to do. But their night had not ended there, their satisfaction that they had come up with a way so ingenuous to infiltrate the property. Their dissatisfaction was carried to a greater extent when Kye and Tye reported that the mine itself had been broken into. The evidence was all over—roaches—tiny remnants of marijuana cigarettes, a partial pack of rolling papers, a roach clip, candle stubs, and even the aroma of recently smoked marijuana lingered at the furthest point back in the mine, the highest and driest area. For a day, Mr. Faehner kept the mine off-limits to tourists to save himself the embarrassment, but it cost him their ire and a few hundred dollars and Kye and Tye their tips. The boys were put to work that day investigating just how the villains had gained entry in view of the fact that the main mine gate was still locked when the boys went to open it and the air shaft halfway through the mine was far too narrow to accommodate anyone bigger than the skinniest person—so much had the earth settled down around its vented airway since it was first constructed so long ago. Halfway through the day, Mr. Faehner came to check up on his detectives, only to find out that they had found nothing to explain it. Disappointed in their defective detective work, he admonished their efforts to their faces.

"Maybe I should incorporate the help of the Beiler boys to solve this mystery if neither of you can't figure this out."

In reaction, Kye, who was perched atop the mine entrance shelter gate—an elongated construct made of thick sides and long top-covering planks all built on a slab of concrete and secured in front by iron-barred gates—nearly fell from his precarious position. He had been examining the areas where the man-made structure and formation rock met, knowing that in some places, there were gaps almost big enough to allow a person to squeeze through into the mine. Possibly, someone had hollowed out one of the holes in the weaker beds of phyllite, enough so as to gain entry. Probably not realizing what he was actually doing, Mr. Faehner likely attributed Kye's fascination with the rock wall as doing something other than what he was supposed to. But Kye did not care. Either way, it was rude for him to presuppose someone's intentions without inquiring. After regaining his balance, he began a charge toward the front end of the shelter gate so he could hold up his fist in defiance of his all-assuming boss and maybe—depending upon the distance between them as Mr. Faehner had immediately departed once his comment had been made—let out a choice explicative or two. But before he could position himself to make such a gesture or call, he found himself, his pursuit, upended. About halfway down the series of boards, he stepped on something that moved. His charge had been made down his left side with 90 percent board to his right. His left foot had landed on two loose boards, which propelled both boards skyward and sent Kye lurching left momentarily, then toppling over, off the roof, and onto the ground. The two displaced boards followed, one clunking him on the head after it hit the ground beside him and bounced back up.

Elated at having discovered how entry into the mine had been obtained, Kye ran off into the woods to find his brother so together they could hunt down their mean old boss and brag of their accomplishment. When Kye located his sibling, he discovered that he too had had some luck in ascertaining some of the answers in the great mystery. Tye, by wandering around in the red-thorn thicket as best he could without getting scratched or torn clothes, discovered a nascent motorcycle trail that started twenty yards into the wild field behind the electrical pylon. Apparently, the bikers covered their tracks by gently walking their bikes far enough into the thicket before clearing out a thin trail for them to access the edge of the wooded hill. There they again dismounted their bikes and walked them over to the side road where up above the Beilers had built their bulwark. The ramp had been a ruse!

Finding Mr. Faehner, hands clasped behind his back, pacing the first floor of the barn, for no apparent reason, Kye and Tye eagerly told him of their discoveries then proudly escorted him back to the mine area so they could prove their assertions.

"Nothing's ever easy," Mr. Faehner said to himself after ordering the boys to reset the planks and fasten them and the whole row of wood with an extra number of long nails.

His mind stimulated by the evident failure, Mr. Faehner sought again the proper solution. He had been outwitted, at least for now. And he now knew that the Hell Riders would be defiant, wouldn't give up without a fight. There could be no truce; otherwise, they would have already entered into a negotiation to have access onto the land.

Later that day, Mr. Faehner hopped into one of the Silver Ford pickups—carry-overs from the Boddinger days—and hightailed it toward the town of Little Conestoga, where reluctantly he would plead his case before the town sheriff and hope for some sympathy. Up and over Silver Mine Road, he sped until he reached a bend in the road where another road, Goods Road, jaunted out from a parallel set of hollow hills very much like the mine's but without the outcropped rocks and trees. These hills were all tillable and farmed. Only one segment of these adjacent lands was like the mine. From where Goods Road crossed over an unnamed run, even smaller than the run beside the mine, there was an extended acreage of rock and tree exactly like the land around the mine. From the single-laned Goods Road bridge on and toward the Pequea Creek, it bordered the Silver Mine property, following the contour of the run itself. The bounded property was owned jointly by several men who hosted what they called the Broken Bottle Club, a club of local men who spent what was left of their time and money drinking, gambling, and target-shooting on the private space of this land. And endured they had through complaints of every kind. And even the influential Mr. Boddinger had failed to stop their shenanigans. The most he had done to curtail their behavior was to limit how often they could shoot up the place. Their disruptive days, since the days of Silver Ford Incorporated, went from thirty days a month down to eight or nine depending on how many weekend afternoons there were in a given calender month. And that was all Mr. Boddinger pushed for, for reason that he was new to the southern end and didn't want to upset too many applecarts.

From the inception of Goods Road, beginning at Goods Road bridge, the way to Little Conestoga was a winding couple of miles that went this way and that, through and around, mostly hilly terrain, farmlands, and fields. His destination was a newer single-story building built in 1978, the year the current sheriff was first elected to office. Faehner remembered him only as another of the local constituents that he could proudly point to and say that he predated them too as concerns his time at the Silver Mine. And there was a time too when he believed that the long-term sheriff might cause him difficulty in his zeal to take over his beloved mine property. Such was the case with the blackmail of Mr. Boddinger. If Mr. Boddinger had not conceded as he had and fought instead, the resulting circumstance could have been different. And most certainly, the sheriff would have played a crucial role in that. It's fair to say, in retrospect, that he might have been prosecuted along with his friends for having even spent the night at the 1800 house without permission. Boddinger might have even thrown caution to the wind and touted the incriminating photographs himself, throwing himself at the mercy of his wife and a discerning community, and won. For sure, the sheriff would have acted on behalf of the remorseful millionaire and taken great pleasure cutting of the heads of the troublesome teens, and held them up for all the township to gaze upon. The sheriff too would have gained respect for acting so benevolently toward a man who, due his financial stature, could have so easily disregarded the local authority entirely and hired personal lawyers on both sides of the case to ensure its result. After all, a pinchpenny such as the younger Faehner was would never have refused the advice and counsel of a savvy young lawyer interested in taking the case just for the public good.

By the time he pulled up in one of the building's empty slots, his musings on how things might have been were over. Now he would face the sheriff as he really was in regard to who *he* really was—the sheriff, the sheriff; Mr. Faehner, once the up-and-coming Silver Mine boy, now the Silver Mine-made man. And from these perspectives, there was no room to lie.

Hopping out of the pickup, he paused to reflect on the significance that this was the first occasion ever that he had resorted to asking the local official for help. Was it a sign of weakness? But before he went in, he dismissed this notion entirely. After all, as a dutiful taxpayer, he would only be getting back from the community what he partly paid for. Right?

Once inside, he took up a seat in one of the cushioned arm chairs laid out in a small row against the back wall. The chair he comforted himself in lay directly in line of the occupied office chair. The sheriff, sitting behind the desk and wholly engaged with another resident, did take note from the glance he had given that the person who had entered did somewhat resemble the heralded thirty-year-old who had somehow, someway, taken over the late Boddinger's stake in township property. To be certain, he popped an eye right, then popped an eye left of the sulky bulk in front of him and identified the man as Mr. Faehner, a person he knew mostly from newspaper stories and television shots. In reaction to the sheriff's diverted attention, the robust figure slammed his fist down on the desk, the pounding of which shook the articles strewn across it and brought the sheriff back to the sense of what he was doing, priority-wise.

Meanwhile, Mr. Faehner took in the view. The office and the decor were vintage late '70s, the walls all dark-grained wood paneling, floor to ceiling, and were offset by multiple sets for multiple windows, off-white Venetian blinds now only partially opened. The floor was parqueted wood tiles, simply designed, and stained the color of yellow pine. Covering over an area consisting of the sheriff's desk and the area in front of it where a single chair had been placed to offer hospitality to those who chose to take it once they approached the desk was a large rectangular-sized piece of off-white carpet, identical in tone to the hanging blinds. On both sides of this central room were doorways leading to other rooms. Their locations on each inner wall was exactly opposite of the other. Both were painted an off-white color, which seemed to match again both the blinds and the carpet. There was a built-in bookcase too, again painted off-white though there wasn't a book of any kind gracing its shelves. The baseboard too was painted in the same accord, and actually, due to the carpet, blinds, built-in bookcase, doors, and trim, there was enough of the white color to offset the overpowering darkness present in the walls. Overtop his head were acoustic tiles, off-white of course, suspended from a drop ceiling. And hanging just over the desk was a huge ceiling fan, for the moment turned off. It had no pull chain, so it must have been operated from a switch somewhere on one of the paneled walls.

After his entertaining examination of the seventies-styled room, Mr. Faehner turned his attention more immediately in front of him to the giving-it-as-good-as-he-was-getting-it person, who, though sitting in the provisional chair—probably placed there more for rendering the more-apt-to-speak-out less-likely-to-do-so due the passive feeling a person gets while being comforted—was right up to the edge of the desk. If intimidation was the tactic, it was paying off. The sheriff, although not completely backing down and still doing a little barking of his own, was becoming a bit more hesitant with his answers as though he were spending some time considering the implications of them. Mr. Faehner, disadvantaged in that he could not see the face of the antagonist, still began to make inferences about him. He was extraordinarily big above the waist, barrel-chested with a neck as thick and sturdy as the sycamore he had used to hop onto the Beiler domain. His arms—biceps, triceps, and below the elbow—were enormous. He did not appear to be towering, but his proportions were well matched to his size, considering he was one huge mass of muscle. As his crown, he wore a topping of curly-cue blond hair, which only seemed to accentuate his physical difference from anyone around him.

Next, Mr. Faehner began paying attention to the conversation, which in the short span of time since he entered the office had turned into an argument of some magnitude. Apparently, the Little Conestogian had recently petitioned the township for an easement, which would allow for the one Michael Zoig to disperse and store parts he would use to repair and restore motorcycles onto a part of an adjacent lot of land, one-fourth acre, which he was the sole owner of. The township, it seemed, was reluctant to comply with the request for fear that Michael might use the easement as a way to establish precedent and therefore be in a position of superiority to ask or demand of the township further future concessions.

Michael was infuriated. First, he laid down the law by insisting that the hard-nosed sheriff refrain from using his full given name and call him only Mike. Then he went on and on about how unjust the denial was, in part because there was no such provision in the township rules or regulations which allowed for denials based upon speculations about the future, of what might happen. Mr. Faehner was somewhat impressed. This Zoig thing in front of him took a back seat to no one.

Watching this, regarding this, this man who wouldn't take no for an answer made Mr. Faehner reflect on the relevance of being such a person, a person such as he was too. His own persistence had paid off entirely, and it was all due to being like Mike. Situation the same, had he been any different, the outcome would have never come to what it did. It was an epic experience. It had been seventeen years of perseverance to bring him here, sitting in the seat of authority, positioned with power, power to do anything. Looking back, he was amazed at how one thing led to another. And he was honestly amazed at himself for not giving up, for the pattern of change had not happened in accordance with any preconceived notion or plan. Most of it happened by chance, not choice. The only choice was in the manner he had of not giving up and allowing circumstances to come about as they did. His credit was in always being ready to take advantage of the opportunities when they came. And they did. He was, as he had always wanted to be, owner and operator of the Pequea Silver Mine.

But the story was not over. Pressed down deep inside of him was the anticipation of his heart's desire, the reason he had pressed on for the better half of his life, through thick and thin, the thing that everything depended on. It had enveloped him the first moment he cracked rock on that opening day in his youth. That first strike, which occurred when he put hammer to rock on the very first eye-catching piece of quartz, was like the opening line of a song cajoling him, cajoling him; "Here I am, here I am, come and find me." It was almost as if the silver had waited, waited all of those seventy-five years for him, for him to come along, someone who was willing to spend his life believing in it. The Faehner of 1973 and the Faehner of 1990 knew, knew in his heart that the silver mine had only been abandoned because the technology of the late last century could do nothing against the mighty forces of nature. The water table, which had been broken into in the second shaft, flooded the mine. The extent of valuable ore had never been depleted. But no one since had been willing to believe it. The geologic conditions were too ripe to have extrapolated only the amount taken while the mine was in operation, even if every bit removed was of pure silver. More existed! Either in the mine or in the hills beyond. And this was why he could take no chances. No unauthorized characters could be given access to the area, where opportunities like the one he had had could occur. The tourists, since the day he became proprietor, had been restricted in the areas where they could freely pick about at the rock. Their forays had always been kept in check by the occasional "Poisonous Snakes" signs they would bump into while searching for silver. These warnings—complete with a carved picture of a copperhead, one of the few venomous snakes which really did inhabit the area—served well to keep the sniffers, the real rock hounds from wandering into territories considered off-limits by Mr. Faehner's concern. For years, they had served their purpose even before Mr. Faehner had taken over the property. Their implementation had begun before the third summer, before the mine really became popular, and without the consent of the previous owner. Nothing was going to come along and ruin the possibilities of the Faehner dream—nothing then, nothing now. The silver was there. The pact he had made with himself about finding it and finding it on his own would be kept.

Zoig, despite his fervor, did not become anything near what could be considered impertinent. He was either very good at holding back his hotheadedness, or his personality was such that he never went beyond a certain point at expressing his dissatisfactions. All the better. It made him appear the winner regardless of the outcome with the chief. Mr. Faehner only imagined what things would be like if the pale-faced giant decided to become disorderly all at once. What could the sheriff do? Rise up from his desk and defeat him. Unlikely. The arms on the imposing figure were so thickly muscled he could, in all probability, snap any handcuffs put on him. Not even a bullet could stop him. But all conjecture aside, Mr. Faehner was still so glad to see that big Mike could spit words without becoming a hitter. This was impressive.

Then, just like that, their words were over. With a departing shot of "I'll be seeing you soon, Sheriff," Mike got up out of his chair, which he had recently reseated himself in, and promptly exited the office. Mr. Faehner felt conspicuous. Never before had he had to come before the sheriff, not even to report the occasional driver who threw trash out of his or her car along Silver Mine Road. He felt awkward. The seconds that ticked by were added exclamation points to the awkwardness that was settling inside him. There was but one thing to do. Alleviate it! Without further pause, he followed his inclination. He surprised both himself and the sheriff by ejecting himself out of the chair as if he had been electroshocked and scrambled for the door. The sheriff was appalled! Outside, he knew his quick reactions were just a bit late. Off in the distance, sight unseen, was the trailing noise of Mike's reverberating motorcycle engine speeding away. Mr. Faehner glanced at the vehicle that had brought him, one of the old fleet of 1970s Silver Ford pickups, no match against a rip-roaring Harley, the motorcycle he had noticed when he drove into his parking slot, now gone. Catching up was impossible. He stood silent for a moment and let the momentum of his memory take hold. In his head, he placed himself back in the office chair paying attention; the words, the words were out in front of him again, and he snatched them one by one. "Let's see," he conspired with his memory. "I recall, I recall." Then out of somewhere came the decisive factor—Recycle Shop! "Yes, I recall it. That's where that guy works, and I know just where it is!"

Referring to his knowledge of the town and its surrounding environs, Mr. Faehner enacted his purpose and constructed the best possible means for getting to where he wanted to go. The route became clear to him, and off he went. Without further delay, he swung the pickup in a backward swerve, wheeled right, lurched toward the parking lot entrance, looked both ways twice, then sped off in the opposite direction from which he came. The destination was only a half-mile distant, and practically no time was lost in getting there. In fact when he did, Mike had only just kicked down his bike and entered the shop. Through one of the shop's dirty windows, Mike noticed the Silver Ford pickup when it pulled in. He did not recognize the man who got out of it and opted to attend to his repair-shop work instead of going out to greet anyone.

Walking over to the lone visible door of the cubicle-shaped, one-story, block building, Mr. Faehner noticed the inordinate number of motorcycles stationed on the premises. All were red-tagged with dates and descriptions denoting—when the bike was accepted for work, what was wrong with it, and when it was expected to be done. Thirteen bikes. Closer inspection of the building revealed flaking white paint on the block and windows, front and sides, with surface rust on the metal casements and glass so smudged with dirt and oil that it had probably never been wiped since the panes were installed. This told him a lot. Mike prioritized his work above all else, and he was good at what he did. He was trusted and reliable. His rough-cut appearance—for he wore a baggy pair of faded blue jeans tied with a cord of rope around the waist and topped off with a thin white T-shirt—was only an extension of his type of person who excluded all else to what was most important to them. The way to Mike was through his business.

Assessing the highly intelligent facial features of the man who entered the shop, Zoig doubted very much that he was someone who wanted to talk about the best way to enhance the engine performance of a sputtering old Honda or knock around ideas about how to increase the thrust of a '72 Endura. This guy was part of the system, maybe a building inspector, or, possibly, a small business advisor. Anyway, not much concerned, Zoig turned away from the uninteresting person and went diligently to work, crouching down beside a black Yamaha on a spread-out canvass drop cloth. Strewn across the dingy work cloth were parts from the bike and the tools required to fix them. Maybe, Mike thought, the stranger would mistake him for a plain worker and not ask any questions. But he was wrong. Mr. Faehner knew he had the right man.

Interested in the shop due his interest in the man who owned it, Mr. Faehner did meander about a minute or two before approaching the motorcycle mechanic now lying on his back under the bike. One of his legs was wrapped around the front tire on the floor. The other leg was stretched up and over it as if he and the machine were engaged intimately. So entranced was he with his work that he and the machine were one. Mr. Faehner looked on in silent disbelief almost hating himself for having to interrupt such a scene.

"Nice place you got here," Mr. Faehner sounded out once he began his walk over.

"It's a dandy!" Mike said with exaggerated expression, hoping the colloquial term would heighten the awareness of the obvious differences between them and make the stranger want to leave.

Mr. Faehner suspected what Mr. Zoig was doing, but rather than be mad about it, he was glad that such a man, big and bold, who had just experienced setback and disappointment as concerns his most precious asset could inject humor so readily into a situation that at this point was only an aggravation. It meant that just like what transpired in the sheriff's office, Mike was indeed in control of his temper, making him someone who could be counted on that way, which—in consideration of the way he was to be relied upon, not to cause or be part of any unnecessary violence if he decided to become part of the plot to reveal the identity of the thugs frequenting the mine at night—was crucial in achieving the best possible result.

"I think introductions are in order," Mr. Faehner stated assertively, at once making Mike realize he was now dealing with someone of importance to him. "My name is Mr. Faehner. I am the proprietor of the Silver Mine. I followed you here from the sheriff's office where I was sitting behind you while you were pleading your case, at least the tail end of it. I'm sorry the thing didn't turn out in your favor. It didn't, did it?"

Interested that a man like Mr. Faehner would want to have anything to do with him even to the point of claiming that he admitted following him back to the bike shop from the sheriff's, Zoig, at once, let go his leg from up over the bike and crawled out from under the frame to a spot on the drop cloth devoid of tools and parts. With a few light groans, he managed himself up off the floor and stood, hand extended, in front of the inquisitive seeker. Mr. Faehner, standing as he always did when he was purporting a position of power with his hands held behind him, made no motion to extend his hand forward purposely. If he and the amiable giant were to pursue anything of a business relationship where he called all the shots, no level of parity could be pertained to, and he had to be sure his inferior was not apt to retaliate. Mike did not. Instead, thinking otherwise, he rescinded his lengthy reach, spot-checked his hand, and apologized for the fact that it had splotches of motor oil on it.

"Sorry," Mike let out in a low-toned voice. He bent down beside him for a cloth rag and began wiping off his hands. "As you probably already know, I'm Mike Zoig, born and raised right here in Little Conestoga. I've got this motorcycle fix-it shop that I started when I was fifteen years old, and I've been running it ever since. As for what you heard about me and my business, that's about me trying to gain a little breathing room here. For all of two years now, I've petitioned the zoning board to allow me an easement on the land right behind the shop so I can legally park bikes there under some kind of makeshift shed so I can keep 'em dry when it rains or snows, that's all. But the sheriff, he's the head of the township board, keeps telling me no. Says it'll initiate trouble everywhere. Says if he lets me get away with it, others will want it too. Told him I studied the county's ordinance book and discovered there's no such thing as not allowing someone to do something such as this just because of what might happen in the future. Laws weren't written that way. And actually, there's already a precedence set, off the books of course, of them allowing things similar to this. Take for instance . . ."

Zoig went on with his story for a bit until Faehner waved him off of it.

"I think I understand, Mr. Zoig. It's a case of the township showing preferential treatment to those whom it wants to. I think I can help. I'll get your easement for you, at whatever the cost, if I can count on you to do a favor for me."

Mr. Faehner went on into detail about the difficulty he was having at the mine and related to Mike what would be expected of him should they enter into an agreement about it. After a few minutes of explanation, he gave him an ultimatum.

"It's your prerogative, Mike. What do you say?"

Mike accepted. The agreement was, tentatively, that upon the condition that Mr. Faehner charm, or somehow otherwise, get the township to grant the easement allowing the bike shop to allot a lot of the Zoig land directly behind the building permissible for business purposes, Mike would agree to make nightly sojourns to the upper portion of the Silver Mine property, a few hours at a time, and hope to reveal the identity of the unwanted cyclists. The offer stipulated that a minimum of fifteen nonconsecutive days of surveillance would be expected but that the fifteen days expected would not exceed thirty calendar days.

Prior to the plan's inception, Mr. Faehner invited Mike over to the mine where he introduced him to the layout of the property, showcasing all of the spots he himself had selected as places to hide out. In addition to this, he took him on a brief tour of the specific areas where the Beiler boys had put up the steel catchers as he had been referring to the road impediments just recently erected.

"I don't want you making the mistake and trying to fly in here on one of your bikes, on one of these secondary roads, and having you end up in the hospital and your bike end up in the junkpile."

As a last matter of concern, Mr. Faehner handed Mike one of his business cards, which had on it the 872 number of the 1800 house, his current residence.

Mr. Faehner was pleased with himself for taking on Mike the way he did, so spur of the moment. Chances were that Mike might even know some of the members of the motorcycle clan; after all, he was into motorcycles, and they were into motorcycles. Maybe some of them were already part of his clientele, and this whole thing would be figured out from the moment he first spied them. That would be easy.

The day came when Mike Zoig realized he would have to go to the mine and spend a few hours waiting and watching for the invaders, if they should show up, from the secluded hilly woods that were a backdrop to the mine, upper pond, and shanty. A notice came in the mail that day informing him that the township board had taken his special-interest concern to heart and had decided favorably, granting him the unheard-of privilege of allowing an appropriation of his adjacent-to-the-shop land to be used to facilitate business-related items as long as such items were kept in a neat, orderly fashion, and at all times were items that could be considered usable—not junk! The price for the special favor he discerned by noting that a waiver had been issued, which in this case meant paid for, to clear the way for the action. In this case, the cost of the waiver was $750.

Motivated by the swift action—five-days' time it took for Mr. Faehner to complete his part of the bargain, Mike set out on that first-day's night, a moon-bright night on one of his better-to-ride dirt bikes, an old 360 Endura, and sped off toward the mine. To get a good feel for the bike, he rode cross-field, property to property, on a good portion of dirt road entirely before spilling out onto the asphalt road at a high point just one-half mile from the Goods Road bridge. Here, Mike stopped in the road berm, revved the engine a few times just to hear the sound, then proceeded onward, downhill, across the bridge, and onto Silver Mine Road where he again opened it up to make it up the backside of Silver Mine Hill.

At the mine, he rolled into the open lot just before the pond bridge and pulled his cycle to the side of the long swing gate. He fumbled in his pocket for the key, then used it to open the chain lock. He was in. He carefully then moved his bike inside the guarded perimeter before relocking the gate again. Concerned that the bikers in question might already be up at the mine area, he used his discretion and walked, bike beside him, up. No one was there. His first inclination was to follow orders, hide his bike himself, and wait in one of the prospective places. Mike considered his objective from his own point of view. It wasn't his style to sit back and blend into the shadows, then try to ascertain the true identity of the biker bunch. Mike was more assertive than that, much more. He wanted a better way. He wanted to get things over with as quickly, as easily, as possible. And Faehner's way might not be the best way to accomplish the thing. What if he couldn't get close enough to identify them? What if they took off the minute he came crashing down out of the woods? What if they got spooked hearing noises in the scary woods but turned aggressive and came after him, possibly with a weapon? No. There were too many uncertainties, too many unknowns. This thing would have to be played out differently.

Standing there, hands on his handlebars aside his motorcycle, in the open space out in front of the mine entrance, he considered his alternatives. And aptly he came up with one. He would become one like them, another banana in the bunch. If they came, he would be there right out in the open, right out in front. He would spend his moonlight hours parading around on the open ground, riding. The first impression they would have would be that he was just like them. And, because in their minds they saw him first, they were being given the chance to make the choice about what to do. They were being given pseudopower, to do or not to do, as they pleased. They were being given control.

So in this regard, Mike hopped on his bike and began hitting the bunny trails, so to speak, within the proximity of the mine, shanty, and pond. It was a warm, windy night, and he began having such a good time that soon he forgot about his troubles and began riding for himself, for fun. Initially, his ostentatious displays were picked up on by an old gray hoot owl perched atop the woodpecker tree. On one too many nights of recent note, the owl had been disturbed out of his favorite observation spot, and the wise old bird, alight, took wing to wind at once and flew to his second favorite spot, atop the old sycamore born to the lower pond.

Within the hour, the envisioned scenario was set to occur. Unbeknownst to Mike who was riding on a level stretch where he could give it all he got along the unofficially named Silver Lane, a group of smaller-sized spotlights were assembling around the electrical tower atop the hollow hill. From the moment all seven motors were cut, the escalating and receding variance from Mike's motorcycle as he sped up and slowed down during his escapade along Silver Lane was heard. Due to their strength in numbers, the bikers chose to stay and investigate just what was going on below them. As quickly and quietly as they could, the group of seven began coasting their motorbikes down through a thicket of sparsely growing red-thorn plants, this the course they had previously shorn the night of their initial unexpected encounter with the steel-cord barrier still in proximity of the hollow-top tower.

When the bikers came together again, they were out front of the shanty, and much to their chagrin, Mike was all the way at the other end of Silver Lane, which meant, if he noticed them at all, standing by their bikes in the dim of the moonlight, he could, if he felt inclined, leave without the slightest risk of being caught. But instead, he felt uplifted. His first night out they had intervened, meaning that, if he played his cards right, this first encounter would also be the last, the way he intended for things to go. And he had earned back the rights of the deal with Mr. Faehner about as fast as was humanly possible. In a sense, he felt Mr. Faehner was going to be jipped—one night for all that expense, come on!

Knowing the contour of the mine area even at night, Mike, upon looking back up before making another run, did notice the variance of huddled shapes and sizes around what would have been his point of destination. He knew it was them. And he knew that they knew he was there. In accordance of his conviction, Mike, astride his bike, headed straight toward the perceived anomaly—them. On his way, Mike pressed his bike for all it was worth, acting quite reckless given the circumstances and even popped a wheelie once he had cleared the narrower lane and entered upon the openness of the mine front. In response to Mike's antics, the seven spectators gave way before he was halfway done his approach, backing up, one and all to the shanty porch and protecting themselves from any inadvertent contact by placing their bikes in front of their bodies. Mike incredibly rode his wheelie, starting from the point where the lane curves over to the side of the mine all the way past the shanty thirty feet away, and up, up, up the sloping road connecting to the pond. In all, he managed to stay up on one wheel a total distance of sixty-five feet, including twenty-five feet of steep incline—a record! Discontinuing only because of how close he was to the pond rim, Mike, fully accomplished, paused, then revved up his bike once more and advanced, headlights glaring, upon the astonished onlookers. Prepared, Mike took it right to the curious crowd before any of them could begin the inevitable Q-and-A period he was sure would take place.

"Before anybody assumes anything bad about me, let me say this: my name is Mike, Biker Mike," he established falsely, deciding only at that moment to avoid using his real last name so they could never know who he really was. "And I come here same as you, to hang out, ride, and sometimes party in the peace and beauty of this private place. That's all. I ain't looking for any fight about who has rights here. I've been coming, since I first put my ass on a seat of a bike, and there ain't nobody ever going to tell me I can't, not even that rich Mr. Faehner, you know, the fellow who owns all this place."

Mike was finished, and he proved it by shutting up and folding his arms obstinately across his chest and waiting for whatever should come next. The members of the motorcycle group were taken aback by Mike's assertive stand. Neither knew the other, they could have been anybody; yet despite this uncertainty, despite being outnumbered, this guy was holding to who he was, unafraid, and telling them as much. It was an antisocial quality they all admired. Then one of the group, a yellow-haired, yellow-bearded hippie type took the matter into his own hands—literally. Still in awe about the outstanding ride he had just been privy to, he raised both his hands out in front of his face and began clapping as a way of expressing his admiration for the stunt Mike had pulled. Feeling the same way he did, the others joined in the applause too.

"Encore!" one of them shouted in a tone above the "clapture."

"Encore!" repeated another cajoling voice.

"Let's hear it for Evel," another of them shouted, terming Mike's performance as comparative to the legendary rider.

Mike had let his bike do the talking just as he intended, and by doing so, and doing so well at doing so, he had won over the notorious night riders before they could blink an eye. Now, besides just being with them, being one like them, he was one of them, if he wanted to be. And he decided that this would be so even before the celebration ceased. One thing though, he decided in advance, this charade would not carry over into another day. He would find out everything he had to before the night was over.

"Introductions, introductions," a scruffy-looking man whose head was tightly wound in a bandanna designed after the Stars and Stripes elicited.

"We're the Riverville Raiders," he said next in an assuasive voice, thereby letting the others know by content and context that he wanted, at least for now, good feelings to prevail. "My name is Easy Rider, this here," he continued, pointing to another rider next to him, "is Candy Man. Over there is Sweet

Cheeks. Then we got Brutus, Rabbit, Choke, and behind him is She Wolf. We're glad to know ya."

Once the Riverville Raiders were revealed, at least in a style, Mike or, rather, Biker Mike sought to keep things moving, that is, get things over with as quickly as possible. He needed to find out where they holed up exactly. If their team tribute was accurate and they really were from Riverville, a small town on the opposite side of the Susquehanna just across the 462 bridge, that would help, but it still wasn't enough. That could just be the place they currently congregate. It would not be enough to go on to try to find them. Their names, their true identities, they were keeping a secret obviously. How difficult would it be to tempt them into telling more?

The only thing Mike could do was play it cool. If he acted as though his life depended on finding out things personal to them, his plot might become known. Then they would simply clam up on him. Mike would have to bide his time and prick his ears for any all-telling comments or reference he could use as a guide. So instead of acting interested, he acted disinterested. In the course of their interactions with him, he acted more the loner than even he first intended, avoiding speculations, insinuations, and any type of inveigling questions despite what was spoken. He abandoned the role of undercover agent and instead took on a role more like the woodpecker-tree owl without taking flight.

Time passed into the night. Mike heard little of much that could help him. But then unexpectedly, a suggestion was made, seconded and thirded, that the group as a whole take off. And much to Mike's concern as well as delight, he was invited along.

"Care to come with us," came the cordial plea offered by Easy Rider who, Mike knew by now, was the leader of the pack.

"Sure thing," Mike shot back in a low-pitched voice.

"Rivervillians, start your engines," Easy Rider announced, himself breaking away from a dalliance with She Wolf.

They were off, Mike included. Though he would have enormously preferred too, Mike couldn't go out the way he came in and couldn't risk excusing himself so he could, then rendezvous with the pack up on Silver Mine Hill for fear that they might realize he was up to something no good. So he followed them, up the rudimentary red-thorn-thick road, in a game of follow the leader, shifting this way and that through the prickly jungle.

To his aid though was the lidless lunar sphere shining an abundant array of reflected light on the epigeal earthlings.

Once on the open road, the clan of clandestine night riders and their cadet sped through the outlying countryside. They wheeled their way into Little Conestoga, then Creswell, then Columbia, and Mike knew they were headed for exactly where they had purported when they turned onto the mile-long 462 bridge crossing the Susquehanna to reach Riverville on the opposite shore. There, the leader led them onto an off-road juncture, a worn dirt path, which slanted directly down to a river-line road. Despite the steepness of the decline, all of the cyclists took the shortcut at full throttle, proving to Mike that this was a route they well knew. Wherever their destination, they couldn't be far.

And Mike assumed right. Less than five miles down the river route, the river rats, as Mike now thought of them, made an abrupt turn right, stopping just outside a chain-link fence at a spot where a two-section gate stood. Wrapped around the poles where the gates met was a security-grade locking chain, which had had at one point a thick-metaled lock attached to it to ward off the unwanted. The chain was simply pulled away from its dummy position until the clan went safely inside, then reattached in a way that made it seem secure.

The enclosure, protected loosely, the remnant buildings and diggings of an old rock quarry abandoned long ago, after the quarry had reached its allowable limit of encroachment toward the nearest, older-established community. Like most old quarries, there was nothing much that could be done with the property once it had serviced itself out of work except to abandon and secure it.

"Trespassing seems to be their theme," Mike suggested to himself once they had all congregated outside what appeared to be the old main building to the facility. Hesitant at first, he followed them in where a party of pot, which the Riverville seven referred to as thunder weed, and loose sex ensued. Obligated as he felt, Mike joined in the fun for what it was worth but was careful not to indulge too much.

But not much beyond that, Mike suddenly slipped out of the company of the others, mumbling to one of them something about having to take a piss outside. Once outside, he simply attached himself to his ride and walked with it to the front gate and escaped.

"And that was that," Mr. Faehner concluded, bringing to an end the mostly secondhand story, which, for the first time ever, had been told from a perspective as though it were his own remembrance.

"But I fail to see the significance of that episode," the reporter said astutely. "I mean, the way they rankled you, just a bunch of bikers."

"You must understand, Mr. Faehner began, "they had come at a time when, after seventeen stressful years, I had just come into my own. I couldn't let anything come undone."

Speaking of Quarries

"Come on, let's go," Mr. Faehner issued in a hurried voice as if he did not want the conversation to carry on and made sure of it by having them vacate the premises at once. True that that was, Mr. Faehner did have another intent—that was to investigate the extent of excess water dumped on the mine by the storm. Vulnerable spots, such as the ponds and the mine itself, were always checked after deluges just to make sure. The condition of the lower pond was good. The pond level currently was about three feet above normal, which meant there would be no overflow problems, and the only adverse thing would be that the swelled portions of low-lying land around the sycamore tree would be sodden for days after the water receded.

"This is why we came," Mr. Faehner declared as he led the way across Silver Mine Road and onto Silver Lane, then past the very same road gate depicted in the story about biker Zoig and the Riverville bunch. On the way up Silver Lane, it was observed that Silver Run was running at about three times its usual capacity but was not in danger of overspreading its banks; so deeply was it cut into the rock and soil. Up at the mine, the harried owner dug into his pockets to retrieve a duplicate key to the mine gate, now closed, in relation to festivities still taking place just a mile or so away in the Silver Hills Country Club.

"This is your lucky day all the way round," Mr. Faehner announced once he had successfully unlocked the iron-barred barrier. "I'm going to check the water levels in the shafts, pump them if I have to. There's going to be literally thousands of gallons of water welling up in them over the next few days. The last they were drained was last week. I'll have to make room for the flood that's coming. And in the process of that, you'll get the special treat of seeing the mine firsthand and without paying for it, I might add."

That quick, the mine lights were shot on and Mr. Faehner, in his element, took the reporter on a guided tour in much the same manner as he would have had this been seventeen years ago and he first privileged to do so.

Over the years, Faehner had devised a splendidly reliable method of checking the depth of the shafts without being able to either see into the depths or gauge them. He learned that by plucking a loose stone into the center of each hole and counting the seconds before the stone plopped in the standing water, he could ascertain the water's current depth. This he learned the first few years by plunging himself down into the mine depths between pumping periods, accurately ascertaining the water level that was, then pitching small stones along an imaginary trajectory and head-counting the intervening seconds until the expected plop was heard. By using this old tried-and-true method, Mr. Faehner announced to his fellow miner that the first shaft was now only fifteen feet deep and the second shaft was, at present, about twenty-five feet deep—the second shaft being far more difficult to calculate, at least from a standpoint of how much water was in the hole due to the additional fact that at the bottom of the shaft the mine length continued a short distance in a forward direction and contained a water-holding capacity equal to a drop-down area of approximately thirty feet as measured in the down shaft. Summing it all up, Mr. Faehner simply explained that there was probably a one-hour's measure of water conjunctively in the mine and that given time, there would be ten times that coming.

"We'll have to dispel this water at once so at least the oncoming water won't reach a level that would saturate the system of ladders in the second shaft or touch the lowest lights and form an electrical hazard."

"Would you like the honor?" he asked his sideling once they had reached the mine front and were standing beside the power switches.

The reporter complied by switching on one pump then another in succession. Both men listened to the accompanying sounds—echoes of the two heavy-duty machines as they went about their indulgence; volumes of mine water filling then flowing through the two fire hoses that a few minutes earlier had lay dormant at their feet along the mine path.

"That ought to do it," Mr. Faehner said, responding to the system's activity. "Come, there's a pipe underground here. It leads out to the run. We can check how much water is being displaced."

Over at the run, the pipe was gushing.

"That's a large amount coming out of there," Mr. Faehner pointed out. "Not bad considering how far and how deep the water is traveling."

"Looks pretty clear," the reporter noted as he watched the crystalline liquid flow rapidly over a little hop of air into the awaiting waterway.

"I considered bottling it once," Mr. Faehner professed. "I had it tested, and it came up 97 percent pure. Almost good enough to drink. But it wasn't practical. The amount of water capable of being supplied by the mine's continuous infiltration and collection system was incapable of sustaining anything business related. In short, there wasn't enough water worth making the expenditure on. And then what if the business should really take off? What if I had barely enough of a water supply to make money off of? What then? There would be no way to supply more unless I hired a full-time rainmaker. And if they succeeded, that would spoil too many a day for the sightseers."

"You could have simply done what most of the other water companies do. Add tap water to the mix."

"No, that's deceitful," Mr. Faehner said in a way that expressed an admonition that he was aware of the practice and a conceit that he was above such an idea.

Then a brief silence of words arose between the two men as they stood staring at the pouring pipe. The condition of it was being perpetrated by Mr. Faehner whose spirit was rising in accordance with the day's most recent developments. Though giving a tour of the mine and turning on the mine pumps would seem like such an ordinary thing, it was not, not to him. The value of things, which on the surface seemed ordinary, were never lost to him, and he felt vulnerable. The mere mention of the old Riverville quarry in the story he had just related brought back another black cloud from his distant past. In relation to it, he lifted his eyes slowly, above the rush of the run, above the rocky bank of the opposite side of the watery divide. There on the level ground above remained the telltale signs of Mr. Boddingers fabled attempt to convert half of the Silver Mine property into a quarry too. The old road built to facilitate dump trucks still outlined the ground space between the run and the hill. Halfway down from where they were standing, in the direction of Silver Mine Road, was the location on the hill where Boddinger broke into the bedrock to examine the rock types and best find out which kind of quarry operation could begin.

It had been a victory Mr. Faehner could not lay claim to, but he knew in his heart it had been one that surpassed all others. His old boss had failed. If he had not, there would be no silver mine left to partake of. It was a terrible thing to think about. He observed the reporter observing him, and he thought to make the most of the situation in view of the time they had at their disposal waiting for the mine pumps to dispel all or most of the water accumulated in the two deep shafts.

"We've got a little time to wait while these pumps do their work. I want to show you a little something of what could have been a big something, make that the biggest something, that ever occurred here."

Under normal conditions, Silver Mine Run could be crossed in many places by simply jumping, one side to the other, where the distance was shortest. But today was different. The little run was overrun by the drenching rain that had just impacted it. They would have to go around.

"Follow me," Mr. Faehner said without pause and began to walk along the bank of the over-fed stream, up past the shanty, up, up the rise, which led to the pond. There they rounded the pond road portion under which was the body-sized pipe, which carried the continuous flow of pond water into the run.

"In case I hadn't mentioned it, both of the Silver Mine ponds were man-made. They were dug out by the previous-to-the-previous owner," he added with jest. "That guy, Mr. Erb, wanted to enhance the property a bit, then sell off lots for development. Of course due the contour of the land, he wouldn't have gotten too many single-sized properties out of it. That's when Boddinger stepped in, they were friends of a sort, I guess, and inveigled him to trade on other property he owned—property much better suited for development. So they swapped, ponds already in place."

"That's an interesting tidbit of knowledge," the reporter acknowledged.

"Nothing compared to what else I'm going to tell you," Mr. Faehner shot back as they now began to journey down the opposite side of the run.

"Oh! Oh, be careful!" shouted Mr. Faehner with an inflection of humor in his voice as he witnessed the reporter slipping and almost falling in the wet undergrowth they were traipsing through. "The areas surrounding the run are treacherous that way. That's why I didn't have us attempt to jump across the run over at the outlet pipe. The banks' rocks are covered in moss and lichens. Even the morning dew makes them death-traps if you try running, jumping, and landing on them. Believe me, I've learned my lesson trying."

"I'm OK," the reporter reported, relieved that he had managed to check his fall and kept from getting wet and muddied.

"Always be ready to grab hold of one of the trees," Mr. Faehner remarked. "Or better yet, if you come across a walking stick, pick it up and use it."

Continuing carefully along the forlorn path, Mr. Faehner made note of the uniform age of the trees that were spread out from the run to the abrupt wall-like side of the hollow hill about twenty feet across.

"You'll notice how uncharacteristic it is that these trees are all the same size. And that's because they are. Thirty-nine years young they are. How about that?"

"What makes that possible?"

"Because that was the year when that old fart, Boddinger, sought to ruin this place once and for all. He intended to make a quarry out of this whole eastern quadrant of the property. And he went ahead and got ready for it even before he sought the township's approval. Thinking it would be an easy-as-making-a-pie transition, Boddinger bulldozed a path from Silver Mine Road up to the upper pond. And from there straight up, the steeper hillside above the pond. Up near the top of the hillside road, he cleared a large quadrangle out of the brush and thorn-thicketed wild, a pristine landscape never before touched by progress or plow. Back behind the quadrangle, he constructed an auxiliary road, which followed an adjoining property line and led out to Silver Mine Road at a point where most of the barn fields were by-passed. In addition to his little road-building project, he ambitiously took it upon himself to blast into the hillside. "Here!" he said, exclaiming his final word due the fact that they had reached the exact place he was speaking of.

Stepping out from the wood-studded trail, Mr. Faehner led them over to a stretch of the hillside, where, unlike the rest of it, was broken, disfigured. A huge seam of limestone, exposed, stood out like a sore thumb against the unscathed landscape. Its healing was a decades-old veil of sprawling honeysuckle vines, which had taken hold in the freshly holed wall and spread opportunistically throughout. Buried beneath the redolent yellow strands was the beginning of what could have been the end of the Silver Mine. Standing before it, Mr. Faehner felt as if he were beholding a shrine, a holy place. His mind was emptied. In a moment of mental solitude, he paid homage to God for laying hand upon the evil plan at a time when the young Faehner boy was helpless to stop him. When he came out of his conscience thought, it possessed Mr. Faehner to speak openly of his innermost self.

"I can only speculate at best, but I believe, like I always have believed, that Mr. Boddinger came here with the intent of making the Silver Mine a quarry. And maybe not just this side either. Quite possibly the entire thing. As you may or may not know, he was a quarry owner from way, way back. He owned the Rock Spring Quarry on the southeast side of Lancaster City. Today, it's just a waterlogged hole in the ground. But back at that time, mid to late '70s, it was a bust-ass business. He had everything. It would have taken little money and little effort to do the same here."

"What stopped him?" the reporter put forward.

At that moment, as if on cue, there was heard the distant but distinct sound—*clippity-clop, clippity-clop* of a horse-drawn buggy moving—first down, then up the dip on Silver Mine Road. Like always, due the specifics of the hollow, sounds were amplified enough that they were perceived as many times louder than they actually were. Mr. Faehner gave an expressive "h'mmm." How ironic was it that a buggy show up right when it was about to be discussed!

"Have many Amish up your way?" he posed to the questioner.

"None that I'm aware of," the reporter shot back.

"Around here, they're everywhere. Around here specifically, they're everywhere too. It was they who saved the mine. It was they—Old Order, New Order, every Order who came together to stop him. They noticed. They live around here, and they noticed. They watched. From their farms and fields, they witnessed the subtle changes that were occurring. They saw the swath of old trees being uprooted. They heard the banging that echoed out of the hollow. They understood what was meant by the arrival of the bulldozer. And they took action. For months, they crowded the provincial township hall and made their voices heard. And there wasn't a listener amongst them. Every man, aged 16 to 106, stood up to be counted. And in the end, they won. They challenged Boddinger one and all and countered every move he made. Though they were a minority by number, about fifty families total, they became a majority in that each and every one of them stood together for this one cause. Boddinger was defeated. He never got over his bitterness either. He stopped doing business with them. Things like buying oats and barley for the horses he stopped buying from Amish farms. And winter corn too. And the one Amish farmer—Beiler, I believe—whose farm and family is just to the north of the upper pond, he ended his business association with altogether. Beiler, up until that time, leased about 150 acres of land on the north side of Silver Mine Road starting across from the Goods Road bridge and running up to the electrical pylon atop the main mine area. Long ago, tobacco was cultivated there. In later years, soybeans. I've been told that the Beiler clan had leased that land from every previous Silver Mine property owner since anyone cares to remember."

"Did you reinstate that legacy once you came into the property?"

The reporter's question took Mr. Faehner by surprise. The funny thing was that Mr. Faehner, though he privately admonished Mr. Boddinger for what he had done in regards to the broken agreement with the neighboring farmer, had never thought to reestablish the old deal. He didn't know why. To himself, he made a silent "h'mmm," then uttered the only response he could—"no."

It made no sense to remain on the subject now that the train of thought had strayed to other places. Mr. Faehner sought to regain the original purpose for their being where they were.

"There's more to this story," he said, then gestured their departure by waving his hand, backward toward the hill against which they were standing, picking up his feet, and moving away. The reporter, before moving on, heeded the advice given to him earlier and made a quick search of the hillside for that all-important walking stick he would use to keep his feet while walking through the slippery woods. The hike took them back to where the nascent road met the pond road. There they took a turn up into the weed-choked hill same-side as the intended quarry and rambled upslope along a gully path.

"This was the bulldozed path I told you about," Mr. Faehner related to his traveling companion in a way that indicated how pleased he was that he was now proving his story. "Ever since, the condition of the road has worsened. It has almost reverted to its former self, all except this huge rut right in the middle. But no matter. No one ever comes up here, except me. No one knows anything exists up here—except me."

The reporter looked at him wondering now what to expect. All he had been told about was the existence of an ancient quadrangle. What could be the significance of that?

When they came to the area once devoid of growing things, it was of course unrecognizable from anything around it. Too much time had passed. Mr. Faehner made no attempt to reconfigure, in the reporter's mind, the approximate boundary lines by sighting and citing landmark points of reference to him from the best of his memory. Instead, Mr. Faehner stood on a balance of loose rock and soil and surveyed the area to their right toward the line of trees that rose up out of the hollow hill. Beyond where they were standing lay a vast rough terrain, an overgrown field of berry plants, red thorns, milkweed, Queen Anne's lace, forget-me-nots, purple violets, crab grass, and a plethora of other wild-growing things. Included in this wild garden was the occasional seed plant from one of the nearby farms, a corn stalk, or a tobacco plant living out its seasonal existence, alone and undisturbed. It had been one year since Mr. Faehner had bothered to make the annual pilgrimage to the vestigial site, and every year he did so, it seemed to get harder and harder to focus in on the elusive last man-made remnant of Boddiger's old plot. But there was one focal point from which the observation could be made and approximated, and after ascertaining it, Mr. Faehner calculated out the direction and strides necessary to reach it.

"This way," he nodded assuredly, then traipsed off on a wayward course into the field.

Plodding ahead, the reporter saw one thing of noted distinction that lay in wait of their plotted path—a small stand of small trees, if you could consider them trees, which seemed to be apart from the tight-together woodland behind them. Upon reaching the spot of trees, the revelation of their ambition became clear. The first thing of note that caught the reporter's attention was that the half-buried set of offset trees were actually mulberry trees, a counting of seven—three of which were climbable, all of which were bursting with juicy, ripe berries. Without any consultation as to the pros and cons of eating wild berries, each man exercised his hands and eyes and selected for themselves the best the mulberry trees had to offer. Once the men had appeased their impulsive appetites, it went without pause or special notice that the object of their expedition lay only a few yards distant from a far-reaching branch of the thickest tree. There, entangled in a jumble of younger mulberries—though in their stage they should be referred to only as bushes—was one of the unsightliest things either man had ever laid eye upon, a green minibus whose contemptible existence made even the wildest of living things want to conceal it from their sight.

Both men walked toward it. When they were within a couple of feet, the reporter—reluctant to go further—began to probe the beast's belly with the long end of his walking stick as if checking to see if the creature was dead or alive. Mr. Faehner approached the front-side step-down door, which of course was wide open and cautiously peered inside.

"You have to be awfully careful around this old bus any more," he stated with a cautious tone of voice. "Nature knows it belongs to it now. There could be anything under the Silver Mine sun living in there. Over the years, I've seen or seen evidence of many different creatures making a home out of it. You'd be surprised. Last time out, I found a nest of black rats who actually ate their way into the mattress of the bottom bunk bed in the back. I sat down next to them without realizing it. I sat my big butt down, and I felt all these muffled movements beside where I was sitting. Then, where the torn-up entry hole was beside me, I saw this hideous black face appear and rise up out of the hole just for a second. An instant later, I felt one of them attempting to bite through the bedding material to get to me. Another second more, and it would have had me, bit me right in the ass!"

"Seems to me the prudent thing to do would be to get rid of the bus entirely. Next time, you might not be so lucky."

"No!" Mr. Faehner declared firmly. "Rats, bats, gnats, I don't care. There's something else going on here that's far more important than hosting an animal hotel. And I won't, in spite of any other consideration, retreat from that purpose."

"What on earth could be so important about allowing an old green hulk of metal to rot way up here?"

"It's the other half of the story," Mr. Faehner admitted. "It's why I brought you up here. I wanted to be able to show you what I was going to tell you about."

"Not the kind of thing you could bring in to kindergarten," the reporter responded in a jovial voice.

"No, it's not," Mr. Faehner returned, laughing as he did.

"This is certainly turning out to be a day for stories," the reporter said in preparation of finding a safe place to settle down, eat more succulent berries, and prop up his ears to hear another fascinating tale of old.

"This old bus is serving a penance, so to speak," the storyteller spoke with an aura of spookiness in his voice. "Left here originally by the disappointed property owner, probably out of spite due his bitterness, the bus remained up here to rot under my tenure as a way of exemplifying to me, to the mine itself, that all it once stood for meant nothing."

The mood of the precursive statement was one that was indicative of great things to follow. And though enticed to entertain his thoughts more through verbal communication, the reporter refrained from doing so knowing full and well that Mr. Faehner's profluent abilities at relating all of the relevant matters of the soon-to-be-heard story would satisfy even the most esoteric of his curiousities. And Mr. Faehner, so adept, was not about to let him down. He went right to work punching out the tale as if it were only a recent memory.

"The hilltop approach on the northeast portion of the Silver Mine hollow was, is, the most remote and unused part of the property. There was nothing to it except a vast expanse of wild field bordered by the thick woods that come up from the hill. It appeared one day right in the midst of this obscure, forsaken wild—without any expectation of it—this ugly green glob . . ."

"What did you find out about it?" Pip inquired of his companion after he returned from an attempt to pry information out of the Silver Mine overseer about the mysterious appearance of the half-sized green bus that as of sometime in the past twenty-four hours parked itself up on the upper hollow hill beside a small patch of mulberry bushes the boys sometimes visited to pick berries.

"Not much," came the disappointing reply. "At first, he was being obstinate, but I insisted and he came around and said that there's some guy that Boddinger gave the OK to for him to park that thing here for a while. He kind of hinted that he's down on his luck or something."

"How long does a while mean?" Pip asked, more to himself.

"Don't know," Jimmy responded for them both.

Knowing the property like the backs of their hands, the boys were sure that given the time and opportunity, they would find out for themselves exactly what was going on regardless of Luckee's reticence or Mr. Boddinger's refusal to tell them.

Later that same day, at a predetermined time and place, the boys met and pronounced to each other their determination to ascertain the identity of the newcomer and the reasons for his appearance.

"I don't believe he's here because he's someone who is down on his luck," Pip expressed in the manner of a true cynic, while leaning over to tie a shoelace that had been untied for the past several hours.

"You're right," Jimmy concurred in a tone that denoted his defiance towards any other possibility. "Old Mr. Boddinger is too mean of a person to care for the welfare of some miscreant."

"Unless maybe he's some kind of distant relative, you know, a black sheep of the family, sort of."

"I doubt even then Mr. Mean would lend out a helping hand," Jimmy shot back.

"Yeah, you're right," Pip agreed, changing his mind at the first objection.

From their vantage point in the lofty upper level of the barn, Pip observed that situationally things couldn't be better. Both bosses' vehicles were gone from their customarily parked positions over by the 1800 house. The time was ripe for the boys to break away from their duties and take off on a little excursion of their own making to see for themselves what might be going on up on the remote hilltop.

Pip removed his eye from the knot hole where he had used it to observe, while in secrecy, the goings-on across the pond.

"It's now-or-never time," he said with an air of finality.

Leaving the back way out of the barn, the boys, once in the open, made a mad dash all at once across the barn lot, across Silver Mine Road, and high-jumped literally into the thicket of wild-growth plants that edged the wooded beyond. They were like two scared rabbits to the eyes of the red-tailed hawk hovering above the tree tops, imagining what could possibly be chasing them.

Once in the woods, it was an uphill climb as the boys made their way up, up, up over root and rock, past tree, thick and thin, avoiding, avoiding, avoiding the ridiculing red thorns that, in view of their propitious positions all over, seemed as if they were purposed to guard the hillside. Due the difficulty, neither boy came away unscathed once they finally found their way out of the close-catching thorns.

"How bad did you get it?" Jimmy inquired of his friend while sucking blood off the tip of his right thumb.

Watching his friend blood-sucking his thumb, and he, about to do the same to the opposing thumb on the opposing hand, put Pip's mind in a whirl about the hilarity of the circumstance. Really, it was either laugh or cry.

"I've been cut, stuck, nicked, pricked, scratched, scraped, and generally turned into a Pip-sized pincushion."

"What else are you but a descriptively walking, talking, thesaurus," Jimmy returned jovially.

For the remainder of the journey, the boys moved with a certain alacrity, the type befitting scrappy fourteen-year-olds and in less time than it took them to cover the initial one-third of distance, they converged on the outer edge of trees only a stone's throw away from the distressingly unsightly green glob. A discussion ensued. Much to the boys' chagrin, they realized there was nothing they could do really to force the situation. The circumstance was too new to them. If they created a disturbance and got this guy out of his tortoise-shell domicile, it might make him mad, and hostilities might begin, touched off by the few rounds of stones the boys first intended to throw.

"We could say we thought it was some mysterious sight, you know, a UGO—an unidentified, objectionable green object. So we pitched stones at it. Who wouldn't believe that?"

"I for one," Pip shot back. "Besides, that would have been called a UOGO, just to let you know. No, we don't know enough yet. If we infuriate this guy, it could mean our butts. He could legitimately be someone who Boddinger knows simply because you never know."

"Well, what are we supposed to do then? Stand here and wait? Wait?"

"Initially, yes," Pip put forth. "Part of good detective work is waiting and watching. It's the part you don't ever hear about. But it's the part that is most important to cracking a hard case. We have to trust in experience."

"I know you, Pip. You've been reading too many *Hardy Boys* mysteries again."

"All good fiction's based on fact," Pip stated authoritatively, admitting to but also standing behind the charge. "Besides, he's not going to stay holed up in there all the time. Eventually, he'll come out. He's got to take a crap sometime you know." The boys' level of levity decreased steadily as the bulk of the afternoon heat beat down upon them, the trees doing little to protect and shade their sensitive skins. Especially affected were the portion layers of their—hands, arms, and legs, which now were afflicted by the many thorn-inflicted wounds. Salty sweat, induced by their perspirations, swelled from their nearby pores, covering and irritating the fresh fleshy cuts. It made them moody.

"When we get back, I'm heading straight for the medicine cabinet," expressed Pip with enough certitude for the both of them.

Jimmy, again sucking on his sore thumb, gave a cernuous acknowledgment with his head and continued pertaining to his most immediate concern. Both boys were only moments away from decidedly abandoning their clandestine position in the verily variegated, sun-spotted, sideline of trees when suddenly the monotonous overtone of heat, sweat, irritated skin and tedium came to an abrupt end. It all came at once, the sight, the sound, the high-level disturbance it caused in their minds. Coming round the rudimentary lead-off road—which led out to Silver Mine Road, way, way beyond the barnyards and adjacent fields—was a hulking, unimaginably tall crane! It moved slowly, sluggishly, across the virgin soil—crushing, uplifting, putting into turmoil everything in its path. At every movement, the bulky metal monster seemed to writhe in protest as though it were a thing of life, laboring over unseen maladies, aches, and pains accrued from countless sessions of forced work. Undiscernibly, it grumbled—metal grinding, gears slipping, voluminous black smoke rising up out of a dark encrusted exhaust pipe. Foot by foot, the clanking metal beast made its way across the slightly sloped hilltop until it came to rest in a position almost center of the open area. For a moment, all was quiet. Then, all at once, the appreciated still was again broken by the disruptive act of a workman clambering out of the machine, then looking back at it, shaking a fist and hurling, what was believed to be high-grade explicatives at the now inanimate object. His objective, of course, was to relieve himself of the obvious buildup of stress he undoubtedly underwent while dealing with the onerous old-time machine unloaded over a mile away.

Only a minute after the cantankerous workman settled down a second piece of heavy equipment came rounding into view trekking along the clear-cut swath made by the crane. A similarly colored bulldozer came into view, its scoop lifted two feet up off the ground, and trekked its way over alongside the crane. This workman hopped out of his heavy-duty machine and joined his co-worker now loitering next to the front-end bucket of the crane. Both men had their eyes fixed on the dirt road, which had brought them into the widespread field as though they were waiting for something yet to follow.

And the something came suddenly, rounding the top path at top-flight speed, swerving this way and that to stay out of the path of the unearthed rocks and ruinous ruts. It was a pickup truck, a transport truck, sent to provide the heavy equipment drivers a means back to where they came from. And that, their place of origin and return, became clear once the pickup was brought to an abrupt stop after nearly sideswiping the dozer. Stamped on the cab-door side was the redolent insignia of the Rock Spring Quarry!

The boys were in shock but had no time to dwell on the matter. The time for their excursion had expired. They had to get back. Abandoning their post, they began an easier descent down through the wooded hill, purposefully remaining near the less-dense field perimeter to stay out of the realm of the menacing red thorns. When they came out of the woods, the boys at once split up. Pip went immediately to the office trailer to seek out the regrettable tincture of Merthiolate for his cuts. Jimmy went off to the barn to shovel excrement out of the donkey stalls. The remainder of the day went by without their being able to get together to discuss what had happened.

The next day down, the boys could hardly wait for the opportunity to go back to the wood's edge and spy on the green glob and now too the bothersome quarry equipment. But it was not to be. The labors, which were assigned to them that day, kept them apart the entire day and kept them each so busy they couldn't even think to go off on their own to do what they so wanted to do. It was two days more until they had a chance to unite and find time to even speak to each other while on the property about what was going on. During those three days, both Mr. Boddinger and Luckee had remained aloof whenever any mention was made as to either the bus or the quarry equipment. The boys were waiting for just the slightest chance and were ready to pounce on the subject but neither one of their superiors gave in.

Upset that their fact-finding mission was turning into a farce, the boys turned their attentions again toward the field where another look around might garner them more clues as to what was actually going on. This time, though, they made no attempt to hide their presence. This time they didn't care. Immediately after a satisfying lunch, they set out on their quest. Instead of making their way through the protective trees, they remained out in the open, going straight to the upper pond, then expecting to hike straight into the thickly covered hillside to where the bus and the heavy equipment sat. But just as they were about to begin their march into the field, they met the unexpected. A wide path had been cut into the overgrowth from a point a few yards shy of the pond road and reaching as far as the eye could see up the hillside.

"This happened right under our noses!" Jimmy exclaimed in a startling voice.

"Probably after we left for the day yesterday," Pip assumed. "Probably to keep us from knowing about it until it was too late too. The dozer did this. That means there's a greater purpose for these machines being here than just having them sit here."

"Why on earth would he have brought a bus, a crane, and a bulldozer on the property if he didn't intend to use them?"

"Well, the one reason I thought was plausible was that he brought them here because he was done using them down at Rock Spring. Maybe he had too much heavy equipment sitting around, you know, getting in the way. This would have been the perfect place to store them without paying for storage. If they were old and past their prime, they could have still been used for parts or sold for scrap or sold to another quarry—one that has a little bit tighter budget. Anyway, that's what I was hoping for."

"You still could be right, Pip. So he put in another road here. He's done that right along. Maybe he put in the road just for the sake of putting in a road?"

"Yeah, well then, what's the crane for, huh? And what about the green machine up there?" he asked while pointing a finger up the field-splitting swath of freshly dug earth.

Now ever more determined, the boys bolted up the tertiary road like soldiers advancing on an enemy encampment. They would not be deterred. One way or another, they would meet the challenge of determining, once and for all, answers to the questions that were circulating in their minds. To their astonishment, they found that the situation had become exacerbated. Now in addition to the crane and the dozer, there were two large dumpers and fittings for the crane, two large wrecking balls, which could be attached one or the other in lieu of the bucket. Stopped in the midst of the mechanical monsters, the boys looked about at the wreckless road that had just become part of their surroundings, the earth-moving machines only recently introduced to the once pristine land, and the Green Glob as the bus had now officially been named.

"So much for our theory about the use of this extent of Silver Mine property for any of the Rock Spring Quarry's overflow of equipment," Pip stated in an honest but disgusted voice. "I don't believe this road was built for the fun of it anymore. And all of this other heavy-duty equipment, it has a purpose, one we don't know about. But the logic is simple: quarry equipment is used for making quarries!"

"I think you're right!" Jimmy shot back without the slightest disbelief. "This guy's up to something really big around here. And he's doing it all on the q.t."

"Yeah, and he's especially hiding it all from us, trying to prevent us from interfering with his master plan, knowing full well we'd be up to taking him on no matter what."

Fearlessly, the boys moved from one machine to the next, taking turns in the operator's seats inside the vehicle cabs, imagining what it would be like to have charge of such a monstrous thing, and, once their fantasies were appeased, looking for ways to throw a monkey wrench into the operation, possibly finding starter keys, which could be confiscated and duly thrown as far as the strength of their arms would allow into the distant thickets. But to their dismay, none of the four big machines contained any hard-to-find sets of spare keys or anything else, which could be considered a hard loss should they have exacted their purposes.

Chagrined, the boys were about to admit a defeat, when much to their surprise, they heard—coming from the immediate direction of the Green Glob—sounds of someone moving about, distinct footsteps on metal that, due to its loose-floor fit, clinked and clanked with every punctuated motion.

"Oh my god! Let's get out of here!" Jimmy elicited in a whispered statement of declaration. Instinctively, both boys took off on foot and raced back down the dirt divide they had come up on. But then, when they had reached the pond road, they stopped.

"Wait!" Pip shouted in a tired breath. "I'm sick of all this. Why are we acting this way, all afraid and everything? This is where we work, not him, whoever he is. This is ours, and we were here first!"

"You're perfectly right," Jimmy offered in support. "But he's not the only person we're up against. What about—"

Pip never let him finish.

"Come on," he urged his friend. And with that, he took off down the round of the pond road, leap-frogged over the rise below it, and bounded toward the front of the shanty. There he dashed inside, and after fumbling about for only a minute or two, he retrieved from the seldom-used back room a pair of Luckee's high-powered binoculars. Jimmy, who had taken the long way around, was just then arriving at the shanty porch and met with Pip the moment he was coming back out.

"Come on," he issued once more and led them both on a trek back up the steep dirt path. At a point halfway up, Pip then led them off into the nearby woods where they continued their expedition. They stopped when they reached a spot just about equal to where the bus stood off in the field near the mulberry bushes.

"While we still have time, we're going to wait here and glean what information we can about this guy by spying on him from the woods. He won't even know we're here."

Because of the height and thickness of the field's left-alone greenery, Pip thought it best to elevate himself so that observations would be made at an optimum. He strung the field glasses around his neck by use of the lanyard and began climbing up a twisted oak whose lowest branches almost touched the ground, then one by one spiraled around and up the gnarled trunk as if they were a staircase leading up to the sky. Once he was positioned, he directed the binoculars toward the bus.

"Voila!" he shouted in triumph the instant his view became fixed. "I see him right now. There he is. And to think we were running from him, from that wimp!"

"What's he look like?"

"The best description I can give is to say he looks like a hippie, a throwback, a someone from the radical '60s. He's the quintessential—and look, he's walking with a hirple! A hippie with a hirple! Imagine that!"

"Easy now, Mr. English. Quintessential? Hirple? Those words don't mean a thing from where I'm standing."

"OK OK, Mr. Pea Brain, I'll try to come down to a more colloquial level, for your sake."

"Oh, very funny," Jimmy returned with a hint of injury from the unintended insult brought on by yet a third word he didn't understand.

Ignorant of his friend's insecurity, Pip went right on with his descriptive analysis of the Green Glob's strange-looking, strange-acting occupant.

"These binoculars of Luckee's are great!" he purported. "The clarity and closeness make it seem like he's right out in front of me. Like, like he's got a bandanna wrapped around his forehead. It's red, white, and blue. It might be . . . yes . . . I think it is . . . the American flag. And you should see this guy's face. No wonder he's alone living in a green bus. He's as thin as and scary looking as a scarecrow! And I don't mean of the *Wizard of Oz* variety! And by the way, a hirple is a limp. This guy's twitching all around like he's got two left feet. He must be on dope."

For a brief minute, Pip only watched as the man in his view went about what looked like a few mundane tasks to tidy up the inside of his mobile residence. Then, he appeared, hobbling out of the bus in exaggerated steps, this time carrying a roll of white toilet tissue. The tissue was bound by a strap of leather strung through its cardboard core and hung around his neck. Pip was taken aback by what he was about to witness.

"Hey, this guy's about to take a crap—nature style," he elicited in a two-toned voice—one of excitement and disgust.

Thoroughly amused by the prospect of what his friend would be seeing, Jimmy shot back, "Hey, we ought to sneak up on him and surprise him while he's right in the middle of a squeeze!"

"No, I don't think so Jim. It's bad enough I have to see it from here."

Pip watched and reported as the man went off a short distance from his living space and performed his necessity over what looked like an open groundhog hole, then wiped himself clean.

"It would be hilarious if a groundhog would rear up and bite him in the, in the rear end, shall we say."

"Know what? I say we go right over there and tell him who we are, after all, whoever he is and whatever he's doing doesn't trump who we are and our place here. Let's go butt heads with this guy and let him know who we are. Let's go!"

The outcome of the encounter could in no way have been predicted. For all the boys knew, they were about to come into contact with a man—friend or foe. But nonetheless, they moved boldly, swiftly, out of the adjacent woods and into plain sight. Straightforward, they marched, trampling over, tripping over, tall spreads of thick-cover grasses and countless spears of tall milkweed until they reached the sought-after stand of mulberry bushes beside which stood the Green Glob and its occupant.

Arms obstinately folded with a look of consternation on his scary face, the man stood in wait, having first heard, then seen as the boys struggled through the field.

"Now what the devil are you two doing out here in this lonesome plot?" he said in an implicating voice before either of the boys had completed their approach.

"Plenty!" Pip fired back in as uppity a voice as he could.

"Is that so," the thin man responded, already realizing that the upper hand that he wanted to establish with the pair of wanderers was lost.

"Yes, that's so!" Pip fired back, delaying once more the specifics of introductions and purpose until he was certain each knew where the other stood as things related to who was going to be in charge of the situation. Energized by his companion's audacious behavior, Jimmy, who had been standing a short distance behind, stepped right up beside him, fists curled, almost hoping for a fight. Both boys, despite their youthful age, were, even by themselves, more than a match for the forty-year-old, and he knew it. He reacted in the only way he could by first, backing up a few feet and keeping his mouth shut to see what he was in for. After a moment more of silence, Pip spoke up.

"We," he said stressing the plural of them, "work here. We've worked here since the beginning. So we're here to ask you what you're doing out here in the middle of this lonesome field. Now what have you got to say about that?"

"Yeah! And you'd better tell us the truth!" Jimmy demanded, ready to use fists, if necessary, as a way of getting to it, if the guy posed as an imposter, anything other than what the boys believed him to be—someone connected to what was going on.

Nervous, the man inched his way sideward and back until he felt close enough to the entrance to the bus that he could leap in if he was leaped at. Then he spoke.

"I'm really sorry to disappoint you boys about my being here so unexpected and all, but I really do have a reason for it. I was brought down by the boss himself in an indirect sort of way to work for him in an indirect sort of way."

"Work at what?" Jimmy interjected loudly.

"Just hold on there, I'm getting at that," the man elicited with an increasing surety. "It's obvious to me that I know something that you two don't despite your being so cocky about all the time you've obviously spent here."

"Tell us. Tell us what you know," Pip pleaded with expectation written all over his face.

"Well, it goes like this . . ."

And the man went through with it, eliciting the story as much as he knew, knowing that he probably shouldn't have, but realizing that he had never been told otherwise. After all, once the quarry got started, how could such a thing ever be hidden. When it was over, the boys walked away, dejected. They felt betrayed. And even more so, they were hurt by the deception that had been carried out in an attempt to keep them from finding out. And that had been their treatment even from Luckee who was supposed to be their advocate, their friend.

The man in the bus meant nothing to them now. His presence, to guard over the expensive quarry machines day and night, was only an annoyance as compared to the definitive problem of having the beloved property converted into one huge hole in the ground.

For four long weeks, the boys lived in a state of constant gloom and doom. Boddinger, so smug and confident that his plan would prevail, even went as far as using the crane's wrecking ball to break into the rock hill across from the kiln—a gaping wound—one large enough to allow the machine free swing as a way of announcing his soon-to-be-won parlay with the zoning board. But something unexpected happened. A hushed uproar went up amongst the Plain Folk of the community. Opposed to the idea of such ideal land being spoiled forever was the Amish community for which the unity in the word community really meant something. The story lapsed into a moment of pause and came out of its surreal surrounding, its conclusion not including the parts of the past, which made it seem like a real-life moment. Mr. Faehner communicated directly to the reporter in a tone now more matter-of-fact.

"And they came, one and all. From farm and field, from near and far, they came. A turgent of Bible-taunting Plain Folk took their turns before the township officials and denounced the quarry plan, all with scripture in their hearts, quoting all their favorite excerpts. One by one, they made their appearance felt. One by one, they won.

The Artist

"Once the great Boddinger initiative was over, so was the purpose of the busman. He hung around for a few days, then just disappeared. He was never heard of or seen again—at least by us. And the Green Glob remained. Don't know why. Everything about it was forgotten. I don't even know if Boddinger knew it was still on the property. He never had reason to go up on the hilltop again. He was furious and never got over the fact that he had lost. Come on. Let's go."

Mr. Faehner and the reporter walked away from the decades-old decay once they had sufficiently filled their mouths with more of the succulent mulberries and after the reporter had advantaged himself to his hiking stick. They left on the same path they had taken to get up and didn't stop until they had reached the bottom round of the pond road. There they took a needed breather to relax their tired legs. The day had grown warm again now that the storm had departed, and Mr. Faehner began to feel even more tired realizing what comforts he was missing out on being displaced from the Silver Hills sanctuary. Tantalized by the thought of the cooler atmosphere and the quenching remedy of a cool drink, he alluded to his hiking companion that there were, at their immediate disposal, drinks available in a cooler inside the shanty.

"Do you have the key?" the reporter asked in a pleading voice.

"I have the key to everything all the time," Mr. Faehner answered back in a prompt, reassuring declaration. And with that, he produced from his pocket the shanty key and unlocked the mine memorial museum. Moving swiftly from front room to back, Faehner went straight for the vintage cooler, which for all of the Silver Mine years had been used to stock bottles and cans of soft drinks for all of the Silver Mine workers. From it, he reached for two cans of grape soda and carried them out to the front where the reporter was waiting. While still a few feet apart, he tossed one of the cans to his thirsty partner then popped open his own can's top. The cans were emptied as though each man were engaged in a competition to see who could finish first, then tossed into a nearby recycling receptacle. Their basic need now satisfied the two men were ready once more to delve into the issues that had brought them together. The reporter, anxious to hear yet another alluring tale, attempted to solicit one by summarizing the story about the Green Glob as though it had been the last.

"That last one about the busman was quite interesting. You've given me just about enough material now that I can . . ."

Mr. Faehner knew exactly what the reporter was up to—pressing him for another story which he was fully ready to comply with—yet he allowed him to continue, his inveigling speech, just to see how convincing he could be. As the reporter prattled on, Mr. Faehner led them out onto the shanty porch so they could stand under its shaded roof and enjoy the nice circulation of air he knew was blowing across it now as evidenced by the sudden panoply of musical notes playing from a wind chime. In his mind was the put-together list of all of the conflicts, conflagrations, contentions, disruptions, annoyances, altercations that had been a part of his experience since he first set foot on Silver Mine land. And on the list, though not on the wall of representation behind his Silver Hills desk was one more—a fiend of a sort—that he deemed worth telling about. Another who had had the audacity to believe that they could make the mine a place of their own and in the process of it eliminate any others who thought to do the same. Ridiculous! Without any statement of preparation, Mr. Faehner began.

"It goes way, way back to near the beginning of the second year here, I believe. It's hard to pinpoint a date exactly. Too bad I didn't keep a diary or journal of the day-to-day occurrences back then. Anyway, as I believe I mentioned to you already, there was an old farmer, Arthur Ender, who was privileged to stay living in the 1800 house from the inception of Silver Ford Incorporated in early 1974 until the end of the year. After that, it was ours, but not for long. Yes, we moved our nascent office operations in there almost immediately, but something happened shortly after that which impeded that whole concept. It concerned an artist. Just like the busman, we had absolutely no idea he was coming.

"It all came about because of Luckee's bar. That's where old man Boddinger got together with Luckee and invited him to come aboard too. Well, the more the merrier. This artist, so to speak, frequented the bar too. And I don't know what, through friendship or pity, one of them had the funny idea of bringing this poor guy down to the mine to live in the house and apply his craft in whatever way he could to add something of a creative touch to the fancy of the place. And it's not like he wasn't without his talents. He's the one who painted those murals of the early miners on the shanty walls. He's the one who painted those Indian-head figures on the front of the mine gate. He sculpted hand-sized figurines of old-time miners—complete with carbide lamps attached to their foreheads—at their predecessors, the Indians, who mined the silver outcroppings long before the first white Americans ever set foot around this area, and he even sculpted a comical figurine of Luckee. I'm sure he would have come up with even more and better designs had he had the time. But in the end, he was his own worst enemy, and that's what got him out of here in less than a year, if I remember correctly.

"I'll never forget the moment when I first laid eyes upon him—him jumping out of the back of Luckee's Silver Ford truck, duffel bag swung over his shoulder, probably carrying everything he owned in the world in it. I was right there to witness it. He was all made-up for the event, I imagine. He had on some kind of a floppy hat, beige colored with a black band around it. Sticking out of the band was a pheasant feather—what was supposed to be an Indian feather, I believe. He wore a pronounced smile on his face, which was thin and ruddy. Flowing out from underneath the floppy hat was a mesh of long scraggly black hair, which looked like it hadn't seen shampoo and water for days.

"He was never formally introduced to me or my partner, so in addition to not knowing his name, we were kept in the dark about why he was becoming a part of the place. My belief was that the reason for him showing up was twofold: first, but not foremost, was for him to apply his craft, his artistic endeavors, where he could to spruce things up a bit, second and most likely the real reason was to keep us in check. By the beginning of the second year,

Mr. Boddinger was always saying that we, meaning me and Jimmy, were getting a little bit too big for our britches as the old saying goes. I think the artist was welcomed down so he could have a permanent resident, someone to keep a perpetual eye on us and what we were doing. For by this time, we were starting to come down occasionally, after work, just to hang out. We never really did anything wrong, but I don't think Boddinger ever trusted us.

"So this artist, so to speak, was given full rights. Letting him live in the 1800 house was like giving him the key to Silver Mine City. He had no car of his own, which meant that it was rare that he ever left, which meant that our coming and going as we pleased was brought to an abrupt stop. Right from the get-go, everything changed. And let me tell you, he savored every second of it. To him, we were just kids in Keds—Keds was the brand name of a popular sneaker back when I was a boy. To him, we were just donkey-shit shovelers. He disregarded us as though we were two pesky flies buzzing around in a room, being shooed away every time they get in the way. Boy, oh boy, he's one person from the past that I would like to have come around one more time, to have see what I've become here. I think I'd let him have a look-see too, then I'd find myself a long-handled, broad-bottomed broom and chase that guy right the heck out of here.

"Resentment grew right from the start. It was almost as though he was advised about how best to handle us. He never spoke up about how he felt in regards to our being there. He didn't have to. He spoke to us with his looks and his attitude. His confidence ran high. He had Mr. Boddinger's blessing. He had the unprecedented privilege to live in the prestigious 1800 house. And we knew what a perfect match his free-loading lifestyle was to Boddinger's penchant for cheapness. In that sense, those two were made for each other. Boddinger paid him very little for any of the art work he did. And he got to live in a great place for free. Considering that alone it was nothing short of a miracle that we ever got him out of there."

"So it was you two who figured out a way," the reporter interjected just to get a word in edge-wise.

"I was much stronger-willed than he was. I knew what I was fighting for. To him, the mine was just a place to live for a while. To me, the mine was my hope, my destiny. And the funny thing was that it didn't ever have to come to a him-versus-us situation. That came about because of the contemptible behavior he showed us. If he had been smarter—befriended us instead—we probably wouldn't have cared that much that he was going to be around for a while. But the way things stood, I felt that it was pretty much him or us. I had to look at Boddinger's perspective. We were, for all intents and purposes, only fifteen-year-olds at the time. In his view, we were definitely expendable. The artist was too. As a matter-of-fact, maybe more so. And I think Boddinger liked that. The artist was completely vulnerable to his whims and will. He depended on him for a place to stay and a way to stay on his work. We, on the other hand, did not. We came of our own volition, and we left of our own volition. Boddinger never knew then of the great expectation I had for the place. I'd of lost if he had. He'd have used it against me every chance he got. Once though, I almost let it get out, but considering the circumstance in which I did let him know that it was my intention and desire to take over his position someday, he probably took it as a joke."

"What was the circumstance?" the reporter asked in an amused voice.

"A birthday cake," Mr. Faehner answered in a complete manner. "Yes, a birthday cake. During that first year, I turned fifteen. On the occasion, I ordered a specially made sheet cake from a bakery in town. I brought it down late the day before. I think it was a white cake with white icing. Frosted over it were the words "Pequea Silver Mine Owner—Chris Faehner" in bold red lettering. I remember the expression on everyone's face the moment I presented it to them. Everyone was aghast. Imagine the audacity. Imagine what they must have felt about me for having dared to do such a thing, me, a fifteen-year-old nobody letting a thirty-five-year-old millionaire know that I had the belief that someday his paradise would be mine! He never let out then and there just what he was feeling, but I knew. I could see it in his eyes—a seething desire to pick me up and toss me right out the door. But Luckee interceded for me as he always did by making light of the situation, commenting what a whimsical thing I had done. And it may have worked for the others. But right then at that moment, Boddinger doubted it was a farce. He did let it go though, for it was never brought up in conversation after that day.

"And you know, there was something else that happened that day that meant something to me, made me believe even more that one day the thing I wanted most would happen—that my birthday wish would come true. A thing that no one else ever found out about. A thing I've never spoken about before. A moment when fate was put to the test, tossed like dice, but came up in my favor. You'll think it's silly. But to me, it was a portent of the future."

"What was it?"

"The cake. Just like I told you, I already had the cake in the house the day before I intended to give myself a party. I had it hidden on a closet shelf in one of the upstairs rooms, where no one ever bothered to go. When everyone was gathered in the kitchen for a hot lunch, I decided to go get it. Carrying the large box down the steps, I tripped when I got near the bottom one. I fell forward, the cake in the air. Landing on my knees, I captured the cake, midair, mind you, without the slightest attempt at trying to do so. My hands extended out, and there it was. I recovered it. There it was. My heart pounded. I realized right then and there that the thing could have turned out quite differently. I could have ended up with a couple of pounds of flour and frosting on me. What a fool I would have looked like—in front of jerk A, Mr. Boddinger, and jerk B, the Artist. A thing like that would have brought them together—maybe jeopardized the eventual outcome of the entire situation—that of the artist's extrication. The way that cake landed back in my arms after I had tripped, after it had been released from my hands, meant only one thing to me. I was immune to the evil power of those who would have wanted to get rid of me. Fate was on my side, and more importantly, known only to me."

"Was it easy after that? I mean, to find a way to make the artist go?"

"No. Remember, they were made for each other. Mr. Boddinger was something of a cheapskate when it came to compensating his workers. And the artist was something of a freeloader, taking advantage of a situation which benefited him immensely. If we had not deliberately set out to get the goods on him, his Silver Mine time would have lasted. How long, nobody knows. And like I said before, it was good that we disliked each other the way we did right from the get-go. That gave us incentive to move forward with the effort to remove him from the property."

And before the reporter even had to ask further, Mr. Faehner began with the story, taking them back in mind, in time, to the time leading up to the artist's unintended departure . . .

"Only a quick look and see," Pip stated sternly. "And don't disrupt anything. He's a neat freak, and he'll notice the slightest disturbance, and we'd be blamed whether we did it or not."

Self-assured, the boys crept up the creaky steps leading up to the top floor of the 1800 house, a place they had been recently banned from in lieu of the fact that the attic, as it was, had been given over to the itinerate artist as a place to live in for as long as he remained associated with the enterprising Silver Ford Incorporated. It was their first chance, since the artist's arrival, to inspect the forbidden hideaway without being noticed. Boddinger, Luckee, and the artist were gone. Boddinger away on business, and Luckee and company had gone off on some trip down in the county to see about buying an old sofa for the artist to put in the top-flight apartment to provide him a sleeping space. Luckily, there was no lock ever put on the door. The only method for keeping people out was the rule laid down by Luckee soon after the artist took up residence and supposedly supported by Boddinger to stay away from any and all of the artist's belongings and from the third-floor attic where most of his things would be kept.

All of the time previously, the less-than-spacious attic had remained empty except for the occasional house spider who managed to slip through the floor space under the door and find a way up and the occasional fly who wandered in from a crack in the thick-stoned wall. But now, the forlorn slant-roofed room had been transformed entirely into what could be considered an adequately conditioned living space suitable for occupancy. The boys couldn't believe it. Right under their noses too. Upon seeing that there really was a reason now to keep them out, both boys began to feel a little uneasy. The room was dim, afforded natural light only by two small side windows, panes of sectioned bubble glass fitted into the gray stone walls but without latches and cords. They were unopenable. There was, however, a single artificial light that the room could be afforded relief from its dingy atmosphere, which before the arrival of the artist, probably hadn't been turned on for years. Pip went quickly to it, the cobwebbed orb dangling from an old cloth wire attached to the rafters. With one hand reaching toward it, he winced as he readied his thumb and fingers to trick the old light on, afraid that it might explode, having to be used so often now after so many years of abeyance. He turned his head and closed his eyes as he pushed in on the switch. The light complied without complaint, and the room became illuminated with a soft yellow tint.

Around the room, the boys' eyes met with the things they had been forbidden to see. And they were aghast at what they saw. Nowhere did they see the things they'd imagined they would if they'd given their imaginations over to it. Nowhere. Not one object. Both Pip and Jim were thinking the same.

"I thought this place would be some kind of art studio by now," Pip supposed after having made a visual sweep of the creature-comforted floor space.

"You couldn't have read my mind any clearer," Jimmy retorted with a similar sense of bewilderment.

The room's contents consisted of the very mundane—an old fabric-worn recliner, a drop-leaf table sitting up against one of the unopenable windows, a few stacks of '60s and '70s vinyl albums, some covered in their original record protectors, some not. There was a put-together shelf standing back behind the albums. It was made with body-long, foot-wide pieces of pine board sitting end to end on cinder blocks, three tiers high. It was apparent that soon the loose-lying albums would be placed upon it.

But the room also included the more prominent; central was a huge bearskin rug resting on the open floor and looking so clean one would think it was never walked upon—a prize in the collection. Around all the walls were the runners-up in this assorted display. Pelts of practically every worthwhile fur-bearing animal indigenous to the areas of the county were mounted to brackets on the side walls. Included were cottontails, muskrat, beaver, and woodchuck, though why anybody would want to keep a woodchuck's coat was beyond comprehension. Included too were three prominently displayed deerskins. A mother's soft and tan and two fawns, white speckles on tan. On top of the deer was the finest specimen of red fox ever. Its lavish red-orange coat trimmed in white shined vibrantly, even in the dim of the attic. There were more, but the boys' eyes then fixed upon the instruments of death to all of these unfortunate creatures. Standing in one of the wall corners was a small assembly of firearms that the boys curiously crept to. Though neither of them were what could be considered an expert in the field of identifying guns, the weapons they looked at were ordinary enough that they could tell, without doubt, what they were.

"Two twelve-gauge shotguns, a 30/30, and a .270 deer rifle," Pip stated firmly as if listing them for inventory.

"So we've got a Dr. Jekyll/Mr. Hyde in our midst," Jim analogized. "A seemingly passive artist and a dark-sided killer!"

"It's a good thing we've been letting things go then," Pip contended. "I mean allowing the situation between him and us continue in a stalemate. If we'd have done anything to really piss him off, he might have gone off after us, shot at us with one of the deer rifles."

"Yeah, then after having done one or the both of us in, you could call it a dearly-departed rifle," Jimmy said in a half-serious, half-joking way.

"Funny," Pip returned wryly. "But seriously, let's get out of here. We don't know when they'll be back. We'd better get going while the getting's good."

Having accomplished what they had set out to do, the boys abandoned the artist's attic and, leaving the house altogether, went for a short walk around the lower pond so they could help each other come to a better understanding of what they had seen and found out about regarding the secrets the artist was keeping. Thoughts they had each been experiencing came out in the space of conversation they had made for themselves.

"You don't suppose he's set his sights on any of the wildlife here, do you?" Jimmy asked with the utmost concern.

"How could he not!" Pip slapped back with disgust. "If it's in his blood, it's in his blood. He's like a wolf in a forest full of helpless creatures. There's never been hunting here as far back as can be determined. From Boddinger's time in the seventies to Erb's time in the sixties, all the way back to when Miller farmed this land back in the forties and fifties, this habitat has been largely protected. These animals do not fear people—not in the sense of fearing for their lives. They would think nothing of the artist if he made his way through their woods with a gun poised in his arms ready to shoot the life out of them. He probably enjoys it for all it's worth too. His life as an artist is just too mundane. And what a way to break up the monotony, engaging yourself in a blood sport."

"You don't suppose he's already knocked off a few of the animals around here," Jimmy interjected. "I mean, some of those pelts seemed pretty fresh if you ask me."

"I don't doubt it," Pip concurred. "The question is whether or not Boddinger knows. I mean, does he or doesn't he know about this guy's wild side. And did he or didn't he give his permission allowing him to hunt on Silver Mine property. I, personally, don't think so. I've never heard it being talked about openly in the time he's been here—that's unusual considering that we're all really just a group of guys, with guy things on our minds. Also, the way everything pertaining to his secret side is packed away up there in the dark. Avid hunters like to show off their trophies for all eyes to see, and then, at the slightest hint that their catches are being eye-balled or discussed, are ready to tell the story behind the kill. Even recreational hunters are likely to do this. But not here. In this instance, his exploits—all past, present, and anticipated future—have all been kept under wraps. Why? And before God Almighty, I hope I'm right in my assumptions. Otherwise, what an upper hand he's got. I mean, he's already proved he's good at his craft and to top that off with him having Boddinger's holy permission to fling his guns around here. Why, there would be no stopping him."

Everything the boys thought was true, except for their concern that Boddinger had somehow lost his mind and was allowing the wayward artist to wield his weaponry upon the hapless creatures of the hallowed hollow hills. What they didn't know though was that secretly, behind their backs, behind the scenes of displayed indifference between them and the artist, there was a concerted effort going on between Boddinger and their newly arrived rival to come up with reasons to let the boys go. Spurred on by the artist, the pertaining conversations, if you could consider them that, usually were brought up as an off-the-cuff remark or even a joke somehow related to the boys' inexperience at life and how was it that the two of them found themselves in such an exulted place and position so early on. Much of the more particular grief was filed against Jimmy whose belligerence in words and attitude were an easy target. But Boddinger knew he couldn't have one without the other. And Pip was, without doubt, the best Silver Mine worker he could have ever hoped for. And besides, he would always say as a way of quashing the seriousness of the artist's intent, "Where else will I get a better couple of shit shovelers?"

Though Boddinger kept it to himself, the persistence of the artist's attempts to try to get him to get rid of the city boys began to bother him. Even though the discontent of the artist had always been related to him in private, he knew that eventually the boys, especially Pip, would catch wind of it. And he sensed in them, especially Pip, the pride felt in being such a part of something special. They would not relent. Inevitably, there would be a showdown. Inevitably, a winner. Another thing too kept him at bay. That was, that there was a practical side to all of this. The artist came cheaply, and the boys came cheaply. To himself, he knew he was saving a ton of money because of having allowed each of the two to hang around as it were. The boys were paid an hourly rate of only $3 for a specified amount of time each week—fifteen hours, the weekend work. Other than that, they were on their own to do as they pleased, working more or less of their own accord, garnering what extent of extra compensations as they could beyond that of their meager pay. Typically, this meant tourist tips. For Pip, they came quite often after the completion of one of his many expert Silver Mine tours. For Jimmy, they came after the occasional special attentions he would sometimes apply toward one of those persons interested in horseback riding. The extent of these subsidiary compensations Boddinger cared little about as long as the standardized acceptance fees were being paid.

So in essence, the situation was a stalemate. In the practical sense of things, to consider one over the other made no sense as long as the status quo remained the same. If push came to shove, Boddinger didn't know which side of the proverbial fence he would want to stand alongside of. And he had no compelling reason to make any considerations about it. As long as the artist and the boys remained relatively calm with each other, though their underlying tendencies might be of a much more hostile nature, Boddinger was more than willing to let things be. He hoped over time that the incessant badgering he was receiving about the boys' youth and inexperience from the artist would wane.

Weeks rolled on like this, this stagnated; one-side-can't-gain-on-the-other scenario. But what Boddinger had hoped for—that time would have eased the tensions—was not to be. Both the artist and the boys refused to give in though they did give up on the idea that an either-or decision was in the realm of possibility. The only way for one side to win was for the other side to slip up, do something to make Mr. Boddinger royally mad, make him mad enough to give someone the boot.

Then came an opportunity, at least what appeared to be a real chance at getting the artist in trouble. It was learned that on an upcoming weekend, Mr. Boddinger had accepted the invitation of an old friend to spend those days sailing down the Chesapeake soaking up the pleasures of life. To the boys, that meant that what would have been a golden opportunity for them to have done the same at the mine, meant now, due to the artist's all-the-time presence, a whole lot of nothing. They were understandably upset. But in their mode of moodiness and resentment, a thought occurred—that the artist would set out to do the thing that they could not—being that the mice could play since the cat would be away. Disappointment could turn to victory.

When all was said and done, the boys had arranged to come back to the property later in the day in the hope that the artist would be up to something no good, and they would catch him at it. Then what? Who knew? It would become a battle of belief—but regardless of that, it was worth a shot.

So as to keep the mission completely undercover, the boys, after walking the two miles to the outskirts of Lancaster, thumbed their way the remaining eight and got off about a quarter-mile short of their destination on Silver Mine Road. When the car that had facilitated them sped off, it kicked up a pile of dry dirt that shot into their faces and settled down upon their clean white T-shirts.

"So much the better," Pip said pointedly. "We should have thought better than to wear white on this kind of an operation. But, hey, that doesn't mean we have to have our faces dusted and dirtied. Come on, let's clean up over in the stream."

Just a short distance away was the Goods Road bridge, which spanned a very small unnamed stream, which followed Silver Mine Road its last mile until it met Goods Road where it then turned slightly back and followed a contoured course at the slope of an adjacent hillside belonging to the Broken Bottle Club, a clandestine group of avid outdoorsmen who spent many days shooting rounds of any-type guns at stationary targets set up in the woods behind the hill. Already in their Silver Mine stay, the boys had heard thousands upon thousands of echoed explosions coming from the afternoon events. It was the one thing that kept them from ever venturing off into the woods cross-creek from the west-side extent of the mine property.

Crouched under the cement bridge, Pip and Jim splashed cold stream water onto their crust-covered faces washing away the bothersome coating of brown. After the quick cleansing both boys realized that dusk was only just beginning to settle. Around them, particularly in the stream ditch they were now a part of, daylight was fading. Dark spots, in places where shadows were apparent as the sun gasped its last, advanced, in streaks and stretches, along the weed-choked bank, to be copied and continued until all was covered in darkness.

"We'll have to wait just a bit," Pip pointed out after he observed the relation of themselves to the encroaching night.

"That's OK, I have to take a crap anyway," Jimmy put in.

The crude remark made Pip cringe with disgust for he knew that in matters such as this Jimmy was as unprincipaled as all get-out. To him the whole world was a toilet.

"Go ahead then, take your crap," Pip retorted.

Already Jimmy had advanced beyond what he considered the scope of visual perception, given the circumstance of the rapidly declining light. Once sufficiently secluded behind a suffocating wall of milkweed Jimmy pulled down his pants, squatted, and began the elimination process. Unfortunately for Pip he was still privy to it—the awful sounds of Jimmy's bowels let-loose. It made Pip wish he was nowhere near. When it was over Jimmy appeared out of the even-darker-than-before stream-scape. And he knew, though he could not see it, the look of Pip's face; disgust undisguised.

"Just communing with nature," he said with a wry smile to his friend who he knew would say nothing at the moment but would inevitably give him what-for at a point later in time.

"Come on! Let's go!" Pip shouted in a half-toned voice.

And with that Pip and Jim scrambled out of the low-lying trench and picked up where they were left off—onward to the old stone house. Boldly, confidently, under the protecting cover of nightfall, they chose to walk the remaining distance right on Silver Mine Road—so seldom did a vehicle travel this road at night, and so easily could one traveling its course on foot spot any oncoming vehicle and elude detection by a quick run-and-duck into the nearby fields.

Just as predicted they made their way, unseen. And, just as they predicted, when they got to the top of the hill they could see, below, that an activity of unusual proportion was taking place inside the usually quiet building. Bright light was shooting out of every window, of every floor, and sounds of an uproarious nature were emanating out of the ones' half-opened. Though this was just what they had hoped for the boys were at a momentary loss over just what they should do. Should they go to the barn phone and call Mrs. Boddinger and anonymously report the disturbance? Should they instead just barge right in to the home and confront the artist? This they contemplated, each, two imperceptible gray dots, resting on the crest of the hill. Finally, Pip came to a decision. "Follow me!"

It wasn't enough that something of a gargantuan nature was taking place in the house. For all they knew Mrs. Boddinger could be there herself hosting some kind of glad-to-be-free-of-her-husband-for-a-while, wild party. Who knew. So to find out exactly what was taking place and who was in the place taking it Pip beckoned Jim to follow him so they could observe, with their own eyes, the goings-on inside.

They positioned themselves at one of the first-floor windows—one that stood beside Silver Mine Road and was seldom, if ever, looked out due the fact that all a person could see out it was the short distance across the road and the tangle of honeysuckle vines that proliferated along the steep roadside. Outside was now pitch-dark so that even the white of the boys' T-shirts did not offend their intended desire—to remain unseen until otherwise decided. So secure were they at their "window of opportunity" that each of them pressed themselves right up against a corner section of the pane and focused, one eye each, into and onto the center of recreational activity. And what Peeping Pip and Peeping Jimmy saw amazed them both. In full view of their investigative operation was the artist attired in full-length, Indian garb; long-legged, ankle-flaired pants with three-inch crisscross stitching down the sides, a brown and tan opened vest studded with tiny turquoise cabochons. And, to top it all off, he was adorned with a full Indian headdress—eagle feathers flaring out of the headband. He was entertaining himself and the others by doing, or attempting to do, some sort of Indian dance which was most likely not authentic. Even so his antics were not without reward. Frequently, during his escapade, two of his female companions, also clad in Indian-fashioned dress, got up from their sitting positions on the floor around him and made feinted reaches for him as if cajoling him to come with them—enticing foreplay for what would come later. There was another man, also Indian-dressed, standing beside an aluminum quarter-keg of beer which he frequently tapped to fill his large plastic cup even when it was most of the way full. Also within his grasp was a large plastic bowl of potato chips which he was devouring between slurps of beer. In addition to the easy-to-observe dancers and squarely positioned beer and chip feeder, glances were made at another couple having fun in a far corner of the side room. It looked like they were down on the floor in a state of partial undress wrestling each other, body to body, from one feel-good position to another.

"It could very easily turn into an Indian-style orgy," Jimmy surmised.

"If it did what would you expect us to do about it?"

"Join in," Jimmy said with a half-smile.

"Very funny," Pip returned. "In the first place we wouldn't be welcome. In the second place there's three girls to three guys in there so the numbers aren't exactly right. In the third place . . ."

"All right already," Jimmy assented. "then how about waiting until the lot of them are just drunker and acting a bit kookier. Then we'll bust in and take control. How about that?"

"I don't know Jim. We'd have them all right but to what end. For all we know Boddinger approved this little get-together. What do you think he'd do to us for sticking our noses where they don't belong. And, even if he had not approved it I don't know if he would get all bent out of shape over an Indian party."

"I think you second-guess yourself too much, pal." Jimmy purported.

"You might be right, old friend, but in this case we have to have something that's worthy of winning a prize."

A few minutes passed and Jimmy, reluctantly, pulled away from the window. Pip pressed on, pressing now his right eye up against the pane, first rubbing his left eye to alleviate the pressure it had been taking being smudged to the glass. With the new eye in he had a clearer view and broader perspective of the situation inside. And it hit him! Something of meaning. Something that now stood out from the backdrop. Something out of place. Something recognized. On the top of the long kitchen counter, pushed off to the side to make room for the various party foods was one of the artist's shotguns. With its tan-colored strap and glisteningly oiled long-barrel it was, without doubt, one of the collection from the artist's attic.

Oh my! Pip thought to himself as he identified the weapon then adjudged its meaning. He quick-turned to his friend who was now standing aloof—distanced from the happenings mentally as well as physically.

"I think we got him," Pip pronounced proudly.

"Got him how?" Jimmy returned with an aura of disbelief.

"Got him in a way that's going to make Boddinger want to boot his butt all the way back Silver Mine Road, that's how," he said assuredly.

"Prove it!" Jimmy said as if it were a dare.

"Look there!" Pip declared without signifying what he was talking about.

"Look where!" Jimmy shouted back in a pitched voice.

Directing Jimmy's attention to the counter space where the shotgun lay Pip described for him his assertion that the artist would, without a doubt, be issuing forth, next day, on a foray through the hollows, hoping to track down anything worth shooting at.

Pip was right. For all the time now that the artist had been around he had been waiting in secret for the perfect opportunity to ply his other craft. He had been forewarned. During the scant interview process prior to his Silver Mine inception, some of it direct with Mr. Boddinger, some of it indirect through Luckee, it did come out that the artist was an avid hunter. And because it did the artist incurred stiff lectures, again, firsthand from Mr. Boddinger, and secondhand from Luckee, that, hunting, of any sort, was forbidden, anywhere on Silver Mine property. The restriction was without exception. But the artist figured differently. Only his art work meant more to him. So, his second-place interest would receive second-priority treatment. And in the case of his affiliation with shotguns and wildlife showpieces that meant a lot.

For a long time coming he had been preparing for it, watching and waiting for that fortuitous day, when, he could set off into the pristine hills and prey upon a community of birds and mammals that had never been fired upon. And he had to be ready for it. In the preceding months he had acted out the intrigue by venturing out into the uplands and lowlands, all the while stopping and spotting for the animals as they moved about, at the sun's first light, foraging for the food and water that kept them alive. And there was the would-be hunter, crouched in position, determining their movements, learning over them, salivating, for that inevitable day when in his hands he would carry the means to thrill and then kill them. Give them that ultimate end-of-life moment that all animals hope for—to be hunted and quickly done away with rather than die slowly of malingering old age or disease.

The Indian party was a third-priority thing. The artist too had been told not to throw any type of wild get-togethers with his old friends from Luckee's bar, nothing that would bother any of the once-every-hour-or-so local who would drive by Silver Mine Road. They're a lot of people who want nothing out of the ordinary to happen in their lives—not even to think or assume that something extraordinary is going on.

There wasn't much to think about. Here was a real chance to catch the artist, red-handed, at something he had been absolutely told not to do. It was now or never.

"Quick," Pip quipped. "Let's call this one in. We can go to the barn and use the phone there, contact our parents, tell them we're spending the night. They won't care."

"Stay the night!" Jimmy protested. "What will we do for food?"

"No problem," Pip stated confidently. We have plenty of time before we have to hit the hay. Hey, that has a figurative as well as a literal meaning here since we'll be spending the night in the barn," he chuckled. "We'll thumb a ride over to Mom and Pop's in Little Conestoga. I've got fifteen dollars on me. How about you?"

"Me! I didn't bring a thing. I thought you had a way planned for us to return home after a while."

"I did if we needed it. That's one of the calls I'm going to have to make. I had a friend's older brother on stand-by. And if that failed I had my much-older cousin—in a pinch."

With the details worked out the boys again set out on foot, back to the Goods Road bridge, onto Goods Road, where at least two or three cars per hour prevailed as compared to Silver Mine Road's one or less. And as luck would have it, they were picked up within minutes by a Little Conestogian, who was more of a motorcycle enthusiast than a car driver, but as circumstance presented itself, he was out at the end of a joy ride, having already dropped off the friend he had been with with his seldom-used Chevy. Such was his mood, so happy-go-lucky, that he actually was glad to see someone in need of a favor and offered them, not only a ride to the grocery, but also a way back.

Back at the barn, Pip and Jim first took care of the business of eating—two one-pint chocolate milks, each a pack of Tastykake cupcakes, and a big bag of potato chips to share. Put away for morning were two sodas and a box of chocolate-covered doughnuts. Before first bites were taken, Pip tabulated the total expense and informed his friend what would be the part he'd be expected to pay back.

"You're a real hardhead when it comes to money, you know," Jimmy said, the way he always did whenever Pip let him have it for owing him back.

"You should be too," Pip pointed out. "Trouble is, I'm never one to owe you or anybody, anything, and that's that!"

"Hey, that old guy sure was nice to us, giving us a ride up and back to the store the way he did."

"Sure. And he's not exactly a stranger either," Pip contended. "I've seen him various times riding cycles on the road around here. He must have four or five at least. He's a nice guy too—always smiling while he's zooming along.

I didn't recognize him though until after we were in the car. He seemed so different being in a car."

The night was deepening. The boys talked and talked until they talked themselves to sleep. Pip had made a point of positioning himself in a principal area of the barn floor with the purpose of being in the right spot that when daylight came, the sun's first reaching rays would shine amid his face and wake him.

Morning came. Pip was awakened but not in the way he intended. Gunshots suddenly rang out, gunshots sounding exponentially due the amplification of the hollow in the hills. Pip shot up. The day was dark. The artist had beaten him to the punch. Pip's rustling about woke up Jim who knew now too what was up.

"He's out there already," Pip stated in a firm tone. "Come on, we have to hurry!"

"I'm with you, pal. But wait one minute. Let me grab a couple of doughnuts for the both of us. You're a hungry eater, same as I, in the morning."

Grabbing a doughnut for each hand, Pip and Jim set out into the dawn, still yawning, still slowly settling into the wooded hills. There was no detail to follow, only their wit. Pip thought hard—about how they would remain undisclosed while they advanced upon the hunter. As daylight approached, it would be almost impossible to remain out of sight, if they intended to get close enough to actually witness the carnage about to be perpetrated. And another thought hit him relating to the difficulty at hand. What if the artist saw them but acted as if he did not, then, without warning, began firing at them, possibly hitting, possibly killing them? It all sounded hideous but, understanding just how the artist felt about them, not entirely out of the realm of possibility. They would be vulnerable to say the least. But Pip was always one for a battle of wits and the Silver Mine's land he knew like the backs of his hands. Before they were out of the barn complex, he had it. They would observe their nemesis from the opposite stretch of hillside and at least get some idea of what he was up to. And they would be safe.

It didn't take long for things to happen. Within minutes, the boys were safely nestled in the higher-up reaches of the eastern hills. The artist was in the west. The shooting had already begun, so well had the hunter staked out his potential hunting ground. Round after round, four in all were fired, each with intent. The succession of the echoing blasts told the story. The first shot might have missed. The second probably hit. The third was a try for the kill. The fourth the kiss of death. The pursuit had not been far for the intervals between shots were each less than a minute apart.

Once the fourth and final shot had been fired, the boys dared not move from the point they had advanced to while attempting to get a clearer fix on just where, on the opposite side, the scene was taking place. Their patience paid off. Ten minutes later, they saw him, the artist, trekking along a rudimentary dirt path that ran the length of the shoreline of the upper pond. His shotgun slung up over his shoulder in a catered position as though it were being rewarded for having performed some special task. All was now quiet, quieter than before, with one less creature adding to the whole.

From their specific vantage point, Pip and Jim only watched as their intended target continued on his way, done for the day. So pleased was he with what he had accomplished in that short span of morning gray that the boys could hear him whistling by as he passed out in front of the open area near the mine. When they were to the rear of him, Pip noticed an unidentifiable object, rusty-red, swinging off the barrel tip of the shotgun, attached to it somehow. The boys didn't know what to think, but they knew there was only one way to find out. Sure that their presence could not be detected now, they raced down out of the woods and over to the pond as fast as they could. They followed the pond path quickly but observantly, looking for clues—footprints, snapped-back branches of red thorns—anything to show where he had been.

Then suddenly, Pip stopped dead in his tracks. He had a premonition, if you could call it that being after the fact. He knew. He knew. Awfully true!

"Come on!" he shouted at the top of his lungs. I know what that dirty . . ."

In Pursuit Of

The story about the artist was divulged entirely, though through the ending of it, Mr. Faehner's enthusiasm in telling it became noticeably less. One would have thought that after an afternoon of storytelling the answer might have been simply that he was now appreciably tired of it. But that wasn't the case. Faehner's fugacious spirit came about because of a lacking he felt, felt keenly. He had opened up his bag of favors, emptied it in front of the opportunistic reporter, but he knew only to himself that the stories—despite their intrigue, depth, or meaning—fell so awfully short of expectation. So did the day. The self-celebration had exacted its toll, reminding him, extolling the opprobrious fact. He witnessed it in their eyes—all glowing centers of congratulatory offering. A thousand eyes had done so this day, a thousand eyes that could not see. Only he. The more he saw in others the appreciation they had for his past accomplishments, the more he felt less about himself. The stories—all the successes—all were only intended to clear a final path. The Silver Mine story was not over.

Oblivious as to what was going on inside his up-until-now-ever-so-loquacious host, the reporter attempted to recapture the high-spirited mood that had prevailed ever since he was first apprehended then brought before the white-bright billionaire. "So he killed the red fox and cut off his tail. And you and your buddy led Mr. Boddinger into the hills to show him the stinking dead body. You left off there, there's more to tell?"

"Actually, there's not," Faehner exacted in a lugubrious tell-all tone.

Not wanting to be implicated for being impertinent, especially after all he had done, indulging the young man the way he had, Mr. Faehner suddenly spoke, eluding to the time. That and a quick walk led them back to the crossing at Silver Mine Road.

Standing outside the 1800 house, the limousine was waiting thanks to Obe's watchful eye. After a handshake and a smile, the reporter was simply whisked away—alone. Faehner deferred. For the moment, he preferred not to face those thousand eyes that would again deceive him into thinking more of himself than he deserved. And ironic it was that they were of his own device. Alone, he was left. Alone, he had to contemplate. For the longest while, he stood. For the longest while, he stared. From the elevation he stood upon, he stared around the boundaries, which surrounded him—the barn, the house, the pond, the old across-the-road path that led to the mine, the hollow, the hills, all of it original, all of it original to the day he first set foot on the property.

Determined, he set forth up a worn footpath, which led along a wayward course to the top of the high grassy hill in back of the stone house. It was the last of its side of the broken hollow hills upon whose once-dominant land everything rough and exterior was removed. The land, put into use prior to Boddinger's ownership, transformed annually into a field of tobacco, wheat, corn, or soybean. It was now as it had been for forty years since the Silver Mine's inception a field of wild grasses, wild flowers, and the occasional wild tree.

But it was more. About halfway along its southern extent, then down and into the steep-sloped woods was the spot upon where so long ago, the famous Richard Faehner, geologist, conducted his on-site survey of this often-not-considered piece of land. The evaluation was complete. Richard knew; so quick did he pick up his belongings on that final day of discovery. Pip knew too. He knew the signs. Whenever one of "Rick's Picks"—as his geological contentions were referred to—were actualized, he would always act in the same self-assured manner and never say a word, at least to the much-younger Pip, about what exactly he had done.

Mr. Faehner found the location, memorialized only by memory, and patted himself on the back for having had the intuition enough to wrest from Rick's patterns-of-the-past the intimation that he was up to something big. And the something big that he was up to was being kept a secret. But any secret can come undone regardless of its size. All it takes is the irrepressible desires and actions of one who believes that there's something of worth behind it. That person was Pip, now the fifty-three-year-old Mr. Faehner. The irrepressible desire was his certainty, established on that first day back in 1973, that the silver in the mine, or mine area, had never been exhausted; that it remained still to be uncovered by the person who sought to seek it. He knew now. There existed beneath the buried bedrock a never-before-exploited mother lode of silver all verified and documented by the late great geologist!

"Good things come to those who wait," was how, for the first twenty-eight years of his silver mine expectancy, Mr. Faehner kept himself in a perpetual state of belief. "Great things come to those who wait longer," was the theme of the last twelve years since the unexpected death of Richard Faehner. For it was then that a twelve-years-younger Mr. Faehner willed a way to exact the truth about his dreamed-for-yet-undiscovered silver. The story of itself, though having taken place so long ago, was only now coming into fruition. The tedious wait was near over—a wait so long most others would have been glad to give it up long before now. A credit Mr. Faehner secretly gave to himself—that he had not. If ever in the history of one man's pursuit, a pursuit guided by only hope, there was an example of the extraordinary, this was it. Determination and the determination to remain determined!

Entering into his own, his private realm of determination, Mr. Faehner dredged up the efficacious tale, the geological tale, about how and when he had received the proof he needed that the silver he had so, so, sought for so, so, long existed.

Locating Rick's campsite off-road in the Mojave Desert proved to be quite a simple task. His whereabouts there, now several years in the making, had become common knowledge to the few locals in the nearby town. The citizens of Red Rock, all fifty of them, had come to know and appreciate the "Diggin Fool," as they had so warmly labeled him, for all of the special interest he had shown in their godforsaken homestead. After all, if he ever found whatever it was he was looking for out in the sea of forsakenness that surrounded them, it might be something quite important, something that could change their lives, something that could put their town on the map, which by itself had a literal as well as figurative meaning since on most United States maps, the town was surprisingly missing. A fact that meant more than a slap on the face, when taking into consideration the obvious truth that there should never be a reason not to. Most tiny towns are often left off due to lack of space. But Red Rock, lying halfway between Needles and Essex, with nothing between, was usually slighted simply because even the cartographers had never heard of it. But all that could change if the world-famous geologist got what he wanted out of the ever-present rock and rim that every day reminded the people just how insignificant they were in comparison to the timeless tedium of temperature and topography that typified them.

Mr. Faehner had only to inquire to the first person he came in contact with to discover the exact location of his relation, when he had last appeared in town, and whom he had last spoken to. And thrilled were the people of Red Rock when they surmised incorrectly that Rick must be on the verge of something big to have brought in such a respectable, intelligent, obviously important person as they perceived Mr. Faehner to be when he appeared out of the eastern extent of Highway 40 that fabled day back in 2001.

Off-highway, he sped out of the northeast edge of the town onto a deserted desert road, which led in a northeast direction a sum of some undetermined miles across a flat of barren red-rocked landscape until, as he had been directed, he came across the misshapen figure of a centuries-dead desert wood, one of a species of extinct desert tree as of yet unidentified in the scientific community. Never had it been viewed by the eyes of an identification expert for reason that the town of Red Rock itself is believed to be a myth.

Mr. Faehner slowed, then stopped when he came to the tree site. His instructions were to veer to the left of the vestigial wood and follow, as best he could, the newly created virgin path through the crumbly rock and soil, made by the sometimes often, sometimes seldom, jaunts to the outer ridge of an ancient dried-up creek discovered by the studied geologist in the late of 1998. While stopped, he did stare at the awkwardly bent character of wood, which looked as though it had spent years upon years in an ever-dying mode, yielding, yielding its once well-formed size and shape slowly, slowly, bendingly, bendingly toward its origin—the earth.

It felt strange to leave it, this tree that once knew it was the last of its kind and prolonged its own dying and death as long as was earthly possible in the hope that life really did spring eternal, and it would yet realize that one of its kind from a lifetime of seedlings would take root around it.

The road, if you could call it that, was like an apparition—first appearing, then disappearing along the red-rock route. The only confidence Mr. Faehner carried with him was that anything other than the prevailing assortment of rustic reds would be hard to miss. And in accordance with the directions given him, this last leg of the journey, this sojourn over the rough and tumble road, would lead him straight to the prestigious professor. He hoped so.

The purpose of all of it, of visiting Rick in the desert, was to finally come to terms with him—about their past, about their present, about their future. Now the time had come to forgive and forget. Now the time had come when finally the financial standing of the one Mr. Faehner outweighed the financial standing of the other. In essence, the roles had reversed. Not so much as to say that the monetary means of the professor had gone entirely in the opposite direction. That hadn't happened. But what had happened was that the Silver Mine proprietor had been, the past decade or so, expanding his opportunities exponentially all over the southern end of Lancaster County to the point where his frequent splurges of investment had actually garnered him considerable ownership of the entire area's landholdings. This difference now between them from the way it used to be was reason enough for Mr. Faehner to believe that change was a possibility. Rick, if he were smart, would reconsider what it all meant. No longer could he look down upon his younger relative, dismiss him as he had in the past as some precocious Pip. Things would be serious now. At least that was the hope and expectation.

What Mr. Faehner wanted was the tool to go on with his own private dream—Rick's expertise. Twenty-seven years before, Rick had discerned—it was then the young Pip's belief—the secret of the Silver Mine's silver. From the surveys that were made on the downslope of the hollow hill, Rick had ascertained information enough to know where in all probability the precious metal lay hidden. And now many, many, years later, Mr. Faehner had decided the time was right to initiate a discourse with the esteemed geologist. It was time for a trade. He had options. Mr. Faehner could, if he wanted, pay Rick outright for the secreted information. The sky was the limit. He could, if he wanted, offer to include him in on it, allowing the prestigious professor yet another chance at fame—without most of the fortune. The convincer might be that the compensation monies could be used to fund some of his other pursuits, such as this time-consuming sojourn in the desert. Nothing was certain. Most likely, it would come down to a battle of wills.

Thirty-five miles of lengthy travel later—a distance sharply in contrast to the just a little ways up the road, he had been told—Mr. Faehner came into view of something "not quite right" right-side, his vehicle. It began as a subtle depression in the red-top, probably only inches wide and deep, but then progressed into a trench several feet across with a depth that could no longer be determined. Eventually, it turned into a chasm whose dimensions could only be imagined. It was something out of time and place. It was desolate.

Rick's desert camp reminded Mr. Faehner of the old saying about being stuck on a deserted island. This island of dirt, clay, and sand was just bigger. The setup was simple despite the fact that Rick's presence was of a duration longer than two years, off and on. He pulled up and parked parallel to Rick's full-sized orange van, which without its white top would have been very difficult to see amid the sea of off-red topography.

Getting out, Mr. Faehner unbuttoned his white shirt and cuffed his sleeves when he felt the already ninety-degree heat pounce upon him after his cool air-conditioned drive. He did notice though that the air was dry, just like it is always said of the desert climate. He felt his throat becoming parched and momentarily reached back into his car for a cold frosty root beer he had resting in one of the front seat cup holders. Before entertaining any other thoughts or ideas, he spilled the quenching contents down his throat, down to the last carbonate bubble. The bottle he uncharacteristically tossed to the side. Somehow, amongst the vastness of the Mojave, the empty glass bottle seemed to add rather than detract from the landscape. And immediately in his mind, Mr. Faehner smiled for thinking that since glass is made from sand, then this glass is only returning to the soil from which it came. Sand to sand instead of dust to dust, he rationalized.

With his hands clasped behind his back, Faehner paced back and forth around the camp. He couldn't help but notice it appeared a little out of sorts. Though Rick never put up much of a fuss trying to turn his outdoor camps into Hilton Hotels, he did keep what he did have in a semblance of order. Outside the van were two collapsable-legged six-foot-long tables—one, full of geological instruments: pick hammers, chisels, small handheld wisp brooms, a compass, Majove maps showing what the desert looked like during different periods in time. Over the second table was a faded olive-green tarp. One of the same ones, Faehner believed, Rick had used on expeditions when they were a team. Faehner laughed. "That guy's the same as when he was when we were doing this together." Saying that aloud served to emphasize it and the meaning of it. At once, the humor left him. A revelation hit upon him. The inside of his head turned into one huge gray-matter cloud spelling out: what if?

What if, what if, what if Rick's the same? resounded in his brain. For despite who he was now—Mr. Faehner, attired in a millionaire's shirt and a millionaire's tie, ampled to the hilt with assets and self-assurance—there was now, with this newly aspected realization, reason to doubt. For if what he said to himself was true—that Rick was now what Rick was then—then there could be trouble. Spurred into action, Mr. Faehner spread his free hands over the drab old multipurpose table cover and lifted it up to look underneath. It was just as he surmised. Relics. Fossils.

"I've done it again," he said out loud in a voice sounding of consternation. "I've horned in in what Rick would consider his private professional space. This place too; like the silver mine; like Plum Point, Maryland; like the amethyst field in Strasburg, Lancaster County; like the location of the new mineral species in Cedar Hill Quarry; like the Devonian fern site near the Juniata River in Perry County; like the geothite fields off Indian Head Road in West Hempfield Township; like the secret starfish site under Highway 81 at the Swatara Gap—Protasterina, yes, that was the name of the almost-impossible-to-find coelenterate—was another of a series of basically unknown localities where Rick—with his special skills and knowledge, had found, studied, collected from, and hoped would remain entirely his." But in each of the previous places and now including this one, the amateur enthusiast, whether when he was the young boy Pip or now the older esteemed Mr. Faehner, had prevailed upon himself to become personally involved with Rick's hard-to-find places.

"I've uncovered yet another one of Rick's interesting finds. How will he react?"

Staring down at the specimen table, Mr. Faehner could tell that Rick's latest discovery was one of significant importance. Several years of spending weeks at a time in a place that wasn't fit for a rock to live in was proof enough of that, let alone the ancient remains of the creatures assembled across the table. Curious, Mr. Faehner examined the museum-quality specimens, wondering if by his own erudition he could hope to identify them. He could, at least in part. All were of a collection of early, previously undiscovered dinosaur-era reptiles—hatchlings and eggs! Rick had done it again, turned the paleontologic community on its head, though they didn't know it yet, by finding and putting together another piece of the puzzling puzzle of life's many mysteries.

"I'll have to tell him before he has a chance to accuse me of horning in on one of his finds. He has to know that I'm not here to obtain this special resource for my own purposes. He takes everything so personally. And he has no stomach for nosy people whether they're of the professional or nonprofessional type. And worse for that matter is the fact that I came out uninvited, unannounced. He's going to be annoyed to no end with me. Rick never did like the unexpected. The only way to win this thing is to beat him to the proverbial punch. I'll go right in with what I've got. I'll beat him down with flattery and explanation, flattery and explanation."

Straight in his head now about what he intended to do, Faehner set the tarp down carefully over the specimen table. Words went through him, words he would use to quell Rick's highly anticipated anger, words he would use to cajole the thinking part of the highly intelligent geologist's brain into dealing with things the way they would be. He rehearsed them in part, "Rick, you're a highly respected member of the paleontological community. I can afford you the opportunity to continue with this specific site. Just think for a moment of the possibilities I can extend to you. Just think, Faehner and Faehner, together we can . . ."

On and on, the scenario played out in Mr. Faehner's mind as he strolled out beyond the camp in the direction of the ravine. The drop-off point was about one hundred yards away making the desert trekker believe that safety, always tantamount to Rick's concerns, was the reason the camp had been established so inconveniently far from the place of action. "Maybe this ravine is unstable. Maybe it's falling in on itself," he surmised out loud.

When he reached the drop-off, he scanned the opening, side-up, side-down, searching for indicators of where exactly Rick was gaining access of the weirdly wide pit. At first, he could ascertain nothing of note, so he began to walk in a direction onward from the position of the camp. After five minutes in which he gained possibly another hundred yards, he noticed something a short distance ahead. A half-minute later, he was upon it. The setup was creative yet simple—a trademark example of Rick's innovative, problem-solving mind. It was a eureka moment. Mr. Faehner patted himself on the back for such eximious work, having in the vastness of the desert realm found so easily Rick's secret camp and now his secret entranceway into the paleontological past. "And now to find him," he stated resolutely. Always extra careful before venturing into the unknown, Faehner made a cautious study of the vista, looking, listening for any indicators that he might be heading into trouble. The landscape was quiet, all except for the occasional swirl of red dust coming off an extended piece of red wall across the divide. The loose soil was being picked up by occasional but strong whirls of desert wind coming up out of the chasm.

Ready, Faehner made a quick but complete examination of the makeshift access. It consisted of two presumably long iron spikes pounded into the topsoil some six feet from the wall ledge. Behind them was placed a thick oak plank with two half-moon grooves cut into its side to fit onto the iron spikes. Apart from each other were two tied-on pieces of bull rope, one much thicker than the other. The thicker piece had a series of per-foot knots obviously for use as a body's stop-and-go descent or ascent. Thirty feet is a long way to go, up or down, either for the experienced or inexperienced rope climber.

Sure as he was, Faehner made the descent. At the bottom some thirty to thirty-five feet below the desert surface, he began to feel a little concerned for his situation. He looked up. From below, the long span from side to side no longer seemed safe. He felt as though he were an unfortunate creature caught inside the gaping mouth of some enormous desert beast ready to devour him. The realization was that from this point on, no matter how far he trekked, this was the only way out!

Onward he went, hoping, praying that the source of Rick's paleontological discoveries was not some awful distance away. To the best of his knowledge, he could say that Rick never acted foolishly. And after two long years in a desert hole like this, he would know by now how to play this thing out. Faehner continued his march across the compact floor, watching, listening for any signs of wall collapse. He was uncomfortable to say the least. Outfitted entirely in fashionable clothes, ones which would have made an impression with Rick, he had not thought to change, not even his leather shoes, when he decided to hunt Rick down rather than wait him out back at camp. But it was too late now. The clothing was now part of the sacrifice, a sacrifice he hoped wouldn't include his well-being.

He stayed on the side he came down on, which gave him an appreciable view of the opposite side but not so much the side he was on. Often were areas where the side jutted out, assemblages of unyielding bedrock. Around these defiant walls of stone, anything could exist. Around the first in a series of three were the sun-baked bones of a rattlesnake. Around the second was the putrefying body of a dead desert rat. It seemed to Mr. Faehner that these geological outcrops held sway over the desert creatures either as a place to come to or a place to come to to die. In jest, he pictured in his head what was just to come when he rounded the next bend.

Rick! Faehner couldn't believe his eyes. Rick! The site of the workings were slightly above reach. Rick had, over a period of extensive digging, managed to extricate almost the entire level below it, creating a shelf against the wall about two feet deep sticking out. He had been using the detritus as a mound to stand on to get at the material he wanted up above. But something happened. Tragedy struck! From the look of things, it occurred in one huge moment. The desert floor below the mound suddenly opened up, sucking the professor right up. Rick's days-dead body was covered to the nose. Instantly, he had been holed and filled in with the desert soil he was using to benefit his efforts. He was alive probably for days, maybe, watching. Like the turn-off tree yielding itself slowly, slowly to the scorched earth, so did the distinguished geologist—unto death.

Mr. Faehner's mind whirled like the dust swirls that picked up and deviled the tranquility of the ancient underground. What were the implications of all of this? The realization kept hitting him harder and harder. Rick was dead. Rick was dead! Rick was dead! A raft of thought and idea ran through his head amid the hard reality that Richard Faehner existed no more. Richard Faehner existed no more. Every time he put into different words that newly disturbing concept, he was overwhelmed. He could have said it a thousand different ways and the outcome would have been the same—disbelief, shock, and disbelief. He entertained the idea of digging him out, rescuing what was left of him from the mouth of the desert that ate him. But no. What if the desert decided for some dessert—him? He could be swallowed up too. No, he must not risk it. He recalled his intention, his original purpose, to extricate from Rick the secrets of the lost silver. That and that alone was what he must work on. And in that mind-set, he did the unthinkable. Rick would be rendered up to the ages. It would take hardly an effort to cover over Rick's already-decaying head and leave him. He would be left behind to become part of a world that had encapsulated him while he was alive. He would become a part of geological history. Faehner pondered the possibility of it all. The body of the esteemed geologist was already perfectly cast in a condition for near-perfect fossilization. What better final purpose could someone as dedicated to his profession hope for than to be offered up to the future of it. Someday, an era or epoch away, Rick's body, preserved, could be excavated by some go-it-on-his-own professional. Rick's red-boned skeleton could be put on display at some futuristic exhibit featuring twenty-first-century man.

Though these thoughts and considerations started in the context of jest, the gesture now fully composed was to be taken seriously. Irony. The plot was to be that essentially, this hole in the ground would become Rick's burial plot until, hopefully, he would become a part of the lasting past and, as such, carried on into the future. His legend would become legacy.

Using Rick's picks and shovel, Mr. Faehner quick-covered the rest of Rick's head, then left the tools in a state such that they had never been used for that purpose. While doing so, he contemplated other implications such as, should he report Rick's disappearance, that he came here and just did not find him. Should he be seen again himself back in Red Rock when he departs. And loner that he was, Rick's absence would eventually be discovered. Take, for instance, his house back in Lancaster. Though paid for, there would still be annual taxes due on it and ongoing utility bills. How would those be taken care of? Would the delinquency of taxes and other bills spark an investigation into it all? And so what if it did? Faehner wasn't responsible for Rick's death. No one could ever prove whether Rick was alive or just missing when Faehner came out into the desert to see him.

There was time. Time. For now, there was time. Time to figure everything out to its best possible conclusion. For now, Rick's body rests near a forgotten little town, outland, in an even more forgotten little part of the desert.

Once the deed was done, Faehner paid Rick a respectful minute of silence, attributing to him all of the worth he had rendered upon the world of rocks and minerals. And he brought up into words the thing kept silent. Silver broke the silent soliloquy. Now that Rick was dead, there could be no parley, no exchange, no silver! He imagined Rick's sordid smile, a death-face smile, knowing. He was taking all of his secrets with him.

With nothing left to do in the ravine, Mr. Faehner made his way back to the entry point, back to the campsite. He felt tired. The strain of it all—losing Rick and probably losing his chances at finally finding out where exactly the

Silver Mine's silver was, made him feel like a popped balloon. At the camp, he began looking over in more detail Rick's little desert enterprise. The specimens, the hatchlings from the primordial swamp or some such place, he decided to take. They would do no good here lying around on a table day after day and would probably be stolen by the first person who happened upon them. Better that they remain in the family.

He packed them up nicely with old newspaper and small cartons, the same as Rick would have done and fitted them into what was left of the compact space of the 5.0. Before leaving for good, he looked around and found Rick's stash of food and drink and helped himself to a couple of bottled waters. One he drank. While quenching his desert thirst, he sauntered about, taking in a fuller appreciation of what Rick was accomplishing. In particular, he eyed a stack of notebooks—worn, torn. Curious, he picked one up and began leafing through its print-faded pages. He was dumbstruck by what he read though most of the content was too esoteric for his full understanding. But that wasn't it. The content wasn't what excited him. What came to him now, clear and concise, was the meaning underlying the meaning—that these erudite words and passages held out yet another message. The dates were clear—1970, 1971, 1972. Mr. Faehner was euphoric! This meant . . . This meant . . .

He tossed the old notebook aside and shouted out with glee, "Richard Faehner, you old magnificent, meticulous mentor! I know what you've done! I know what you've done! You've left behind your Silver Mine records. This work out here in the nowhere of the desert took you thirty years to bring to fruition. Thirty years! And so too you expected to someday ring out the knowledge of the Silver Mine silver. The silver! Mine!"

Back to Lancaster

Exuding with a confidence unlike any he had experienced for a long, long time, Faehner took to his 5.0 like Speed Racer would have if he were late for the beginning of a cartoon race. Ahead of him were the 2,699 road miles back to the east, back to Lancaster. There would be no dawdling, no stop-offs along the roadsides of the western provinces to see: Native Americans selling wares, ancient lava flows of solidified volcanic cinder, Amarillo's famous steak-eating diners, the puffy pink of the Mary Kay plant in Oklahoma City. There would be no particular attention paid when crossing the mighty Mississippi at Memphis or at Knoxville where the road turns finally north in the Appalachian Mountains. Indifference would be shown to the spectacular views along the Blue Ridge during the long Virginia ride. The five-day trip out would be made back in three—that was the goal. No other considerations held merit.

The trip back as intended was uneventful, but after three nine-hundred-mile-a-day rounds of driving, Mr. Faehner was in no condition to carry on with his plans. Upon midnight at the end of the third tedious day, he found respite in a tiny ten-room motel just off the Pennsylvania Turnpike less than twenty miles distant from Lancaster City. There, he plopped $50 down on a room that was $35, then dropped his fatigued mind and body on the fourteen-hour bed and expended a full twelve hours of it on a much-needed sleep. Once awake at noon the next day, he treated himself to an hour-long meal, a hungry man's compensation for a missed breakfast and a late lunch. The refreshment did him good. The revitalized blood flowing in his veins served to replenish his ideas. He knew what he must do.

But daylight would not do. He had to wait, wait until the day faded into dark. Then, if detected, the only notice of him would be the figure of a man at home as if everything were as it should be. He would answer no knockings, pick up no phone, but just go about his business in the sparingly lit, shade-drawn house, searching, searching for the hoped-to-exist notebook, folder, or paper-clipped collection of loose-leaf containing the secrets of the silver.

Waiting proved to be an ordeal. With his adrenaline on high, he very much felt the need to be doing something, anything, rather than nothing. Many times, he was tempted to just go home to the estate, Silver Hills, or even the Silver Mine just to keep from constantly pacing and impatiently fidgeting as he had been doing ever since he had last gotten out of the 5.0. But he fought and restrained himself. What was going on was far too important. He wouldn't risk being deterred by anything or anybody. This was it—the culminating factor in a lifetime's search lay waiting for him if he just practiced patience. He held on and, in the end, ended up staying, paying for another day's lodging just so he could stay put at least for a few more hours. He had to get into the Nevin Street house. Rick was already many days dead. Who knew who had found out? Who knew whether, at any moment, another relative would be contacted and make their way ahead of him to the house for any reason whatsoever? Rick's personal papers would never be turned over to him or anyone.

So he whiled away the hours, watching reruns of some of his favorite childhood sitcoms—*The Munsters, The Andy Griffith Show, Leave It to Beaver, Gilligan's Island, Sanford and Son.* Before dusk, he traveled down the road to a diner and ate. After eating, he took off for Lancaster, hoping beyond hope that a lifetime of waiting would be found to be worthwhile.

Knowing that his Mustang, despite its own intrigue, would not be recognized as belonging to him or anybody worthy of anybody else's attention, he decided to park it directly in front of the end-of-row, two-and-a-half-story home. The neighborhood was dark and quiet. Rather than remain conspicuous by remaining in the car for an unwarranted length of time, Faehner quickly got out and approached the other Faehner house. He had no key, front door or back, so he had no expectation other than breaking and entering to get inside. If caught, he had thought up a solution to breaking the law—Rick was dead, he would tell them that. He had to retrieve the valuable papers he had already made arrangements for. They were his now, and he had to have them. Who could argue the fact that desperate times call for desperate measures? Valuable papers such as these could not be put away for months, years perhaps, while court dates waited. Any astute business person would tell you that.

With that contingency story in mind, Mr. Faehner by-passed the front of the house entirely without even a glance toward the porch or door and instead headed nonchalantly along a little strip of sidewalk that ran down the side of the house aside the alley. Backyards from Chestnut Street homes abutted the alley across from Rick's, all but the area specific to the first half of his property, which had across from it the rock shop. The rock shop was where, when Faehner was a mere boy of twelve through fourteen he worked, cracking rocks and minerals into specimen-sized pieces suitable for sale at some of the more prestigious museums and institutes of science and learning around the United States of America: Smithsonian Institute of Natural History, Franklin Institute, Academy of Natural Sciences, and other institutes. Mr. Faehner glanced over at the padlocked building, then paused, taking himself inside as it was those long years ago. He pictured himself in steadfast pose, angling and striking the many select types of bulk material used. They were simpler times. They were happy times. They were how it all began. It was the experiences of working in the rock shop that led to the discovery of the mine. It was a profound realization that it all came about because of his interest in colorful rocks. The memory of it came back to him. His home on Pine Street was only two blocks away. His school, Sacred Heart, was only half a block up on Nevin. His relations—George, Era, and Rick Faehner—lived here, a point between the two. He remembered how he would walk to and from school and how, while in the seventh grade, noticed the colorful chips of rock and mineral that were daily swept out of the shop and into the offset beside the alley. At twelve, he had never been formerly introduced to these family members, at least he had not remembered being so, so when the first day came when Era scolded him for taking some of the excess bits of yellow sulfur, black anthracite, tan siltstone, orange orthoclase, blue quartz, pink quartz, and red volcanic cinder, he did not know who she was, and likewise, she did not know who he was. But the twelve-year-old that he was did not give up. He saw no harm in gathering discarded pieces of, what were to him, interesting but worthless bits. He was right. Era's objections were not based on what he was taking, but that he was taking. But he persisted. It became a ritual—him turning the corner of the alley, looking first to see if she was around, then to observe the ground outside the shop for anything new to pick up. If there was, he would very quickly swoop down to get it. If she happened to witness it, oh well. Each became bolder, that Faehner trait, innate. Era took things further. She began standing right outside the shop at times just before and after school so she could, just by her presence, thwart the obnoxious kid. The gloves were off. Only one week of this Faehner put up with before he outright confronted her for the right to do as he pleased—pick up the rocks. An argument ensued. Words were exchanged. Era, unable to deal with the persistent child, next began flinging rights-of-property issues at him—about the rocks, about the very spot where he was defiantly standing. It was Rick, who, just by coincidence happened to be standing just inside the shop and overheard the crux of the heated debate, came out to quell the escalating shouting match. His immediate inclination was to put a stop to his mother's outlandish behavior as he considered it, realizing that it was ridiculous seeing a woman of her years getting into it and being one-upped by a boy barely old enough to like girls.

Era backed off, so mindful was she of the prestige her only son had recently come into: a Ph.D. in mineralogy, 1970, Penn State University, and a Ph.D. in volcanology, 1971, Penn State University, and a Fellowship in the Great Britain Society of Gemology. He was without doubt her golden boy. Nothing he said or did was wrong.

It took a lot to make Rick mad. He was good-natured and bothered not about the little things in life. His mind was well disciplined, made so by the many years of study he had endured earning the three degrees. But his mother was another matter—entirely. She was always too, too much in his business. And that's precisely what this was—his business!

It was through Rick's intervention and characteristic calm that allowed for the matter to settle. Impressed by the boy's initiative, Rick then proceeded to make the proper introductions with Era, who added that not only was he Richard Faehner as he purported, but that he also possessed more degrees than most college professors! She was so riled up at having the chance to extol her son's virtues that she became flushed and began to breathe heavy. Rick rushed to her aid, supporting her by squeezing and holding onto her shoulders. Once he deemed her fit to be left to herself, he mildly scolded her for letting her temper get the best of her, again, then insisted she go back across the alley and back into the house. He sealed the deal nicely by complaining he was hungry and could she fix him a sandwich to eat.

That done, he turned to the boy, who was by now obviously being entertained by the comic scene and, in the mood of the moment, offered him a riantly expressive face. The connection was made, much to Rick's disbelief, that the both of them were in fact Faehners.

Always the savvy businessman, Rick, always on the lookout for a fresh pair of rock-cracking hands, inveigled his young nephew into trying out a pair of work gloves. The pay—$1.65 an hour—not too bad for a young boy working for the first time. Mr. Faehner let flow the many memories he could recalling how naturally he took to the workaday world. He found out a lot about himself as he hammered away day after day in the confines of the one-story block building—his remarkable work ethic, his efficiency, his way of working things out in the face of adversity, his never missing a day of work. He swelled with immeasurable pride when he thought of it all. And then the darkness took over. He remembered where he was now in the scheme of these things; that that one notion of Rick's, of going on a whim to the silver mine, and how it put into motion the whole of the rest of his life; that he was standing here in the dark just days past his esteemed uncle's death, choosing to break into his home to find, once and for all, the believed-to-be papers signifying the existence of everything, the only thing he wanted from life any more. Twenty-eight years had gone by. Twenty-eight more he would have waited.

Quickly, his mind went back to the matter at hand. Under the cover of night, he needed to determine which was the most advantageous means of entry into the old Faehner house. He knew it inside and out despite the fact that he hadn't been inside himself for all of twenty-six years. Rick, his mother, and his father were not people who liked to change things around just for the sake of change. He knew the house, its contents were, in all likelihood, the same and in the same place as they had been his last time in. The cast-iron Stegosaurus still stood beside the vestibule door. The gold-patterned, three-cushioned sofa still sat in the living room, the downstairs middle room. The vintage 1970 Zenith television set still stood up against the staircase wall, across from the sofa. The gold-striped wallpaper still adorned the walls of every downstairs room. Nothing had changed. Everything was the same.

He weighed out his options before him. One option he had was to break into the cellar cap—the domed metal lid placed over the sunken cellar steps located beside the property fence. It was an ideal way to enter, at least from a perspective of remaining obscured from observance. Once under the protection of the cap, all of his movements would be undetected. But there were other obstacles—two in fact. There was the to-the-outside door, which had to be gotten past; and there was the to-the-kitchen door, which may be locked as well. And who knew what sort of lock was on either, if any? He might have to use devices to break past them. And for that, he was unprepared. He had no pry bars, sledge hammers, or long-handled chisels in his vehicle. And, despite what Hollywood has made us all believe, kicking down a hard door is harder than you think. In most cases, it can't be done, especially when constrained by cramped spaces. Breaking into the back kitchen door would be altogether too noisy, and he could be noticed even if he didn't notice anyone noticing him. That's the way old neighborhoods work; someone sees something, watches for a while, then calls the police without ever coming out, without anybody else ever knowing who did what. Being in the apparent depths of an obscure dark alley didn't ensure anything. It was far too risky.

The only other means of possible entry was by use of one of the back-of-the-house windows of which there were three possible choices. One was the double-wide kitchen-sink window set facing directly into the backyard. The only way it could be reached would be to stand up on something and pry open one of the slides—these windows slid side to side. It didn't seem feasible. With what there was to stand on, one would end up being pretty off balance while trying to break open one of the slides.

Another one of the back windows rested just around the corner of the house from the double-wide windows. It though stood all by its lonesome with no real way to get at it except for a ladder, and that was out of the question. The only favorable window was also the easiest to get at. It stood at the end of the back porch where the main body of the house jutted out from the kitchen part. It looked into the living room. For all practical purposes, it was the one.

Mr. Faehner knew the window well. It was indigenous to the house, 1910, when windows were hung on pulleys with weights. The upper and lower portions were held in place by a simple latch lock. This latch was loose, had been, since he first knew about it. He stepped up to it, jiggled it, jiggled it again and again and again. Soon, the latch was off its catch. He was in. Before crawling through, he thought about utilizing the one implement he did have handy—his Brinkman flashlight. But no, he reasoned out, imagining what some nosy neighbor would think then, seeing the flicker of light. That would define "intruder"! "They'll have to think that I'm Rick, that I'm just here, just got back, and moving around the house same as I would any other time I came back from an extended trip. I would be out of sorts with things and just trying to get caught up with whatever was happening here." Wary, he slowly, carefully, climbed through the opening using his trusty flashlight to feel for things in front of him. There was the corner table and lamp on top of it that he had forgotten about, and when he was halfway through, he used his free hand as a guide to navigate the field of darkness away from the obstacle. Finally, his hands reached the carpeted floor, and he lowered himself inside. Without delay, he stood and reached again for the window case and closed it. Leaving it open would have surely been a mistake.

For the moment, he refrained from turning on the flashlight, concerned still as to how best to go about things. He thought about it—the one way or the other of either using the house lights or using the Brinkman to do what needed doing. The debate was on. Using the flashlight meant using little light, which would impede his ability to find any of Rick's important papers, especially if they were recorded, as he believed, twenty-seven to twenty-eight years ago. They obviously wouldn't be right out in view. But using the flashlight also meant that the likelihood of being noticed, at all, in the house was limited. The bad aspect of that was that, if he was noticed and someone saw the tiny beam of light flickering about in the darkness, they would be sure to call the police. On the other hand, using the house lights meant having plenty of light to search for the documents, which meant finding them quicker. And the quicker, the better. But it also would be a signal to any curious neighbor who knew Rick well enough to come up to the house unannounced, welcome him home or whatever. Faehner pondered that maybe the answer would be to wait until later, after eleven or twelve, and try it then when any of the snoopy neighbors would be asleep. But he was too anxious to wait. Too many things could go wrong in that span of time. Finally, he found his compromise. The downstairs would remain dark. Upstairs, only, he would turn on the regular lights. That way, if anyone would come to the door, he could ignore it as if he couldn't hear. The point being that a downstairs light is always an invitation to those who would want to pop in on someone, whereas an upstairs light is not. A reasonable person would take it as a sign that that someone wants to be left alone, that they've retreated for the day. Secure in this belief, Mr. Faehner, using only the scant amount of moonlight coming in through the partially curtained window he had just entered, crept toward the staircase across the central room. There he steadied himself, then continued tiptoing up to the darker beyond. The experience was surreal to him—stepping alone, in the dark, in a dead man's house. What would he encounter? Who? Could Rick's audacious spirit have found its way home from the desert? Knowing?

Like everything else in the house, Rick's room was the same—the same room he had grown up in as a child, the same room he had kept while he attended high school and college, the same room he had occupied once he had earned his degrees. In this house, everything stayed the same. Knowing that, Faehner, once he had reached the top-flight step, moved off in a straight-ahead direction. Rick's old room was directly above the kitchen and overlooked the tiny strip of backyard behind the house. He crept on, ghost or no ghost. Bothering him only was a slight misgiving—that he felt like something of a miscreant for having broken into the house, for having left Rick's body, for desiring to take what didn't belong to him. But the quiver of uneasiness lasted only but a few seconds. His behavior was being dictated by a condition that had been building in him for most of his life, and it took precedence in him unlike any other. There would be no turning back. There would be no bother to feel bad—about anything! It daunted him that he should spend the least amount of time lamenting his uncle's demise, in terms of it being finally the catalyst for coming into the secret of the silver.

Boldly, he entered Rick's forbidden realm, and boldly, he would partake of it. With great purpose and meaning, he flicked on the light and began his quest to find answer to the question that had plagued him from the past.

He had no real memory of it. During those long-ago years when he worked in the rock shop, he had always known which room in the house belonged to Rick, but he had never actually, as far as he could remember, been in it. He did specifically remember Rick popping his head out of one of the side windows to speak more directly to his mom or pop. That was how he knew. The only thing different than what he expected was that there was no bed in the bedroom. Apparently at some point in time, the room was given over to the more important aspects of his life. An outdated computer sat in one corner, screen blank, plugged in, and apparently fully functional. As a person who came into his profession during the early 1970s, it was hard to imagine Rick as anybody adept at using a computer. Such was the same for Mr. Faehner though he was fifteen years younger, and he himself had had to force himself to learn the ways of the newer technology.

Randomly, he went around searching piles of papers, stacks of old files, and boxes of old folders. Most were labeled by category and date, which would have made the process easier if there weren't so many to look through. To narrow the search, he ignored anything dated 1976 or later. He focused only on the research from 1975 or before. Twenty long minutes passed before he realized that there was another realm within the room that would need to be explored—a closet!

Somehow, he was drawn to it. Something inside him told him that inside the closet was what he was looking for. The something whispered to him, "Come to me. Come to me. Look inside. Look inside." He did.

The third box he pulled out had a huge 1975 printed on the top lid and all four sides. Underneath the bold black date was written Silver Mine Prospectus. This was it, Faehner knew. Here he had it in his hands. Hardly did he stare at it before throwing off the cover and delving deeply into the documents it contained. It was everything he had hoped for—page after page of detailed summary about the mine, its structural geology, its history, its prospect. And then the revelation came! Twenty-eight years of uncertainty came to an end! A hand-drawn map and a simple clarification statement told of it! The believed-to-be mother lode of silver by reason of scientific study, by explanation of one of the most brilliant minds, existed in the content of land located across the unnamed stream that bounded the western extent of Silver Mine property alongside the Pequea Creek! But it belonged to the Broken Bottle Club!

The Silver!

The significance of what he recanted in that epochal twenty-eighth year jarred the pattern of his thinking and brought him back to where he was—standing on the precipice of his own hollow hill overlooking the exact extent of land identified in the prospectus. Obtaining it had been the result of twelve longer years since the day it had been given its credence. But it was a rare event indeed that he should spend his time coming up to it, like he was doing now, for he coveted it so deeply that to come in sight of it enveloped him with a string of dissatisfactions—grief, sorrow, lament, envy, discontent, frustration that he could not contend with. Despite his invariable determination to find the sought-after silver, he was not without his weakness. For forty long years, he had kept up his pursuit; and for forty long years, he had had to do battle with the devils that had tried to shake him. At times, it had seemed like he was in a never-ending tale whose telling someday might have been without conclusion. Even now, even at this moment, the ending wasn't clear. Would or would it not include the result he had purposed for the most of his life? Would he find silver?

The land he now fearlessly faced under which the silver supposedly lay had been, all of these past years, owned and occupied by the Broken Bottle Club—a band of older-aged men who used the woodland as a weekly getaway from wives, from work, so they could indulge themselves in practices they dared not engage in while in the convention of society. Their time, they spent, mostly Saturdays, Sundays after services, enjoying all of the vices that were forbidden them while in the company of conservative friends and other contemporaries. Smoking, drinking, gambling, swearing, were their routine dalliances, though, on occasion could be heard the sweet-pitched laughter of disreputable women. What tied the occasions together was the affinity the men all held for the sport of target-shooting. And every get-together was sooner or later marked by the loud echoing shots made by rifles and handguns. It became their undoing.

From the day after the revelation about the silver was made, Mr. Faehner was furious, furious that such a group of good-for-nothings were able to mock the sacred ground they stood upon, cavorting, carousing as they did while, just below their fool-footed feet were tons of silver just waiting to come to the surface. A strategy was laid in place that day, a harangue that would be carried out to its fullest. The Broken Bottle Club would be broken!

Initially, the attack would be carried out in a subtle, indirect manner, a way in which no one connected to the club would know who was initiating the thing. Complaints were made. Anonymously, Mr. Faehner began to make calls to the local authorities about anything he really could so the Broken Bottle Club would become known as a place of bad influence, a disturbance, in the community. He posted signs in the woods and walking paths around the areas of the park nearest the club warning his patrons of the annoyances and even possible dangers they were in by approximating themselves too close to the places where they might hear foul language even on the Lord's Day, see a foul club member urinating or defecating in what was thought was an isolated spot in the cross-hollow's woods, be put in harm's way by a stray bullet fired off by a drunken BBC'er. But it was a gamble. It could have produced a problem, making his own Silver Mine guests feel uncomfortable and upset enough that they then take it out on him, making their grievances known to the only person they knew to be in charge. This happened. As a way to counter this, Mr. Faehner then posted on all of the same signs the telephone number of the Little Conestoga sheriff's office. Then people's issues were made to the person they were intended—the sheriff and deputy. Then an issue would be made about the trouble that the Broken Bottle Club was making.

The process was slow to develop. The members of the BBC were all members of the larger community. And apart from the things they did while in the woodland were all somewhat respected by their constituency, even their wives who either didn't know or didn't care to know what went on down at the club. The club too had been around for more years than anyone could remember and without the least complaint against them. How could it be that years and years of recognized peace and quiet all of a sudden turn into something so irksome? Mr. Faehner realized this too, that it would be a struggle to change the mind-set of the community against a club that was, in truth, nothing more than an annoyance, and that only to the very few who knew and disapproved. And their disapprovals were mainly directed at the fact that the proclivities that went on there were also done on Sundays. This was why, for a time that stretched into years, Mr. Faehner refrained from making any personal complaint. He needed to assure anyone who might think otherwise that there was no ulterior motive for him to castigate the not-very-often-thought-about group.

When the issuance began, the complaints made to the township officials were of a minor nature. Every so often, Mr. Faehner, pretending he was someone other than himself, would make a call by barn phone or cell phone to the Little Conestoga sheriff's office or the township office to get a hold of a township supervisor and voice a concern about something the members of the Broken Bottle Club were actually in the act of doing, had recently done, or had been doing for a relatively longer period of time. To make sure he would get them, Faehner acquired, and carefully read over, a copy of the township ordinances so he could direct his sometimes true, sometimes made-up allegations at violations that were part of the statute and, if proven, would implicate them.

The first call he made, he identified himself as a weary traveler who had to stop alongside a stretch of Goods Road near some little concrete bridge, which crossed some small stream, unidentified on his road map. He was a sightseer who had the misfortune of getting a flat tire and had to stop to replace the tire. When he got out to do so, a band of what looked like old men came flying down the Goods Road hill, windows down, music blaring, vehicle careening, and nearly struck him. Just ahead of him, the carload of unconcerned men suddenly veered off into the wooded hills apparently just to joy-ride off-road. Having the advantage of owning all of the land to the east of the BBC gave Faehner the ability to call in on the club about times that were real, about instances that at least could have occurred by reason that the men were there when the instances supposedly took place. Mr.

Faehner spent an appreciable amount of time dwelling over the details of each and every fictitious call, but he also curbed his enthusiasm in that he had to caution himself to wait, sometimes months between calls, so that the complaints would seem random and not appear part of any scheme to undo the controversial club all at once.

Two months after the initial call, he phoned in from the Silver Mine barn and said he was a Mr. Jones, and he had been out canoeing on the Pequea Creek that day, and when he had just gotten past the area of the creek he knew belonged to the well-known Silver Mine owner, he heard a lot of gunfire going off in the woods right-side of the creek. Concerned for his safety, he immediately paddled his aluminum boat to the right-side bank of the channel, thinking that the height of the bank would protect him if any bullets, real or perceived, should strike too close. As part of the allegation, he even made noises to describe the *ping, ping, ping* he said he heard coming down around him. "And," he pointed out to the mystified sheriff, "I was a victim of the shooting, inadvertent or not!"

This, the sheriff had no choice but to take seriously. He dispatched his deputy the next day to investigate. The bottle club was taken to task for what was being described as a blatant disregard for the safety and welfare of others. They were warned. They would have been prosecuted, but problem was, the Mr. Jones, the innocent victim, was nowhere to be found. He, whoever he was, had failed to follow up and make a formal complaint by stopping in on the sheriff and signing papers about the incident. So the bottle club was spared. The sheriff, in doing his duty, even went so far as to advertise in the *Conestoga View*, the town's weekly paper, asking Mr. Jones to come forward and accept a personal apology from the club for what had happened.

Mr. Faehner was angered. "So they would have gotten away with a slap on the wrist, eh. An apology! For having nearly killed a man! What kind of a place is this really!"

Mr. Faehner had to caution himself. He had got caught up in the episodic event and wanted too much, too soon, even though in his panoply of preplanned ideas, he had realized that it was going to be a long, slow process to break the club. Now he wondered, had he made things better or worse. In looking back at it, the club had received a blow by receiving bad publicity, yet the fact that the accuser, the notorious Mr. Jones, was reluctant to come out in the open, more or less meant that maybe the stronger side of the opinion of what really happened favored what the club was contending; that it was doubtful that even an errant bullet could have sprayed in the opposite direction of where they were firing. The truth would remain in controversy.

"It was clumsy of me not to have considered the situation far enough into its progression to realize that I would have had to produce a witness," Mr. Faehner said in regret. But he would not give up. There was no other way. Prior to acting out his plan, he had thoroughly researched the history of the Broken Bottle Club. What he discovered was no surprise. The land the club was situated on had been put into that service seventy years ago. It had been handed down, father to son, for three generations. It was collectively owned, which meant that as long as there were sons to hand it to, its legacy would continue.

To go on aptly toward his goal, to succeed at it, meant having to set aside any meaningful sense of time, again. To wait. Already twenty-eight going on twenty-nine years of his life had been spent trying to wrest the secret of the silver from his now-deceased uncle. Having begun the quest so early in his life gave him time, adequate time, to reach for what was his. But no longer. Now forty-one, he felt life slipping past him. He felt vulnerable to age. He had been the supreme Silver Mine property owner for a decade now, and he pondered why he hadn't ever attempted to quash the Broken Bottle Club before whether he knew it or not that the precious metal lie beneath their soil. In most every other direction, he had made it a priority to confiscate the contiguous land. Why not the club's? Why?

The answer was simple. In the year when Rick had conducted his survey, he felt secure that the silver, if there was silver, lie dormant, waiting in the geological underground somewhere in the vast extent of Silver Mine property. The riches would be extended deep, not out, from the original source—the mine. Situated almost a mile distant from the land in question, one would never think that the bulk of the ore would exist so far away. But thinking is never the same as knowing. The flaw in this line of thinking was that the silver mine itself had not been the main source of the deposit. The mine, its mineral wealth, had only been a finger's worth of an arm, a body, of pure metal. The miners of the past only mined what they could. When the veins played out, so did their enthusiasm for retrieving it. The water table they had broken into in the second shaft had only dampened their spirits. The silver was already gone. A tumult had spread across the formation an eon ago, separating the main body of the silver from the little bit that remained in the area of the mine. Nobody ever knew.

Dr. Richard Faehner. It was he who supplied the answer. Unrelenting as he was at everything he purposed for, he had delved into the in-depth study of the hypothetical contingencies concerning the geological "upset" that he knew existed in relation to the mine, the body of rock around it. The ancient upheaval he knew might have caused such a disparity in the surface layering of rock would have had to upset the formations below. Deposits of any embedded material would have been broken, especially the silver, which in this case was prevalent within 150 feet of the surface. The silver was there for the taking. It had only to be believed in. Once again, Mr. Faehner tipped his thoughts to the memories of those godforsaken years, twelve troublesome years of unrelenting wait; each minute of each day, of each week, of each month, of each year, like a tiny drip of water trying to fill up a large pool, one drop at a time. His head began to throb, thinking about the whole of it. It could have been his undoing. He didn't know what saved him, helped him persevere, except that he accepted *it*, whatever it entailed, as his fate, his destiny. He knew that no matter what else happened or no matter how long it took, he was bound to the principle of the idea he had laid down before him those long years ago. His life would be the pursuit of it—incomplete without it. He contemplated it. He contemplated himself in a way that no one else could. It was mind-boggling really, what he had done. Done! What a satisfaction it was to think to use that word. Unfortunately, he could not, not yet. The final outcome was not yet decided. But for that, Mr. Faehner was almost as glad. To think to have the thing over with, one way or the other, offered him relief. The dreaded wait would finally be ended!

He recalled the series of defining instances when the Broken Bottle Club had been rendered into a serious state of disarray, one from which it could not recover. There were tasteless tactics implemented during the last two years of the bottle club's reign when Faehner really fought to overthrow them. Faehner was at his wit's end, waiting, watching, wondering about how best to best them. He decided to draw from his experience the same type of retaliatory measures he had employed against the men who had attempted to thwart him while he was on his first quest to own the mine. Those measures, he reasoned, had even worked against the likes of Boddinger, a millionaire, a man who in his life had reached a certain pinnacle of power. Yes!

In his recollections of things already tried, he knew that the incident involving Mr. Jones had received the most attention from the local authorities. He needed to take that concept—one of contending that the clubbers were being reckless with the rules when it came to protecting other people, or living things, from their errant sprays of bullets whenever they got together for shoots. People, of course, could never be compromised. But animals, on the other hand, could. Like what had been done to the artist so many years before, Mr. Faehner put together a proof-provided plan to implicate the BBC for the wanton act of shooting local deer out of season. The evidence would be circumstantial. It was an unfortunate thing to do, but he had to do it. They would fall, one by one, for the sake of the Faehner future, bringing about the culmination of prestige and fortune represented in all the years worth of his Silver Mine endeavor. There would be no ifs, ands, or buts about it. Forever, already, he had waited. The time was now, or it would be never. "And besides", he rationalized to himself in a more personal moment, "we would just be killing them off a little ahead of schedule. Rare is the deer around here or anywhere in the state for that matter that lives beyond a third year. Sportsmen abound here."

To pull off the plan, he inveigled the help of a hunter he knew, a hunter who owed him a huge personal favor, a hunter who could not refuse him. Hecky, upon receiving word from the prestigious Silver Mine owner, responded immediately to the request. "I'll do whatever it is you want me to do," were his few, select words in reply. Then, when the phone was hung up, he recalled vividly the time only a few years back when he had been spotted, by a few Sunday tourists, tracking a wounded twelve-point buck down out of the mine-side hollow hill and across the frozen upper pond. The hefty deer, mortally hit, slumped when it tried and tried and tried again to regain itself on the slippery ice sheet. Hecky, unaware that a number of tourists were finding their way out of the mine at the time, followed his trophy out onto the ice and delivered, for all eyes and ears, the final blow to end the animal's life. Then, still not minding the fact that there were witnesses to his unlawful act, he dragged the "deerly" departed cross-ice to a cleared section of pond edge. Hastily, he abandoned the kill and returned soon after with a pickup, and, with the help of a companion, picked up the carcass, never once concerning himself with the facts—he had been seen, he had been identified by description, and his pickup's license had been jotted down. Faehner dealt with him personally as the report had come to his attention first. He dealt with Hecky from a position of power. Instead of turning him in and having him subjected to all of the fines and punishment, Faehner, always someone who would advantage himself for future gain, wanted this one to use as he could for some distant return. Hecky, for all intents and purposes, was had. He never thought of all the years that had gone by since the incident on the ice and how hard it would be to put together all of the incriminating pieces of that day's puzzle. For instance, the true witnesses of the actual event were all out-of-staters—New Jersey people. Their names were handed over on a slip of paper to the then-incensed Mr. Faehner, but no summary of the report was ever made. No authorities were ever alerted. And Mr. Faehner never saw anything himself. Now if turned into something big, it would be a controversial thing, not really the type of definitive evidence you want to have when making a legal challenge. But Hecky didn't see it that way. He owned up to the fact that he had done wrong, and he didn't want to hide from it. In fact, he was glad for the fact that now, if he did what Mr. Faehner expected, it would fix things up between them. He preferred to live his life in peace and in the good graces of the richest man in the county! All the years that had passed since the day he trespassed on the mine property and did-in the prized buck whose head was now stuffed and mounted atop his fireplace, Hecky had lived knowing that someday he might be called upon to deliver some kind of appeasement for the benevolence that was bestowed upon him the day he cold-killed the creature. He was now ever so glad for a way to, once and for all, rid himself of the burden of debt he had felt all this long while.

So to make things right, Hecky snapped into action. Still an avid sportsman, he knew exactly where to go to accomplish what he must. Muddy Run was an outdoor person's paradise located only a half-hour's drive south of the mine. Activities in the vast land-acre preserve included boating on the huge man-made lake, fishing galore, overnight camping, hiking, kite flying, and the like. Surrounding the park was a perimeter fence, which protected whoever or whatever was inside from whoever or whatever was outside it. This included the local population of deer who, over the many years of the park's existence, became keen to the fact that the area inside the gated barrier was a place of sanctuary from the patrol of fall hunters who annually came after them. Often, they congregated in places near the fence, and often, they made attempts to jump over it. Some did due to the fact that the gate was not that high. The ones that made it never left. Newly arrived deer often remained in clear view of the boundary line to encourage those left behind to continue trying to clear it.

These congregational zones were perfect places where an attack on the deer might be tried. The trick was to get in close enough amid the sparse old-growth trees that dotted the valleys there and take deadly aim at the deer, vulnerable whenever they abutted the fence line and had fewer places to dart away to if attacked.

But Hecky knew what to do. On his first day out, he staged a foolproof setting, one that was sure to get him his deer. At a predawn hour, he unloaded a large bag of store-bought apples around a selected area of outside fence. Some he cut into halves to release their tart smell into the windless air so the deer could more easily sense them. Then he waited. Around the backside of a huge hickory tree, he kept his silent vigil, watching, as the glow of the morning sun changed the shadows of night into visible images.

It was as if he was dreaming when the first glance he made under the pale sky, he spotted three young deer right on top of the scattering of fresh-cut apples. He didn't hesitate. Taking direct aim, he let loose three rapid shots from his .270 rifle. All three were direct hits.

The result of Hecky's job was as if a bottle was broken on the head of every member of the Broken Bottle Club. The dead deer had been positioned as if they were fleeing from the club's land, were shot, and dropped while attempting to leap over the unnamed stream, which bordered with the Silver Mine property. A unanimous call alerted the Little Conestoga sheriff's department. The community was outraged. Hefty fines were imposed. The clubbers all pointed fingers at each other while one, then another, touted innocence. The cleverly-created conflict could never be resolved. And in the minds of the members, the trigger-happy fool was the one, among them, they thought it to be.

The next-to-last chapter in the Broken Bottle Club's existence came about by Mr. Faehner employing yet another tested method worth getting someone into trouble. Just as he had done to the millionaire man, Boddinger, he set about to capture real-life images of the BBC men having their way with the wayward women that, on occasion, frequented their Sunday socials! To do so required the hiring of another wayward person, a misfit, who would do what was asked without question. He called upon a person of old—Mike Zoig!

The goal of this game was to have old Mike infiltrate the club as a one-time guest and take photographs of the widowed and married men with the wild women, doing the things they were called upon to do. Then, with the evidence in hand, the BBC members would have quite a bit of explaining to do, particularly with their, wives, sons, and daughters. The community too would be deeply affected by the controversial news—that their once-innocuous little club was becoming something to be ashamed of. And like what happened to Boddinger, it might not even have to go that far. For him, just the threat of what could have happened was enough to make him relent—certainly not repent. In the same way, the clubbers would be exposed and exploited. In the same way, they would be forced to relinquish something of their own. In this case, it would be their cherished woodland. And they would never set foot upon it again!

The trick of it all would be to make it happen. It was an idea much easier said than done. Snapping a few implicating photos of a passed-out Boddinger was certainly of a much easier nature than what would be required when trying to do the same around a bunch of ill-behaved women and men who were up and carrying-on to the best of their abilities. Would it even be possible?

Then there was Zoig to consider. What would happen to him as a result of the undercover operation? Wouldn't he be implicated too? After all, wouldn't he be there, be a part of it. But in a way, Faehner reconsidered, that might be better. If Mike was the only one who did not get his hands dirty from the mess that would be created, it might arouse suspicion, and that wouldn't do. And if Mike did get caught up in the fray, did it really matter? Who would he have to vindicate himself to? He wasn't married. He had never been married. He had no brothers or sisters. And as proprietor of Little Conestoga's only cycle parts and repair shop, his business was too important to dismiss for his one day of dalliance tantamount, in his case only, to having a little fun. If this was what could be expected, then only one question remained. Could he get in?

The answer was simpler than when posed. Zoig, though a close-friend-to-no-one sort of guy, did know just about every man and young man in the close-by community. To those who enjoyed spending free time rolling out on the country roads glued to their bikes, Zoig was something of an idol. When he went out zooming, everybody stopped and stared, wishing they were out too. So as it was, everybody at the Broken Bottle Club knew and thought highly of the motorcycle man. Faehner did too. Since the days of old when he and Mike first joined forces to break up the band of Riverville riders, the two former teammates liked and respected each other. Whenever they encountered each other out in the open, they interacted—sometimes in a somewhat simple way, acknowledging each other with a point or a nod; other times by engaging in brief stints of conversation. There was not a lot between them, but the "what" that they had, they had. It had never faded. It would never fail.

When Mr. Faehner approached Zoig, he was not disappointed. He was his same compliant self, ever ready to keep the desire of association open between them. After all, who wouldn't want to be appreciated by the richest man in the county? A deal was made. A settlement of money was reached. And Zoig was supplied with a sophisticated T-1 cell phone capable of transferring digital photos by satellite as soon as they are captured. "Just the push of a button," Faehner reiterated while displaying the device to him. "Just the push of a button, and your pictures will immediately be sent to the monitor on my computer desk. There I will process them as quick as I can. Then once I signal you that everything in OK, it doesn't matter what happens to the camera. I'll have what I need."

Mike didn't ask questions. In fact, the only thing he felt compelled to say was that he was no shoo-in to get into the club, especially when they would be up to no good. "It could take a week. It could take a month."

Mr. Faehner laughed and left. Mike had no idea just how irrelevant that tiny amount of time seemed when compared to the eternity he had already waited. Faehner knew already of how much uncertainty he faced. He knew he was close but knew that no matter how close didn't matter, not in the least. At any moment, at any junction, the venture could come undone. The possibilities existed. The Broken Bottle Club might not relent, which in this scheme meant sell out under duress. Mike might fold under any pressure he might face. If he told anyone what he was up to, somebody might get wise to the fact that Mr. Faehner was up to something. And a billionaire doesn't usually get involved in things that aren't up to a certain standard. Who's to say someone couldn't figure it all out—of what Faehner was really up to, of forcing the clubbers off their land so he can rightfully take the silver that's been his for most of his life? And the greatest doubt of all still existed—the silver. What if it didn't exist? It was shocking to think about in terms that sent his ambitions all the way back, all the way back to day one!

The time he waited was well worth it. The events took place in perfect form as though they were parts in a well-rehearsed play. Mike Zoig came through without a scratch. No one was the wiser. By the consensus of the members of the Broken Bottle Club, no one among them, owner or guest, was considered suspect. The real culprit, they concurred, was someone from the outside, someone off-property somewhere who used a high-powered, high-definition camera with a telephoto lens that snuck down into their private little world. Not a dispute arose among them as to how it all happened. Their only concern became, as soon as the photos were revealed, what to do about it.

Copies came—one, two, three a week to each of the sorrowful sinners. Each was relieved, time and time again, when it was they who retrieved the large envelopes from the daily mail. It was the same for everyone, the manner in which they were sent—one picture saying a thousand words, no sender's name or address, no requests or demands, no idea of what it was all about.

Mr. Faehner bided his time. It was purposeful. He wanted each man to consider the consequences, of what might come. He wanted them to dwell, over and over, on the trouble that was sure to come. Each man did. They began paying more attention to the loved ones in their lives. They began attending services regularly if they did not already. They began praying at times when they found themselves alone. But most of all, they found excuses to be in proximity of the mailbox whenever the mail carrier arrived. Sunday became a blessed day, not so because they went to church but more so because there was no mail delivery to worry about. Months went by this way. The club fell quiet. The men, when they did convene there, did so only so they were free to speak to each other about the situation they were all in. They were all at their wit's end about what to do. Several times several of them were on the brink of confessing to their wives what they had done, thinking it was better to face up to it before rather than after. "I'd rather pay for it now than pay for it later," one of them summed up his feelings. "It's probably better she hears it from me instead of someone else." But he never did. Neither did the others. Then something happened. Each of the owners received a registered letter in the mail. Each, while signing for it, thought, "This is it—the blackmail!"

The letter was an invitation. All of them were being asked to convene in a conference room of the Silver Hills Country Club on an evening of the following week. What was it about? The letter didn't say. The letter did say that the proposed meeting was tentative, and if any of the expected landholders could not or would not come, the meeting was off! That was it, short and sweet.

In a manner much like how Drayton, the Pequea holdout was dealt with, Mr. Faehner approached the meeting with an all-or-nothing attitude. This was the final act in dealing with people who could oppose him. The strife he had been secretly delving out to the Broken Bottle Club was now twelve years in the making. He could not believe it himself, that he had allowed it to go on that long. But it had, and here he was. Just as he had done to so many others he was about to face, he remained, by himself, in the secluded observation room adjoining his private office. There, for a time, he waited and watched as the roomful of clueless Conestogians dawdled. His purpose was to find out what they knew or, rather, what they thought they knew. But in a relatively short span of time, he realized they knew nothing. So this was it!

Mr. Faehner entered the room in a stunning white suit offset by a blazing pink tie. Gripped firmly in his both hands was a bulging carryall bag, which he transported, then emptied on the oval mahogany table around which they were seated. The contents spilled out in front of them, their eyes in awe at the sight. Sparing not a word, Mr. Faehner made to them his first and final offer. "There it is, gentlemen. My offer for the property. Take it or leave it. $250,000!"

The men sat and stared. Inches from their eager hands was the sum of all their desires! The Broken Bottle Club was broken!

Mine!

The next day's dawn started in a spectacular splash of silver light, which shone overtop of the Silver Hills hill. It spotlighted the capitulated dome of the relinquished bottle club's land as if it were on display. Mr. Faehner continued to stare as if in a trance. The culmination of forty-years' effort and hope was upon him. He wondered how his fate would be decided. He was alone just as he wanted to be. It was how he had faced all of the life-leading situations of the past. It was why he had not told the young reporter, to whom he had told everything else, that he was standing on the verge of something so remarkable. Moments of realization were his own in life, and that's how he wanted it. The climax in the quest to find the silver whether ecstasy or agony would be his to discover.

He turned from his view, fretting the fact that there was more time to endure before the scheduled work began. Passing by a small oval mirror hung like a picture frame on one of the inner walls of his office, he took note of the fact that he was still attired in yesterday's Easter-egg suit, now all creased and crumpled from spending a tireless night, crunched up on a two-seater sofa in his office. He looked a mess. Having no other clothes to change into and reluctant to go to his estate, he spent a little time in front of the mirror pressing his whites, along with his wrinkled yellow tie, with his hands. Hungry, his first inclination was to run up to the little store in Little Conestoga and partake of what used to be the original Silver Mine breakfast fare—chocolate milk and chocolate-covered doughnuts. Heck, he thought, as traditions go, why not have that chat with Pop for good luck.

Convincing himself, he hopped into the limo and sped the short mileage to the store. It was a splendid trip, splendid experience. He and Pop even sat on the porch, sunlight streaking across their hands and legs as they leaned back in their creaky wooden rockers, exchanging tidbits of news. Faehner indulged himself, opening both containers—the cardboard carton of chocolate milk and the package of mini delights. Pop, ever so relaxed, rocking back and forth, even asked for a doughnut, something he had never done before due its seeming impoliteness. But Pop sensed something special about the day—the way Mr. Faehner was pertaining to it, spending every moment with it. It was as though something really important was about to happen to him. The only other time Pop remembered him like this was on his wedding day. Because of that, Pop knew something special was about to take place.

"Yesterday, you were about to tell me something, son," Pop reminded him in such an endearing way as if to elicit a response. "Then Mom came up, and you clammed up tighter than an oyster trying to protect its treasured pearl."

Mr. Faehner offered no immediate response. He kept on munching his morning delights and swigging his chocolate milk. He yawned often.

"Stay up late last night," Pop said in comment to the observation.

"I didn't sleep a wink, Pop," he said while stretching his mouth wide open once more.

"There's got to be a reason then, son."

"There is, Pop."

Mr. Faehner looked at the trusted old soul and imparted to him a feeling of consideration and kindness. There was nothing he couldn't say. And he propped Pop up for what he did. The expectation of what should happen over the course of the next few weeks flowed out of him, and Pop was eager to hear it. And when they were done, Pop was quick to quip, "So you came here to say that you waited forty years to say it." Then Pop stopped, going over in his mind the construct of the previous sentence, wondering if he had put it together in the way he had intended for the meaning he had hoped to get out. Meanwhile, Mr. Faehner went on, addressing the issue and its complexities. He finished by saying, "Now don't breathe a word of this to anyone. OK, Pop?"

"I promise I won't tell a soul," Pop spoke as if taking a vow, "not even Mom."

"Won't tell me what?" Mom suddenly asked as she made her way out past the screen door to find Pop. Pop looked at his porch partner for the answer, and Mr. Faehner nodded approvingly. To him, in a way, Pop was his pop, and Mom was his mom. He got up and stretched his arms until he knew they were longer, then headed off the porch. "Bye to you all," he said with a wave. "And," he was adamant to point out to Mom, "that makes two days in a row that I came to see you."

The fact that he had heeded her expressed desire to see him more often made Mom all warm inside, and as she watched him leave, sure that he would come back soon, she touched her heart. Once he was gone, Pop told her. "Sit down, Mom. I have something to tell you . . ." The little trip to Little Conestoga to see Mom and Pop lasted only a short while, relatively speaking. Only half of the tedious duration was over. Back from the early morning excursion, Mr. Faehner wanted nothing more to do but to be near where the ground-breaking work would begin. Arriving at the little concrete cross-over bridge at the junction of Goods Road and Silver Mine Road, he paused momentarily and glanced over at what used to be the property of the Broken Bottle Club—now his! He glowered when he thought about them, all the time he had wasted as a result of their obstinacy, all—when knowing in the end things inevitably would have turned out the same. His attention turned toward the little run, which no longer seemed like a divide. He pulled the limo out past the bridge slab and guided it into a small glen on the Silver Mine side of the waterway. He got out and stepped through the thick grass to the bank and stared down into the water one direction, then the other, and thought it a shame that such a rustic little run should go on without a name. Not anymore! He owned it now, both sides, and everything in it! It would be named!

He pondered the possibilities as a plethora of potential prospects poured into his mind. One after another, he considered them: Crossing Creek, Broken Bottle Run, Silver Stream, Split-Silver Run, Silver Line Run . . . It went on. Indecision. Finally, it came to him. The significance of the run is that it was the crossover to the secreted silver—that was it! The run would be named Silver Crossing!

Time was almost up. Soon the loggers and road builders from the paper company would arrive and begin work. Long ago, the contingency plans had been drawn up for the time immediately following the takeover of the Broken

Bottle Club's land—that whenever that occurred, the company would come right in and begin their work. The woodland, as it was commonly referred to, was aptly named. The entire hill acreage was replete with Pennsylvania hardwoods. Walnuts, beeches, oaks, locusts, maples, hickories dotted the landscape. Their value alone was enough to cover the costs of the contract. Other trees taken would be cut up for firewood—mostly the dead or dying. There was no exchange of money, only services for wood. Both would profit.

When the first of the paper company's vehicles arrived, Mr. Faehner was making a first-ever stroll along Silver Crossing, remarking to himself that it was a first-class run of special beauty. He vowed to himself in private ceremony that if the day did come that resulted in the finding of an extraordinary amount of silver ore, he would have a huge quantity of it broken up, flaked into heavy bits, and scattered into the entire length of Silver Crossing. The stream would then glitter and glisten in the reflection of the day's sun. It would be a proper christening.

As Mr. Faehner advanced upon the crossing, he witnessed a cavalcade of company vehicles approaching from the long slanted road. The lead vehicle—a company pickup, with its insignia barely visible—had already pulled up beside his vacated limousine and halted. Stepping out was a haughty-looking character, the foreman, who, immediately upon touching the ground, charged back up to the bridge and began hand-signaling the drivers of the other vehicles to pull off to the side of the road. One by one, they lined up, exited their transports, and hurried toward the bridge for further instructions. By the time Mr. Faehner arrived at the bridge, the foreman was already barking out orders to the assembly of workers. He was immediately impressed by the discipline that was evident in the deference the men showed their boss. He knew that the business at hand would be handled right. Even more impressive was the line-up of earth movers and tree-hauling vehicles behind them. It was the equipment essential for phase one of the tedious operation—cutting roads and clearing trees in the woodland.

When the pep talk was over, Faehner approached the foreman and formally introduced himself. Previous to this, he had only made contact with high-ranking company officials. The foreman greeted him cordially.

"Hello there, sir," he said while offering a hand for a shake. "You must be the big wheel here. My name is Chuck. And the rest of these guys are my tree fellers." Chuck chuckled out loud, hoping Mr. Faehner got the joke he been making for the past fifteen years, substituting fellers for fellows but meaning that they do fell trees.

Mr. Faehner smiled. Before he had a chance to comment, Chuck had already turned and signaled for the work to commence. He then turned back to Mr. Faehner and assured him that everything was going to be OK. Chuck was right. He knew exactly what was expected of him, and he was an expert at meeting those expectations. Prior to this day, he had visited the site several times and knew what needed to be done. Maps had been drawn up and gone over, over several pots of coffee. It was a basic plan. A workman's road would be put in running parallel to Silver Crossing, just opposite the road on the Silver Mine side of it. This road would be used to gain access to the various areas of the hefty hillsides, which rose up sharply from the stream base to their high points, which were on average from 100 to 150 feet up off the road level. The only piece of land level to the stream bank base was an acre of back-behind, adjacent to the Pequea Creek—the area where the members of the former Broken Bottle Club congregated. The road that would be built up into the steep hill would be difficult to make.

The other objective of the hired-on tree fellers, or fellows, as one would wish to call them, was to clear away a significant portion of the old-growth trees and haul away the timber for its best possible purpose. Stripped of its trees, the high hill would be ready for the real excavation—the removal of its rock and topsoil so areas of the underlying rock could be exposed. Then, another team of experts would come in and get at the business of blasting away at the dolostone and layered phyllite to reveal the thick veins of quartz, believed to exist. It is in and amongst these quartz veins that the silver would be contained.

An obstreperous noise went up as the machinery was put into action. From a starting place across the Goods Road bridge, bulldozers, graders, cranes used for lifting and loading, and various transport trucks inundated the once-pristine land. A plethora of white-capped men inundated the hillside slopes. Out in front was a smaller force of blue-capped individuals sent to identify and mark the good-wood trees. Trees that were good for specialty building such as walnuts, maples, and oaks were marked with a white stripe. Trees that were deemed good for general purposes such as pines and poplars were marked blue. Trees that were only good enough for pulp wood were marked red. Trees that were good for nothing, invasive trees such as ailanthus, would be annihilated. All of the dead and dying wood would be cut up for firewood, free to the men who wanted it.

To the paper company, the fifty acres of timber was a treasure-trove on its own. Such an array of fine-quality hardwood was hard to come by. They took down the trees in an exemplary manner, knowing what most people did not—that money really did grow on trees! In what was a continuous round-the-clock effort, the paper company workers labored away at their arduous task, toppling, cutting, loading, and hauling away logs of every sort and size in keeping with their ten-day commitment. There was incentive, even in carrying their workload through the overnight, thinking it best to keep their promise to someone who could, on a whim, buy out their business down to the last wood chip and think nothing of it. It had happened in the county before—to a winery, to an orchard, to an entire town—Pequea!

During the overnight hours, the progress was marked by the added commotion of high-powered generators, hauled in to provide spotlight illumination for the late shift. By day, an anxious Mr. Faehner stood vigil over the changing landscape across Silver Crossing, maintaining just this amount of distance from the ongoing activities, enough to be a part of it but yet be apart from it. He remained reserved. There was simply no way to know the final outcome, but at least there would finally be one, one way or the other. He found it hard to nourish himself in the ways he had been accustomed to—eating big meals once or twice a day. His stomach wouldn't let him. It was all tied in knots. His stress-induced daily intake now included a morning routine of chocolate-covered doughnuts splashed down by a pint of fresh chocolate milk, courtesy of Mom and Pop. Lunches usually consisted of two plain hamburgers squirted with ketsup and mustard—no pickles or onions please—topped off with an orange or grape-flavored soda. The food was good for him, body and soul, and he wondered with absolute objection how it ever came to be considered junk food. By night, mentally tired but hard to get to sleep, Mr. Faehner retreated to the comfortable confines of the nearby Silver Hills, his towering tribute to his obsession. There, he paced all about the place, tracing back, past to present, all the events that had led up to the current day, whichever that might be, to see it all happen again and again. Possibly to soothe his soul. Possibly to bring together the insufferable years, to make them seem like less of a lifetime—forty days instead of forty years.

So much of his life had been spent in pursuit of the intransigent silver that, in reality, his life had been spent. Who was to say how much longer he had—a day, a week, a year? And if his life should end after any of those increments, would it have been well-spent?

But though Mr. Faehner had kept the revelation of what he was doing his own personal business, that is, with the exception of what he had recently revealed to Pop, who then told only Mom, there was no way really to confound the natural curiosities found in the everyday people who happened to know or find out that something of some kind of relevance was going on on the newly acquired, piece of Silver Mine land. As word got out, people started to come. The first to notice as expected were the patrons of Silver Mine Park and Campground who were the closest in proximity to the everyday disruption. Next in line were the community residents of Little Conestoga, those who happened to pass by the once-serene sylvan setting and now saw it every day being inundated by an influx of men and machines. These locally curious onlookers began taking time to go out of their way, again and again as the days progressed, to pass by along Goods Road or once in a while even pull into the Silver Mine glen just past the Goods Road bridge, stop, and try to ascertain for themselves just what was going on. The papers said nothing. Try as they did, Mr. Faehner kept himself as intransigent as the silver he was so desperately seeking. He was unavailable to the press. He began to receive unsolicited phone calls, letters, and e-mails, inveigling him to respond to the inquiries all titled "What's Going On?"

Rumors spread. Some, who thought themselves clever, wrote editorials to the local papers speculating, hoping to be the first to get it right. Ideas popped up like mushrooms after a three-day rain in the summer: a clubhouse, a canoe launch, an elaborate creek-side retreat, a cultivation area for the rare Dutch elm, once all but wiped out in the Lancaster County area by disease.

To remain safe to himself as the hillsides were cleared, Mr. Faehner retreated to the Silver Hills side of the Pequea Creek. There, every day, he watched. What remained at the end of the tenth day was a stump-studded hill with one rudimentary dirt road spiraling up. On that auspicious occasion, as he stood ruminating the future of the huge dirt pile he had created, one obnoxious reporter, standing cross-creek from the evasive Silver Mine owner, thought to take a whack at getting his attention by folding up a handwritten note into the shape of a paper airplane and flying it successfully across the divide. In his presence, Mr. Faehner unfolded the plane, read it, folded it up again, then flew it back—no response. No one was going to know.

They came. In the vast procession of onlookers that came, he saw them. Each of them rather blatantly made no apparent attempt to conceal their identity. Seeing them, their figures standing amid the daily ration, was as if seeing figments of one's imagination—ghosts from the past. But there they were—flesh and blood realities.

Mr. Drayton came first. On just the third day of the reckoning, he pulled up in an outdated car, unidentifiable except to an expert of vintage vehicles—though this car was vintage by aspect of age only—, alongside the Goods Road bridge, got out until he was beeped at by a slew of oncoming traffic, then, after a moment's hesitation of fighting past his concern of feeling unwelcome, guided his car into the well-attended glen beside Silver Crossing. Mr. Faehner, just getting back from a quick trip to Mom and Pop's for a two-hamburger lunch, jetted past the unforgettable character in his classic 5.0, noticing him while having to slow down just a little so he could negotiate the turn to go up-hollow, as he considered it, whenever he had to go from a turtle's pace at the turn to a rabbit's speed quickly to successfully get up the hill. Mr. Drayton, of course, knew nothing of the white Ford and, therefore, did not know he had been identified. Mr. Faehner didn't care and, in a way, was glad to see him. The act of him coming out meant that there were no lingering hostilities between them—there had never been on Faehner's side. "Let him enjoy the show."

Next to come around was the widow of Mr. Boddinger who Mr. Faehner still felt a high level of respect and compassion for. Her husband had cheated on her, and Mr. Faehner knew that. And so far as he knew, she had never done or attempted anything directly against him. She, he thought in a whiff of selfless air, might have been the only other person capable of being told the truth and trusted to keep it. At seventy, or about that age, she was thin, frail, white-haired, but still kept up her appearance, wearing just the proper application of facial make-up—rouge, lipstick, eye shadow to allow her to look nice. Mr. Faehner knew who she was only for the sake of having been in her presence about a dozen times during the past decades—in public places such as stores or restaurants—and heard someone introduce themselves to her and she to them. He never did. She didn't know him to see him as most people didn't even though his picture at times made the headlines, so ordinary was his look. So dignified was she as she meandered along the bank of Silver Crossing, Faehner decided then and there that when future events came up, those pertaining to the Silver Mine, she would be invited. It struck him as to how differently things could have gone in regard to her—both Boddingers really. If Mr. Boddinger was a nicer man . . . If Mr. Boddinger would have taken the young Faehner boy under his wing . . . He thought. The Boddingers would be the ones . . . Mrs. Boddinger would be the one . . .

On the eighth day, the Artist—as he had been officially dubbed long ago—made his presence. While sitting cross-creek from where the corner of the old Silver Mine boundary bended back toward the campground, just a short distance back from where he usually watched the activities, Mr. Faehner spotted, remarkably, him. He couldn't believe his eyes. Not once in all the intervening years had he seen him. Not once. But there he was now in full view, standing boldly, brazenly. There was no mistake about it. The topper, in proof of it, was the unbelievable fact that atop his head was the same, yes, the very same floppy hat! It had to be—beige colored with a black band around it! Sticking out of the band was a somewhat worn, somewhat wilted pheasant feather! He wore a thin smile and had pronounced red cheeks. Flowing out from under the hat was a mesh of long scraggly gray hair, which looked like it hadn't been shampooed for days or weeks or possibly thirty-nine years!

Mr. Faehner regarded him with a mix of feelings. How easily he could shout across the Pequea and order him to get out. How easily he could let go, let him know that the Boddinger decree that he get the hell out still stood. He imagined himself crossing the Pequea bridge and confronting the interloper. "Get out and stay out!" But the words weren't necessary. Their two life paths had already met long ago, and the Artist had been defeated. It was not necessary to do the same again. And in a weird sort of way, it was important for him to be here, important for them all to be here. Oh, how he wished it were true for the others—for Mr. Boddinger, for Luckee, for the guy who possessed the Green Glob, for the infamous Dr. Richard Faehner. My, oh my, how he wished they were here. They would be witness to the most important day in Silver Mine history! They would marvel at the man who when he was a boy extolled the possibility of this day to come. They were the ones to whom it would have mattered most—that they who saw him as a wonderlust boy could now see him as a man who sought after and got what he wanted, despite them, despite them all!

By the end of the logging enterprise, Mr. Faehner was being inundated by letters from media services, all asking him for exclusive rights to know what was going on on his little Silver Mine add-on. Most were laconic. Mr. Faehner was a man of few words, fewer with the media, and to get to him one would have to act like him. A few he opened while whiling away the late-day hours up at Silver Hills. They were from every place he ever heard of and many places not. News agencies from as far away as California and Canada participated, cajoling him. After a couple of days of regarding some and disregarding others, it suddenly struck him that from among the throng of inveigling messages, none belonged to the *Hazleton* reporter. Thinking this impossible, Mr. Faehner checked and double-checked stacks, these times searching for post office marks, any from in or around the small Pennsylvania town. There were none. What a disappointment. Mr. Faehner began to think into it. "Of all the people who I thought would be interested . . ."

But the time was not now to spend reasoning over the mysterious absence and apparent lack of interest of the young reporter who, above all and above all else, had been granted the grandest of interviews—the inner view of his entire life. Pressed on by the matters of tomorrow, Mr. Faehner abandoned his immediate concern over the reporter's lack of concern until such a time that he could more fully and freely entertain it. The final thought he gave it was an expressive "He will miss it. For everything I gave him, he will miss it."

At dawn on the eleventh day, the matter of the effort to extrapolate the intransigent silver took on a far more serious nature. A security force of twelve armed men came and stood guard over the entire perimeter of the attention-getting dirt cap—called such because it could hardly be referred to as a woodland now. Black-lettered "Caution" tape was strung out around all of the borderline with the guards taking up positions the same distance from each other so that the entire property boundary was protected, sight to sight.

Shortly after the perimeter was secured, another contingent of experts arrived at the scene. Mr. Faehner almost smiled when he noticed ironically that the black-lettered, yellow-painted van denoting the detonators exactly matched the color combination of the perimeter tape. It certainly made him feel right—that things were coming together. Deliberately missing from the assembly of experts was anyone experienced in formation geology. Instead, Mr. Faehner chose to rely on his own ingenuity or, rather, that of his deceased uncle's. Rick was exclusive, dead or alive. His work, so esoteric, so set apart from the others in his field, was unique. It could not be improved upon, not by a lifetime's worth of erudite study. Rick, as a geologist, was second to none. It was in this vein that Mr. Faehner knew he could depend upon the use of Rick's age-old notes on how to proceed with the silver-extrapolation process. And the fact that the construct of the findings did not include exact detail of where precisely the main body of silver might be found in relation to the topography of the newly acquired land was of no real concern. As it was, Mr. Faehner was prepared to blow up the entire hill, deep down and into the bowels of the earth, if necessary, to reveal the precious ore. One thing though did cross his mind now that the long-planned-for event was about to take place and so prominently had relied on the promise of Rick's resourceful research. It was something of a bit of a dilemma. He asked himself, should he now or ever relate to any interested parties such that it was, without question, the fruits of Rick's labor that had led directly to the belief that the silver existed. True, that it had always existed in the free-wondering mind of the boy that first stepped foot on the Silver Mine land so long ago, but it was only made certain by the talent of his late, great, uncle. The question would come up, he knew. Once the silver was found, they would know that he was after it. They would know that he knew. It was a tedious task to decide what to do. But for now, Mr. Faehner wanted only to find his elusive silver. Everything else would have to wait.

Without a consulting geologist, Mr. Faehner was the go-to guy for the team of explosive experts. He told them blandly just to go ahead with the overall instruction—to blast away all the cap rock in specific areas of the hill. These designated areas, of dolomite and phyllite mostly, had no significance whatsoever except that they were areas that seemed intriguing, at least on the surface of things.

Drilling began. At all of the pointed-out places higher up on the hill, holes—five feet, seven feet, eight feet—were bored out of the principal rock. In them, cartridges of dynamite were inserted, ready to detonate. Time-delay fuses were set, and precautions were made to make certain everyone was cleared of the compromised area and at a safe distance from the pending explosions. It was without precedent, this blasting away at will that went on.

Series of simultaneous explosions shocked the hillsides and hollows of the surrounding countryside. The reverberations echoed so vibrantly that even a mile away in Silver Mine Hollow, anyone present might have believed that the silver mine itself was being blasted back into operation. Even a mile distant, the repercussions reached a decibel level above the safety standard. The workmen and Mr. Faehner all wore protective equipment—earplugs of various foams and soft plastics and strap-on sets of old-style muffs. As part of his wanting to get into the moment, Mr. Faehner deliberately did not wear his when the initial sets of charges went off so he could hear, first-ear, the sounds of the excitement. It was exhilarating! He was amused by the contrast between what he had just experienced and the reminiscent echoes of the shootings made by the now-unmentionable members of the now-unmentionable club. Stragglers who remained outside the danger zone thought to remedy the situation by hand-capping their ears but were caught unexpectedly by never knowing when the next blasts would occur. One by one, they eventually gave up.

Between the series of explosions, there were one-hour intervals when further set holes were being bored into the rock. As the blasting continued, these intervals became increasingly longer, made so so that dozers could be used to climb and clear the broken rock away from the excavation sites higher up on the hill's sides. This is how things went on—setting, blasting, clearing, for the better part of a week. Only at the end of every day did Mr. Faehner, guided by one of the technicians, venture up to the three gaping holes and examine them for traces of the silver ore he sought.

For the first four days, nothing of significance was found as the hill holes reached depths of 52, 66, and 74 feet respectively. On the fifth day, however, something of significance did come to light. A thick rich vein of smoky quartz was revealed in the two deepest "shafts'" as they were referred to now due their depth. The deposit discovered along a range of depth from 81 to 93 feet in the two deepest shafts about 170 feet apart meant that the band was connected, and if there was silver underlying it, it should be connected too. What a possibility! Mr. Faehner remembered from when he was a boy that Rick had explained to him how the silver was always found in relation to the quartz. That night of the fifth day, Mr. Faehner, alone again in his Silver Hills sanctuary, got caught up in the practice of reiterating Rick's words. Those reverberating words sounded, sounded, sounded in his head. And to alleviate them, let them out, he began repeating them, over and over, for himself to hear. "The silver is always found in relation to the quartz. The silver is always found in relation to the quartz. The silver is always found in relation to the quartz."

The upheavals continued throughout the sixth day though due the newer depths of the three shafts the loudness of the periodic explosions were lessened. The impact to any person standing outside the safety zone was such that personal ear protection was no longer necessary. Mr. Faehner was glad to remove his. At one point in the early afternoon, one of the technicians approached Mr. Faehner from across Silver Crossing and shouted that there was going to be a delay before the next blast because they were going to set a bigger charge. Mr. Faehner thought nothing of it other than there must be trouble. There must have been an encounter with some particularly hard rock that required the power of extra dynamite to remove it. He felt chagrined. He said nothing for what was there to say. He was no expert in the field of blasting holes out of rock in the ground.

He paced away the long delay, hands clasped behind his back. More and more, he felt tormented by the expectation. But what was the expectation to come? What would it be released as? He stood on the threshold of all things. Would it come to good? Would it come undone? Would there be exultation, or would there be emptiness?

The moment of truth had arrived whether it came in a minute, an hour, or a day. Everything that his life had stood for was being put on a stage with the whole world watching. What would be its outcome? For the world would decide too what was its worth. Would they approve once the secret came out? Or would they have reason to mock his apparent self-conceit? Would he come out of it bright, shining, like the silver he seeks? Or would he come away marred by mystery—why would a man spend a lifetime in pursuit of what was a childhood fantasy?

Mr. Faehner hardly noticed when the charges went off. He didn't look up. Scarcely did he hear when the tiny particles of silver, shot out by the blasts, sprinkled down from the sky and into Silver Crossing.

A Difference of a Year and a Day

Addendum

The turn of the afternoon hour had passed, and Mr. Faehner raised himself up out of his chair and began pacing the office floor, his hands clasped firmly behind his back. So serene was the mood—of him, of the usually busier Silver Hills Country Club that in the lack of background noise and distraction, he could faintly hear, or so he thought he could, the subtle movement of the wall-hung clock. Every tick seemed to speak—in the order of every second—late, late, late . . .

Suddenly, five minutes into the tedious delay, the main office door was swung open, and a young man, dressed for success, so to speak, stepped in. The two familiar faces looked upon one another expressively as if each had some great need to say something to the other. Both of them recognized it. Mr. Faehner spoke first. "You're late, you know," he said in a subtle but direct voice.

"I know, I know," the reporter admitted in a subdued tone. "There was a parade of Amish buggies all the way down Silver Mine Road that I had to follow, then swerve around, follow, then swerve around for miles. Sometimes, I had to wait—"

"No! That's not what I mean by late," Mr. Faehner interrupted.

"Well, what do you mean then?" the reporter got in in his defense, like a child who had been scolded would if they knew they had done nothing wrong.

Breaking out into smiles, Mr. Faehner clarified his earlier statement.

"You're late," he reiterated as an open remark. "I mean a year and a day late!"

"A year and a day?" the reporter asked quizzically.

"Yes, a year and a day," Faehner repeated. "This time, last year, just after you left, you never came back, came back to find out what was going on around here. You never called or contacted me. How come?"

"Oh," the reporter let out in relief.

"You would think that all of that late-breaking news would have had you running right back here for a second round of my personal attention. And you, who I thought was so bold and enterprising, not a word out of you."

"I followed the news, like everyone else. I know what you found in that little woodland aside your property. It's all included."

By now, Mr. Faehner's mind was all about silver. The reporter's "It's all included" had gone right by him. What he had on his mind was something that needed to be said.

"The extent of the silver-mining operation is beyond expectation. Tons and tons and tons of it have been extrapolated already. Tons and tons and tons of it await. So far, there's been enough pure ore taken out for someone to build a silver city. In anticipation of more and more to come, I've already taken hold of the succession of properties over west of the main site. It's a day-and-night operation now—blasting, clearing, loading. I haven't got much time to do much else except . . ."

The conversation went on for hours with the reporter being filled in on everything that had to do with the new mining operation. He himself had to be the one to ask about some of the other things that he had been told about during their previous encounter. Among them were questions pertaining to the town of Pequea, the Susquehanna ferryboats, the winery, and more. Both men were treated to a round of royal laughter when Mr. Faehner told about seeing the Artist and Mr. Drayton again. He never mentioned Mrs. Boddinger. Then, when the talk about silver had meted out, the reporter finally spoke up.

"The reason, Mr. Faehner, why I never came back when you thought I should was because I became very busy, very busy pertaining to you. I never wrote a newspaper article on the event of your celebrity. Instead, I wrote a novel! About you! About your life! About the experiences of your life! It's now all put into word—your ambition, your determination, your passion, your desire to make your own end. It's all there."

"I don't know whether to laugh or cry," Mr. Faehner quipped. "Tell me now, in your book, how does it all end?"

"Happily ever after."